INTO THE WILDERNESS

Blood of the Lamb Book One: *The Crossing*

If you haven't already read Book One of the trilogy,
here is a plot summary:

On a tiny atoll off the coast of the small Pacific island, Oneue̅re, Maryam is raised to believe that she and the other Blessed Sisters are special: that when they Cross to the Holy City (the rotting cruise ship Star of the Sea*) at the onset of puberty they will serve the Lord and His Apostles with willingness and joy. But Maryam is wracked with doubts, alone, it seems, among her peers in questioning the Apostles' power and control. She finds herself cast in the role of human sacrifice—her blood siphoned from her body to save the lives of the Apostles from the deadly plague, Te Matee Iai. Her realization that she and her fellow native servers are nothing more than expendable slaves to the white elite forces her to question everything she once held true—her faith, her allegiances, and her desire to serve.*

Weakened by blood loss, she tries to escape back to the village where she was born, aided by the very person who received her blood: Joseph, who is as shocked as Maryam by the Apostles' bloodthirsty deeds. But her father, faithful servant of the Apostles, rejects Maryam, and it is only Joseph's quick thinking that saves her from his violent response. Now gravely ill with Te Matee Iai, Joseph, along with his mother Deborah, convinces Maryam to flee the island, revealing their most precious secret: a boat built by Joseph's late father to aid his family's escape. Maryam, although terrified by the prospect of sailing into the "void" created by The Tribulation that consumed the Earth, reluctantly agrees—but only if Joseph and his mother will accompany her, and if she can take her best friend Ruth.

She hatches a plan, allowing herself to be recaptured by Joseph's cousin Lazarus, the cruel and unpredictable son of Father Joshua, and is taken back to the Holy City, where she is publicly humiliated, then bled again, then locked up and left to die. But through her great determination, and the help of her good friends Joseph, Ruth, and blind old Hushai, she and Ruth flee the Holy City in the night and rendezvous with Joseph at the boat. Just as they are about to leave, Lazarus takes Ruth hostage, insisting that they take him, too. With the pursuing villagers nearly upon them, Joseph and Maryam reluctantly agree, and the four set off together—sailing forth into the void . . .

Now read Into the Wilderness, *the second book in the trilogy, to find out what happens next in this gripping and powerful series.*

BLOOD OF
THE LAMB
BOOK TWO

INTO THE
WILDERNESS

MANDY
HAGER

an imprint of Prometheus Books
Amherst, NY

Published 2014 by Pyr®, an imprint of Prometheus Books

Cover image of hands © Roy Hsu/Media Bakery
Cover image of wire © Koolstock/Masterfile
Cover design by Jacqueline Nasso Cooke

Inquiries should be addressed to

Pyr
59 John Glenn Drive
Amherst, New York 14228–2119
VOICE: 716–691–0133 • FAX: 716–691–0137
WWW.PYRSF.COM

18 17 16 15 14 • 5 4 3 2 1

Library of Congress Cataloging-in-Publication Data

Hager, Mandy.
    Into the wilderness / by Mandy Hager.
        pages cm. — (Blood of the lamb ; book 2)
    First published in New Zealand by Random House New Zealand, 2010.
    ISBN 978-1-61614-863-8 (hardback) • ISBN 978-1-61614-864-5 (ebook)
    [1. Fundamentalism—Fiction. 2. Refugees—Fiction. 3. Islands of the Pacific—Fiction. 4. Science fiction.] I. Title.
PZ7.H1229In 2014
[Fic]—dc23

2013031833

Printed in the United States of America

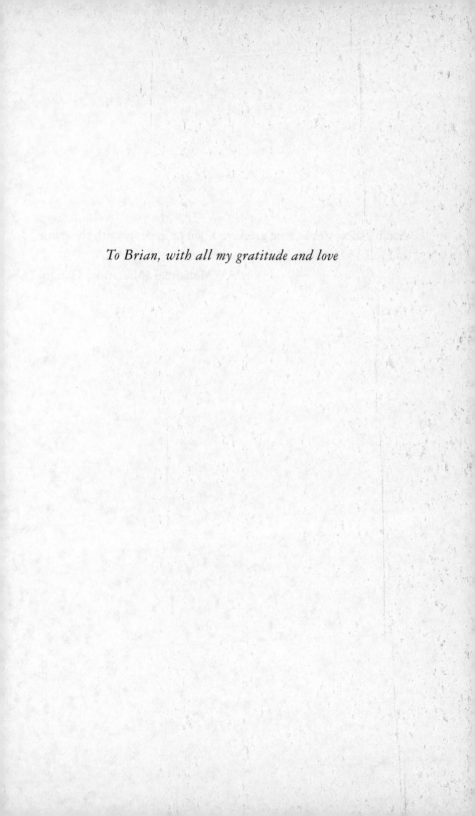

To Brian, with all my gratitude and love

Satan's successes are the greatest when he appears with the name of God on his lips.

Mohandas (Mahatma) Gandhi

CHAPTER ONE

For the first hour after they escaped Onewēre, the sea fought the boat and its fledgling crew as if it was trying to break their resolve and send them fleeing back to land.

But as the craft finally found its centre of gravity and settled into the rollicking motion of the swell, Maryam relaxed back against the carved aft rail and took in the enormity of what they'd done. Never in known history, old Hushai had said, had anyone successfully escaped the Apostles' tight controls. Yet here they were—four disparate travellers, two brown Blessed Sisters, two white Apostles—heading off across the ocean with only scrappy vestiges of faith and this untested sailing craft to aid their flight.

Poor Ruth, so reluctant to set forth, clung miserably to the side railing and purged streams of bitter bile into the sea. Yet not once since they'd crossed the reef that separated their small island home from this dark sea had her lips stopped forming the protective incantations of her prayers. She feared they sailed into nothingness, a world destroyed by the Lord when He sent forth His punishing wrath.

Maryam longed to comfort her, but she knew the time was not yet right—nothing she could say now would allay Ruth's fears. Her friend must find a place of peace within herself if she was to survive this reckless voyage. And if that peace was found through prayer, then Maryam was pleased for her, even if she could not find the same accommodation for Him in her own heart.

Joseph adjusted the position of the tiller and hunkered

down next to Maryam, briefly freeing up his left hand to wrap his arm around her shoulders with a reassuring squeeze. "Are you all right?"

She turned to him, brushing streaming lengths of hair from her eyes, and nodded. "Are you?"

His short dismissive laugh was scooped up by the wind and carried off into the night. "I feel like I'm in a crazy dream—that any moment now I'll wake up strapped to that bed again and realise my uncle Joshua has unearthed our plan."

Lazarus, who had earlier retreated to the sheltered canopy that spanned the two hulls of the boat, now poked his head back out into the wind, his fine sand-coloured hair catching the moon's cool light. "Don't underestimate my father. If he sets his mind to come in search of us, we *will* be caught."

Ruth groaned, shooting Lazarus a horrified glance before she returned to her prayers.

"Keep your musings to yourself," Maryam snapped. Her fury at Lazarus's hijacking of their plans seethed in her still. "Your presence here has put us even more at risk." *How dare he?* That he could have treated Ruth so—held a knife to her throat and threatened to use it if they did not let him come—only fuelled her hatred of him. He was cruel and arrogant, already too close in spirit to his controlling father ever to change. *How did they get stuck with him?* If the Lord had wanted to punish her for her wilful disobedience, Lazarus's forced inclusion in their escape plan did the trick.

"You've picked the thorn instead of the flower, cousin." Lazarus laughed as he sought out Joseph's eye and jerked his head towards Maryam. "If I was you I'd watch your back. This one really is a witch."

"It's *your* back that is still at risk," Maryam retorted. "You are not welcome here and if you think that distance from Onewēre will dull our memories and poor opinion of you, think again."

Beside her, Joseph sighed and dipped down to whisper in her ear. "Don't waste your energy," he urged. "This is a very small and unstable platform on which to conduct an all-out war."

His reproach stung her, though she knew he was right. This anger supped on what little strength she had left after the Apostles of the Lamb had taken so much of her blood. Still, she drew away from him.

"I'm *not* a witch."

Joseph grinned at her, tension playing hide-and-seek behind his eyes. "Well, I don't know about that. I think you put a spell on me!"

She softened at this, relieved by his lightness of tone. He was still on her side. Even now, she was amazed that Joseph had thrown away his chances for privilege and comfort and chosen, instead, to join her in flight from the Holy City. His kindness shone from him like the miraculous globes that lit the rooms in the great hulk from which they'd run.

She glanced back over her shoulder, scanning the dark horizon for one last glimpse of Onewēre, the only home she'd ever known. But there was nothing now to mark the place they'd come from, merely the lumpy outline where sky met sea—where the stars were swallowed by deep inky darkness and, below, the moonlight fractured on the breaking peaks of swell. They were truly alone out here, perhaps the first to have sailed this route since the immediate aftermath of the Tribulation that consumed the earth. Her heart registered her fear and tension in a jittery dance.

"Are we on course?" she asked, trying to focus on the few small things they could still control.

Joseph flung his head back, pointing to the familiar stars that formed the Maiaki Cross in the southern sky. "If we keep the Cross aligned to our left throughout the night, we should be fine." He fumbled in his pocket, drawing forth a circular object that he pressed into her palm. "Here. This compass shows the direction we're heading. If we use it with the map, we're sure to find our way."

Maryam studied the compass in the wan light of the moon. A delicate arrow-like needle swivelled from a centre point, while around the border of the enclosed face a calibrated measure marked off north, east, south and west. She turned it in her hand, watching as the arrow swung towards an invisible force to starboard of the boat. "How does it work?"

"Give it here!" Lazarus rushed from the shelter of the canopy and snatched the compass from Maryam's hand. "It has a way of finding north," he said, ignoring the fury in Maryam's eyes. "Something to do with magnetic force."

Maryam turned back to Joseph. "But why then did your mother make me study the book of stars?"

"Back-up," Joseph replied. "Besides, she thought you needed something to occupy your mind while you waited to escape."

For a moment Maryam felt outraged, remembering the strain and effort it had taken her to learn the patterns of the stars. She'd been so drained from blood-loss it was difficult to think at all. But perhaps Mother Deborah's intuition was right—if Maryam hadn't had to focus her energies on the star guide, she truly would have gone mad with worry that their plan would fail.

Joseph seized the compass back from Lazarus now, returning

it safely to his pocket as he called to Ruth. "Do you feel up to coming over here? It's time we talked."

Ruth bit down on her bottom lip as though damming back her nausea, and nodded. She crawled across the cramped deck space and tucked herself down next to Maryam as Joseph began to speak.

"If I've worked things out correctly from the map, we should be heading straight for Marawa Island, the closest land-fall to our own. My father discovered its existence years ago, when he first started planning our escape."

Lazarus cut in again, seemingly unconcerned that he re-ignited Maryam's hostility each time he spoke. "Now I under-stand why he would sneak aboard and lock himself inside the library for days on end. I thought he was just toying with Father."

"Who cares what you thought," Maryam nipped back at him. "Let Joseph speak."

Joseph looked from Maryam to Lazarus and shook his head. "Peace now," he murmured, tiredness sweeping his pale face. He glanced up to check the angle of the string of feathers flying from the tip of the forward mast, and adjusted the tiller to ease the twin hulls a fraction more downwind. At once the boat settled into a more comfortable roll.

He began to flesh out the details of the boat's creation for Ruth and Lazarus: how his father Jonah had built it, using sketches from an ancient book. How he had hidden the craft within the sacred cave, desperate that one day he, his wife and son would escape the clutches of his power-hungry brother, the Holy Father Joshua.

"Uncle Jonah and me as well!" Lazarus interrupted. "I take it they had no plans to return?"

Joseph merely shook his head.

"And you? Do you ever plan to go back?"

Maryam snorted. "Go back? For what? For your mother to bleed me dry of life? Your father to take my dear friend Ruth here and defile her again?"

Joseph gasped and turned shocked eyes to Ruth. "I had no idea. I'm so sorry," he said, as though the sin was his and not his uncle's to resolve.

"Don't speak of it again," Ruth mumbled, firing a resentful glare at Maryam. She swallowed hard, as if struggling past a seasick lump inside her throat. "What's past is past."

Maryam was not surprised by Ruth's desire to wipe the sins of the Apostles from her mind. Ruth had always been the docile and accepting one while she, Maryam, was much slower to forgive. Her anger and disgust at what Ruth and she had endured would never abate. They had *believed*; been raised to hold the Holy Fathers up as sacred spokesmen of the Lord. That the Apostles had deceived them both, abused their trust and bodies as if they were nothing more than slaves—than animals—churned around inside her still. She might have escaped the island physically, but the memory of it was etched forever in her brain. And the fact that Lazarus had forced his way aboard just made it worse. The son of Father Joshua was tainted by his father's blood.

She breathed in deeply, calling on the strong salty scent that rose off the sea to calm her. It was all-pervading, free of any verdant hint of land, and so oxygen-rich she was ambushed by a yawn before returning her attention back to Joseph. "How long until we reach this place, this Marawa Island?"

Joseph shrugged. "I think perhaps three or four days."

Ruth groaned. "Four whole days?" She was struggling to keep her eyes open, the motion of the boat and the after-effects of their flight from the Holy City now taking their toll.

Maryam, too, felt the lulling call of sleep. She stifled another yawn and shifted to awaken her leaden limbs. "Then we should plan to sail in shifts, two on, two off, to get some rest." But no sooner had she spoken than she realised she could hardly pair Lazarus with Ruth. Nor were she and Ruth experienced or strong enough to take on a shift together—they'd need either Joseph or Lazarus on hand to help control the two huge woven sails. The only alternative—to co-operate with Lazarus, to work with him while Joseph and Ruth were sound asleep—filled her with dread. She'd never forget the way he'd dosed that poor female server with the stupefying anga kerea toddy, and most certainly would have abused her had he not been stopped by Brother Mark. Or her own terror at his attempts to overpower her at the pool near Joseph's home. She did not trust him and had no idea how she was going to hold her fear of him at bay.

"You rest now," she told Joseph, worried he'd taken the most strain during their wild flight across the reef. The killer plague, Te Matee Iai, still stalked somewhere inside him, and although the transfusion of her blood to him had slowed its march, she knew his body still was frail. "And Ruthie, you go rest as well."

"But that would mean—"

She brushed Joseph's arm with her hand. "Believe me, I'll call you if I need your help!" Now she turned to Lazarus, all playfulness fading from her voice. "Just keep away from me. I'll work the tiller; you do the ropes and sails."

He saluted, mocking her resolve, but quickly scrambled to

the place at the prow where the deck between the two hulls narrowed to a thin walkway, only two planks wide, that cantilevered out over the oily black sea. At the walkway's end he nestled against the carved figurehead of a warrior, whose inset shell eyes stared off towards the unfathomable west. Instantly, Maryam felt the tightness in her chest diminish a little.

Joseph and Ruth struggled to their feet and retreated to the shelter that straddled the two sturdy hulls. A dense thatch of pandanus leaves shrouded the tightly lashed bamboo frame, forming a roof and walls to hold out wind and rain—a dry place to sleep and shelter for the stores Joseph and his mother, Deborah, had packed inside.

Maryam shifted into the seat Joseph had vacated, huddling down as she took possession of the tiller for this first night shift. It fought against her, as if wanting to swing the boat around, and she had to lean into it, using her body-weight to hold it firm.

Up to the south, the Maiaki Cross was the only familiar marker in the cloud-rinsed sky. She tried to recall the constellations she'd studied in Mother Deborah's book, as well as the lessons from old Hushai's tales of their ancestors' fabled travels. But she couldn't recognise any other feature in the vast network of stars. What kind of navigator was she, to sit beneath uma ni borau—her ancestors' great roof of voyaging—and not even recall the simplest of stars?

Yet as she willed her panicked pulse to slow, some of the familiar blueprints of the stars emerged and grew more solid, like the peaks of Onewēre's highest mountains when the mist that cloaked them in the squally months began to clear. There was the crab-like constellation Tairiki off to the north; that hungry shark Te Bakoa, with his gaping mouth and glowering red eye, lurking around the reef of stars in the north-east. And there, flowing between them all like a silted tidal stream, the wash of stars the Apostles called the Milky Way.

That these ancient markers had not altered since time first began, and even now had not deserted her, was somehow soothing. When all else around her was uncertain and unknown, at least she could rely on these shining beacons to guide their way.

Maryam could just make out Ruth and Joseph inside the shelter as they tried to settle on the sleeping mats. Poor Ruth. She was so scared, and so reluctant to take on this voyage, it was impossible for Maryam not to feel responsible for her safety now. For a wild moment she was tempted to push the tiller hard around to head them safely back to land. But then the horrors of the previous weeks returned to her, and she knew the only escape from the Apostles' cruel control lay in fleeing the Holy City and never looking back.

How innocent she and Ruth had once been: to believe they were the special ones—the Lord's Chosen, Blessed Sisters raised to obey the Apostles' stringent Rules and to think of sacrifice as the fulfilment of devotion to a loving Lord. How foolish that thinking seemed, when all the time those same Apostles planned to steal her blood to save themselves from Te Matee Iai, proclaiming that it was the Lord, and not the life-blood of the Blessed Sisters, who was protecting them from the plague's harsh grip. As for Ruth, destined to a life of shame, her body used to serve her masters as nothing more than breeding stock . . . no! No matter what hardships now lay ahead, nothing could be worse than that.

As the night wore on, Maryam fought the ever-growing compulsion to drift off to sleep. She had not yet regained her strength after the last transfusion, feeling the way it sapped her and resenting it even though the last donation was of her own making to save Joseph's life. Even now she was unsure whether she had given enough blood to cure him—his frailty still worried her. If he should succumb to Te Matee Iai again . . . she dared not think of the fight she'd have on her hands to save him then, knowing how angry he had grown when she'd been bled that second time. It nearly killed their fledgling friendship on the spot. And if he knew she had hidden within her small bundle of clothes the very instruments of torture used to take her blood, just in case he needed more, she doubted she could stem his rage. Lazarus would undoubtedly steal her blood without a care, but Joseph was far more compassionate— a special quality in a world where "goodness" was merely a word used by the Apostles to maintain control.

Suddenly the sails started flapping and both booms swung madly across the deck. The tips of the hulls dug deep into the swell and the whole vessel pitched and reeled off its course.

"What are you doing?" Lazarus shrieked, water surging over him. He scrambled down the deck, shaking himself like a village dog after a dip, as Maryam tried to bring the tiller around and the stern rudders fought against the forward momentum of the swell. But they refused to respond, and Maryam had no idea what to do next. It was Lazarus, hauling on the sturdy woven jute ropes, who finally reined the sails in and edged the prow back around towards the west.

"Idiot," he cried, his features reduced to a sharp mask of derision in the night's dull light. "If you can't stay awake, then leave the tiller work to me."

He stood over her now, a threatening silhouette against the

sky, and Maryam felt consumed by shame. She knew he thought of girls as lesser beings, and it mortified her to have proved him right. But she tightened her hand on the tiller, quickly checking the heavens to confirm their course. "I'm sorry," she conceded. "It won't happen again."

He snorted at her words. "If you're as good at sailing as you are at keeping secrets, then I fear we're doomed."

She looked up at him sharply. "What do you mean?"

"Come on," he jeered. "Do you *really* think I just accidently spotted you and your faithful lap-dog Ruth as you stole away? Are you really that stupid?"

Still she did not understand. She'd presumed Lazarus had simply happened on them as she and Ruth fled past on their way to join Joseph at the boat. Was he now saying this was not the case? Much as she hated reacting to his mocking, she had to find out what he meant. "You already knew?"

Lazarus slowly adjusted a rope, dragging out her uncertainty with obvious relish. Finally he squatted down next to her, replying in a voice spliced through with scorn. "I've been watching you," he drawled. "You're different from the other Blessed Sisters. Trouble."

"I don't care what you think of me," she struck back, "when you had so much, and yet you chose to use it to cause others pain."

For a split second her words stalled him, but then he regained himself. "Is the master blamed for beating the stupidity out of his dog?" He shook his head. "You people beg for pain—you crave it—all in the name of sacrifice to the Lord."

"You think we have a choice in this?"

"Yes I do!" He caught her gaze and held it. "And you,

prickly little stonefish, are my proof of that blind stupidity!"
He laughed, applauding himself, the percussion of his hands
loud in the night. "When I found you at Joseph's house after
your first ridiculous attempt to escape, I knew there was something up. I've followed you, sweet Maryam. Stood outside the
door while you lay there drunk on toddy as you let my mother
give Joseph more of your blood. I've listened to your secret con-
versations and know your fears. Believe me, I know more about
you now than you know of yourself."

"But—" Maryam's words died on her lips. He'd known of
their escape plans and yet not revealed them to Father Joshua?
Why was that? And why, come to think of it, had he fought so
hard to come aboard? He had everything back in Onewēre's
Holy City: status as the son of the Holy Father, freedom, health.
Why would he give it all away? She lowered her eyelids to avoid
his brash stare, secretly studying his face through her long dark
lashes. He was handsome, no doubt of that, but the sheer mean-
ness of his spirit bled out through his eyes and curled his lip in
a perpetual sneer.

"I know what you're wondering," Lazarus smirked. "You
can't comprehend how anyone would shun such privilege and
luxury. Am I right?"

Despite herself, she had to nod.

"Then think on this. Before this night, I knew what every
day would bring. I knew I'd someday take over the reins of
my dear father and that, thanks to the sacred blood of Blessed
Sisters like you, I could cheat the Lord of my death until I felt
the time was right." He shrugged. "Well, I'm sorry, Sister, I
want *more*."

"More?" *Just how far did his greed extend?*

He stood up abruptly, turning his back on her to scan the sea. "I doubt you've got the imagination to understand."

Maryam dug her fingernails into the timber tiller. He made her feel so—so—*beneath* him. That was it. As if she was worth nothing.

"I understand that you are no better than your father," she said. "That everything you touch is poison in your hands."

Lazarus spun back around to face her then, looming so close she could smell his stale breath. For a moment she feared he would strike her, but instead a seductive smile stole across his face. "Now, now, Sister. Allow me to prove you wrong." He reached out, brushing his damp hand down the side of her face as tenderly as a man in love.

She flinched, her arm rising of its own accord to knock his hand away. "Never touch me again," she hissed at him, furious heat spiralling up her body until it burned her ears. "The Lord forgive me, but I hate you more than words can say."

"Hate?" he said. Then he shrugged. "Then this should make for an exciting voyage. You see, the thing with hate, dear Sister, is that it needs love to define it, like night needs day."

With that he turned on his heel, leaving her alone now to digest his words.

CHAPTER TWO

The rest of Maryam's shift passed in a tired blur. She struggled to stay focused through the darkest hours of the night, and with great relief relinquished the tiller to Joseph as the first tinges of pink tickled the horizon in the east. Then, despite the cramped conditions in the small covered shelter and her proximity to Lazarus, she fell asleep almost as soon as she crawled onto the sleeping mat. The steady motion of the sea rocked her, and the exhaustion she'd been fighting now swept her away.

Mid-morning light was streaming in when Joseph shook her by the shoulder. "Wake up," he urged, "there's something you have to see!" He seemed lit by excitement as he tugged her by the hand.

"Wait," she whispered, fearing Lazarus would hear. But when she looked about she saw that he'd already risen and was at the tiller. She smiled at Joseph. "How do you feel?"

"I'm fine." He beckoned her. "Come on!"

She reached out to stop him. "No, really. Are you well?"

He sighed and his eyes lost their focus for a moment, as if he'd turned their gaze inward to assess his state. Then he slowly grinned. "I promise you, I feel great!" He tugged her hand again. "Now, please—come or you might miss them!"

Them?

Maryam scrabbled from the shelter after Joseph, struggling to shake off the fog of sleep. The light that bounced off the sea was dazzling, and it took a moment for her eyes to adjust to the glare. While she'd slept the boisterous wind had dropped away, and they were now sailing on a warm light breeze.

"Maryam, look!" Ruth's excited call drew Maryam to the front of the boat.

Ruth pointed down into the spray of water churned up by the bows. Scuffing just beneath the surface, playing with the air bubbles the hulls threw up, a pair of enormous fish sped along in tandem, their dorsal fins slicing through the water as they raised their rounded snouts to breathe. They were roughly the size and shape of sharks, but shared none of their leering, sinister presence.

"Are they dolphins?" she asked, riveted as the creatures swivelled their heads to the side, studying her with intelligent eyes, their mouths curved upwards in what could only be a friendly smile. She had seen their fins cut through the sea before, way out from land, but never observed them up this close.

"I'm fairly sure," Joseph answered. "My mother spoke of seeing them when she was learning how to sail beyond the reef and—oh, look!"

One of the dolphins sped ahead, flinging itself out of the water in a graceful arc. It seemed to hang in the air for a long moment, then dived into the swell again, spiralling deep, out of view. Maryam leaned over the bow and watched as the slick dark shadow of it re-emerged from the opalescent depths and the creature returned to its playmate with a flick of its powerful tail.

Behind them, at the tiller, Lazarus whistled to attract their attention. "Look behind!" he yelled, and pointed to the boat's duel wake. There, bringing up the rear in a joyous procession, another dozen or so dolphins tracked their progress through the sea.

Maryam felt her spirits lift. "You see!" She turned to Ruth. "There *is* life out here, beyond our shores."

She threw herself flat onto the deck and dangled her arm over the side of the hull, sifting the refreshing spray of the water through her fingers. Beneath her, the closest of the dolphins rose on the peak of the swell and nudged her hand, brushing the full length of its sleek body along her touch. Its skin felt as velvety and firm as melon flesh, and Maryam found tears prickling her eyes as she received this unexpected proof of life.

She looked at Joseph, excitement lifting her voice. "Did you see that?"

"It doesn't seem afraid at all," he said.

"Why would it, when it has free rein of this vast ocean?" *Fear is something you have to learn first hand*, she thought, remembering her own shocking swing from bliss to dread after she had Crossed from the atoll to the Holy City. Could anything be worse than knowing those you most trusted had betrayed you? She reckoned not.

Joseph nodded thoughtfully, then slapped his belly. "Come on," he said, offering Maryam his hand to help her to her feet. "I'm starving! Now we're all rested, let's have some food."

There was no argument with this. Together they reefed in the two sails while Lazarus lashed the tiller to hold the boat steady on its westward course. Now all four climbed into the shelter to unpack the stores. There was bread enough to last five days and they fell upon it hungrily, wrapping salted fish into the thick chewy slabs they broke off from a crusty loaf. Lazarus was uncharacteristically quiet, intent on his food as the others speculated on the scene back in the Holy City when it was discovered they were gone.

"I fear for Hushai," Maryam said. "If they find out how much he aided us, they'll make him pay." The old blind man

held a special place in her heart, and the thought of him suffering on her account churned her stomach.

"My mother promised she'll try to temper Uncle Joshua's
rage," Joseph assured her. "Besides," he laughed, "unless those
villagers who followed us actually saw the boat, they'll have to
scour the whole of Onewēre before they realise we have gone."

"And if they saw the boat?" Ruth pressed. "Is it possible
they have the means to follow us?"

All four turned as one to scan the sea behind them, but
there was nothing out on the horizon line to suggest anyone was
giving chase. Nothing at all, in fact, bar sea and sky.

"I don't know for sure," Joseph said, "but it seems unlikely
they'd think it necessary. They're so arrogant, I doubt it would
occur to them we could escape without killing ourselves." He
turned to Lazarus. "What do you think?"

Lazarus finished chewing before he replied. "I doubt they'd
do it openly, even if they do have such a craft as this—and I've
never heard word of one if they do. But my father will be furious
that I have gone. If he comes after anyone, it will be me."

"And you didn't consider this before you forced your way
aboard?" Maryam turned to him angrily. "They may well have
been content to pray that Ruth and I were swallowed by the
sea, but you . . . don't you see how your selfishness has risked
us all?"

Lazarus's eyes narrowed. "Selfish! Were you not already
forcing your dear friend Ruth here to accompany you? I did you
a big favour—she was ready to retreat."

"Stop it!" Ruth broke in. "I am not a scrap of bait for you
to fight over. We are here now—all of us—and if we don't work
together we all could die."

"Tell that to your crazy friend. *I'm* not the one who keeps this up," Lazarus said.

"How dare you!" Maryam spat. "Your very presence here—"

"Enough!" Joseph raised his hands. "You two are going to drive me mad! You have to form some kind of truce." He ignored Maryam's furious glare. "However it came to be, we're here now and we work together, like Ruth said." He leaned back and rummaged in the shelter. "Let me show you the map. It's where we're going now that matters most—not where we've left."

The map was pocked with age, its corners tattered and the ink degraded. In the seams where the paper had been folded, the writing had faded clean away. Joseph pointed to a tiny speck within a wash of blue. "This is Onewēre here."

They pored over the fragile chart, amazed. Here, at last, was evidence of the world outside their small island home and its minute satellite atoll. Hardly visible amid the blue that signified the sea lay strings of tiny dots that spoke of land elsewhere, and there, dominating a good half of the map, what seemed to be a huge landform. Maryam tapped her finger on it, leaning in to read its name. *Australia*. "What place is this?"

"I once saw pictures of it in a book," Joseph replied. "A dry land, with earth as red as pomegranate seeds. They had many great cities there, with buildings reaching right up to the sky."

"Why, then, aren't we heading there?" Lazarus asked. "Surely it's so big that, even with the fallout of the Tribulation, the people there must have survived."

"My parents were wary of it—they knew so little of its customs they did not think it worth the risk." Joseph pointed to a little island west of Onewēre. "This is Marawa Island, here.

It's spoken of fondly in the old legends—was known once as a place of trade."

"Your parents thought that made it safe?" Ruth asked.

Joseph shrugged. "I guess." He drew a line with his finger between the two islands. "The best thing is it's directly west of Onewēre, so we should be able to find it, even though it's still quite small."

There was sense in this, Maryam realised. She'd always known the ocean was unimaginably vast, but to see it laid out like this—as if the Lord had looked down and mapped it from His throne—underlined how insubstantial they and their sailing craft really were. "Do you remember how the legends went?"

"Not really. Only that they claimed the two islands were once so close in their dealings they were like brother and sister. Then the missionaries arrived on Onewēre and drove the siblings apart. While the people of Onewēre took up the Lord's sacred word, their brothers and sisters on Marawa Island chose to turn away."

"We're heading for an island where heathens rule?" Ruth's eyes grew as round as cockle shells.

"Who knows?" Joseph replied. "The Tribulation changed everything. Besides, I'd rather heathens than my uncle's Rules."

"How can you say that?" Tears swelled in Ruth's eyes. "Do you not still love the Lord?"

"Enough of this," Maryam broke in. "We've set our course and now must wait to see what it delivers up." To get into an argument with Ruth over her faith would achieve nothing but hurt all round. Nor did she want to reply directly to Ruth's question, knowing in her heart that her answer would only cause her friend pain. Instead she reached over and patted

Ruth's back. "It's okay, Ruthie," she whispered. "No one will wrench you from the Lord."

Ruth brushed the tears from her eyes and forced a smile. "It's just that all this is so—big . . ."

"I know." Bigger and scarier than Maryam could imagine. She turned her mind from it. "But we are here—you and me, together. Safe. And the dolphins prove there is life beyond our shores. We have food to eat, a map and that strange compass thing to guide our way. What could possibly go wrong?"

Ruth merely shrugged.

*　*　*

Throughout the day they all took turns to steer the boat, working hard at learning how the sails responded to the shifting winds. It was hot work. The sky was cloudless; the sun's heat sapped their strength and drove their thirst. Maryam and Joseph checked through the stores and doled out the fresh water as frugally as possible, just in case their journey lasted longer than they'd planned.

Yet, despite the hospitable sea conditions, there was an inescapable awkwardness among the group. With no space for privacy, even the most natural of acts proved stressful, the girls insisting that the boys turn their backs when they needed to relieve themselves—leaning out in an ungainly fashion from the deck—one standing guard for the other, making sure the boys kept to their word. But there was no such modesty from the boys: Maryam and Ruth learned only through excruciating experience to turn away the moment Joseph or Lazarus made his way up to the front deck between hulls.

The lack of privacy impacted in other ways as well. Whenever Joseph settled down beside Maryam, Lazarus was there too, as if he could not leave them be. It did not help that Joseph seemed to welcome his cousin's company, laughing with him about old friends and shared experiences. She felt cut off from him, sensing that the person she had known was occupied elsewhere. At times he tried to draw Maryam into their conversation, but he seemed not to appreciate her fear of Lazarus, and looked confused and wounded when she turned away.

This unspoken wedge was further widened by Ruth's constant anxiety. She could not seem to shift her dread. Late in the afternoon, the two girls retreated to the shade of the pandanus thatch and Maryam tried again to reassure Ruth about what might lie ahead.

"I'm sure Joseph's parents wouldn't have chosen Marawa Island unless they thought they would be welcome there."

"How would they know? The Apostles said—"

"The Apostles lied to us, over and over again. They said there was nothing out here, that all of it had been consumed, yet here we are."

"Here? We're nowhere, Maryam. Perhaps this is exactly what they meant? We could be stuck on this stupid boat for ever, with no sight of land."

Her words hit Maryam harder than she dared to show. She had not thought of this. What if the void the Apostles spoke of was this endless sea? They could be trapped on board until their reserves of food and water were all gone. What then? "But the map . . ."

"What of it? It was drawn back before the Tribulation destroyed it all. Besides, the Lord said those who turned away from Him would not be saved. At least at home we knew the Lord watched over us. Now that we have turned our backs on His Apostles, surely He will punish us?"

"But He *didn't* watch over us, Ruthie, that's my point." Maryam began peeling a ripe mango, the sweet sticky juice running down her wrist right to her elbow. "And if He did, then He allowed all those terrible things to take place. To go unpunished."

Ruth clapped her hands over her ears, shaking her head wildly from side to side. "Don't say such things . . . really, don't—"

"I'm sorry, Ruthie. I'm sorry. I didn't mean to upset you so." Maryam reached over and wrapped her arms around Ruth's heaving frame. "I promise I will keep you safe."

"How can you?" Ruth wailed. "I know you've tried . . ." Her next few words were indistinct, washed away by shaky sobs. ". . . from Father Joshua and he still—took—me against my will."

For one heart-stopping moment Ruth raised her head, her bloodshot eyes meeting Maryam's. The pain in there was so intense it struck at Maryam like a fist. So *this* was where all Ruth's turmoil stemmed from. So much had happened in the hours since Ruth had confided in her as they fled the Holy City, Maryam hadn't fully processed it. How stupid of her not to have realised that Father Joshua had taken Ruth and left her broken, filled with shame. How Maryam hated him. Wished him to Hell.

She took one of the softened kunnikai leaves that wrapped the fruit and pressed it into Ruth's hand so that she could wipe her tears. Then she shifted slightly, until she could see more clearly into her friend's face. "Tell me of it," she whispered, remembering how it had eased her own aching heart to tell Mother Elizabeth of her abuse at the hands of the Apostles—though she would offer Ruth comfort and understanding in return, not betrayal as her beloved mentor had.

"I can't," Ruth wailed. "It was so—so—"

"Speaking it aloud will help," Maryam insisted. She knew how these things festered inside if they were left unsaid.

Ruth blew her nose loudly on another kunnikai leaf and took a few deep calming breaths. "He told me to go down to the storeroom to collect more toddy." Her voice quivered like the call of a wandering tattler bird. "Then he followed me. He locked the door from the inside so no one could enter, and then he came at me . . ."

As Ruth spoke, Maryam felt her heartbeat gaining speed, as if she was in the room alongside Ruth. She knew the kind of arrogant sneer that would have lit his face—had seen it as he'd beaten and humiliated her before the entire congregation after her first foiled escape.

"He told me the Lord had picked me for his bride. That I should—" Ruth wrung the sodden leaf between her hands. "That I should . . . surrender to him . . . with willingness and joy, just like the Rules."

Oh Lord. "Did he hurt you, Ruthie?"

"Hurt? He pushed me up against a wall." A deep crimson blush flared up her neck. "He—forced—his way inside me, and when I cried out at the pain he clamped his hand over my mouth." Now Ruth was overwhelmed by sobs, and hid her face in her hands.

Maryam felt sick to her stomach. Was she wrong to have

pressed Ruth to speak of such horror, when to do so might have caused further distress? She was out of her depth.

"It's all my fault," Ruth mumbled now. "I must have done something to anger the Lord."

This Maryam understood. She had wrestled with similar doubts when she first realised that life with the Apostles was not as she had always dreamed. But she knew now that to take responsibility for the cruel actions of others was wrong—kind old Hushai had made that clear. "It's *not* your fault! The man is evil, plain as that."

"But he's the Lord's chosen one—"

"No he's not! He's not chosen by the Lord at all—he just uses this to force his will." She remembered Mother Deborah's words the day she showed Maryam the boat. *The thing that you must know is this: the Apostles of the Lamb were formed from a desire for power, based on greed.* Ruth's treatment at the hands of Father Joshua was proof of that. Then there was the stealing of Maryam's blood; the deaths of Sarah, Rebekah and kind Brother Mark. Proof upon proof, mounting up.

Ruth let out a shaky sigh and raised her head. "Every time I close my eyes I see his face," she whispered. "How am I supposed to live with this?"

"By fighting back." The words were out even before Maryam had thought them through. But it was true. "The best revenge is our escape."

"And if he should come after us?"

"I really don't believe he will. We're nothing to him, merely slaves. I reckon he'll be glad we're gone."

"Who'll be glad?" Joseph squatted at the entrance to the shelter.

Ruth shot Maryam a frantic look, warning her. "No one— just the talk of girls," Maryam said.

Joseph grinned. "Well, then stop your chatter now—it's time the two of you sailed this boat alone!"

"Ruth and me together?"

"Yes, why not?" Joseph pulled a serious face. "All of us need to know how to operate tiller and sails, in case one of us should get hurt."

Maryam looked over at Ruth, uncertain if she was recovered enough to do as Joseph asked, but Ruth was already getting to her feet, a bright smile pasted on her tear-streaked face.

"I claim the tiller," Ruth said, refusing to make eye contact with Maryam. "You're on sails."

There was nothing to be done but play along with her, but Maryam feared that Ruth would still have to face her demons if she was ever to regain her peace of mind.

*   *   *

There were times during the following days when Maryam almost forgot they were fleeing from danger into an unknown world. They broke the monotony of the sailing shifts with fishing competitions that quickly turned into all-out gender war. The girls had the knack for teasing the most enormous fish onto their lines, though often lost their bounty as they tried to pull it in; the boys' strike rate was lower, but they hauled their lines in with such efficiency the fish had no chance of escape. Neither side would concede inferiority, however: it fell to the losers to gut the fish—and they would often still be arguing over technicalities long after the sun had set.

Mostly Lazarus pointedly steered clear of Maryam, and his arrogant dismissal galled her, but she tried as best she could to keep the lid on her animosity, hoping her forbearance would win Joseph's regard. Her heart thumped painfully whenever she bit back her instinct to shout at him, but the worst of it was that she couldn't tell if Joseph even appreciated her effort. They never seemed to have a moment alone.

At times the boat glided so effortlessly through the ocean Maryam could close her eyes and trick herself into believing they were on nothing more challenging than a pleasant outing, and would return to the comforts of home at the close of each long hot day. After weeks of fear and tension, this mood of calm relaxation was magical. Even Ruth showed signs of unwinding, laughing to the point of choking over Joseph's disappointment when he excitedly hauled in a streamer of seaweed he'd mistaken for a fish.

As the afternoon of their third full day at sea drew towards its end, Maryam leaned against the forward mast and watched as Lazarus scaled and gutted an ingimea, the giant yellowfin tuna she and Ruth had reluctantly asked the boys to help drag on board. Lazarus was agile with the knife, there was no doubt, and his long strokes through the ingimea's flesh were bold and sure. She shuddered. To think that only three nights ago he'd held this same sharp blade to Ruthie's throat.

The ingimea was as large as a small dog, with enough flesh on it to last for several days. When Lazarus had finished carving it up, Maryam soused some of the fillets in lime juice for their evening meal. The rest she packed in salt to preserve from spoiling in the days ahead: there was still no sign of land, and already, with an extra mouth to feed, their fresh stores were starting to run low.

As they gathered together in the last of the light to share

their feast of fish, a line of thick black rainclouds boiled and rolled together on the western horizon, the lowering sun streaking the dark vapours with fine shots of silver.

"I think we'd better reef the main right in," Joseph said. "They're heading straight for us. Maryam, can you give me a hand?"

Pleased to have been singled out, Maryam rose to help him untie the ropes that held the massive sail aloft. As Lazarus and Ruth hurriedly stowed away their abandoned meal, she and Joseph lashed a good half of the redundant sail back to the boom, their eyes sliding constantly towards the menace in the west. The clouds were not approaching, but hung with a foreboding presence as the travellers sailed towards them: it was only a matter of time before the boat and rainclouds met.

At the tiller hours later, Maryam's brain whirled hopelessly round and round the problem of Ruth's fragile mental state, and she hardly registered the approaching storm until a shift in the motion of the boat drew all her attention back to the task at hand. The wind seemed to be coming from all directions, buffeting the sails and making the tiller hard to control. The sea churned in a sloppy chop and, at the ropes, Lazarus fought to keep his footing as he hauled the mainsail right down to the boom. The dark bank of clouds loomed overhead now, blotting out all trace of stars, and the air grew thick and charged around her. Yet still the rain refused to come.

Joseph appeared from the shelter, early for his shift, and gingerly made his way along the deck to Lazarus's side. "You go and rest now," he told him. "I can't sleep."

Lazarus did not argue. He staggered down the swaying deck and crawled into the shelter to settle next to Ruth.

Thank goodness she's still fast asleep, Maryam thought.

Joseph busied himself re-securing all the ropes, then edged his way back to Maryam's side. He smiled at her through the gloom. "Finally, we have a chance to be alone."

Maryam's heart skipped a beat. So he was missing their old closeness too. She inclined her head towards the clouds. "I think we might be in for a good soaking soon."

Joseph grinned. "Nothing can put a dampener on things when I'm with you!"

"Wait until you've sat till dawn in pouring rain and then say that!"

"You're on," he said, gently wrapping his hand over hers to help adjust the tiller as a squally backwind slewed the boat.

Warmth radiated through her from his touch. She sneaked a look at him as he raised his head to check the unpredictable wind in the stream of feathers atop the mast. His features were straight and fine, his nose so much more defined and sharp than hers, and his fine blond hair could not have been more different from her own thick curtain of wiry black curls. She thought him beautiful, as striking as the ancient European kings painted in the murals on the walls of the dining room in the Holy City.

"Why couldn't you sleep?" she asked, her heart galloping as he rubbed his thumb along the line of her little finger.

"Can't you guess?" He turned his eyes to her, and even in the darkness she could feel the intensity of his gaze.

She nodded. "I'm worried too."

"Bad guess!" He laughed, the sound a point of brightness in the night. "Every time I close my eyes, all I can picture is kissing you!"

Maryam was glad the shadows hid her tingling blush as the memory of their stolen kisses back on Onewēre filled her mind.

35

She swallowed hard, her mouth suddenly very dry as he leaned in close. "I have thought—"

His boldness swept her words away and for one long moment nothing else existed except the concentrated merging of their mouths. Maryam felt her body melting, her bones transformed to whirlpools as his tongue met hers. When finally she pulled away to draw a breath, she could hear the race of blood thrum through her ears.

"You know how much I care for you, don't you?" Joseph whispered. "I think I knew it from the first time I saw you at my father's funeral." He ran a finger down her arm, lowering his gaze as he traced his name against her skin. "And what about you? Do you like me too?"

"Of course!" she laughed, amazed by the uncertainty in his voice. "We agreed already that we're friends, remember?"

"No," he said, his brow creased to a frown. "I mean, do you *really* like me?"

How could he even ask it when only moments ago she had given herself over to his kiss? "I do," she confessed, terror and excitement competing inside. She didn't know what else to say. It was the truth, but she felt as if she teetered on the edge of a precipice, and there was only a perilous, uncharted region far below. Instead, she wrapped her arms around Joseph's shoulders and pressed him close.

He littered her hair with tiny kisses, his breath panting out hard and fast, and she closed her eyes, allowing the pressures of the outside world to fall away once more. But a predatory face intruded on the swirling pleasure in her head—Father Joshua as he forced himself on Ruth. She pulled back abruptly, guilt competing with pleasure in a confusing dance.

"I'm sorry," she babbled, "but I can't stop thinking of poor Ruth."

"Ruth?" A hint of impatience crept into Joseph's voice.

"She suffers cruelly from the assault by Father Joshua. I don't know how to ease her hurt." It was totally the wrong time to be telling him this, she knew—their intimacy was retreating like the tide—but she badly needed to share the worry. She wanted Joseph's help.

Joseph stared at her intently before sighing. He released her from his embrace. "I suspect it's something only time will heal," he said. "I've heard my mother speak of the fallout from such an—" He held his hand aloft as the clouds finally decided to release their load. "Oh-oh . . . It's here."

Plump drops splashed around them, bursting like tiny explosions as they hit the deck. Within seconds both Joseph and Maryam were soaked.

"Quickly," Joseph ordered, "get under the shelter now and try to sleep. I'll man the boat."

It pained her to break their precious moment, but the rain was falling more steadily now, running off her hair and weeping down her face. She rose up on her tiptoes and kissed the wet tip of his nose. "Shall I wake Ruth for her shift?"

Joseph shook his head. "No, let her sleep. Perhaps with rest her mind will find some kind of peace."

Maryam sent him one last smile, warmed, despite the rain, by Joseph's kind and thoughtful heart.

CHAPTER THREE

The downpour lasted until dawn. Maryam hardly slept, tossing and turning as she replayed the conversation and the unsettling kiss from the night before. Why, oh why had she raised Ruth's problem with Joseph then? After so few opportunities to be alone with him, she'd distracted him from the little time they had.

When, finally, the rain had stopped and the sky was growing light, she could stand her swirling thoughts no longer, and crawled out of the shelter to press a nourishing ball of te kabubu paste into Joseph's hand.

"Please, eat this," she said. "It'll help to warm you and keep up your strength." Then she handed him her one spare shirt. "Here. Use this to dry yourself."

He looked wet and miserable, his skin paled to a stony grey and wrinkled from the long exposure to the rain. Purple pools of tiredness smudged beneath his eyes. As he stripped off his own soaked shirt he sneezed a spray of te kabubu out across the deck and shrugged.

"Well, the good news is it looks as though the rain has passed." He pointed east, to where the bank of clouds had retreated. To the west, the sky transformed to vivid blue.

Maryam scanned the western horizon and spied a flock of birds reeling in the distance, far ahead. "Look! Doesn't that mean we're nearing land?"

Joseph shielded his eyes against the glare. His face lit up. "You could be right!" Again he sneezed, the force rocking his whole body. "Keep a good watch on them—it could mean Marawa Island is up ahead."

Despite her relief, Maryam was swept by a terrible fore-boding. "Is it protected by a reef?" she asked. She thought back to their wild flight from Onewēre. Even when they'd known the position of the corridor between the deadly shelves of coral, they'd struggled to manoeuvre the big boat safely through. Just how would they navigate a completely unfamiliar reef?

He guessed her thoughts. "If we approach in daylight we should be right. I'm fairly sure it's just a case of watching for changes in the colour of the sea."

Fairly sure? She didn't want to question Joseph's authority, but his words failed to comfort her. They were sailing as blind as old Hushai, in a boat so large it seemed to have a mind of its own. If they should make even the tiniest error of judgement . . .

Joseph rubbed his hair as dry as possible with Maryam's shirt and stretched his arms towards the heavens with a tired yawn. "Thanks for your help. Can you take the tiller now? I need some rest." He draped the two damp shirts across the pandanus thatch to dry. "Keep an eye out for the wind, it's stronger than it looks—and wake me if you see anything that remotely looks like land! I'll get the other two to help you."

When Ruth emerged from the shelter, Maryam noticed immediately how much less strained she looked. She had more colour in her face, and even smiled when Maryam pointed out the flock of birds.

"I dreamed we landed in the Lord's own realm, and the Lamb greeted us Himself and made us welcome."

Lazarus, refreshed too, laughed. "And just what did He look like, oh great oracle of the high seas?"

His sneering slapped Ruth's cheeks with pink but she did not falter in her answer. "Like He looked upon the cross. His hands and feet were marked with blood, yet from Him shone a sacred light."

There was such awe and longing in her voice it made Maryam want to cry. Despite what Father Joshua had done to her, Ruth's faith was secure. The familiar touchstones of the Holy Book helped keep her sane.

"It's a sign, Ruthie," Maryam reassured her. "The Lord is telling you all will be well."

"Either that or He's telling her she's soon to meet her maker because we're doomed," Lazarus drawled.

Always ready with a put-down.

"Take the tiller, Ruth," Maryam ordered, seizing Lazarus by the arm and towing him up to the front of the boat. Some things could not be left unsaid. "Don't toy with her," she whispered to him furiously. "I don't care what you say to me, but leave Ruth be."

He rubbed the place where her fingers had dug into his elbow, and a caustic smile twisted his mouth. "Let me get this straight. If I leave your friend alone, then I can say whatever I like to you?"

She nodded reluctantly, realising she'd backed herself into a corner. There was nothing she could do but take the hand he now held out to her. Still, she conceded only one half-hearted shake before tugging her hand back quickly from his grasp.

"We have a deal then," he said.

"I guess we do." She hated how he looked at her, like a hunter eyeing up his prey.

"Then right now I have this to say—" He rubbed his toe

along a join between the timbers of the deck. "I saw you kissing my cousin in the night."

She found she could not look at him, and studied instead his restless foot. His toes were long, each joint clearly delineated beneath his pale skin. "What of it?" she challenged him, knowing there was no point in denial. But it infuriated her that he seemed to know what she was doing or thinking at every turn.

"Nothing, little Sister. Nothing." He leaned in towards her, his voice now serious and hushed. "But be careful where you rest your heart. Your blood may have given him a boost, but, believe me, Te Matee Iai does not give up its own so easily."

Her gaze flew up to his, but she could not read the content of his eyes. "What is it you're trying to say?"

"Only this: those who use the Blessed Sisters' blood to halt Te Matee Iai's progress are not cured, merely given a reprieve."

"Reprieve?"

He ran his hand almost tenderly down one of the ropes, and sighed. "Have you not wondered why so many of your Sisters have already died? Or why more and more are picked each Judgement time to fill the ranks? The need for blood—*ongoing* need—is as endless as this sea."

"You mean—" Her question died as the meaning of his words struck her full force. He was saying Joseph still could die. But even as she processed this, out of the corner of her eye she saw an unfathomable emotion ripple across Lazarus's face. Of course! He was teasing her, knowing full well how much his prediction would cause her grief. "You're lying," she accused him. "I heard your own mother say she could maintain his strength."

"Maintain, yes. Keep him alive without more blood? Not a

chance." He looked pleased with himself, as though he believed he'd dealt her a mortal blow.

"You really *are* detestable. What kind of person would wish his cousin dead merely to score a point with me?" The answer came easily enough: *a liar and heartless beast.*

She turned her back on his deceit, hurrying down the deck to join Ruth at the tiller. From now on, she vowed, she would not rise to his bait, no matter how he taunted her. And if he thought he could lie to her—well, he was wrong.

* * *

The wind rose to a gusty westerly, hitting the boat head on and making a hard slog of progress as they tacked from side to side to make leeway towards the west. Maryam and Lazarus were forced to work together, adjusting the heavy sails each time they made a turn. It was arduous and concentrated work, and by noon the sun blazed directly overhead, the harsh rays bouncing off the water and striking at Lazarus's pale unprotected skin like open flames.

Maryam had just ducked into the shelter for a drink of water when she heard Ruth give a strangled cry from her station at the tiller.

"Sweet Lord in Heaven! Come and see this."

Maryam rushed to her, following the line of Ruth's arm as she pointed out in front of them to the south-west. There, at the very edge of the horizon, something broke the regularity of the hazy border between sea and sky.

"Can you see it too?" Ruth demanded.

Maryam blinked and looked again, clambering to the very

prow of the boat to see if she could gain a better view. There *was* something there, she was sure of it.

"I can!" she called back, her heart banging out its excitement despite the wilting effects of the sun. But the shadowy apparition was further to the south than any land they'd plotted on the map. *Time to wake Joseph*, she thought. *He will know.*

She charged back down the deck and ducked into the shelter, where Joseph lay sprawled across the bedding, his face flushed and his breathing thick and laboured in the stifling heat. She shook him by the shoulder.

"Joseph! Wake up! We think we might have sight of land!"

His eyes shot open but took a moment to focus on her face. "What?"

"Land!" she repeated. "Come take a look."

He stirred himself, reaching for the map as he followed her outside.

She pointed to the mysterious lump on the horizon. "See? Right there!"

He cupped his hand over his eyes, peering intently into the distance before turning his attention to the map. "It *has* to be Marawa Island," he agreed. "There's nothing else even remotely near us."

"Praise the Lord!" Ruth cried, her anxiety extinguished by the joy that swept the group.

"We'll need to sail harder on to the wind if we're to reach it before nightfall," Lazarus said.

Maryam knew he was right, but even now could not bring herself to acknowledge him. Instead she turned to Joseph. "How long, do you reckon, until we're there?"

Joseph shrugged. "Hard to tell. But we'll need to leave at least an hour of light to find a safe way through the reef."

"And if we don't?"

"Then we'll have to circle it all night, well out at sea, and wait till morning."

"You're joking," Ruth wailed. "You mean we'd have to wait all night?"

"If you want to reach land safely, we really have no other choice."

"In that case, let's get moving," Maryam said, looking up to check the position of the sun. "I figure we have about seven hours of good light." She studied Joseph, who still looked flushed. "I'll make some lunch, then let's see if we can move this boat more quickly."

He grinned at her. "All right. You're on!"

Never was a meal prepared and eaten in such haste. It was as if they'd been infested by a swarm of ngongo bugs, the itch to reach land so great that sitting still was all but impossible. The race was on as soon as they had swallowed their last mouthfuls of the stale bread.

Joseph, Lazarus and Ruth took charge of the ropes, while Maryam swung the tiller in an endless cycle of hard tacks. Their concentration was palpable; no one spoke bar the odd curt call for help. After an hour the heat and sustained effort began to sap their enthusiasm, and still the island remained a teasing shadow at the far edge of their world. But they slogged on, breaking only for much-needed water, and by the passing of the second hour the island was clearly outlined against the sky.

"Have you thought about our tactics once we land the boat?" Maryam asked Joseph during a brief break for water rations. Now that the island lay before them, thoughts of their likely reception weighed heavily upon her. What if the people of Marawa were hostile to strangers? What on earth would they do then?

"I'm sure when they've heard our plight they'll take us in."

"You're assuming they'll understand what we're saying," Lazarus chipped in. "You said that they turned away the missionaries——what if they can't understand a word we say?"

"That's where I'm counting on Maryam and Ruth to help. My father was convinced that all the islands once shared the same far-distant ancestors, so hopefully they'll recognise some of Onewēre's words."

"But I can hardly remember how to speak it," Ruth said. "Blessed Sisters are forced to speak English once we're taken at the Judgement."

"I can understand our language when it's spoken, but I'm not sure I can string whole sentences together and make sense," Maryam added. "What if we say something wrong?"

Joseph gestured helplessly. "I have no idea," he said, frustration clipping off his words. "I never said it would be easy."

Maryam glanced up at him sharply—it was so unlike him to snap. She saw now how drained he looked. The rings under his eyes had darkened almost to black. "Let's focus on one problem at a time," she said, hoping to relieve him of some stress.

"Maryam's right," Lazarus said. He, too, seemed to be studying Joseph intently. "Let's get there first, then worry about how we'll be met."

Joseph leaned against the starboard rail, closing his eyes for a moment before he proceeded back to the ropes to start up the whole tacking manoeuvre once again. Meanwhile Lazarus rummaged in the shelter, returning with a large clay pot now emptied of fresh water. He flattened himself along the forward deck between the hulls and scooped sea water up into it.

"You look overheated, cousin. Let me help!" With this, he poured the water over Joseph's head.

Joseph gasped and wiped the salty water from his eyes. But he was smiling, Maryam noticed, as he wrestled the pot from Lazarus and rushed forward to refill it, chasing after Lazarus until he, too, was soaked right through.

"Beautiful!" Lazarus spluttered, retrieving the pot. "Now for the girls!"

Soon all four were scrabbling for some kind of container, hurling water over whoever was at hand, laughing and squealing in shock and pleasure at the unexpected release of tension, until not a person or a strip of deck was left undrenched. When at last they'd had enough, they sprawled on the deck to dry themselves before somewhat reluctantly returning to their tasks.

Two hours on, and the island took on a more solid shape. It rose to a perfect peak on its most northern side, with a plateau to the south that gently fell away into the sea. It was still too far distant for anyone on board to tell if there was jungle or where villages might lie, yet to see the island growing real before their eyes filled all four with renewed drive.

There were more birds in the skies above them now, and a startling array of creatures in the watery world below. Fine-winged storm petrels hovered on the highest air currents. Frigate birds, with their curious red pouches, reeled and screeched directly overhead, as if they were cheering the travellers onwards as they battled the stubborn headwind, accompanied by a forward guard of streamlined flying fish.

It was impossible not to feel excited by the prospect of

reaching land. Though the Apostles had claimed there was nothing beyond the small sanctuary of Onewēre, the four escapees now had proof that life—albeit only birds and fish so far—existed beyond Onewēre's distant shores. It boded well, reinforcing Maryam's growing conviction that the Apostles' dire talk was nothing more than wicked lies to maintain fear. She closed her eyes and tilted her face towards the sun, allowing the golden light to filter through her eyelids and collect behind them in a warm pool of hope.

Joseph's coughing distracted her. He was doubled over, trying to regain his breath.

"Time for a break," Lazarus announced, pointing to the shaded shelter. "I'll take the tiller for this tack while you three rest out of the sun."

Joseph raised his head, his eyes watering from the choking fit. "But we need to maintain—"

"We've time enough," Maryam cut in, grateful to Lazarus, despite herself. He understood his cousin well enough to know he'd never take a break while others worked.

She nodded her thanks as Lazarus took over the tiller, then she scrambled to the shelter to pour Joseph a drink. He flopped down beside her, his breathing laboured and his eyelids ringed with red. As he took the cup from her she noticed how his hand shook and how he winced as he tried to get comfortable.

"Are you all right?"

"I'm fine," he said, falling back onto the sleeping mat. "My body's just discovering muscles I didn't know it had."

"I know what you mean," Ruth said. "I've got blisters from the ropes." She held out her hands to reveal raw strips where the ropes had run through her fingers and chaffed her skin.

"Let me go on the ropes then," Maryam offered. "You work the tiller, Joseph, and Ruth can be our lookout now that we're close to land."

"What about you?" Joseph said. "You have to preserve your strength—it's still only a short time since I took your blood." He sniffed loudly, wiping his runny nose with the back of his hand.

"I'm in better shape than you," Maryam countered. "You look as if you've caught a chill."

"It's nothing, while you—"

"Listen to you two! It's not a competition as to who is feeling worse!" Ruth laughed.

Maryam felt herself blushing. Ruth was right in a way. It was as if she and Joseph were circling around, worrying about the other at their own expense. The difference, though, was that she knew her strength was rebuilding, while Joseph's seemed to ebb away. And this mattered to her—mattered more than she could ever put into words. But she also knew that the only way Joseph would get the rest he needed was if they made it to land.

"Thank you, Mother Ruth!" she said, trying desperately to lift the mood. "Now could I humbly suggest we have a snack and then put all our effort into reaching the island?"

* * *

The sun was losing its heat when they finally approached the reef that protected Marawa Island from the open sea. They could see the waves break across its back in a seemingly continuous ring that divided the dark blue of the ocean from the luminous mottled turquoise of the shallow water inside the reef.

The island was clearly visible now. Lush impenetrable-looking jungle spilled down from the cone-like peak right to the edges of the glistening coral sand. Overhead, dozens of birds competed for the updrafts, their cries clearly audible above the boil of the surf. If there were people on the island, there was no sign—it looked as pristine and uninhabited as when the Lord first formed it.

They slackened off the sails, allowing the boat to wallow on the swell as all four made their way up to the prow and studied the way the waves broke on the thick ring of reef.

"I can't see any opening," Joseph said. He pointed to the plateau at the southern end. "I think we'd better circle round and see what's on the other side."

"I agree," Maryam said, trying to put from her mind any reason why the place should look so deserted. "Surely there's a passageway if your father said they traded with Onewēre in the past."

Together they worked to haul in the sails, leaving only a small storm jib that was much easier to control. Lazarus took command of the tiller; the other three stood up at the bow to scan for rocks or coral shelves that might hole the boat. Progress though the sloppy swell was slow. Many times Lazarus was forced to manoeuvre the craft around abruptly as one of the others warned him away from a threatening dark mass beneath the water. It was not worth the risk.

Then, as they rounded the headland at the south end of the island, a whole new vista opened up to them. The plateau folded in on itself, forming a perfect crescent-shaped bay. At its centre, strange conical parapets just peeked out from the tangled mass of jungle, weathered to a streaky grey.

"Do you see that?" Maryam shouted. Her cry carried to the birds, which picked up the duel between excitement and trepidation in her voice and relayed it in raucous echoes out across the bay.

"There! Look!" Ruth's voice, too, flew high as she pointed to a smooth channel of water amidst the waves churning against the reef. "There's a break!"

"You're right!" Joseph turned to Lazarus. "Do you see it?"

Lazarus nodded. "What do you think?"

"Let's approach it slowly and see if it's wide enough to sail through." Joseph looked to the girls. "Be ready to reach for the ropes if we have to spin away at the last moment."

All thoughts of the strange building were pushed aside as the four put their energy and concentration into crossing through the passageway between the deadly coral shoals. With Maryam keeping watch out on the starboard hull and Ruth to port, Joseph straddled the carved figurehead to scan the sea below as Lazarus steered a wide lazy loop away from the island. Then he turned the boat and aimed it directly back towards the break.

Maryam glanced at Lazarus for a moment, grudgingly acknowledging his natural skill and the intense aura of concentration that lit his face. He was in his element, boy against nature, and in that moment his whole aspect changed. It amazed her, this sudden likeness to Joseph, the way he radiated the same determination and strength of spirit. For a brief second his gaze swept hers.

"Focus," he snapped. "Keep your eye out for snags."

She flushed, knowing she deserved his warning yet hating how he always made her feel in the wrong, especially when *he* was the one who should be shamed by all the sins he'd perpetrated in his own short life.

Staring down again at the rough edges of the reef, she found herself holding her breath as the hull started to slide past the jagged branches of coral with only a tiny fraction of space to spare.

"Ruth," Lazarus shouted, "how's your side?"

"All right," she said. "But don't come any further over this way."

"Maryam?"

"Same as Ruth."

"There's a huge rock just through the other side to port," Joseph called out from his vantage point. "As soon as you're confident we're through, swing to the right."

All appeared to be going as planned until, without warning, the boat was picked up by a surge of swell. The sea compressed through the narrow channel, shunting the boat forward, so that it slewed sideways at alarming speed. The right hull slammed up against the mass of coral, and a terrible scraping sound filled Maryam's ears as she was jolted off her feet and sent flying. Ruth screamed as the side rail caught Maryam square across her stomach, winding her. Somehow she managed to grab hold of the rail just in time to save herself from pitching overboard into the sea. But the pain was excruciating, and tears sprang to her eyes. She fell back to the deck, struggling for breath as the boat again lurched forwards on the swell.

"I'm okay," she panted, motioning for Joseph and Ruth to stay at their posts. She forced herself to lean out past the rail to check for damage, fully expecting to see the timber shredded beyond repair. But by some wondrous miracle, the hull, though scraped and splintered, remained intact.

"It's fine," she gasped, her voice wavering now though the worst was past.

"We've cleared the rock," Joseph yelled. "And it looks as if we can sail straight up to the beach."

Maryam wiped the tears from her eyes and tried to put her pain aside. There, ahead of them, the dense jungle reached long trailing fingers of vegetation down to the sandy shore, while a ragged procession of square boulders marched from the low-tide line up towards the dark understorey of the bush. Below her, the water was so clear she could see multicoloured fish dart between each individual stone and shell beneath swaying strings of seaweed.

With the hiss of the reef behind them, the air was alive with a barrage of birdsong and the clamour of insects rejoicing in the last of the afternoon's warm light. No one spoke as the boat glided in towards the beach. Instead, each of them nervously eyed the dark shadows of the bush for any sign of human life. The strange building they had spotted was now hidden from view and the trail of hewn boulders was the only hint that anyone had ever been here before.

They lifted the rudders and allowed the boat to slowly drift and beach itself on the smooth sandy shore, Maryam's heart beating so hard she could feel a pulse throbbing wildly in her temple. It was the moment she had dreamed of—safe at last from the Apostles' controlling grasp. But even as she climbed across the rail and splashed into the warm shallows, a niggling uncertainty took hold of her. She had no idea what she feared the most: meeting the people who inhabited this island, or the awful possibility that no one lived here at all.

CHAPTER FOUR

The first thing that struck Maryam as they secured the boat to several of the huge boulders was the staggering abundance of bird life. A colony of brown boobies lined the soft sand at the rim of the vegetation, their rich brown feathers puffed up and their piercing black eyes watching the intruders' every step. Petrels, terns and shearwaters filled the sky, and from the dense jungle came a cacophony that seemed to make the air vibrate, as though warning the four that they did not belong. The smell, too, was overpowering—the fetid pungency of bird droppings mixed with the salty scent of kelp and the earthy undertones of the composting leaf-litter from the jungle floor.

There was no obvious sign of human settlement and, from the beach at least, no hint of the strange building they'd seen from the boat.

As soon as her feet touched dry land Ruth dropped to her knees in prayer. "Oh Lord, thank you for bringing us safely to Marawa . . ."

The other three regrouped behind her, swaying slightly as they adjusted to standing on firm ground again. Maryam felt a rush of excitement. *They'd made it!* Whatever else happened, they'd escaped the Apostles and sailed an unfamiliar craft across an equally unknown sea. Had she still believed the Lord was listening, as Ruth did, she'd have thanked Him too. But, for now at least, it was enough to feel pride in their own achievement.

"So, what do we do now?" she asked.

"Eat," replied Ruth, as she wound up her prayers. "I don't

know what it is about the sea air, but I'm hungrier than I've ever been before."

Maryam laughed. "That's no surprise." She prodded her friend in the soft roll of fat around her belly. "But don't you think perhaps we should make a camp first?"

"I vote we go in search of that building we saw," Joseph said. "It may be that we won't need to camp if we can find the people who live here."

His words stirred up Maryam's nerves. For as long as she did not know the outcome of their search, she could still hope all would be well. But the thought of launching straight into a new adventure made her knees go weak. "You think there's time for that today?"

Joseph studied the position of the sinking sun. "I'm guessing we've got about another hour before it grows too dark."

"Then let's waste no time," Lazarus said. He hurried over to the edge of the jungle, searching the ground before he spied a weighty staff of wood and picked it up. "Come on."

"What's that for?" Maryam demanded, fearing she already knew.

"Protection."

She glanced over at Joseph, expecting him to tell Lazarus not to be so stupid. Instead, he nodded his agreement, made his way over to his cousin's side and scooped another hefty piece of driftwood off the sand.

"Are you mad?" she said. "If we approach them with weapons we're just inviting trouble."

"There's no way I'm walking unprotected into what could be a trap," Lazarus countered, chopping the air with his staff.

"Trap? That's crazy talk. No one even knows we're here."

Joseph smiled nervously. "I'm sorry," he said. "I'm with Laz on this. Until we know otherwise, it's best we're prepared for every possible response."

"But you promised we'd be made welcome," Ruth protested.

"That's my hope," Joseph replied. "But I'm not letting you girls walk into anything unprepared." He looked intently at Maryam, as though silently willing her to acquiesce.

Maryam shook her head. The boys were right to be cautious, she supposed—and she was touched by Joseph's desire to protect both her and Ruth—but it seemed ridiculous to invite trouble where there might be none. "All right. But as soon as we meet them and it's clear we have nothing to fear, you must promise you'll drop the sticks immediately, as a show of faith."

Joseph smiled his relief. "That's fine with me."

"And you?" Maryam challenged Lazarus.

"Perhaps," he conceded. "But I'll make up my own mind when the time is right. I'll not have *you* dictating how I act."

"I'm *not* dictating—"

"Good," he interrupted. "Then we're in agreement. Let's be off." He marched towards a break in the undergrowth and disappeared into its depths.

"Laz! Wait!" Joseph called, running now to catch him up. In a moment he, too, was swallowed by the dense curtain of trees.

Maryam grasped Ruth's hand and ploughed in after him, panicked by the thought of being left behind.

Enclosed by the trees, the rich loamy odour of humus was almost overpowering, and the air itself was damp and thick. They plodded on, still swaying slightly, ducking under low-slung branches as startled birds took to the air in a flurry of flapping wings and shrill complaints. Five minutes . . . Ten . . . Then, up ahead through the maze of trees, Maryam saw the boys halt in their tracks and gaze around in stunned silence. A shiver trickled down her spine. Whatever they had seen there did not bode well.

As soon as the two girls caught them up, it was horribly apparent why the boys had stopped. All around them lay the remnants of what must once have been a village made from stone. Now it was almost one with the jungle itself, consumed by a thick tangle of creepers, moss and grasses, and invasive trees. For as far as they could see in each direction, disintegrating stonework littered the ground, displaced by huge trees that twisted up through the collapsed structures, suffocating them in sinewy roots that spilled over and down like water transformed to wood. In some places it was impossible to tell where plant and stone divided, the streaky limestone faded to the same dirty shade and texture as the rough-cast bark.

Ruth gasped, her hand shooting to her mouth as her eyes shocked wide. "It's all true, just like the Apostles said. Everything has been destroyed." She dropped down to her haunches then, rocking backwards and forwards as she moaned.

"Hold on, Ruthie," Maryam said, though she knew the consolation was meagre. "Until we've found that big building we can't be sure."

"You think the jungle would have grown like this if people still lived nearby?"

Maryam shrugged, not risking her voice with a reply. Ruth was right. It was clear that no one had ventured to this place for more years than she cared to guess. She crossed to Joseph's side, and reached out for the comfort of his hand.

"What do you think?" she whispered, examining his face to try to read his thoughts. His skin reflected back the same ghostly pallor as the stone and trees.

"We carry on until we find the other building, like you said." He squeezed her hand. "But maybe you should take Ruth back and wait for us at the boat."

"You're joking! We stick together no matter what."

Joseph looked over to Lazarus. "What do you think?"

"Sister Maryam is right for once. Until we know exactly what we're up against, it's better we don't split up."

Ignoring his insult, Maryam smiled at Lazarus, thankful that for now he'd put away his bravado. She squatted down next to Ruth. "Come on, Ruthie—please don't give up on this yet."

Ruth's haunted gaze rose to hers. *"Thus with violence shall that great city be thrown down, and shall be found no more . . . for who knoweth the power of thine anger? Even according to thy fear, so is thy wrath."*

This, from the Holy Book, shook Maryam right down to her bones. If it was true that this village had been destroyed by the Tribulation, then everything else they had been told about that terrible time in history could well be true. When Mother Deborah told Maryam of the ship's log and the solar flares, she'd made it sound as if she believed the destruction was only temporary—that she was sure most life had been restored and Onewēre was not alone in its revival, despite the Apostles' claim that the Lord had chosen only them and their disciples to remain on Earth. Was it possible for the underlying story of the Tribulation to hold true, even while the Apostles lied about so much else? And if it *was* possible, what did that mean for the four of them now?

"I'm sorry but we have to keep going, Ruth. We really have no other choice." Maryam forced herself to rise, and offered her hand to hoist Ruth back up to her feet.

Ruth caused no further argument, but followed after Maryam as though she sleepwalked towards death. And, indeed, it felt as if they were fighting through the outskirts of Hell, crumbling stonework tripping them, webs of roots and creepers snaring their arms, legs and hair as they pushed through the undergrowth in the growing gloom.

For fifteen minutes more they persisted, struggling and panting as the ground began to slope uphill. And still there was no end to the destruction, nor any sign of the great towering structure they had seen from out at sea. The jungle was slipping into darkness now, the birds settling down to roost and the clamour of the insects dying with the retreat of the sun.

"That's enough!" Joseph finally called, turning to the other three as sweat poured freely down his face. "We'll search again tomorrow, but for now let's go back to the boat and settle for the night, or else we'll end up lost in here."

No one argued, so they turned and stumbled back along the way they'd come, the darkness setting snares for them as tiredness and disappointment took its toll. Maryam struggled to match the pace set by the boys and, in her haste, missed her step as she clambered over a fallen log. She fell heavily, catching her back on some crumbling stonework, and hit the ground hard. For a moment she just lay there, stunned. Her elbows had been torn open by sharp shards of stone and her tailbone pulsed with pain.

"Maryam!" Ruth scrabbled after her, frantically digging through the pile of mossy dislodged stone to free her of its leaden weight. Then she let out a blood-curdling scream, and Maryam saw her wildly fling something into the undergrowth. "Oh Lord! Oh Lord!" Ruth leapt away, shuddering uncontrollably.

"What is it?" Lazarus was beside her now, grasping her shoulders firmly and trying to calm her while Joseph rushed to Maryam's aid.

Ruth shrank from his grasp, but pointed at the pile of rubble. "A human skull. I saw it—it was just there. It was—" Again she shuddered, before she was beset by tears.

Joseph was supporting Maryam as she gingerly rose to her feet. "Where does it hurt?"

"Everywhere." She tried to smile. Her tailbone ached so much she thought she would vomit, and her elbows stung. But worst was the humiliation. Why was she the clumsy one who always seemed so foolish and ridiculously weak? She shook Joseph's hand away and set off again towards the beach, biting on her bottom lip to hold in the pain. Right now she cared for nothing more than escaping her embarrassment—the supposed skull and Ruth's distress would have to wait.

"Maryam, hold on!" Joseph crashed after her, leaving Ruth and Lazarus to take up the rear.

"I reckon you imagined it," Lazarus taunted Ruth.

"I swear I saw it!" she protested. "It was smooth and round, just like a skull."

"So, tomorrow, then, when we return, I'll find it lying over there?" He pointed to the tangled branches.

"Yes, you will."

To hear the two of them squabbling was for a moment strangely reassuring. But Maryam's distracted amusement quickly fell away as the effort to keep moving while every muscle in her body cried out for attention made the last quarter of an hour fighting through the tumbledown village a painful chore.

When finally she broke through the undergrowth, sidestepping her way past the nesting birds, the relief was so intense it released her tears. She limped down to the water's edge, groaning as she knelt to wash the sticky blood from her elbows.

She ignored Joseph as he came and squatted close beside her. She still felt too belittled by her own weaknesses to meet his eye. He said nothing, just reached across with his index finger and carefully brushed away a tear that had collected in the thick lashes beneath her eye. Out on the horizon, the sunset lit the sky with rusty pink and gold. She let the beauty of it wash over her, and slowly leaned in towards him until her head rested on his shoulder and the comfort of his body helped the pain recede.

"This is not what I imagined," she confessed.

Joseph slipped his arm around her waist. "You're incredibly brave, you know?"

"No, not brave at all."

"But look what you've endured already. First the bloodletting, then my Uncle Joshua's wrath. Even today, twice hurt enough for any normal girl to weep and wail, yet you—"

"Stupid and stubborn perhaps," she interrupted, "and certainly clumsy—but not brave." She shifted on her knees, trying to cushion her aching tailbone. "Braveness is a conscious act—like yours, standing up to my father when he would have seen me bound and beaten, or passing up your chance for a comfortable life. All I've done is run away."

He grinned. "Well, you're right about the stubborn part!"

She feigned annoyance, nudging him so hard he lost his balance and fell onto the tide-lapped sand. "Watch yourself," she warned.

Behind her, Ruth laughed. Maryam glanced back, expecting to see that Ruth had been spying on their game. But she was still up near the edge of the jungle, laughing as Lazarus tried unsuccessfully to light a fire. And he was playing to his audience, striking the flint with such a pompous lack of skill it made Maryam smile as well.

"He should hand the flint over to Ruth. We've been lighting fires like that since we were small."

"He used to know," Joseph said, standing now to brush the coating of wet sand from his legs. "When we were little he used to come and stay with us. My father would show us how to hunt and fish, and make a fire from almost nothing to cook what we had caught." He offered his hand to Maryam, but still she had to suppress a groan as she straightened out.

"You like Lazarus, don't you?" she asked as they walked back to join the others.

He nodded thoughtfully. "I do. Until the last two or three years we were as close as brothers, and then something—I don't know what—seemed to come over him. He changed."

"He scares me," Maryam said. "I don't trust him at all."

"Give him a chance. I think maybe he'll be better now he's free of his father's expectations."

"I hope you're right," Maryam said, though her doubts remained. She knew the other side of Lazarus's behaviour—had experienced it firsthand.

They had reached the makeshift fireplace Lazarus and Ruth had built from scattered rocks.

Lazarus glanced up. "Right about what?" he asked.

"That I can teach you how to light a fire properly," Joseph joked. He snatched the flint from Lazarus's hand and went to work, whooping with delight when a spark caught in the mix of twigs and dry leaf-litter at his second strike. He blew gently on the smouldering kindling, and fanned a tiny flame to life. "Now, *that*, cousin, is how you start a fire!"

Maryam and Ruth applauded, while Lazarus took his defeat in good grace. He even volunteered to scour the beach for burnable wood, hauling over great logs as Ruth and Maryam filled their arms with brittle branches from the jungle's edge.

Soon the fire was built to a reassuring blaze, spreading a warm pool of light across the darkened beach. They huddled in its protective orbit, skewering the salted fish on sharpened sticks to heat. Behind them, the jungle pulsed with life. Noises that at home Maryam would have taken for granted—cracking sticks, rustling leaves, strange grunts and calls—took on heightened meaning now. Unknown creatures, even hostile islanders, could be out there watching . . . waiting . . .

At first they spoke of nothing more than memories of life back on Onewēre, seeking the comfort of much happier times. Ruth and Maryam told the boys of their childhood on the atoll after they were Chosen in the Judgement—carefree days coloured by the expectation of greater things once they Crossed to the Holy City to begin the Lord's work. When they could go no further, tacitly agreeing not to dwell on their lives after their Crossing, Joseph and Lazarus picked up the conversation.

To Maryam's surprise, the boys' lives sounded quite normal. Joseph told them about how he'd been brought up amongst the villagers, while Lazarus regaled them with stories of the mischief he'd got up to in the Holy City. All the angry sourness faded from his face as his humour and storytelling skills took over, and Maryam began to see the person Joseph liked. Yet she held a little of herself back from him, mindful that he still could suddenly turn on her and revert to the cruel-hearted boy she'd come to know.

As the night deepened, tiredness stilled their tongues, and the enormity of what they might face in the days ahead started to hit home. Maryam stirred the embers of the fire with a stick, releasing tiny sparks into the cloying air.

"So what's the plan?" she asked at last, knowing she was merely putting into words what others were thinking. Although the throbbing of her tailbone had eased a little, thanks to their small supply of Mother Deborah's herbal tonics, and the grazes on her elbows had dried and stiffened to protective scabs, anxiety ached right through her like a wound.

"First we must locate that building," Joseph said. "And then, if it too is deserted, I'm willing to climb up to the top of the mountain to see if there are any signs of other villages around the coast."

"Is that wise?" Maryam had seen how, as the night progressed, he breathed less easily and a fine slick of sweat now gleamed in the firelight on his face and neck. She was sure he had caught a chill, and he had little in reserve to fight it.

Lazarus tossed another log on the fire. "That's stupid, cousin. I'll go. You need to rest."

"I'm fine," Joseph grumbled. "It's nothing that a good night's sleep won't fix."

Lazarus rolled his eyes at Maryam and Ruth. "He's as stubborn as his father. You can see now why Uncle Jonah stormed out when my father was proclaimed Holy Father instead of him. Like my dear cousin here, he too could not accept there were some things best left to others."

"Stormed out? You've got that wrong, *dear* cousin."

Lazarus shrugged. "Come on now. You know how much his leaving hurt my father, but if it helps you to believe otherwise that's fine with me. I'm tired. I need to get some sleep."

He rose abruptly then, and stalked over to the boat. The others watched in silence as he dragged a sleeping mat from the thatched shelter and took it off into the darkness along the beach.

"What was that about?" Ruth asked.

"It seems he doesn't know Uncle Joshua threatened my father with death should he remain in the Holy City or try to interfere in any way." Joseph slapped his hands against his hips as though to punctuate the end of the conversation before he rose. "I think it's time we all turned in."

"But I don't understand," Maryam said. "Both you and your mother told me your family left the Holy City by choice."

"That's true as well. The path that Uncle Joshua was taking made them sick to their stomachs—but Uncle's threat left them with no other option."

"Why have you never told me this before?"

"The threat extended to never speaking of it. It was not safe to mention until now."

"But—" Surely Joseph's father did not believe his brother *really* would have him killed? What of family bonds? Then she remembered her betrayal at her own father's hands. *Family bonds did not always guarantee safety after all.*

"Enough now," he cut in. "Stirring it up again will do no

good. He's my cousin and we're stuck together, good or bad."
He began to collect more driftwood to feed the fire through the
night. "I'll sleep here to tend the fire. If anything is roaming
round, the flames should hold it well at bay."

His tone discouraged any further comment, leaving Maryam
no choice but to retreat with Ruth to the refuge of the boat.
There they curled up on the sleeping mats, trying to ignore
the way the craft tilted back towards the sea. After three nights
rocked to sleep by the motion of the waves, they found it hard
now to relax, with every tiny sound loud in their ears. By the
time Ruth had finished her prayers, Maryam knew she wouldn't
sleep. She just could not get comfortable. Her tailbone was too
bruised to lie on, and her stomach still tender from her flight
into the boat's side rail. Besides, she had much to think on. She
waited until Ruth's breath had slowed and evened out before
creeping from the boat.

Joseph lay by the fire, his eyes shut tight. His capacity to
shake off his uncle's threat against his family amazed her—she
was certain she did not have it in her to let such a long-term
grievance go. Her father's rejection of her still swelled inside
her like a boil needing to be lanced. This was what she loved
about Joseph: the open warmth and generosity of his heart, so
unlike her own. *Loved? No, put that foolish thought away.*

She passed him by and made her way down to the sea. The
tideline was alive with teams of questing crabs, reminders of
that fateful night, weeks ago, the evening before she Crossed.
She remembered how she'd felt back then, standing with her
toes bared to the warm lapping tide as she stared out at the
magical lights of the Holy City—the great fortress called *Star
of the Sea*. How excited she had been. How filled with awe. If

she'd known back then what was to befall her, would she have gone so passively the next morning? She sighed. Perhaps. The teachings of the Holy Book and the Rules were hard to spurn.

And now here she was again, seeking the constancy of the tide to calm her in the face of more uncertainty. For a moment she envied the crabs, hidden safely in their hard protective shells, able to bury themselves beneath the sand as daylight neared. If only she was half as brave as Joseph thought.

Under the cover of darkness, Maryam shed her clothes and waded into the water up to her thighs. She twisted her thick plait of hair around her hand and tied it into a high knot atop her head, then sank down into the tepid sea until it cradled her in its buoyant arms. She did not venture any deeper, mindful of unseen predators, and rested her knuckles on the grainy sand to resist the gentle tugging of the tide. At first the salt stung her elbows but she knew that it would do them good. And it eased her strained muscles and bruises almost as much as it calmed her troubled mind. She looked up to the stars, charting her position subconsciously as she located the Maiaki Cross. Somewhere, way across the sea, it shone down on her father's home. Would he have been so angry and unforgiving if her mother had lived?

"Maryam, is that you?" Joseph's query shook her from her musings, and she bobbed down, hiding her nakedness as she tracked his voice. He stood at the edge of the water, backlit by the fire.

"Shhhh," she whispered across to him. "You'll wake the others."

"Hang on a minute! I'm coming in!"

Before she could argue, he had stripped off his clothes and

waded in, his hands strategically placed across the parts she feared to see. He squatted down and made his way across to her clumsily on bended knees. "Are you all right?"

"I'm fine," she said. "I just needed some time to think."

He was right next to her now, the water lapping at his shoulders. "You look like a seal," he murmured, reaching out to tuck stray tendrils of her hair back into her plait. His fingers lingered on her neck, cupping it, his thumb circling the fine curls at its nape.

She could hardly breathe. His hand slid to her shoulder, drawing her around until they faced each other, only a hand's-width of lapping water between them. She knew she should pull away, put distance and propriety between them, yet she couldn't—*couldn't*. It felt as though the tide pressed up against her back to trap her there and she was powerless to intervene.

Never before had she been so conscious of her body. She knew Joseph had glimpsed it when Father Joshua stripped her bare before the entire congregation of the Holy City when she'd first Crossed. But now it really mattered to her, and she felt ashamed. She'd always been so small—Mother Elizabeth's "te bebi"; she'd been late to get her bloods and was still as lean and lacking curves as a young boy. Would he think her ugly if he saw her now?

The whites of his eyes shone silver as he leaned across the distance, every fraction of an inch heightening her apprehension, until he met her with his lips. All the strength in her legs gave way and she floated up against his chest, nipple meeting tingling nipple with a terrifying recognition as the kiss transformed to something so heated she truly felt that she would burst.

He drew back from her, panting, holding her gaze as his fingers slid down from her shoulders to tentatively brush her breasts. Even as her body trembled, her hands rose instinctively to push him away.

"Don't," she whispered, barely able to find the air to force the word out past her lips.

His pupils were so dilated his eyes looked black. "Do you want me to go away?"

"Yes," she said, then panicked. "No." She didn't know. "It's just I'm so small and ugly," she blurted. *Stupid.* That's not what she had meant to say.

"But you're beautiful," he said. "You must know that." He took her hand, rising to his feet so quickly she had no time to protest as he pulled her up as well. And now he grasped her other hand, hoisting her arms out from her sides to stop her as she tried to free them. "Oh Lord," he said. "You have no idea *how* beautiful."

She locked her eyes on his face, terrified to look down at his nakedness. She was a Blessed Sister, her body sacred and her life forever destined to be sacrificed to the Lord. It was a sin, this act—this wonderful and overwhelming act—her elders had told her it was not allowed.

"This is wrong," she said.

He dropped her hands and instantly she shielded her pubic hair. "How can it be wrong?" he asked. "I love you."

She closed her eyes. *He had said it, used the word!* But did his saying it make this right? She wanted more than anything to think it so—to take away the nervous hurt she heard now in his voice. Maybe if he *really* did love her . . . *how could something driven by such shared longing be a sin?* She stepped in close to him and gently ran the palms of her hands along the muscles of his arm. His skin was so smooth, the fine hairs soft and downy as they rose in goosebumps at her touch. He grunted and pulled her to him again, crushing her with a kiss that left her in no doubt of his desire.

She was lost now, unable to think rationally. She pressed up against him as his touch explored her inch by inch. Gave herself over to it, her own fingers spider-walking down his back until they traced the hard curve of his hips. As his hand brushed past the hair that guarded her most private place, her eyes shot open in surprise.

There, over Joseph's shoulder, she saw a stark silhouette on the beach. Lazarus! Awake and watching.

With a tormented cry she pulled away, splashing through the sea. She didn't even pause long enough to scoop up her clothes—just ran back to the shelter of the boat, leaving Joseph totally abandoned to the tide.

CHAPTER FIVE

The night seemed to last forever as Maryam drifted in and out of tormented dreams. Father Joshua was there, and the baying congregation of *Star of the Sea*. And her father's voice was there as well, ringing in her ears when she awoke fully just after dawn: *Take this faithless whore and cast her out.* At the time his words seemed so unfair, yet now she feared her actions last night proved him right.

How could she face Joseph now? She should have sought him out immediately, explained to him why she had run. Would he hate her? Would his love have died the instant she fled? With a heavy heart she forced herself to rise and seek him out. Maybe it was not too late.

Already the birds had started up their din, squawking and creeling above the chirp of the crickets warming themselves in the first rays of the sun. Maryam poked her head out of the boat's shelter. Joseph's sleeping mat lay deserted beside the smouldering remains of the fire. There was no other sign of him at all. Lazarus was there, though, swimming confidently across the bay. She released a long and shaky breath. How on earth would she deal with *him*? She had no doubt he'd use what he had seen the previous night to cause her pain. It was part of his make-up, plain as that—he could no more control his brutish nature than a snake or shark. Today, for sure, she'd be his prey.

She climbed down from the boat and tossed a few more sticks onto the fire to stoke it back to life. The smoke helped drive away the army of biting insects that swarmed around—

already her arms and legs were covered with inflamed itchy spots where they had bitten during the night. She peeled a pawpaw and ate it quickly, trying to soothe the terrible knot in her stomach each time she thought of Joseph.

Lazarus swam in to land some distance from her, and she turned her eyes away as he rose from the sea. A picture of Joseph in all his aroused glory flashed through her mind, and a stabbing ache ran through her. *Where was he?* But now Lazarus came striding up the beach towards her, wearing only shorts, his sleeping mat and shirt tucked under his arm. She could feel a blush roaring up her neck to consume her face, so busied herself by tidying the campsite, hauling Joseph's sleeping mat onto the deck of the boat and returning with a metal pot in which to heat some water to brew up a potion of te buka leaves that would stop her insect bites from festering. It would be good for her grazes too. Dear Mother Evodia had long ago taught her all about its special qualities for staving off infection in the humid heat.

Lazarus had stopped a short way off, and was staring intently at the hard-baked sand. He glared over at Maryam and, seeing she was watching, beckoned her over.

"I think you'd better come see this," he called, his voice dripping suppressed rage.

She ran over to him, not brave enough to meet his eye, but scanning the ground to see what it was that held him there. As she approached, she saw something had been scratched into the hard crust of sand. *Gone ahead. Will climb the mountain on my own.*

Lazarus rounded on her. "This is *your* fault, you stupid girl." He slewed his foot over the sand, smearing Joseph's message with one angry sweep.

"I didn't do anything—"

"My point exactly." He surveyed her as if she were a piece of rotting meat. "Couldn't you have just given the poor lovesick puppy what he wanted? Can't you see that he's ill?"

"I know he's got a chill, but he—"

Again he gave her no chance to defend herself. "How in all heaven can you be so blind?" He slapped his hands against his face, leaving white handprints on his sunburnt cheeks. "You had me fooled. I actually once thought you might have had some brains."

"What is *that* supposed to mean?"

"He's dying, you imbecile. You think your blood has saved him—but if you really cared for him you'd have seen how he's succumbing to Te Matee Iai again."

She was struck dumb, the pain of his accusation so intense she felt she'd been flogged. *Dying? No, he couldn't be.* She'd given him her blood, and the marks of Te Matee Iai had gone away— she'd seen this with her own two eyes. And yet . . . hadn't this been nagging at her all along, causing her to fuss over him so? Perhaps she'd known, but couldn't stand to face the truth.

"If he climbs that mountain now, in such a weakened state, there'll be no hope." Lazarus looked furious, but Maryam was stunned to see tears wash across his eyes. "The effort will totally destroy what little resistance he has left."

She wrapped her arms around her head, trying to blot out the truth of his words. If only she had closed her eyes again last night, given Joseph the one thing he most needed then to soothe his soul. Was it really so much for him to have asked of her—to share in his affection? She'd failed him. Failed the one person, besides Ruth, who'd only ever shown her honest unconditional love. She dropped her arms and raised her face, determining to meet her remorse and faults head on. "I'll go after him," she said, meeting Lazarus's scornful eyes. "If I hurry now—"

"Stupid *and* not logical," he spat. "The last thing we need is you getting lost or injured in the jungle, while Sister Sanctimonious jumps at imaginary skulls and loses the plot again." He scooped up his shirt and wrestled it over his wet shoulders. "No, we'll go together and we'd better do it straight away. Go wake Ruth."

Maryam hated how he seemed to think he had the right to order her around. But she knew she had to swallow down her compulsion to defy him, for Joseph's sake. Time was short. She turned and ran, relieved to see that Ruth was already emerging from the boat.

"What's all the yelling about?"

"It's Joseph. We need to go after him, and do it now!"

"Go? Where has he gone?"

"We have to hurry. He's gone to climb the mountain alone."

"So?" Ruth rubbed the sleep out of her eyes.

"Please, just come." Maryam grabbed for Ruth's hand, tugging her towards Lazarus, who waited at the jungle's edge. "I'll tell you all about it as we go."

*   *   *

They followed roughly the same route as the previous afternoon, clambering over the ruins of the crumbling village with more confidence and determination now that they were better mentally prepared for its dire state. They were aided too by the improved light that filtered down through the trees as the sun rose higher in the sky.

As they walked, Maryam gave Ruth a quick censored version of the night's events, though left out her late-night swim. "The trouble is, we've no idea what time he left."

"I doubt he'd be so stupid as to try to walk there in the dark," Lazarus pitched in. "I reckon he most likely left just before dawn. That would make him an hour or so ahead at most—if you two are fast enough, we just might have a chance to catch him up."

"But we've no idea which route he took," Ruth grumbled.

"Then pray, Sister, that your Lord will help us find the way."

As they approached the place where Maryam had fallen, Lazarus, who was leading, let out an amused snort.

"Nice one, cousin!" He pointed to the collapsed wall. There, strategically placed on top of the pile of dislodged stone, sat a disintegrating skull, its hollow eyes calling their bluff.

"I *told* you so," Ruth crowed, before fanning her hand out from the side of her face to block the grisly sight from view.

Maryam, too, averted her eyes, needing no further reminder that they raced with death. The quest to find the people of this island was completely irrelevant to her now—there was but one life she was desperate to find. Lazarus's accusation banged mercilessly around inside her brain: Joseph's disappearance was her fault—*hers alone*. How could she not have seen that the plague was returning?

But then a tiny prick of doubt entered her mind. What if Lazarus was lying to her yet again—using her confusion and her guilt to punish her for his dislike? It was possible: he had no scruples and, although he tempered his behaviour in Joseph's presence, without him there were no guarantees. She found herself studying him for any subtle hint that might unmask him at this game. But Lazarus's sense of urgency seemed real: he crashed through the undergrowth without restraint, clearing a path for her and Ruth in his wake.

For almost an hour they tramped in virtual silence, pausing only to yell Joseph's name. There was no response except the echoing call of the birds, crying out in alarm as the three trekked past. Lazarus was following some kind of track now, a thinning in the thick labyrinth of jungle that seemed to shroud the whole island.

The tumbledown village disappeared behind them as the gradient grew steeper. All three of them were panting, the humid jungle air sapping their strength; even strong-limbed Ruth fell behind Lazarus's breakneck pace. The girls had to concentrate to keep him in their sights as he pressed onwards. Then, as they pushed through a thicket of scratchy bracken, they almost ran straight into his sweat-soaked back.

He had halted, breathing hard as he stared up ahead of him. A crumbling stone stairway rose steeply from the jungle floor, two strange sculpted creatures flanking its point of ascent.

"I think we might have found our mystery building," he said, sounding awed. He ran his hand over one of the statues, tracing the swirling lichen-stained relief cut into the stone.

Maryam had never seen anything like it: it looked like some kind of malformed dog, decorated with an intricately carved breastplate above the sturdy taloned feet of a bird of prey. Time had eroded the stone, and its crumbling edges had fallen away, but its threatening nature lingered still. Beside her, she heard Ruth start to pray.

"Come on then," Lazarus insisted, launching himself up the uneven steps two at a time.

"I have a bad feeling about this," Ruth muttered, seizing Maryam's arm to hold her back.

"We have no choice," Maryam countered, but she squeezed Ruth's broad hand all the same. "We've got to find Joseph before he wears himself out."

She tried to push aside her guilt, but it would not shift. Regardless of Lazarus's concerns for him, she had to locate Joseph and let him know how much she cared. And, if her worst fears were realised and Lazarus was right, she had to persuade Joseph to accept more blood. She had the means to save him, hidden back inside the boat, and would not rest until she did.

They ducked beneath the overgrown canopy of branches, stumbling on the loose slabs of stone that teetered and shifted beneath their feet as they climbed. Soon they reached a landing, again bordered by more fantastical creatures—this time two squat figures, their mouths twisted in leering smiles, fat pointed ears and long segmented noses that curved up like thick coils of rope. Beyond the landing rose another flight of steps, though its final destination was hidden by an enormous uprooted tree.

Lazarus was first to tackle it, using the forks in its branches as footholds to help him clamber up its side. As he crested the top and straightened up, he released a slow awestruck whistle and shook his head. "Holy Mother! You're not going to believe this."

Maryam pushed Ruth ahead and hoisted her up to the first foothold. She followed quickly, her thigh muscles screaming as she stretched her legs to their limit to scale the gnarly trunk. Then Ruth in turn reached over to haul Maryam up before straightening to take in the view. "Oh Lord."

Before them stood a tall gateway formed from tiers of sectioned stone. The slabs were cantilevered in towards the centre, forming an arched supporting structure for a massive head. It was impossible to comprehend how the huge blocks of stone must have been laid in place, let alone carved to form the fleshy lips, broad nose and lidded eyes beneath the elaborate domed head-dress that rose up to its pointed peak. Lush creepers sprouted from cracks and fissures in the stonework like unruly hair, while a patchwork of lichens gave the face a strangely lifelike hue: soft mossy greens colour-washed its eyelids, and a speckled array of blues and golds flushed its grainy sculpted cheeks.

Beyond, Maryam could see glimpses of a large complex of buildings, equally ornate and pocked with age. Without a word, they climbed down from the tree trunk and stepped in through the gateway to this other world.

They appeared to be standing at the edge of a sizeable plateau completely ringed by crumbling walls. Many of the smaller buildings that must once have filled the site were so degraded by weather and time that only remnants of their walls and rough foundations remained. Grasses, shrubs and bracken thrived amidst the crumbled terraces and jumbled piles of stone, providing homes for the many birds whose droppings splashed the ruined stonework with pungent streaks of white. Behind it all, the mountain rose as a perfect backdrop to the scene.

But it was the structure at the very centre of the complex that captured Maryam's eye and drew her towards it: an enor-mous square building, its corners four discrete towers, their vertical indented walls stepping up towards the heavens, each topped by a parapet which, in its turn, was further capped by a domed roof of stone. *These* were what they must have spotted from the boat. The blocks of stone that formed the outer walls

had been chiselled to fashion vast reliefs peopled with innumer-
able tiny figures locked in time.

Maryam ran her hand along the pitted stone as it dawned
on her that each individual panel told a kind of ancient tale.
Some seemed to represent the lives of the people who must
have lived here: boys and girls, men and women, many of them
scantily clad apart from ornate jewellery and oddly styled hair.
A number depicted great armies toting clubs and spears as they
battled a series of nightmarish beasts. Others revealed the workings of strange rituals, all focused on the recurring image of a
smooth-faced man who sat cross-legged in their midst, his hair
caught in a topknot and his relaxed hands lying palm-upwards
in his lap. There was a rare kind of serenity in each rendition of
his face, while those pictured around him appeared to look on
with awe. *Was this their God?*

Ruth had followed and was studying the carvings too.
"I don't like the look of this," she said, sweeping her arm to
encompass the whole site. "No wonder the Lord struck them
down. It's clear they worshipped heathen gods."

Lazarus arrived now as well, and he snorted at Ruth's words.
"What happened to the Lord's great capacity for forgiveness, huh?"

She rounded on him, hands on her hips. "You know the
teachings just as well as I do. The Lord sent forth his Tribulation
to rid the world of non-believers. Only the Apostles and their
Chosen ones were saved."

"Your head is so filled up with teachings—do you *ever* have
an independent thought?"

Tears welled in Ruth's eyes. "If you'd all listened to me in
the first place we wouldn't find ourselves stuck here now. You
knew there was nothing but death and destruction beyond our

shores, and yet you chose to disbelieve . . ." She stormed off to the far end of the site.

"She has a point," Maryam said. "It's obvious no one here survived."

"You saw the map. You think that *nowhere* out there in the world others exist?"

Maryam shrugged. "I don't know. If we'd found people living here it might be different, but—"

"That proves nothing." He kicked at a stray stone, sending it clattering across the ground. "Besides," he said, inclining his head towards the mountain, "until we've searched the whole island we can't be sure." He walked away from her. "Let's be off."

She didn't argue. Instead, she jogged across to Ruth and squeezed her shoulders tight. "Let's find Joseph, then I promise we'll take the time to talk this through."

Ruth nodded, misery etched across her face, but she allowed Maryam to guide her after Lazarus, who once again presumed to lead the way.

They circled around to the back of the great building, working their way through more disintegrating ruins until they reached the northernmost edge of the fragmented wall. Again, an ancient carved head atop a tiered stone portal seemed to watch them pass, as they came upon a narrow rocky track that wound up through the undergrowth and disappeared into the trees.

Their journey now was all uphill, the ground dry and unstable beneath their feet. The sun had risen higher in the sky, its heat growing oppressive despite the shade of the over-hanging trees. Maryam cursed herself for not thinking to bring food or water. Somewhere up ahead, perhaps, they'd find a stream, but meanwhile she scanned the vegetation for something to eat. Eventually, through a thicket of scrubby trees, she spied the serpent-like air roots of a wild fig her people called te biku.

"Food!" she yelled, launching herself off the track towards the tree. She could see that it was fruiting, but many of the figs had already been picked over by scavenging birds. She searched around the thick sinewy roots at its base and collected the ripest of the windfalls, discarding those already pecked. By the time Ruth and Lazarus broke through the scrub to join her, she'd collected roughly a dozen of the leathery purple fruit and piled them together at her feet.

"Eat," she said, tearing one open and biting into the moist pink flesh to suck every last scrap of the nourishing seed mass from its skin.

The other two fell hungrily upon the figs as well, and soon the pile was reduced to nothing more than discarded skins. The sweetness helped to boost their energy, and Lazarus climbed up into the tree's nest of branches to harvest another tasty load. He removed his shirt and cushioned the figs in its fabric before tying the improvised holdall around his waist.

As they set off up the track again, Maryam tried to concentrate on where she placed her feet on the rocky ground. But Lazarus's bared back distracted her, and she found herself watching how his shoulder blades rotated as he swung his arms. Then a funny thought struck her, and she laughed.

He spun around defensively. "Are you laughing at me?"

She couldn't stop; the joke seemed so apt she couldn't resist telling him, if only to prove she was not quite as dull-witted as he thought. She gestured at his naked chest. "Perhaps you should have picked some of the fig leaves too!"

She knew he'd understand—they were all far too steeped in the stories from the Holy Book not to recognise her reference to Adam and Eve.

A startled grin flashed across his face, transforming him for just a moment before he spun away. "Very funny," he drawled, punishing her now for making fun of him by setting a much faster pace.

For another half an hour or so they toiled on, pausing only once when Lazarus glimpsed a large brown snake ahead and called a halt until it slithered off the track. It was the first living thing they'd seen, besides the insects and birds, and its presence was somehow comforting and strangely apt.

At last they heard the flow of water and deviated off the track to search for its source. A short distance into the undergrowth they found a stream, its water clear and refreshing to drink. All three downed handful after handful until their thirst was quenched.

"Can we rest a moment?" Maryam asked.

Lazarus merely nodded, untying his shirt and doling out the remaining figs. He plunged his shirt into the stream, wringing it only slightly before he dragged it back on. Maryam wished she, too, could strip away her sweat-soaked clothes to cool off, but there was no way she would consciously reveal herself to him. Instead, she made do with splashing water over her face and neck, allowing it to trickle down beneath her shirt.

She closed her eyes, listening to the gentle murmur of the stream. The sound was soothing, even cheering, in the face of her nagging concern for Joseph. *Where was he?* What if they'd somehow bypassed him and he'd returned to the boat to find them gone?

All at once a rhythmic thumping and scraping intruded on her thoughts. Her eyes sprang open just as Lazarus scrabbled to his feet and rummaged in the bushes until he found a sturdy stick. He raised it, ready for confrontation, and jerked his head to indicate the girls should stay put. Ruth clutched hold of Maryam's hand, her eyes wide and fearful as Lazarus stalked through the undergrowth towards the noise. It seemed to be coming from the track above, and Maryam's mind flashed images of the fierce-looking warriors depicted in the stone. What if the people of Marawa were now approaching, filing through the jungle with their sticks and spears?

She spied another fallen branch and seized it, all her peaceful intentions flung aside. If they were going to be attacked, it was not fair to expect Lazarus to bear the brunt of it alone. She crept after him, leaving Ruth to bring up the rear.

As Lazarus neared the border of the track he paused. He checked back over his shoulder, his face registering surprise when he discovered Maryam so close behind him, staff in hand. His brow furrowed as their eyes met—it was clear now there were footsteps thundering down the track towards them, and moving at alarming speed—yet he waited for her to join him before the two of them edged right up to the brink.

They could see uphill to where the track curved round a corner, following the contours of the terrain. The sound was so close now, Maryam knew at any moment they would be revealed. She held her breath, her pulse hammering in the base of her throat as she gripped the staff with both hands and raised it up defensively against her chest.

Then movement flashed into her vision—but it took her a panicked moment to register that it was Joseph hurtling down towards them. Lazarus laughed, lowering his staff as he stepped from the shelter of the trees, right into Joseph's path. "Cousin!" he called, his voice lifting with obvious relief.

Joseph's feet locked up, his expression switching from shock to alarm as his feet slid out from under him and he was launched into a skid that ended only when he crashed right into Lazarus, sending them both sprawling out across the track.

Both boys lay on the rocky ground in a knot of arms and legs. Maryam rushed over to offer Joseph her hand, taking in the heightened colour of his face and the mass of scrapes and grazes he'd sustained. But he ignored her, untangling himself from Lazarus before rising on shaky legs to brush away the dirt. Lazarus, too, was grazed, and he winced as he fingered an egg-sized lump on the back of his head.

By now Ruth had arrived as well. "Joseph!" she cried, "thank the Lord it was you!" She turned to Lazarus, who looked pale despite his sunburnt skin. "What happened?"

Lazarus grinned unconvincingly. "Nothing much. We just ran into Joseph here."

"Crash might be a better word." Maryam glanced at Joseph, hoping her attempt at humour might lighten the mood. But he showed no sign of having even heard. One of his knees was bleeding and his elbows looked swollen and raw. He refused to look at her, instead directing his words to Lazarus, who had sat down again to pick dirt and gravel from a seeping graze along his calf.

"I climbed right to the top—it's got the most amazing view, right out over the entire island."

"And?"

"The news is bad. It seems we really are alone."

"I knew it," Ruth cried out, stamping her foot. "We're worse off now than if we'd stayed." Her chin started to wobble and Maryam knew she was close to tears.

Once again she wrapped her arm around Ruth's shoulders, feeling like all she ever did was try to temper Ruth's distress. But it served her right. *She* was the one who'd bullied Ruth into coming on the voyage in the first place, even if responsibility for the final act of coercion lay at Lazarus's feet. "At least we don't have to worry about being attacked," she said, trying to keep her voice upbeat, though the combination of Ruth's constant anxiety and Joseph's blatant hostility made the effort almost impossible. She turned her head away as a tear escaped and tracked down her cheek; she wiped it on her shoulder with a self-disgusted shrug. A deep breath later, and she composed herself enough to fake indifference.

"Let's get you both back to the stream," she said. "If you wash your grazes now to clean them up, I've already brewed some te buka leaves back at the boat that should help them heal."

Lazarus rose to his feet and mumbled agreement, then limped back towards the stream as Joseph followed closely behind.

Ruth's gaze turned from the boys to Maryam. "What's going on? Joseph just cut you dead."

Maryam sighed and shook her head. "I've ruined everything, Ruthie. I've shamed my family, put my friends in danger, dragged you to this awful place, and now Joseph—"

She looked at Joseph's retreating back and bit back a sob.

CHAPTER SIX

The humidity built to such intensity Maryam found it hard to see past the film of sweat that had dripped into her eyes. She wiped it clear and looked up to study the sky through the canopy of leaves. The sun was being strangled by a mass of ominous dark clouds.

Ahead, the boys limped downhill in single file. Joseph had steadfastly refused to engage with Maryam in any way. His rejection was so unyielding she had given up trying to breach it, falling instead into her own dark hole of wretchedness. Beside her, Ruth was brooding too. Maryam felt as if each of them harboured such a store of suppressed rage or hurt that at any moment it could erupt like rogue lightning and raze them all.

They could just see glimpses of the big ruined complex when the first fat drops fell from the sky and pocked the dusty track, stirring up the air with the tang of rain on dirt. The tree-cover counted for little as the first drops gave way to a furious deluge that instantly transformed the track into a muddy stream. They ran now, their feet flicking the mud up around their legs.

By the time they reached the plateau all four were soaked, and still the rain pelted down. It wasn't like the squally winter rain that sometimes deluged Onewēre. It was tepid and offered little relief from the rank humidity that thickened the air and made every inhaled breath a chore. In Maryam it had brought on a headache that jarred with each step.

"I say we take shelter in the big building," she called to the others as they made their way through the ruins. She was desperate to stop.

No one bothered to answer her. But the boys veered off their direct route towards the stone gateway that led down to the beach and headed, instead, for the parapeted building at the heart of the complex. They huddled in its doorway and waited for Maryam and Ruth to catch them up. Inside, a wide entrance hall was flanked by the shattered stairwells of the two frontal towers, its once smooth tiled floor littered with the accumulated debris of wind and time: crumbling stone, dried leaves and dirt, stinking mounds of bird droppings and feathers. A host of parasitic plants sprouted from fractures in the floor and walls, as if they'd pushed up through the earth to rightfully reclaim what once was theirs—their florid display at odds with the dull brown stone of the structure that supported them. Rain leaked in through the cracks to form puddles that snaked through the filthy flagstones in dusty streams.

Rows of thick stone pillars formed the backbone of the building. The two most elaborately carved of them stood at the entrance to a gloomy room beyond the hall. Maryam, Joseph, Lazarus and Ruth edged towards it in silence. Something about the decayed majesty of the building and the stifling gloom set their nerves on edge. Maryam's head pounded in time with her heart as they stepped over the threshold and tried to take in the dimensions of the room.

It was an enormous space, almost as big as the atrium of the Holy City, *Star of the Sea*. The flagstones had been laid in symmetrical patterns, and a pathway of darker stone drew them in towards the raised dais at the far end.

There, in the dull half-light, a huge stone figure looked

down upon them. He sat cross-legged on the dais—the same calm-faced man Maryam had seen depicted on the carved reliefs outside. His hands, lying open on his knees, were spread as though to beckon the four unexpected guests; a secret smile seemed to hover on his pronounced lips. His eyes were lowered modestly; his chipped stonework face was streaked with dark trails of rain as if he wept.

"Oh Lord in Heaven!" Ruth cried out. She alone had stopped staring up at the figure, and was clutching Maryam's arm so tightly Maryam could feel her pulse fighting against Ruth's panicked grip. Ruth was pointing a shaky hand at the ground beneath the statue's broad bare feet.

At first Maryam was not sure what she was looking at. Some kind of tangled mass: a pile of sticks, branches and smooth rounded stones.

Lazarus released a long slow whistle. "Meet the former people of Marawa Island," he said, his voice barely a whisper above the orchestra of rain.

"People?" Yet, even as Maryam spoke, her brain began to make sense of what lay before her. This was not the wind-blown refuse of the jungle—these were bones. Hundreds of them, heaped below the dais and spreading out across the floor to either side. She shook her head, hoping her eyes were playing tricks on her, but when she'd blinked again there was no doubting it: the pile of bones was real.

She looked at Ruth beside her, and they held each other's gaze. Then Ruth began to speak. *"And it shall be, if thou forget the Lord thy God, and walk after other gods, and serve them, worship them, I testify against you this day that you shall surely perish."*

Her words struck to the core of Maryam's doubt. Every

time she turned her back on the Apostles' teaching, it was as though the Lord sent forth new evidence that His words were real. She brushed Ruth's hand from her arm, so overwhelmed by the dark shadow this new test cast on her spirit she had to escape her friend's needy grasp. She backed from the room, unable to tear her eyes from the spectre of the island's dead: the bleached brittle bones of men and women, old and young, heaped together as if they'd died in one desperate moment, trapped in time. Long leg bones, disconnected at their knobbly joints. Spidery fingers pointing into space. Whole networks of collapsed ribs and twisted tracks of spines. Slick rounded skulls with their hollow eyes and empty nose-holes. And, most heart-wrenching of all, tiny disjointed bundles of bone held tightly in a mother's dying embrace.

And when Judah came toward the watch tower in the wilderness, they looked unto the multitude, and, behold, they were dead bodies fallen to the earth, and none escaped.

The Holy Book's words tolled in Maryam's head as she turned and fled the building. Up until this moment she'd still held to the faint hope that somewhere on the island other people lived to welcome them to this new home. It did not seem possible that she and her two dear friends had fought so hard to reach this place—escaped the cruel clutches of Father Joshua and risked their lives out on the open sea—only to find the island as deserted and bleak as the desolation that now possessed her heart.

Great painful sobs rose up from the pit of her stomach and broke free. It was so unfair—*so unfair*—that all the hopes she'd held for the future now lay as dead as those poor islanders in their crumbling tomb. She could not stop the tears that seemed to draw from every cell of her body to leave her as depleted as when the Mothers had drained her of her blood.

A hand roughly shook her shoulder and she startled to see Joseph's wary face above her. He looked drained too, his skin grey and unhealthy beneath the veil of rain. "Come inside," he said. "We've found a corner that's dry and free of bones."

She could not bear to respond, seeing the hurt and confusion behind his eyes as further proof of the total failure of her dreams. Instead, she slumped her head into her hands, willing him just to leave her to digest the truth. *All is lost.*

Joseph, however, did not comply. He reached down and firmly grasped her by the arm, coughing as he hauled her up with one impatient jerk. He towed her back across the compound, saying nothing until he pushed her, none too gently, beneath the shelter of a crumbling tiled roof that slumped between two chipped columns of weathered stone.

He took her by the shoulders then, forcing her to meet his gaze. There was a graze just below his right eye, fresh from his collision with Lazarus, its edges blue and puffy where rainwater had soaked into the broken skin. For a moment neither of them spoke, Maryam dizzy from the effort of holding his stare while knowing how he hated her—that she'd lost his love. Her heart drummed out its pain, reverberating loudly inside her head.

Finally she drew in a deep breath. She had to tell him now, while they were alone, what had caused her to abandon him. "I'm sorry. I—"

"*I'm* sorry," Joseph echoed. He released her shoulders and took one of her hands in his own, his words tumbling out now as she listened, open-mouthed. "I never should have touched you," he said. "It was just you looked so beautiful. I feel terrible—and know how much I shamed you—frightened you—I couldn't face you this morning, after what I'd nearly done. I feel so ashamed. So bad—"

"Stop!" Maryam raised her free hand and pressed her fingers to his lips to silence him. He'd run because he thought he'd hurt her? Done her wrong? "It wasn't that at all," she said, a great wave of relief welling up inside her as she realised that perhaps he didn't hate her after all. "Lazarus was watching us. When I saw him there I panicked—that's why I ran."

"He was *watching*?" Joseph shook his head slowly as though processing what she had said. Then a smile dawned in his eyes. "You don't hate me?"

Relieved laughter burst from her. "You don't hate *me*?"

He did not answer her, just swept her up into his arms and held her tight. She nestled her head into the crook of his neck as she fought back the urge to cry again. Then he kissed her sopping hair and she raised her face to him, her ear catching in his rain-soaked collar and dragging the fabric away from his skin. As her gaze travelled up his neck towards his lips, something purple registered at the very corner of her vision. She pulled back, suddenly nauseous, and yanked the wet shirt away from his neck. *Oh Lord.* There, in the recess above his collarbone, the ugly telltale marks of Te Matee Iai mottled his skin.

"No!" The word burst from her lips with such force she saw him flinch.

He released her; his arms hung like dead fish at his sides as he tried to work out why her focus was fixed in such horror on his skin. Then the light faded from his eyes. His voice grew flat. "The marks are back?"

She nodded, hating that she had to tell him. She reached up

and cupped his face, pressing her lips to his. At first he did not respond, his lips tight and resistant, but gradually the steady pressure of her own lips softened him, and he drew her hungrily back into his embrace. It was almost brutal in its intensity— not a kiss of passion, but fraught with desperation and fear. Then the rhythm of his breathing changed, and he pushed her away as a ragged cough exploded from his chest.

He was consumed by it, doubled over, hands on knees, trying to bring the choking spasm under control as Maryam frantically rubbed his back. She could feel the way his spine jutted out beneath his skin, and the straining of his muscles as the cough ran on, and saw now that the purple mottling had spread around his neck, tucked just below his hairline too. She felt sick and light-headed. *Lazarus was right.*

"We can fight this," she declared as soon as the fit was over and he'd regained his breath. "My blood—"

"Don't speak of it," he snapped. "You must not risk your life for mine."

"But I don't care."

"Well, I do—and we will not have this conversation ever again." The severity of his tone left no room for further argument.

As she churned over every possible retort, the sudden return of the birds' clamour distracted her. The rain had stopped as quickly and dramatically as it had started, and the birds once more thronged above. Already the sky was breaking through with blue, the rain-clouds rolling off towards the east as steam rose from the sunlit ground. And now Ruth and Lazarus were walking towards them, and although there was nothing accusing in Ruth's expression, Maryam felt a tug of guilt at having left her friend alone with him. Worse, she didn't want to face Lazarus at this awful moment: her face flushed hot as she imagined how he'd rub it in now that his fears for Joseph had been proved right.

"So you found her," Lazarus said, shooting Maryam a dismissive look. He jerked his head up at the sky. "While the weather's clear let's get back to the boat and have something decent to eat, then we can talk."

"How can you think of eating now we know this island is forsaken by the Lord?" Ruth said.

"Easy," Lazarus replied. "For a start my stomach doesn't care so long as it's been fed. And, secondly, whatever happened here was long ago—the only thing that matters now is what we decide to do next."

"*We?*" Maryam said. "Since when did *you* have any say in what we do? And since when did you become our self-appointed leader?" He may've been right about Joseph, but it didn't give him the right to seize control.

"Since you started acting like such a flake."

"A what? Look, just because you have a love affair with yourself it doesn't give you the right to judge how others act."

"It does if you're clearly—"

"Oh, spare me!" Joseph threw up his hands in frustration and marched off towards the stairway that led back down to the beach. "Come on."

For a moment the other three just watched him stalk away, each of them seemingly locked up in their own dark thoughts. But as Joseph reached the entranceway to the stairs he was wracked by another bout of coughing, and he stopped to support himself against the massive gateway of sectioned stone.

Maryam found her eyes drawn to Lazarus, who scrutinised her right back. *Here we go.* Despite her dislike of him, and her certainty he'd take the revelation out on her, she found herself pointing to her collarbone and neck and shaking her head. *He's Joseph's cousin, after all. He has to know.*

He blinked, and blinked again, as the meaning of her charade struck him full force. His shoulders slumped and he let loose a drawn-out sigh. "So it begins," he murmured.

Maryam did not know how to answer him, rattled by his lack of fight. Instead, she jogged after Joseph, who had recovered his breath enough to descend the stairs. Whatever happened now, she would not let him out of her sights. He needed her, she reasoned, almost as much as she needed him.

* * *

It was impossible to find firm footing on the boggy ground, and all four of them slipped and fell on the tortuous downhill track. They were mud-coated and bruised when they finally reached flat land again and waded through the remnants of the overgrown village near the beach.

Joseph barely talked, answering Maryam's concerned questions with only a brief word or two as he struggled to keep his coughing under control. It seemed that now these spasms had started, they would not relent. He moved ever more slowly as the last quarter hour of the trek stretched out to double that and then some more. By the time they broke through the trees at the border of the beach he looked completely defeated. He didn't bother washing off the crusted mud, just climbed aboard the beached boat and collapsed on the deck with a wheezy groan.

Maryam clambered after him. She poured him a cup of water and helped prop him up a little so he could drink. His colour was terrible, so pale she could see the veins beneath his skin, and on his chest and neck she could see blotches of red forming next to the purple mottling. It frightened her, knowing full well that by the time the mottling and the breathing problems appeared the plague's victims were already caught fast in its grip. Without a transfusion of blood, there was no doubt he would die.

Lazarus climbed aboard and squatted down next to Joseph. "Come on, cousin, let me take you down to the sea to wash off this mud."

Joseph barely raised his head. "It doesn't matter. I'm fine."

"I think Lazarus is right," Maryam said to him, laying aside her defensive armour for now, for Joseph's sake. "You can't risk an infection from those wounds." She tucked her hand under his armpit to help him up, and glanced over at Lazarus to indicate that he should do the same.

Between them they supported Joseph down to the sea. She had a terrible sense of history repeating itself as she recalled the night her friend Sarah had died. Only then it was Joseph who'd helped her answer Sarah's dying wish to escape the confines of the Holy City to breathe fresh air. That was the night Maryam had first fully understood that she too would die if she remained in the Holy City. The Apostles had drained Sarah of so much blood her body could not sustain itself, and yet they truly did not care—there was always another docile Sister to replace her, to be bled to death.

Now they walked Joseph out into the sea until the water met their thighs. While Lazarus supported Joseph in his arms, floating him on the warm tide, Maryam gently washed him clean, running her hands along his thin arms and legs to rinse away the mud. His skin felt burning hot despite the cooling effects of the water, and she tried to freshen his face, scooping up water in her palm to carefully trickle it across his forehead before sliding her hands down his cheeks to wipe away the grime and further flush out the graze.

She felt as though she was trapped inside the worst of dreams. Only last night they had embraced in the water here, desire the only thief of breath. But now Joseph was struggling for every lungful, his rib bones straining up against his skin as he fought for air. She did not know why the symptoms of Te Matee Iai were thus: the deep ugly blotches, the fight for breath, the terrible coughing and weakness, the rapid decline to death as every part of the body seemed to scream with pain— but it was something passed down from the Tribulation, that much she knew.

Old Hushai had told her this during one of the long nights before her escape. How the Tribulation had caused blindness, terrible weeping sores, babies born grossly deformed. All this, and then Te Matee Iai, which could consume whole families, generation after generation, yet did not appear to be passed by contact or through the air. It was as if Te Matee Iai was some terrible taimonio—a demon—who could possess a man's body at his birth and one day decide to rapidly and painfully bring on his death. That the Sisters' blood somehow halted this tai-monio in his tracks made no sense to her, and yet it did. She could only suppose that whatever poison the taimonio slowly leaked into its victim's body was diluted by the transfusion of a Sister's blood.

Once again that was Joseph's only hope. She somehow had to convince him to back down and let her help.

Joseph started coughing, the spasms so fierce that Lazarus lost his grip on him and Joseph slipped under the water. Maryam lunged for him as Lazarus dragged him back to his feet. He was choking and spitting out sea water, mucus flowing freely from his nose. When the spasms finally stopped, he shook off Lazarus's hands and rinsed his face.

"No need to drown me, cousin," he said, forcing a faint smile. "My time will come soon enough."

"Don't say that!" Maryam pleaded. "You've just overdone it today. Come now and rest while we make you something to eat." She ducked down quickly into the water to wipe away the mud and grime from her own body before trailing the two boys back to the boat.

Ruth had relit the fire and dragged the sleeping mats outside, piling them one on top of the other clear of the still-dripping trees. Now she held out a dry shirt and pants. "Why don't you put these on and rest here," she called to Joseph as the group approached. The girls turned their backs as Lazarus helped him change out of his wet clothing. Then Joseph lay back on the sleeping mats and closed his eyes. No one spoke, yet they all seemed instinctively to understand their roles.

Lazarus began scouring beneath the thick undergrowth for drier firewood, while Ruth prepared a stew of salted fish and root vegetables from their stores. Maryam took her infusion of te buka leaves and gently dabbed it over Joseph's scrapes and grazes, murmuring the kind of mindless platitudes she'd used for the young Sisters when they were hurt and needed care back at home.

"This'll get you right in no time," she said, trying to ignore the nagging voice inside her head. *No it won't. The only thing that can save him is your blood.* The voice would not let up on her. *You have the means to do so, right in the boat.*

It was true that buried at the bottom of her small pile of clothes she had the instruments that Mother Lilith used to take her blood—she'd stolen them on the spur of the moment, just before they fled the ship. But would she know how to use them, even if she could convince Joseph to accept her aid? She did not want to think of this, it scared her so. One mistake, one needle misplaced or calculation of volume wrong, and she would end up dead.

As Joseph slipped into a restless sleep she tried to distract herself by helping with the search for wood. The downpour had left everything soaked, and it took a lot of foraging to find anything remotely dry enough to burn. Eventually, she and Lazarus had stacked enough driftwood and brittle dead branches next to the fire to last them until later, when things had dried out. Although the day was hot and humid after the rain, there was something about the crackling, dancing flames that soothed.

Maryam and Lazarus perched on rocks they'd shifted to form makeshift seats around the blaze as Ruth doled out the hot fish stew, yet still no one was moved to speak. They ate hungrily, but it was as if each of them was locked inside their own thoughts, preparing for the moment when they'd have to tackle what to do now all hope of rescue was lost.

As soon as Maryam had finished her meal she carried a steaming bowl of stew across to Joseph, tenderly shaking him awake. "Eat now," she murmured to him as he roused. "It will help you build some strength."

He propped himself on one elbow, but his hand shook as he raised each spoonful to his lips. It was painful to watch him struggle so, and Maryam sat beside him biting back the urge to help, guessing he'd refuse her offer if she tried. Already the red welts around his neck were darkening to purple, but as he ate she was relieved to see a little colour creep back into his face. When, finally, he had finished as much as he could, she helped him get up to join the others sitting by the fire.

"We have to talk," he said, studying each of them in turn.

How like him, Maryam thought. *So frail, yet here he is still trying to hold us all together.*

He started to cough, but managed to swallow the irritation down again before continuing. "It's clear there's no one left here. We must decide what to do next."

"We should go back," Ruth burst out. "Admit the Apostles were right about the Tribulation and leave this awful island."

"You must be joking! Surely you can't honestly think we'd be better off back there?" Maryam felt sick at the thought.

"What would you have us do?" Ruth replied, two bright spots of colour branding her cheeks. "If we stay here under the eye of these heathen gods, the Lord will punish us as well. And if we sail on it's clear that all we'll find is more proof of the Lord's great wrath. You have to face it, Maryam. Make a choice. The Lord or death."

"You can't seriously believe that?" Lazarus flung the last juices from his meal into the fire, causing it to spit and hiss. He turned to Maryam. "And you wonder why I hold you servers in such low esteem when the prey now argues to walk back willingly to its trap. How stupid is that?"

"That's not fair," Maryam retorted, but she found she could

not meet his eye. What he said was true enough, but she understood Ruth's fear. For them to turn their backs on the teachings of the Apostles ran contrary to everything they'd been raised to think. To act upon. And to believe. It was just possible that the trials they now faced were punishment for her rejection of the Lord and his Apostles' Rules. She could not stop thinking about this: whether if she'd repented her sins and resolved once again to love the Lord and trust his chosen spokesmen, Joseph's life might not now be at risk. "I don't know about you others, but right now I think our priority should be healing Joseph."

"You mean stay here?" Ruth's eyes were wide.

"No . . . Yes . . . I don't know." It was impossible to stay calm while her mind was spinning so. Right now all she cared about was Joseph. "All I *do* know is that he needs our help." She reached her hand out to him. "Please, Joseph, you have to let me try."

"This discussion is so pointless," he said, refusing to take her hand. "How do you want me to take your blood—drink it perhaps?" His tone was so scathing she felt heat consuming her face.

"Wait!" she cried. "I can answer that!"

She did not pause for his response. She ran over to the boat and scrambled up onto the deck, unearthed the bloodletting instruments and carried them triumphantly back to the fire. "Look," she said, holding the strange array of objects out to him—the needle cannulas, the tubing, the one-way valve. "We have the means."

Now real fury engulfed him. With a grunt he raised himself to standing, swaying slightly as he tried to seize the instruments from her. She dodged him and circled around the fire.

"Please, you have to let me help you. I don't want you to die." Her words were not coming out as she had planned, her throat constricting and her nose and eyes aching with the effort of damming back tears. She stepped towards him, holding out the instruments as if they were holy relics, and whispered, for his ears alone: "If you really loved me, you'd let me help."

His eyes flashed horror at her words. With a cry like a caged animal he lunged at her, wrenching the tubing from her grasp and flinging it into the fire.

"No! You mustn't do this!" She was devastated, heart-broken, and filled with rage. Somewhere close by Ruth was screaming at them both to stop, but neither Ruth nor Lazarus existed for Maryam in this moment—this was a one-on-one battle between her and Joseph. A fight to the death. His possible death.

Joseph came at her again, all flailing arms and kicking feet as he tried to wrestle the delicate instruments from her. They were breaking, snapping under the force of his assault, and she found herself sobbing—shrieking—as they fought.

Then, suddenly, Lazarus had stepped in between them. He grasped her wrists with such a steely grip she was powerless to stop Joseph from snatching the rest of the precious life-savers away. "That's enough!" Lazarus roared, dragging her now across the sand as Joseph pitched the broken cannulas and valve into the flames before succumbing to another dreadful fit of coughing.

She dug her toes in, trying to stop Lazarus in his tracks, but he was fired by anger and he did not stop until he had marched her, sobbing and wailing, into the bush and then a good distance further along the track. When he finally released her, he slapped her face.

"How dare you?" he shouted, as she nursed her cheek in her hand and tried to get her hysterical sobbing under control. "Do you have any idea what you just asked of him?" He glared at her. "Do you, damn it?"

"I just want to save him," she cried, sinking to her knees. She was exhausted now. Bereft. "You wouldn't understand this, but I love him."

"Love?" Lazarus sneered. "You call that love?" He blew out a furious breath, his fingers linked above his head as he looked up at the canopy of trees. Then he inhaled deeply and crouched down beside her, his anger barely held in check. "The only way he can stay alive is if he keeps receiving more blood. Don't you see? You can't cure him, no matter how much you wish you could. He'd have to suck you dry and then, because she's probably stupid enough to offer up her blood like you, your best friend Ruth would die as well. Do you really think my cousin would agree to that?"

"But—"

"There are no buts. First you would die. And then, most likely, Sister Ruth."

"But listen," she tried again, reaching out to touch his arm. Somehow she had to make him see sense. "My blood would keep him going long enough till we find somewhere else to land."

Lazarus looked down at her hand, so small and brown against his skin. Embarrassed now, she drew it away. When he spoke again, he sounded almost kind. "He will never take it, Maryam. I know him too well. So, you can either fight him on this and waste your last days with him, or you can show him love, and hope that we can find somewhere with the means to make him well."

She hated him. Hated that she knew he spoke the truth. There was nothing she could do to save Joseph. She was going to lose him and it hurt more than she could bear. Unless, as he said . . .

"You really think there's somewhere out there that we might find help?"

He shrugged. "I've no idea. But, truthfully, it's Joseph's only real chance." He stood up again, and offered her his hand. "Are you brave enough to try?"

Was she? Could she set forth again, when all the evidence now pointed to the truth of the Apostles' claims about the Tribulation's total destructive force? But, then again, how could she not?

She pushed herself to her feet, ignoring his proffered hand. "I am."

CHAPTER SEVEN

On their return to the beach, Lazarus took himself off to the shelter of the boat and Ruth, who'd collected up the plates and pots from their meal, was down at the water's edge, rinsing them out. A putrid smell hung around the camp as the last of Mother Lilith's instruments melted in the embers and sent forth acrid black smoke.

Joseph lay resting on the sleeping mats, his eyes suspiciously red. He looked so miserable that Maryam, yet again, was wracked with guilt. He was mortally ill and she had only made things worse. She sat down at the end of his makeshift bed and ran her finger along the line of his toes.

"I'm so sorry," she said to him. His toes were long and bony, the nails chipped and in need of a good trim. "I will not speak of it again."

"Good," he replied, folding his arms across his chest. He cleared his throat. "And I'm sorry I fought with you."

She ran her hand up the long broad bone of his shin. She couldn't keep from touching him. Beneath her fingers his fine blond hairs were caked with tiny salt crystals that made them gritty and slightly sticky to her touch. "We'll find somewhere to get you help, I promise."

"Maybe," he said, sounding unconvinced. He reached down and stilled her hand, pulling it towards him until she was stretched right out beside him on the mat. "That's better," he said, rolling onto his side so he could see her face. He reached over and brushed her wiry tangled hair out of her eyes. "I always feel better when I'm next to you."

She buried her face into his chest, smelling the briny freshness of the sea on his skin, and fought back tears as the sweetness of his nature knocked away all her defences. How would she live without him if he died? But she knew she had to push the thought away—it was too big, too all-consuming—and right now the best way to help him was to be brave herself. He did not need the added burden of her grief.

"You know last night?" she whispered. "What you said about loving me?"

He nodded.

"Did you really mean it?"

He smiled, twisting a strand of her hair in his fingers. "What do *you* think?"

She prodded him playfully on the arm. "You say!"

"Oh . . . all right!" He raised himself up onto one elbow, so he stared directly down into her eyes. "I love you, Maryam." He kissed her lightly on the nose. "Satisfied?"

For a moment they both just grinned, eyes locked on each other without the need for words. But then the moment was broken as he coughed and sank back down on the mat.

"Rest a while," she said to him as she sat up. "Right now I need to speak with Ruth."

He nodded, his eyes still watering from the intensity of the coughing. She leaned over and kissed him on the cheek, whispering into his ear: "I love you too."

A smile etched his face, accentuating how tired and drawn he looked, and Maryam felt a deep aching inside her chest. She pushed herself off the mat, reluctant to leave him, but knowing he needed rest and that Ruth was down brooding at the water's edge.

She was crouched in the shallows, scouring the pot with sand. Maryam squatted next to her and collected up the rinsed bowls at Ruth's feet.

"I'm sorry," she said, noting the tight line of Ruth's mouth and her defensive hunch. "I just can't bear the thought that he's dying."

Ruth increased the swirling motion of her hand as she worked the sand around the pot, answering only once she'd rinsed it out and checked it was thoroughly clean. "I know that. But you've forgotten there are four of us, not just you and him. And I'm scared of dying too."

Fear flared in Maryam's mind. "You're not sickening as well?"

"No. But to stay here or travel on into nothingness is certain death. I understand why you wanted to escape—to risk this—but we've proved now there is nothing beyond Onewēre's shores. It's time to go home before we're *all* dead."

"But don't you see? If we return home we'll end up dying anyway. One way or another they'll make us pay."

"Not if we repent," Ruth said. "The Lord opens his heart to sinners if they ask."

Maryam scooped up a bowlful of water, trickling it slowly back into the sea. "It's not the Lord I'm scared of, Ruthie. It's Father Joshua."

Ruth's nostrils flared. "Well, you *should* be scared of the Lord. We've broken His Rules."

"They're *not* His Rules." *How could she so easily put aside Father Joshua's assault on her? Did it not still haunt her? Make her sick?* But Maryam knew it would be cruel to dredge the memory up when Ruth herself seemed able to suppress it. She'd need to try another tack. "Please," she said. "I promise that if we find the next place is as hopeless as this, I'll take you home. Meantime, can't you just give Joseph one more shot at life?"

Ruth stood up, clutching the pot as if it were a lifeline. "How do you think all those people died?" she asked, deflecting Maryam's question.

"I don't know. Perhaps they tried to shelter from the Tribulation. Who knows?"

"The Lord knows," Ruth answered. "He knows all."

Ruth started walking back towards the boat, forcing Maryam to tag behind. As they approached the fire, Maryam glanced over at Joseph's sleeping form and halted in her tracks, studying him as he restlessly dozed. Deep shadows of sickness hollowed his eyes; his mouth drooped open in his effort to breathe. Already his face had taken on the bony features of a skull.

"Poor Joseph," Ruth whispered. She sighed as she reached out for Maryam's hand. "If you really want to make me promises, then promise me this: that you'll truly and sincerely pray to the Lord for forgiveness and for a message about what we should do next. He will come to you, Maryam, if you seek him out."

Ruth was grasping her hand tightly, urging her to comply. She didn't seem to realise the irony in her request: that she expected the Lord to give Maryam the answer to their predicament if she prayed, while Ruth herself prayed constantly but had not received the message straight from Him.

"I promise," she said, her pulse throbbing in her temple as she recognised she had no other choice. She did not want to be responsible for forcing Ruth to continue on against her will. Not this time. "If that is what you wish."

Ruth laughed. "The Lord be praised," she said. With that

she clambered up onto the boat and, ignoring Lazarus—who had laid the map out on the roof of the shelter and was studying it intently—disappeared inside.

Maryam sighed. She reached for the small smooth pebble she always carried in her pocket—the special one Ruth had given her before she'd Crossed—and stared into its luminous blue depths. It reminded her of Onewēre, of the clear cobalt water that surrounded her much-loved home. The little ones would be having their afternoon nap about now, while old Zakariya supervised the older Sisters as they tended to the garden and the other daily chores. Life was so simple there: no doubts, no fear, just the overwhelming belief that the Apostles' word was sacred and that the Sisters were destined to serve, in the words of the Rules, with readiness and joy.

She remembered the eve of her Crossing, how she'd stood at the water's edge and stared across the water to *Star of the Sea*. How, somewhere deep inside, her fears for the future stirred and woke. At the time she'd put it down to natural nerves, but now she wondered if she'd had some kind of premonition of the horrors she was to endure. Yet, if she'd voiced her fears aloud, no one would have listened, just as Ruth even now could not comprehend the total terror that overwhelmed Maryam at the thought of returning home. Ruth might believe the Lord would protect them from Father Joshua's merciless wrath, but she did not. Still, a promise was a promise . . . she would go and pray.

It was hard to find a place where the constant racket of the birds did not intrude upon her thoughts. In the end she walked to the far end of the beach and stripped down to her underwear to swim. She entered the warm sea and lowered herself into its buoyant embrace, staring up at the wispy clouds as she floated on her back. Her ears were submerged just below the waterline, blocking out the most irritating of the birdcalls and replacing them with the sea's soft whisper and the reverberation of her own steady breaths.

Dear Lord, forgive me for my sins of doubt and pride, and for thinking ill of your Apostles and resisting their will. Even as she thought it, a tiny voice sneered somewhere deep inside her head. She knew she was lying to Him, that she would never forgive the Apostles nor give in again to their harsh rule. She'd have to try harder than this if she was to honour her promise to Ruth. *I'm sorry, Lord, I truly am. Please give me some kind of sign . . . tell me what we should do next.* Then, with more conviction, she added the thing that mattered most. *And, Lord, please, please don't let Joseph die.*

The gentle swell rocked her in its arms while a flock of golden plovers swirled overhead, calling to each other as they dipped their tawny speckled wings and soared back in towards the land. *You know, you know*, they seemed to cry, their piercing call penetrating the layer of water and reaching her ears. The message was so clear, so unexpected, she lost her equilibrium, and suddenly sank beneath the surface. She dropped her feet down quickly, rising out of the water with a noisy splash as the last of the plovers disappeared into the camouflage of the bush.

You know.

Was this her mind playing tricks with her, or did she really hear the words? And if she did, who was addressing her? What did they mean? Maryam squeezed the water from her thick plait of hair and waded back up the rain-pocked beach to retrieve her clothes, trying to make sense of what had happened as she did so. Ruth, no doubt, would say the words came from the Lord, but she was not so sure—especially as the message seemed to say that she should trust her own instincts and resist returning to the Holy City.

It was all so confusing. Perhaps the purpose of prayer was really just to tap into the mind's vast unconscious store, to allow a person's deepest desires or truths to surface from its depths like bubbles of pure air? It was possible—after all, the Apostles justified their actions by saying the Lord had spoken to them in their prayers.

Whatever the cause or reason, she felt sure now that the right thing to do was to try to save Joseph, and he'd not be cured if they returned to Onewēre, even if he did agree to take more blood. She could see now that Lazarus—for all that she hated him—was right about this. The Sisters' blood alone could not restore Joseph, merely prolong his life, and there was no way he'd consent to that. They would need to find help beyond these shores—venture further into the great unknown—if he was to be completely cured. So it must be.

She glanced over to see that Joseph had woken and had joined Lazarus in his scrutiny of the map. She jogged back along the beach.

"Good swim?" Joseph asked, flashing her a tired smile as she climbed aboard the boat.

She nodded, ducking into the pandanus shelter in search of Ruth. Ruth sat cross-legged in the shade, mouthing the words as she read from the Holy Book. She glanced up with such an air of confident expectation Maryam felt herself blush. Ruth was not going to like what she was now about to say.

"Well?" Ruth said, placing her marker into the Book as she clapped it shut.

Maryam considered her words carefully. "I asked Him and was answered."

"I knew it!" Ruth said, smiling broadly as she reached over and wrapped Maryam in a warm embrace. *"Ask, and it shall be given you; seek, and ye shall find.* Matthew Seven."

Indeed, Maryam thought. *My point exactly. Each sought the one answer they most longed to hear.* She pulled back, taking Ruth's hands and looking at her steadily. "We must go onwards, Ruthie. That's what we are meant to do. I know this isn't what you wanted to hear, but that's the essence of the message I received."

Ruth shook her head as though dazed. "You're sure?"

Maryam merely nodded. To say more would be to invent a story, and she loved Ruth far too much for this. All she could do was reason using the only language Ruth would understand. *"The Lord sent forth the Lamb into the wilderness to test Him, and the people of the Lord as well.* Perhaps He's testing us, Ruthie—just like in the Holy Book."

She reached over and took up Ruth's Book, flicking through until she came to the chapter on Isaiah. She knew the phrase she needed was in there somewhere—something designed to bring strength and hope again to Ruthie's heart. Then she found it and began to read, fervently hoping the words would fit.

"Then the eyes of the blind shall be opened, and the ears of the deaf shall be unstopped. Then shall the lame man leap as an hart, and the tongue of the dumb sing: for in the wilderness shall waters break out, and streams in the desert. And the parched ground shall become a pool, and the thirsty land springs of water: in the habitation of dragons, where each lay, shall be grass with reeds and rushes."

Ruth closed her eyes and fat tears rolled down her cheeks as she listened to the words. A shaky sigh escaped her lips before she looked again at Maryam. "Very well. If this is what He asks of me, then I will go."

* * *

All four poured over the map as the late afternoon sun beat down on the back of their necks.

"I think we should make haste towards the next nearest island on the map," Maryam said.

"I don't agree," said Lazarus. "There's a good chance, from what we've found here and what we know of our own history, that all the people of the small islands *were* destroyed by the Tribulation. I reckon we head for this big island here." He jabbed his finger at the large landmass labelled Australia.

Joseph cleared his throat. "But my parents rejected that idea when they first planned their escape."

"Why?" Maryam asked.

"I'm not really sure. All I know is that they rejected it."

"But didn't you say it was once a great country? Surely, if they were so advanced, the chances are they'd have survived? Think of the wonderful things the people of that time could do—make energy from the skies, turn sea water into fresh . . ."

Joseph shrugged. "I don't know." He wiped his hand across his face, swaying with tiredness.

"I say we go," Ruth broke in.

All three turned, startled to hear her voice an opinion at last.

"We could spend the rest of our lives sailing from island to island and find no help. If you really want to keep going with this crazy plan, we may as well just head for the place most likely to have the medicines we need."

"That, Sister," Lazarus said, raising an eyebrow at Ruth, "is the most sensible thing I've ever heard you say."

Ruth flushed, and scuffed the deck with her bare toes. She could not meet his eye.

"But how long do you think it'd take to sail there?" Maryam asked.

Joseph measured the distance between Onewēre and Marawa Island with his fingers. "The trip here took just on four days," he said, plotting the expanse across the blue-tinted ocean between Marawa and the enormous landmass that was Australia. The journey was three times as long. "I guess that means about twelve days."

"Twelve days?" Ruth's eyes bulged as she took this in.

"Too long," Maryam and Lazarus said in unison. Maryam ignored his smirk, and turned her attention back to the map. "In that case I think we'd better try for somewhere closer." She scanned the dots that signified islands, hoping one would miraculously stand out as right. But there were too many, and she felt baffled by the choice.

"I think you should head for the place where you most want to stay," Joseph said. "There's no point doing it for me."

"How can you say that?" Maryam reached out for him, skimming her hand down his arm. "You're going to survive, Joseph. We'll see to that."

"Indeed, cousin," Lazarus chipped in. "You must not give up now, when we're so close."

Joseph threw his arms into the air, shaking off Maryam's hand. "Do you think I don't understand how sick I am? You forget that I've just watched my father die in the same way." His face was flushed and sweaty, and his sudden movement seemed to dizzy him. He reeled backwards, and would have fallen had not Lazarus seized him by the arm and supported him until he'd stabilised.

Maryam turned away as he struggled to regain his composure, and tried instead to focus on the map. It was hard to see anything through her tears. But she would not give up hope of saving him. Refused.

"There," she announced, stabbing her finger at a clump of islands further west of Marawa Island. "What about these?"

The other three leaned back in over the map, Lazarus wrapping his arm around Joseph's shoulder as if he were simply being friendly, but Maryam could see the muscles of his arm were straining as he continued to support Joseph's weight.

"Why these and not this?" Lazarus countered, pointing at a larger island to the south. It sat alone, within the pool of blue.

"These are closer to Australia," she explained. "If there *is* more possibility of help from there, it makes sense to get as close as we can." She flicked her gaze to Ruth, hoping she'd approve so they need waste no more time. "Besides, with so many islands so close together, surely we're bound to find *someone* who can help."

Lazarus smiled and gave Joseph's shoulders a playful squeeze. "It seems the rain has cleared both their heads! It's a good suggestion. I agree." *How arrogant*, Maryam thought. Acting as if the decision rested with him, when he was nothing more than a stowaway. But at least he was not making the decision harder, and for that, she supposed, she was grateful. "Ruth? What about you?"

"I guess." She hesitated. "You won't forget your promise should we fail?"

Maryam felt the boys' attention fall on her as she replied. "No. If we find those islands offer us no sanctuary, we will return." She stared squarely at Lazarus, daring him to challenge her. Relief swept over her when he did not.

"All right," she said, trying to tamp down the trepidation swilling in her stomach. "If everyone's agreed, let's organise ourselves today, then set off again tomorrow at first light."

Each nodded their agreement, then backed away, leaving the decision to hang in the air over the map like an unwelcome cloud.

*   *   *

Maryam lay next to Joseph as the fire burned down to orange embers, and gave herself over to the pleasure of rest and a break in their preparations. They had renewed their water stores at a nearby stream, amassed a good haul of crabs and shellfish to add to the stash of coconuts and breadfruit they'd discovered nearby, and Lazarus had speared two good-sized fish to fill their bellies before they set off. The sea lapped peacefully against the shore, the long line of its foamy surf iridescent in the scrap of moonlight, while only the odd night bird called from the trees—a welcome reprieve from the day birds' constant squawk and creel.

For the rest of that day Joseph's energy had waned to such a point they'd ordered him to rest, and he had spent much of the evening dozing as the other three worked on. Now Ruth lay sleeping in the boat, and Lazarus had taken himself off up the beach again.

Joseph lay on his back now, with his arm tucked under Maryam's head, and pointed up towards the stars. "See that one," he said, indicating a bright star at the very edge where the horizon met the sea. "That one I call Tekeaa, after Sister Sarah."

Maryam felt as though her heart flipped over in her chest as her friend Sarah's dying words came back to her: *When you look up to the stars for help, I will be there.* It was Joseph who'd remained with Sarah—Tekeaa to her birth parents—as she died. Joseph, who now faced death himself. She rolled over to look at him, and saw how his face gleamed in the fire's dying light like the pale underbelly of a stingray in the sea's dark depths. He was caked in sweat, his shirt glued to his skin.

"I will not let you die," she said. "We *will* find help."

Joseph leaned towards her and kissed her forehead. "Shhhh," he said. "Don't spoil our time. Tomorrow we will all be trapped together on the boat again. Tonight is ours." His teeth flashed as he grinned at her. "I wish I had the strength to swim . . . I'd take you back out into the water and see what arose!"

Maryam felt herself blush, and slapped him jokingly. "I think I have a fair idea!" How she wished she could transport them back to the previous night, before Lazarus's spying had driven her away. Even the thought of their passionate meeting had the power to drive strange stabs low down into her abdomen—not painful, yet urgent and unsettling all the same.

She closed her eyes, trying to imagine what it would be like to lie with him in that sinful way. But, despite desire, her mind shied away from it. She wanted to be close to him—knew her body came alive under his touch and that it was obvious he felt the same—but the idea of taking it any further terrified her, even though she now lay beside him in this loving way. It was all too confusing—the last thing she wanted was to ruin their precious friendship by doing something she might regret. Or Joseph might. What if she offered herself to him and then, when he truly looked upon her, he found her too small or ugly to love? The uncertainty, the possible shame, tied her stomach into knots, and for a moment she was glad Lazarus had interrupted them. Maybe she just wasn't ready for that final step. She snuggled in against him, savouring his closeness and the knowledge that, until she felt the time was right, he would not force himself on her as others might.

Joseph's sweat smelt sour and stale. *How uncomfortable he must be in that sticky shirt.* Before she'd even thought it through, she leapt from the sleeping mat and scooped up the container of water she'd placed beside the fire in case he was thirsty in the night. If she could not give him the pleasure he so desired, at least she could help to ease the discomfort of his illness and show him how she felt for him through lesser acts of love. "Take off your shirt!"

For a moment he merely stared at her, his forehead screwed up in a look of confused disbelief. But, then, a smile twitching the corners of his mouth, he did as she asked and handed Maryam his sweat-drenched shirt. His ribcage pressed tightly up against his skin, and the purple bruising of the plague spread dark shadows around his neck. She turned her eyes from it. For this short time she would close her mind to what it meant. She bundled up the shirt into a ball and poured a little of the water over it. Then, most tenderly, she began to wash his face. His eyes widened in surprise but, as she continued to wipe away the salty sweat, he closed them, lying back and tucking his hands under his head with a beatific smile.

The minutes seemed to stretch and slow: all she was aware of was the steady rhythm of the tide as it beat time to the soothing journey of her hands. She rinsed his face, his neck, his shoulders, the soft hairs that grew under his arms, his chest, and, finally, his white concave belly, which quivered and contracted beneath her touch. Then, with hands made brave by the deepening darkness as the fire burnt itself out, she carefully undid his belt—daring not look at his pressing groin. A dart of longing shot through her but she willed herself not to get caught up in its dangerous barb. Instead, she focused on the cleansing as he raised his hips to help her slip his trousers off, and then she washed his legs and feet, working the damp cloth into the cracks between his toes.

When she dared glance up at him, she found him watching her with hungry eyes. Again, her abdomen contracted. *Lord, forgive me for my brazenness.*

"Come here," he rasped, barely able to speak the words.

She shook her head, never so doubtful of her own self-control as her blood seared through her veins and her pulse beat out a primitive call to act. It would be so easy now to give in to the urge . . . Instead, she reached with trembling hands for the blanket she had used to prop his head, and spread it over him to keep the evening chills away.

For a few tense moments he closed his eyes and she watched his struggle to accept her decision play across his face. But then he sighed and met her gaze, holding out his hand to her. She took it without hesitation now, confident he understood, and slid herself back down beside him until they lay there touching nose to nose.

CHAPTER EIGHT

Maryam woke well before dawn, lying on her back beneath the blanket she had shared with Joseph after the residual heat of the fire had fled. Today they would set off again. She knew she should be frightened but right now all she felt was a kind of bittersweet joy, remembering how she had fallen asleep in the comforting embrace of Joseph's arms.

His breathing was laboured as she rolled off the mat and made her way down to the sea before the others awoke. A waning moon still lurked in the grey pre-dawn, its face a cool silver above the breeze-ruffled surface of the sea.

She washed and dressed while the sun rose and lit the horizon of the eastern sky. Red light filtered through a veil of streaky clouds, as if staining the heavens with blood. She shuddered at the sight, aware that such colour did not bode well. Somewhere out beyond the horizon a storm must be brewing. But they could not afford to delay their departure—every hour mattered when Te Matee Iai was on the move. They would just have to pray the winds were working in their favour, pushing the storm away to the east.

Lazarus walked up the beach, barely glancing at Maryam as he went to work rebuilding the fire. Joseph awoke at the noise and instantly began to cough, the harsh sound competing with the snap of wood as Lazarus broke up brittle branches to stack in a pile. Joseph met Maryam's worried gaze, trying to smile through the spasms that rocked him as he coughed.

"Good morning," he said to her, once he'd caught his breath. "Did you sleep well?"

"I did," she said. She passed him a cup of water. "Did you?" She could feel Lazarus's scathing gaze upon her as he worked.

Joseph gulped the whole cupful down, then stretched and rose shakily to his feet. He grinned. "Never better in my life."

From his position by the fire Lazarus snorted. He blew on the small dry ball of bracken he'd pushed into the embers until a wispy trail of smoke streamed into the air. "I hate to break up your little love nest, Sister Maryam, but I suggest you wake up Ruth. We'll need a good breakfast before we get under way."

His tone was typically superior, as though he spoke to a lesser being. But Maryam decided not to let his attitude rankle her this day—there was too much at stake for argument. Instead, she simply nodded and climbed aboard the boat. The tide was coming in steadily, lifting the boat from its bed of sand to wallow in the restless shallows as though raring to go. Its timing was perfect—they would need the high tide to manoeuvre the boat back out to sea.

"Time to move," Maryam said, grabbing Ruth's exposed leg and shaking it. She slid her fingers to the sole of Ruth's foot, tickling at the hard pad of skin with her jagged nails.

Ruth squealed and rolled into a ball, tucking her feet out of Maryam's reach. "Don't!" Then she peered up into Maryam's face, not quite meeting her eye. "You did not sleep in here last night?"

"No," Maryam murmured, heat flooding up her neck. She busied herself collecting the ingredients for breakfast, leaving Ruth to make of her answer what she wished. The night had been too special—too private—to share even with her.

"You didn't let him . . . touch you?"

The unbridled disgust in Ruth's voice filled Maryam with

shame. She understood Ruth's reaction but she knew Ruth would not believe she could strip Joseph, bathe him, and lie next to him for the whole night without committing some sinful act.

"No. I stayed with him to give him comfort, that was all," Maryam said, backing from the shelter. "I didn't want him to be alone." She knew she sounded brusque and impatient but needed to cut off any further questions before Ruth pressed her into confessing something she'd misconstrue.

"What about me? You didn't think that maybe I was lying here alone in need of comfort too? We're sailing off into the void . . ." Ruth shrugged, unable to finish her sentence. Her eyes filled with tears.

Why was *she* the one who always had to consider others, Maryam wondered. Was she not allowed, for once, to indulge her own selfish needs? She sighed, immediately regretting such an uncharitable thought. Of course Ruth needed her as well: she was younger, and lost and frightened in an unknown world.

"I'm sorry, Ruthie. I didn't mean to leave you feeling all alone. It's just I'm scared Joseph will die." She hated having to say the words, worried that giving them voice might somehow make them real.

Ruth's defensiveness relaxed a little. "Don't worry, we'll save him. I'm sure of that. If the Lord told you to continue on our journey till we find him help, then He will watch over Joseph and keep him safe until we do."

Maryam forced a confident smile. "I'm sure you're right. But look, we've a lot to do before we go. Can you help with breakfast?" She turned and quickly climbed down from the boat, desperate to draw the conversation to a close. There was nothing to be gained from it, and she hated holding back from Ruth.

By the time they'd eaten the last soused remnants of Lazarus's fish, the red had faded from the sky, leaving them with the beginnings of an overcast day. Already the heat was so oppressive that Maryam found herself covered with sweat despite her early morning swim. There was a strange charged feel to the air, as if it had soaked up all their anxieties. But there was no turning back now: they had all agreed to carry on.

They carefully extinguished the fire and packed the last of their belongings back into the boat. The plan was simple enough: Joseph would work the tiller while the other three ensured they made it safely through the passage in the reef. Lazarus and Ruth, much stronger than Maryam, untied the mooring ropes from the series of boulders and Maryam carefully coiled them on the deck. She prepared the small storm-sail, ready to raise it as soon as they had cleared the beach, then took up her position at the prow—directing the others as they manhandled the boat around in the shallow surf.

As soon as she could feel the boat floating free, Maryam ran back to raise the sail. She felt the wind tug at the woven cloth as Ruth and Lazarus gave the boat one final shove towards the reef then leapt aboard, water spraying out around them as they hauled themselves onto the deck.

Now Lazarus helped Maryam secure the sail, then the three of them took up their positions to help guide Joseph as he steered directly for the break. The tide was nearly at its zenith, and Maryam realised that the obstacles they'd encountered on their approach to the island were diminished by the increased depth of water under the boat. Accompanied by the reeling, shrieking host of birds, they made it out through the passage without a glitch, and soon found themselves sailing smoothly on the ocean's broad rolling back.

Once the mainsail had been lifted and secured in place, they gathered together by the tiller to discuss their route. The direction of the wind was hard to gauge, the pennant strung from the big main mast flapping and curling in a confused dance. But long ribbons of cloud were travelling westwards with them, and so they pushed the boom of the big mainsail out to its farthest extreme, allowing the sail to balloon with air as they set a broad reach downwind, straight for the west.

Joseph handed the tiller over to Maryam, taking himself off to the shelter to steal some rest. Ruth and Lazarus sat down next to her, shifting only when they were needed to adjust the ropes. As the boat skimmed the short chop, gliding effortlessly down the rounded peaks of swell, the undulation of the sea lulled each of them into an insular, meditative mood.

By the time they'd been at sea two hours, Marawa Island once again appeared the stuff of dreams—a lush exotic backdrop that belied the death and destruction hidden at its core. How often she had found this true, Maryam thought—what looked good on the surface was rotten beneath.

Behind them, the clouds had now formed into a murky bank. Its dense dark underbelly clung close to the horizon line while, perching on its brooding back, lighter wind-wracked cumulus boiled and tumbled in a knotted mass.

Lazarus shook his head slowly as he studied the sky, his mouth pinching into a tight thin line. "We'd better keep an eye on that. If it gets any closer we'll have to haul down the sails."

"Perhaps we should head back for land?" Ruth offered,

sounding briefly buoyed by the thought of a reprieve from this new voyage.

It is tempting, Maryam thought. She'd have loved nothing more than to fly back to the safety of dry land. But they were making good progress across the sea, and to turn back now was to rob Joseph of what precious little life he may have left. "We have no time," she said, surprised to find herself looking to Lazarus to back her up.

He grunted, turning away from the looming storm clouds to meet Maryam's eye. "Let's tie down everything that could wash loose," he said. "At least, then, if it does catch up, we'll be prepared."

"Good plan," she said, wishing she had thought of this herself. "Ruthie, how about you take the tiller and I'll help secure the boat?"

Ruth, her eyes growing wide with worry, shuffled over on her knees to take Maryam's place at the tiller as the other two began to lash the storm-sail to the outside of the shelter wall. Then, with the sturdiest of the ropes, they tied the shelter itself even more securely to the beams that formed the structure of the deck, all the while watching as the storm bank seemed to deepen and darken in the east, moving ever closer with alarming speed. Already it had consumed Marawa, shrouding it without a trace, and the wind that drove the clouds now raced ahead and started to cut up the sea.

Between them, Maryam and Lazarus reefed in the main, reluctant to take it down completely in case they could still outrun the storm. The sky had emptied of birds, their incessant noise replaced by the creaking of the boat's timbers as it sliced its way through the increasingly sloppy chop.

Disturbed by all the activity on deck, Joseph had now re-emerged from the shelter. He stood face on to the wind, holding tightly to the aft rail as he studied the steady build-up of the clouds. The light seemed to have been sucked from the sky, turning everything around them to a dull and chilling steely grey. Maryam finished tying off the last of her ropes and joined him at the rail.

"Let's hope it passes over us as quickly as yesterday's rain-storm," she said, covering his long white fingers with her own small brown hand. She huddled into him, and they swayed in unison as the wind stirred the sea and pitched the hulls.

He flipped his hand over and wove his fingers in through hers. "I fear it could be much, much worse."

She did not bother questioning his judgement—born and raised on an island in the middle of the vast ocean, all of them knew how to read the skies. She, too, knew the signs were very bad.

"You must stay inside the shelter once the weather strikes," she told him. "The last thing you need right now is to worsen your chill."

"That's ridiculous," he said. "You'll need me if the sea gets rough."

"Maryam's right," Ruth broke in. "Between the three of us I'm sure we'll cope." Her tone belied her words; she sounded tremulous and very young.

Now Lazarus joined them at the aft rail as well. "You must make sure you keep dry," he said to Joseph, punching him play-fully on the arm. "You're wet enough without another dunking from the skies!"

Joseph blushed. "I thought I'd left my mother behind," he countered, trying to smile. But, standing so close to him,

Maryam could see how his reference to his mother saddened him. His chin quivered as he fought to get his feelings for her back under control.

His dignity was saved by an unexpected gust that squalled across the water, throwing spray up in its path as it whipped the tops off the choppy waves and slammed directly into the stern. As the wind hit the sail, the whole boat heeled dramatically to port, pitching the four off-balance and leaving them scrabbling for footing. "Quick," Lazarus cried to Joseph, "for the love of the Lord get back into the shelter now."

Joseph reached for Maryam, blatantly kissing her on the lips right there in front of Lazarus and Ruth, before he made his way back to the shelter—the angry hunch of his shoulders leaving none of them in any doubt of his displeasure at being relegated back inside.

Maryam had no time to worry about the others' response, as another squall raced across the sea towards them. Already she was pushing Ruth aside from her position at the helm, making ready to counter the force of the wind as it hit the boat and pitched it like a child's toy. She gripped the smooth wooden tiller with both hands, using the full weight of her body to hold it to its course, while Lazarus shouted curt instructions to Ruth as they tried to stabilise the flapping sail.

These two vicious squalls turned out to be the first harbingers of the storm itself. The sky was now a solid mass of black, the clouds swarming so close above their heads it felt as if the whole roof of the world was caving in and pressing down on them. And the waves it pushed at them were huge and angry, licking up against the hulls as though they would swallow them whole.

As Ruth and Lazarus struggled to bring down the main and raise the storm-sail, another wave hit them full force. Water crashed over Maryam and Ruth fell heavily, her head barely missing the solid wooden mast.

"Are you all right?" Maryam yelled, her heart rapping out messages of warning from her chest. They had no help, no one to tell them what to do, if one of them was badly injured.

Ruth rose gingerly, fighting the ever-increasing see-saw of the boat. Her teeth had slammed into her bottom lip, blood trickling down her chin. She wiped it away roughly, working her way over to the shelter at the centre of the boat. "Extra ropes," she cried to Joseph, snatching them from his hands the moment he offered them up. "Here," she said to Lazarus, throwing him one of the ropes. "Tie yourself to the boat." She flung a second rope at Maryam. "You do the same." She secured the third around her own waist with shaky hands, lashing it to the base of the mast as best she could.

"Good thinking," Lazarus called, and Maryam saw a brief flash of pleasure light Ruth's frightened face.

And it *was* a good idea: the instant Maryam secured herself to the boat she felt again more in control, freed at least of the fear of being swept overboard. But lightning was crackling overhead and the doleful roll of thunder seemed to vibrate right through her. And to make matters worse, stinging rain began to fall. She hunkered her head down into her shoulders, silently cursing every time another wave washed over her and down her neck.

Up at the mast, Lazarus and Ruth were struggling to change the sails. They fought hard to bring the main down, but the wind caught the thick woven sheet and tore it from Lazarus's grip. It billowed out again, filled with violent air, then, with a sickening retort, it ripped away from its bindings, shredding itself on the side rails before it plunged into the sea.

Lazarus threw himself towards the edge, desperately trying to catch hold of the sail before it sank beneath the waves. His lifeline was stretched to full measure as he slithered under the side-rail and hung down into the frothing wake.

"Lazarus, no!" Maryam screamed at him. This was total foolishness—one rogue wave and the rope surely wouldn't hold. It was one thing to rely on their ropes to secure them while still on deck, but leaning out over the sea like that, Lazarus tempted fate.

Ruth must have had the same thought, for she lurched over towards him and grabbed him roughly by his feet, hauling him backwards despite his loud and furious demands that she leave him be.

"Get your hands off me, you stupid girl. Without this sail we're lost."

"Forget it," Ruth screeched back at him, reeling him in with the rope. "Better a sail lost than someone's life." She was strong, Ruth, and stubborn when she set her mind to it, and Maryam could only watch with admiration as she put all her effort into dragging Lazarus back aboard.

Meantime, the sail filled with water and disappeared beneath the foamy surface of the sea.

"Damn you!" Lazarus cried, scrabbling back up to his feet. He raised his face to the heavens, closing his eyes against the hard pellets of rain. "Damn you to Hell."

This was too much for Ruth. She sprang at him and slapped his face. "Never, ever curse the Lord like that again. We need Him now to keep us safe. I will not let you risk our lives."

Maryam might have laughed had she not been so preoccupied—Lazarus had clearly never seen Ruth so riled before, protecting her Lord's good reputation like a distraught mother would her child. He made to swing back at her, but the boat was floundering now without a scrap of sail to steady its progress, and he was tossed away, crashing against the denuded mast.

"You'll keep," he finally managed to spit at Ruth, rubbing his shoulder before he shrugged and began collecting up the storm-sail, keeping it tucked in the lee of his torso as he struggled to lash it to the mast.

"What on earth is going on?" It was Joseph, emerging from the shelter. Maryam could hardly hear him above the noise: the wind, the rain, the groaning timbers of the boat, the clash of thunder from the skies.

"We lost a sail," Maryam yelled back, using every scrap of air inside her lungs to reach his ears. She motioned him to stay inside, but he was standing now, steadying himself against the roof of the shelter.

Ruth was helping Lazarus raise the storm-sail, their tiff put aside as they wrestled to stay upright while the wind increased and the waves built. Above them a bolt of lightning split the sky, followed only seconds later by a clap of thunder so prolonged and deafening that all four ducked as if they feared the sky would shatter and fall.

The next hour became one long fight for survival, as the wind screamed in the rigging and the swells became virtual mountains, the boat surfing—out of control—down their sides. Deep in the troughs, it seemed the waves behind would break right over the top of the boat, reaching out for them with icy spray. Never in her life had Maryam felt so terrified. The storm-sail strained against its ropes, the boom swinging and jolting as the hulls crashed from trough to trough. Timbers groaned and cracked, lashings stretched to breaking point, and all the four could do was hold on to the railings with all their might. No one spoke now; each was locked in a private nightmare fight as the black clouds intensified overhead, turning day to gloomy night. The deck was awash, making the timber treacherous and slippery, and it was almost impossible to stay upright as the bucking hulls were jostled forward on the surge of sea.

The soaked crew huddled together by the tiller, clutching onto each other for support while Ruth prayed aloud. She turned her head to look behind, and let out a terrified wail just as Maryam, too, saw the great wall of water that rose above them, its crest taller than the main mast at its peak. Time froze in that one instant just before the wave was set to break, looming over them like an enormous building, and before the boat began its frantic scramble up the next swell. But, as it broke, the last of the wall of water caught them, crashing down with such force Maryam feared she'd drown in it and would never again break free to air. Inside the tumble of confused sea they held on to each other by sheer force of will, fingers digging into arms and legs to hold them safe.

When at last she burst free of its fury, Maryam saw the damage the wave had wrought. The pandanus thatching of the shelter was almost entirely torn to shreds, and flapped precariously now in the roaring winds. And the storm-sail, their one means of forward momentum, had been ripped clean away from the mast and trailed in the water in the gap between the hulls.

Joseph lunged as though to rescue it, but Maryam threw herself after him, holding him back.

"Leave it," she cried out to him. "You're not tied down." Her voice was whipped away by the wind almost as soon as it left her throat, yet there was no doubting her intent.

He turned to her, his face so pale his colour reflected the surface of the foam-washed sea. Consumed by white water, the sea itself almost mirrored the cloudy boiling of the sky while, in the small patches between the spray and foam, the depths were black as night. He called back to her, but his words did not have the power to break above the howling wind.

Then Lazarus was edging on hands and knees towards the fraying sail. Twice he was thrown onto his stomach by the pitching boat before he managed to reach the spot where the sail dragged. It was held by barely a thread and, as he tried to haul it in, the last rope snapped, sending it—their final remaining hope—down to the ocean's depths. Maryam and Joseph together fought to work the tiller, trying to gain some kind—any kind—of steerage or control. But it was impossible: the force of the water was so ferocious Maryam feared if they pushed it any harder the tiller, too, would break. Tears of fury and exhaustion in equal measure welled up in her.

Just as Lazarus crawled back to join them, Maryam glanced past him off to starboard, and now it was her turn to scream. A towering spout of water had been whipped up from the sea and was racing beside them. She had seen such things before from the safety of the atoll's shores, and old Hushai had warned her of their danger in the days leading up to her escape.

"Into the shelter!" she yelled, pointing to the pulsing, unearthly, spiralling umbilical cord of condensed wind and sea.

She abandoned her futile battle with the tiller and clawed for Ruth's hand, tugging her across the slippery wooden deck.

Lazarus and Joseph needed no such encouragement, and were scrambling towards what remained of their shelter. They tumbled in and huddled together at its centre, while their stores washed about them in total disarray. The roaring of the wind and the pressure in their ears was almost unbearable.

They could hear the churning vortex of the waterspout as it passed them by like a thousand demons released from Hell. When the roar finally died away there was a lessening of the pressure in the air and, despite the continued attack of the storm itself, all four found themselves smiling with relief that this ordeal was over. But it was not. Another huge wave had built behind them and now it scooped up the boat as if it were nothing more than feathers on the breeze. The hulls pitched onto their prow—suspended in an endless moment of impossibility—then, just as suddenly, completely overturned.

Maryam's lungs were near-bursting as, buried by furious water, she tried desperately to hold her last precious breath. But she was thrown against the shelter's timber frame, tumbled and twisted, minced and mashed, in a thick soup of flailing bodies and broken stores. Her hair streamed out over her face, tying itself in strangling tangles tight around her neck.

Just as she thought she could hold her breath no longer, she felt the boat flip over on its axis. Water streamed from the shelter as the craft righted itself on the roiling surface of the sea. Maryam crashed down onto the deck, her arm twisting under her, and somewhere close to her she heard a crack. Pain splintered her mind, and all else seemed to ebb away. Only in a fleeting moment of clarity did she register that the bone inside her arm had snapped.

CHAPTER NINE

Maryam could hardly think past the stabbing pain. Around her, the shelter lay in ruins. The wooden framing had splintered and the whole structure slumped at a precarious angle towards the prow. Their stores had been devastated, most of them washed away or broken as the boat had flipped. Ruth was bleeding from a gash on her forehead and Lazarus was retching up sea water; Joseph coughed so violently he surely risked expelling his lungs.

Nausea swept over her as she looked down at her left arm and saw the reddening lump where the broken bone pressed at the skin just below her elbow. When she tried to straighten it the pain was so appalling she nearly passed out and bright flashes of light fractured behind her eyes.

Around them the storm raged on, the boat tossed helplessly on the vicious waves. Without the shelter of thatching they had no protection from wind or spray, and Maryam felt a chill settling over her—her whole body was soaked and shaking, and nausea was rising up so fast she couldn't hold back the strings of burning bile that rose into her mouth.

Lazarus was the first to recover, ripping off his shirt and roughly tying strips around Ruth's head to stem the blood. Ruth's eyes were glazed, as though her mind had fled the scene. She sat amidst the slushy rubble, rocked at will by the seas, emitting an unearthly moan. As Lazarus worked to patch up Ruth, Maryam saw angry red grazes puffing up along the central line of his spine, and noted in a strange detached way how he winced each time his body twisted with the jolting of the boat.

Now Joseph was crawling over to Maryam, the ugly marks of Te Matee Iai so pronounced around his neck and chest the skin looked black. His lips were split and seeping blood, his eyes so bloodshot she wondered how he still could see.

"Are you hurt?" Joseph rasped. Up close she realised he was cut and bruised as well.

Maryam nodded, unable to speak. It took every scrap of concentration she had left not to scream out with pain. She forced herself to raise her arm, presenting it for him to see.

"Oh no! Is the pain bad?"

Somewhere inside her dazed brain she laughed. *Bad? That depends on the scale.* Was it worse than their predicament? Worse than everything she'd survived up until now? All she could manage in response was one tiny nod of her head. *Yes, it burns just like the fires of Hell.*

Behind Joseph, Lazarus had finished strapping up Ruth's head and was crawling towards the shelter's doorway, balancing himself on the shattered framing as he pushed his head out past the remnants of the thatch, straight into the full force of the storm.

He did not last long—the rain drove straight into his face—but he'd seen enough. He tipped back into the shelter and dropped his head into his hands. The other three watched him, preparing for the worst as he finally lifted his head. Shock bruised his eyes and washed him ghostly pale.

He cleared his throat, his Adam's apple sliding up and down several times before he spoke. "We've lost the mast. The big one. It's snapped right off."

Maryam heard the words clearly enough, despite the roaring of the wind, but she couldn't really comprehend what he'd said.

Lost the mast? What did that mean? She tried to think through the consequences but the constant lurching of the hulls ramped up her pain. She moved her arm, attempting to brace it more securely against her chest, but the torture was too much for her, wrapping itself in a tight band around her forehead and pressing at her brain. She cried out, unable to hold the well of agony inside her now. Then she blacked out.

*   *   *

Was it hours or days before she regained sufficient sensibility to think? She'd been locked in a nightmare daze, jumbled images washing in and out of her consciousness as the storm raged on. Day like night; night, lit up by lightning, just like day. Constant pitching and jolting. Thirst and hunger. Pain on pain.

When she finally managed to focus properly on the carnage around her, she registered that at least the others were accounted for and now asleep. Ruth's blood-smeared head rested in Maryam's lap, one hand stretched out and clutching at a bamboo strop, the other holding tightly to her sodden Holy Book. Joseph lay curled up next to her, his breathing shallow and laboured. He was bolstered against rolling by Lazarus, whose arm reached tightly around him even in sleep.

It was impossible to tell if it still rained; the gale was so fierce the spray drove horizontally into her face. The wild wind shrieked in her ears, and as the minutes blurred again into hours, its caterwauling conjured up a host of disconnected voices. *Take this faithless whore and cast her out.* Her father's voice, so clear she startled and cast around for him, before she realised how ridiculous that was. *This is your fault, you stupid girl.* That, she knew was Lazarus, and yet he lay there sleeping at Joseph's side. But the voices were so real, the hairs on her arms rose up as she heard Ruth's voice above the wind. *I testify against you this day that you shall perish.* Again, the proof before her eyes belied the phantom voice.

It was as if she'd died—been pitched through some terrible tempestuous limbo to a place where all the voices of her past laid bare her many sins. Perhaps it was the Lord Himself who now berated her, making her pay for her treachery towards Him by casting her straight into Hell. Was *this* the Tribulation re-enacted? Sent forth to punish her for her disbelief? She tried to pray, pushing past the consuming pain that dulled her mind: *Forgive me, Lord—and, if you can't, at least somehow protect the others here and make them safe.*

As if to answer her, lightning flared overhead, illuminating the wreckage of the boat. Beneath its cold, furious flash the faces of her friends transformed to masks—hollow-eyed death masks that left her accused of responsibility for their fate. Her chest ached with the burden of repressed sobs, yet she found she couldn't cry. Everything inside her had been sucked away, leaving only the husk of her, held together by her pain and guilt.

Dizzy and exhausted, she closed her eyes. *Nanona! I am here!* Her mother's voice! *Only she knows my real name.* Maryam spun around, certain the voice was right behind her, forgetting that she cradled Ruth's head in her lap. Ruth stirred and groaned, her eyes springing open and fixing on Maryam's face.

The only thing Maryam could think to do to soothe her was to stroke her blood-streaked hair, crooning wordless comfort as Ruth's eyelids flickered again and closed.

Maryam forced herself to focus on the real world, to take stock of their situation with her rational mind. Although Lazarus was bruised and battered, he did not seem to have any major injuries that she could see. Ruth's head wound had clotted underneath the makeshift bandage, but the effects of the blow she'd suffered were less than clear. Somewhere in her memory Maryam was sure she'd learnt that if someone's head was badly knocked they shouldn't be allowed to sleep. She couldn't recall the logic of this now, just knew it was important to act.

She gently rocked Ruth's shoulder, and Ruth reared up, her head knocking Maryam's broken arm. The jolt shot stars of pain up behind her eyes, making her pant so as not to vomit all over Ruth's dazed face. Once she'd recovered enough to think again, she saw the exercise was in vain. Ruth had slipped back into her slumber and would not be roused.

Instinctively, she turned her attention to Joseph, whose chest was fluttering in time to his feeble, bird-like breaths. The skin around his lips was blue, his fingers so white they looked transparent in the scrappy light. She wanted to reach out to him, to wrap him safely in her arms and make him warm, but she just could not summon up the will to move.

Then a vicious gust of wind hit the boat side-on, shunting it sideways so that one hull teetered between the ridges of the waves. As the boat tried to right itself, a terrible splintering rent the air. The aft handrail ripped clear from the deck and flew into the sea, leaving only splintered fragments in its wake.

Forward, Maryam was stunned to see the figure of the warrior remained in its position at the prow. He was hanging in there for his life, slapped by waves and blinded by the whirling spray. How was it he'd survived, when destruction reigned all around? Had his ancient fighting spirit kept him safe? She didn't know. But she wished for a little of his spirit too, instead of the heavy pall of hopelessness that weighed her down.

She closed her eyes, overcome by drowsy seasickness as the boat pitched and rolled. *I give up*, she conceded to the Lord. *Take me now.*

* * *

It was pitch black when next Maryam woke. Neither the moon nor a single star was visible in the sky, but the wind and rain had stopped at last. The sea was still huge, its motion unrelenting, but at least now it seemed the worst had passed. She could barely make out the shadows of the other three, though she could still feel their presence close by—a kind of innate warmth that reached out to her soul.

"Is anyone awake?" Her voice was croaky and not at all like her own.

"Sister Maryam?" Off to her left, Lazarus stirred, and now she could make out his silhouette against the eerie iridescence of the white-capped waves.

"Are you all right?" she asked, relieved to hear another voice—one that was real.

Lazarus snorted. "I still live." She heard him groan as he shifted towards her. "My back has taken the worst of it, but I don't think anything is broken, just badly bruised. And you? How is your arm?" The genuine concern in his voice made her want to cry.

"Right now it feels strangely numb." She didn't dare move it: for the moment, the pain had gone. "And Joseph?"

Even through the pounding of the waves she heard Lazarus sigh. "He sleeps now, thank goodness. Did you hear him ranting a few hours back?"

"No. What do you mean?"

"It's the fever, I think. He was calling out to his father, Uncle Jonah, as if he were here." She could see him a little more clearly now her eyes had adjusted to the gloom. He bent down over Joseph's sleeping form and spread his hand across his brow. "He's still burning up."

"We need to get some water into him, to bring his temperature down."

"I thought of that. But I couldn't find any containers."

"We've lost our water?"

"Maybe when it's light we'll have more luck finding something in this mess." He stretched his arms above his head, stifling another groan. "How is Sister Ruth?"

"I'm not too sure. You did a good job stopping the blood, but I'm worried that the blow to her head has done some harm. What do you think? Should we wake her or not?" The comfort of sharing her worries, even with Lazarus, was immense. Just to voice her fears aloud made them less hard to bear.

"Why? I don't think I could cope with her hysterics right now."

Maryam bristled at his arrogance, but, in truth, she found she agreed with him. It was hard enough to keep her own swirling fears at bay. "I suppose you're right. At least while she is sleeping she's calm."

For a while they slipped into silence. Maryam knew that if they had lost all their provisions—especially their water—they were doomed. But try as she might to put the thought from her mind, it seemed it would not shift now that she had placed it there. And it made her so thirsty thinking of it; her mouth tasted sour and her throat felt swollen and parched.

Joseph's weak voice floated up from the dark. *"But with an overrunning flood he will make an utter end of the place thereof, and darkness shall pursue his enemies."*

"Joseph!" Maryam carefully shifted Ruth's head from her lap and crawled towards his voice. "You're awake!"

"Apparently," he said. Despite the frailty of his voice, his irony gladdened her heart. But then he began to cough, so weak now he could hardly regain his breath between the spasms. Panting, he said to her: "I *saw* my father, Maryam. He was here."

She was at his side, drawn by the immense heat that radiated from him, and bent down to kiss his dry, cracked lips, trying to ignore the pain that re-ignited in her arm. Joseph's breath smelt vile, as though dredged up from the grave.

"I'm sure I heard *my* mother too," she said. Why argue with him, when his belief in his father's presence must surely have brought him comfort? She brushed his hair away from his forehead, feeling how his whole body shivered beneath her touch. "What can I do to help you?"

"Nothing," he said. "Just knowing you're here is help enough." She felt his hand brush her leg, and then his fingers caressed her skin. His touch still had the power to ignite the skin beneath his hand.

She longed to lie down beside him and seek the comfort of his body next to hers, but her arm was vulnerable to any movement. She had to secure it somehow, to reduce the shock each time she moved. The rope she'd used to tie herself to the boat would do, but it was still attached to the foot of the broken mast, and to retrieve it now, while it was still dark, was difficult and dangerous. She'd have to wait till dawn.

Instead, she propped herself against the leaning frame of the shelter, bolstering herself against the slapping of the hulls, and tried to doze. Her thirst nagged at her, tipping her into restless half-dreams in which she and Joseph stood hand in hand beneath the waterfall they'd discovered in Onewēre's lush jungle, her tongue out to lap up the spray. It was so cool, so fresh, so utterly quenching that she almost cried when she was jerked back to reality by the crashing of the boat. Her throat was so dry and bloated every attempt to swallow became a conscious act and felt as if she were trying to swallow down her own tongue.

The hours until dawn seemed endless as she drifted in and out of dehydrated sleep, and so it came as a surprise when she opened her eyes from another of her thirsty dreams to find the early morning sun now shone down on them from a cloudless sky. The seas had calmed back to a choppy roll, and Ruth sat awake beside her, staring blankly out through the ravages of the shelter at the empty sea beyond.

Now it was possible to see around her, the reality of their situation struck home. The boat lay in tatters: timbers splintered, bindings snapped, and the meagre remnants of their carefully prepared provisions lay overturned in waterlogged piles. She and her three companions looked as wrecked as the boat itself: battered and bruised and broken, soaked and adrift in hostile sea they could not drink.

Worst of all was Joseph, whose feverish face now clearly showed the markings of Te Matee Iai. While the others had dark rings of tiredness beneath their eyes, Joseph's skin was bruised almost to black. The purple rash had now consumed his neck completely, the skin blotchy and inflamed, and he was covered in deep ugly bruises, some as wide in span as an open hand. He did not seem aware of his surroundings, just lay there on his back, his eyes half-closed as he struggled to breathe.

Lazarus appeared to be sleeping, curled into a ball that accentuated the bruising on his spine. As Maryam watched he shuddered, murmuring something she could not decode. His hand shot out, his fingernails digging into the sodden deck, before he dropped back into a more peaceful doze.

Ruth's plaintive voice cut through her thoughts. "I want to go home."

Hysterical laughter bounced around inside Maryam's head. *If only it was that easy.* She reached over for Ruth's hand to comfort her. "At least we're all still alive," she stammered. It was difficult to talk when each dry breath was forced. *Water . . .* That was what they needed now.

She struggled to her feet, the movement juddering her arm. She clenched her teeth against the pain and climbed through the wreckage to the outside deck. Amidst the debris, the mast lay broken from its splintered base. Maryam's stomach flipped: if it had fallen even an arm's length further over to the right, it would have landed right on top of them and crushed them all.

The sea was surprisingly tame after the fury of the storm. But there was little comfort in it. The ocean rippled endlessly in all directions, and there was no sign of land. Could they possibly still be on course, or had the storm pitched them into waters they did not know? There was no way of knowing. Maryam had no idea where the compass was and, until night fell again, they'd have no way to plot the stars.

She tracked the rope that bound her back to the point where it was tied, and put her concentration into freeing the knot. It was hard to do one-handed, her fingers fumbling as they caught on the swollen and frayed fibres. But at last she managed to unravel it, and hauled the rope back over to Ruth.

"I need your help," she said. "I want to strap my arm to hold it still."

Ruth nodded and proceeded to wind it around Maryam's body as she cushioned her broken arm against her breasts. She screwed up her eyes, breathing through her mouth to fight off the pain. Ruth worked as quickly as she could, eventually tying off the rope at the point where it looped back over Maryam's shoulder. Maryam kept her eyes shut, focusing on calming her breaths until the pain settled to a slightly more manageable ache.

Now Maryam cast about for any sign of the water containers, grunting with relief as she spied an unbroken earthenware jar amidst a pile of other debris wedged against the one undisturbed shelter wall. She and Ruth rushed to rescue it—and, miraculously, a cup as well. But Maryam's elation was extinguished as she realised all the other containers had been smashed. If they were careful perhaps they had enough to last the day, but nothing more.

Very cautiously, Ruth poured the precious water into the cup Maryam held at the container's lip. The sight of it set Maryam salivating, and it took all her strength not to gulp it all in one thirsty rush.

"Here," she said to Ruth. "You go first." She couldn't take her eyes off the cup, as Ruth swallowed down its contents. When, finally, it was her turn to drink, she sipped her share in tiny mouthfuls, savouring the sensation as the cool liquid worked its magic and soothed her throat.

Now she carried it over to Joseph, and Ruth lifted his head while Maryam offered him the cup. He lay passively in Ruth's hold, his eyes fixed on Maryam's face as he took a sip. Immediately he choked, sending him into a spasm of coughing that left him limp and short of breath. Again they tried, little by little quenching his thirst. By the time his share of the precious water had been drunk, he seemed exhausted, weakly waving Ruth away as he closed his eyes and sank back to the deck.

"Give Lazarus his share now," Maryam told Ruth. She was reluctant to leave Joseph's side, so eased herself down beside him, wriggling her one good arm under his head until it cushioned him in her embrace. The deck was cruelly hard and dug into her hip, but she didn't care—he was desperately sick, and he needed her: that was enough.

Revived a little by the meagre amount of water, Lazarus and Ruth began to sort through the wreckage and take stock of what they had left. It was a dispiriting result. The map—their precious map—was gone, and the book of celestial navigation was so waterlogged the pages tore under Ruth's fingers as she tried to separate them out. In terms of food, all they could salvage were five coconuts (and their life-saving milk), a bunch of six bruised bananas, one container of te kabubu powder (hard to digest unless mixed with water) and one squashed round of goat's cheese— hardly a feast, and barely a fraction of their original store. Their best find was another half container of water in a broken urn, which they carefully secured in place against the wall. It was not a lot to keep four needy bodies alive—especially when they did not know how far they had been blown away from land.

They decided to divide the goat's cheese first. Maryam gratefully ate her share before breaking Joseph's into pieces small enough for him to eat. But he shook his head, and clamped his lips tight together as she tried to force the soft crumbly cheese between his teeth.

"Come on, cousin," Lazarus urged him. "You must eat." He squatted down beside Joseph and gently touched his fingers to the pulse in Joseph's neck. He closed his eyes, concentrating on the pulse, then slowly met Maryam's gaze. He frowned and subtly shook his head. "He's very weak."

"Perhaps if we mixed up some te kabubu so he can drink it, it might give him strength?"

"We can try, Sister, but I fear the time for food has past."

No! He could not be saying this. Maryam slipped her arm out from under Joseph's head and launched herself upright, determined to give her plan a try. She would not fail him now.

Ignoring the stabbing pain that shot through her arm, she shook some of the te kabubu powder into the empty cup. Next she scooped a little of their store of water in on top and stirred it into a thin creamy paste. She licked the mixture from her finger to check it was not too thick to swallow: the flavour was insipid but the consistency just about right. *Please Lord, please. Don't take him yet.*

She knelt down at Joseph's side, carefully raising his head until it rested in her lap. "Come on," she pleaded with him. "Just try to take a little of this." She dipped her index finger into the paste, then placed the finger to his lips. He opened his eyes again, staring up at her with a glassy lack of focus as he licked the paste away, his tongue as dry and ridged as a lizard's. "Good. That's good," she said, dipping her finger in to repeat the process.

Again he licked the te kabubu paste away, and her heart seemed to lift and soar. She would save him, she was sure of it—all she had to do was keep him nourished and hydrated until they drifted into land. She smiled down at him, determined to raise his spirits with her warmth, just as he whispered something she could not hear.

She bent down over him, as far as her arm would allow. "What did you say?"

"Remember that I love you," he whispered, the scent of the te kabubu not strong enough to mask his putrid breath. He could barely keep his eyes open, the lids drooping as he struggled to hold her gaze. His breath came in rattling bursts, with long gaps between each exhalation.

"I love you too," she murmured back, aware of the tingling in her nose that warned of tears. There was something way too final in his words, as if he used them to say goodbye. She would not let him think like this. Had to give him back the will to live.

"Tonight we'll plot the stars with your mother's book," she burbled, hoping to catch him up in the confidence she now feigned. The book, of course, was now too sodden to read. "If we can roughly figure out where we are now, then we can watch the wind and currents, and calculate the closest land. We will make this work, Joseph, I promise you. We've come too far to—"

Her words froze on her lips. He had not breathed. *He had not breathed!* She waited, willing him to inhale. *Come on. Come on.* His eyes still fixed upon her face, but there was no focus at all now, no light, no life. She dropped the cup, not caring that the precious paste now spilt, and grabbed him by the shoulder, shaking him.

"Breathe, Joseph, you have to breathe."

As her heart pounded with panic, he dragged in another rattling breath. His body jerked, shocked by the additional air, and his eyes cleared of their haze and settled on her face. He smiled, and slowly mouthed her name.

She smiled back at him, transmitting her love for him out through her eyes. *Thank the Lord he is still here.* "That's better . . . you had me going then!" She trawled her finger through the spilt paste, pressing it to Joseph's lips. "Come on now, lick it up," she prompted him, shaking his shoulder ever so slightly to rouse him into action.

As she did so, she heard something clink beneath him on the deck. She rolled him a little, reaching into his trouser pocket to see if she could make him more comfortable by removing whatever lay inside. Her fingers touched on something small and round.

She drew it out, and for a fleeting moment was confused by what she held. The compass!

"Look," she cried out to Lazarus and Ruth. She waved the compass at them, buoyed by the thought that now they had another means to claw back some small sense of control. She tossed it to Lazarus, remembering he'd seemed to know how the strange little object worked. "Does this help?"

"Damn right it does," he replied, studying the compass face as Ruth bristled at his blasphemy. "This helps a lot." He leaned over, grinning broadly at Joseph. "Trust you to come to our rescue, cousin. What you won't do to make a good impression on the girls!" He chuckled at his own joke, prodding Joseph playfully on the arm.

Joseph did not react. His head lolled limp and unresponsive

in Maryam's lap. She looked down at him, and her stomach contracted as she saw how his eyelids drooped over his eyes.

"Wake up, Joseph! You can't give up on me now."

Again she shook him, leaning right down over him despite the pain that seared her arm. She put her ear to his sweaty, discoloured chest. Listened for the beating of his heart . . . for any hint of breath.

It could not be. There was nothing. No pulse. No breath. No hint of life. She shook her head, willing it not to be true. He could not leave her, could not just die here like this in her arms. She jiggled him, again and again, calling out his name as though she could summon his spirit back from the brink. Beside her, Lazarus and Ruth moved in to still her hands, their faces bleached, eyes wide with shock.

"Leave me!" she screeched, twisting away from them to scoop Joseph's sagging body up into her one good arm. "I will not let him die."

She pressed him to her in an awkward, agonising embrace as she howled out her anguish. "Don't die. Don't die. You just can't die . . ."

Her head was bursting with a buzz of tangled noise; her eyes too full of tears to see. Terror at the thought of losing him took her by the throat and pressed the cruel point home with such dizzying force she could hardly breathe, her lungs filling with an ache she knew could not be purged. It was not fair. For the first time in her life she'd found someone who made her feel loved and treasured, and the Lord, in His wrathful vengeance, chose to punish her by taking him away.

She raised her tearful face to the heavens, wailing out her pain. "I hate you, Lord. I never will forgive you for this act."

She pressed her lips to Joseph's, as if her own life force could somehow revive him, but it was pointless—death lay upon him like a pall.

A wave of grief overwhelmed her, stealing her breath and, with it, her desire to live, leaving her as cold and flat and lifeless as the body she clutched so urgently against her chest. But now, as Ruth laid a tentative hand on her shoulder, she understood the awful and enduring truth: this kind sweet boy was dead, and nothing—*nothing*—she could do, or say, or give to him, would ever bring him back.

CHAPTER TEN

The hours melded into one long numbing nightmare as Lazarus and Ruth tried repeatedly to prise Joseph's lifeless body from Maryam's clasp. But she would not budge. The Lord might have stolen his life away, but she refused to relinquish Joseph's corpse as well.

How the Lord had played with them all: demanding loyalty and love, yet giving none back in return. He had rained His punishment down on her, and left her as bereft as poor Job in the Holy Book. *He leadeth priests away spoiled, and overthroweth the mighty . . . And taketh away the understanding of the elders . . . the heart of the chiefs of the people of the earth. And causeth them to wander in a wilderness where there is no way.*

Job's words swirled inside Maryam's head, his anguish giving voice now to her own. It was as if Job understood her pain, had seen her struggle with the Apostles and knew the fault lay not with her—despite the Lord's cruel vengeful acts. *Behold, I cry out of wrong, but I am not heard: I cry aloud, but there is no judgment. He hath fenced up my way that I cannot pass, And hath set darkness in my paths . . . he hath broken me down on every side, and I am gone . . . when I looked for good, then evil came; and when I waited for light, there came darkness . . .*

A hand shook her shoulder, breaking into her thoughts. "Maryam, please," Ruth beseeched her. "You must put him down and drink some water or you'll perish too."

Maryam looked into Ruth's face, but it was as if she was trapped inside tree resin: could see out past the lucent wall but could not move, respond or feel. Her survival counted for nothing now—with the snuffing out of Joseph's life, she found her own will spent as well.

She pulled Joseph even more tightly to her, revelling in the pain it caused her arm. *Let it hurt.* Let it overwhelm her until it blanked this day forever from her mind.

Ruth continued to stare at her helplessly. She plucked at Maryam's sleeve. "We must give Joseph the last rites, Maryam, or else his soul will not go to the Lord."

The sound of Maryam's laugh was harsh and mirthless as it welled up from her depths. "You think his soul is not already pure enough to meet Him? Then damn the Lord."

Ruth gasped, her face flushing an angry red. She grabbed Maryam by the shoulders and shook her. "Stop this! Stop it, or you will commit us all to death."

Ruth's threat washed off her—what did she care? But the shaking she could not ignore, as it juddered her bound arm and drove sharp shards of pain into her brain. She cried out, and Ruth dropped her arms back to her sides as if burnt.

"Leave her," Lazarus broke in. "We have more pressing problems right now." He rose from his brooding, taking the compass from his pocket and placing it carefully into the upturned palm of his hand. Maryam watched, dizzy from pain and totally detached, as he studied the arrow and slowly turned in a half circle until it lined up with the marker to indicate north. Now he glanced out to sea, pointing to his left. "It seems we've been blown south. We need to go back that way if we want to find the islands to the west."

"But how can we do that?" Ruth glanced around the crippled boat. "We haven't even got a sail."

"I don't know." Lazarus shrugged. "If only we still had the map." He wrapped his fingers over the compass, weighing it in his hand. "Let's clean up what we can, and think about our options then." He glanced over at Maryam, a deep frown forming between his eyes. "I tried to warn her . . ." He shook his head, then moved away to start picking through the wreckage on the deck.

For more than an hour and a half Lazarus and Ruth worked around Maryam, trying to make sense of the shattered bamboo, stores and thatch, sorting whatever they could salvage into small piles. They failed to shift the fallen mast, so were forced to work around it, sidestepping the chiselled timber each time they crossed the deck. The sea, at least, was calmer, and eventually a little order emerged from the chaos. But it was only when the deck was cleared of its debris that they discovered yet another calamity. Something had punctured one of the boat's hulls, up near the forward mast, and water was slowly seeping in.

"Damn, and damn again," Lazarus cursed, ignoring Ruth's righteous glare. He rummaged through their meagre possessions and pulled a pair of Joseph's trousers from the sodden pile. He called Ruth over, and together they worked to stuff the fabric tightly into the hole, using a piece of broken wood to tamp down on the folded layers until they were firmly wedged in place.

"Will it be enough?" Ruth asked, her voice drenched with worry.

Lazarus was bailing out the excess water with the help of a broken jar. "You'd better pray so," he replied. "If it doesn't, we're sunk." He handed Ruth another scoop and indicated that she should help him empty the storm's residue from both hulls.

Maryam watched them work, so removed from their actions it was as though she saw them through a veil. She didn't care about the hole, would be relieved now just to sink and drown. *Joseph is dead . . . Joseph is dead.* The words would not stop ringing in her ears and she felt diminished by them, as if her own body dried and congealed around his corpse to form a human shroud. She stroked his hair, his arms, his back. Could feel his body cold and stiff beneath her touch.

She knew, in some small recess of her brain, that she should lay him down now—put him to rest—but every time she made the move to draw her hand away she panicked, terrified she'd never have the chance to hold him in her arms again. It hurt so much. More than the desertion of her mother and, later, the news of her mother's death. More than the rejection of her father. More even than her cruel treatment at Father Joshua's hands. Every cell inside her ached.

The sun had finally broken through the clouds, bearing down and stealing every scrap of moisture from her skin. Her tears were sucked up by the stifling heat before they even left her eyes and her mouth cried out for water, but still she could not move. She could see Ruth and Lazarus finish up their bailing and sensed they were discussing her, but she did not care. Let them think whatever they wanted of her, she would not desert her love.

Ruth came over and squatted down beside her, offering a cup of water. "Here," she said. "Please drink. You know Joseph would want you to."

She understood what Ruth was playing at, could see her game. But she found she could not resist what might be Joseph's wish; besides, the urge to drink was now so overpowering it was impossible to fight. With Ruth's help she took the water sip by sip, hating how her body kept on fighting to survive while his did not.

When the cup was empty, Ruth cleared her throat. "I know you don't want to let him go. I understand. But if we leave him in the sun like this, he'll start to—" It seemed she could not bring herself to say the words, but Maryam's mind filled in the gap. *Bloat and stink.* If they left him in the sun, his body would soon start to smell and decompose.

She shuddered, the terrible reality of it reaching through her veil of grief. She could not do this to him, could not expose him to such humiliation just because she needed him. But when she tried to release him, her hand refused to heed her call.

"I can't," she whispered miserably. "My hand will not let go."

Slowly, Ruth reached over and started to prise Maryam's fingers away. As they began to loosen, and his body started sliding from her grip, Maryam panicked, as if she might hurt him if she dropped him now, and so she rallied all her strength and helped Ruth lower him gently to the deck. He would not lie flat, his body set into the mould of her embrace. She tried to move his limbs, to straighten him, but was frightened he would break. The horror on Ruth's face bled into her consciousness, and in the end she reluctantly conceded defeat. Yet despite the ugly markings of Te Mate Iai and the awkward frozen rigor of his body, to Maryam he truly looked as if he slept; as if at any moment he would wake and smile up at her with his luminous blue eyes.

"He told me he loved me," she murmured.

"Of course." Ruth nodded as tears tracked down her cheeks. "His love for you was plain to see."

"Was it?" Maryam almost smiled. She ran a finger around

Joseph's mouth to brush away the dried remnants of the te kabubu paste still on his lips. They felt resistant to her touch, etched in stone. *Joseph is dead, Joseph is dead.* To think that only hours ago he'd kissed her with these lips.

"I must wash him," she announced, the thought rising unbidden into her mind. "To make him ready for his journey."

Now that she had decided this, she could not sit still. She sprang into action, wrestling off his grimy shirt—no easy feat with only one useful hand and a corpse that now refused to bend—and leaned down between the hulls to dip the fabric into the sea. She pressed it down onto the deck to wring out a little of the water, then began to bathe his skin, biting down on her lips to fight back tears. The last time she had washed him . . . no, it hurt too much to think of this. She blocked it out.

When she had finished, she scraped her nails through his sticky, matted hair to smooth it down. *What now?* There was no place to bury him; no raft or pyre to set alight upon the sea. Much as she longed to keep him by her side forever, she knew she did not have the strength of will to watch him bloat and rot. There had to be something, some dignified way of setting his soul free of this body that had failed him so.

For the first time since Joseph's death she really looked around her, scrutinising every corner of the boat with a deliberate eye. They had no choice but to give his body over to the sea, she realised, yet the thought of just pitching him overboard—leaving him to float at the mercy of scavenging seabirds—made her stomach swill. She needed something to lend him weight, to sink him. Then, entombed beneath the vast protective blanket of water, his body would find rest down on the ocean floor.

With this in mind, her eye kept returning to the anchor stone. It was surely heavy enough and, with its carefully chiselled rope-hole and smooth edges crafted by Joseph's father, it seemed a fitting companion for his journey to the depths. Yes, this course was best.

She turned to seek out Lazarus, but for a moment could not place him. Then she spied him, crouched behind the one remaining shelter wall. His back was hunched and heaving, his face hidden in his hands. He was crying, sobs breaking from him in hoarse gusts of pain. It hurt to watch: no matter how much she despised him, she recognised the bond he and his cousin shared. Her own broken heart went out to him, and she felt selfish that she'd blocked him from sharing in Joseph's last minutes on earth.

She drew in a shaky, jagged breath. She had to open up her heart to Lazarus and put her dislike for him aside. It was how Joseph would have wanted it. *This* was the final gift to mark his passing; the way to dignify his kind, warm-hearted life.

Lazarus startled when she squatted down beside him and slipped her one good arm around his shoulders. "I am so sorry for your loss," Maryam said, struggling to hold herself together. He looked completely devastated, nothing like the cruel, confident oppressor of the past. "He told me he loved you like a brother. That in his heart he knew you were good."

As soon as the words were out, she wondered if she spoke the truth. But, seeing the fleeting glimmer in his eyes, she knew it didn't matter if the words were not exactly as Joseph had said. They were what Lazarus needed to hear now; what *she* would want if the situation were reversed.

She rubbed his back, feeling the tremor in his muscles as he fought with his emotions. She was amazed he did not pull away from her embrace. "He *was* my brother," Lazarus mumbled. "The only member of my family who I truly—" he choked, swallowing hard before he spoke again, "—who I truly loved."

He broke down once more, sobbing with such fury that Maryam could not contain her own raw tears. And now dear Ruth slipped down to join them, enfolding both their wretched bodies in her strong brown arms. Beneath them all, the boat rocked sideways in the swell as if it, too, was moved to offer comfort. When, finally, their tears were spent, Maryam drew her arm away—wincing as she registered just how much her injured arm still ached.

"I think we should bind him to the anchor stone and send them both down into the sea."

"Perhaps . . ." Lazarus sniffed loudly and wiped his nose on his shirt sleeve. He slowly eased himself upright, his eyes locked on Joseph's twisted corpse. "I can't believe he's gone."

"We must say some words over him," Ruth insisted. She glanced warily at Maryam. "I don't care what you choose to say, but it would be wrong not to say something to release his soul."

Maryam acquiesced. Whatever her own broiling grievance with the Lord, Joseph deserved to be sent off as they'd been taught.

"You say whatever you want to, Ruthie, it's fine with me." She felt exhausted now, all the fight cried out of her. She glanced at Lazarus. "We're all agreed?"

He nodded, seemingly swept by exhaustion too. He made his way over to the huge crafted stone and locked his hands around it, bent his knees and just managed to lift it up. Then he dropped it down again and eyed Maryam's strapped, useless arm.

"Sister Ruth, can you help? If we lift it together, it will not be such a strain."

"I'll try," she said.

Together Lazarus and Ruth lifted the anchor stone with ease. They hauled it over to the side of the disabled boat, and Maryam helped as best she could to lash Joseph's body to the stone. It was so wrong, strapping him to this cold unforgiving weight—felt more like a punishment than something conceived from love.

When they were satisfied he was securely tied, Ruth stepped forward with her bedraggled Holy Book. As she flicked through the pages, panic seized Maryam again. To cast him overboard felt like a sin. To never see his face again . . . his startling eyes . . . his upturned lips . . . She could feel herself trembling, feel her breath growing ever more shallow and fast. Then Ruth began.

"I've chosen Revelation," she told them. "It just feels right." She took a deep breath, closing her eyes for a moment before she started to read. "*He said to me, These are they which came out of great tribulation, and have washed their robes, and made them white in the blood of the Lamb. Therefore are they before the throne of God, and serve him day and night in his temple: and he that sitteth on the throne shall dwell among them. They shall hunger no more, neither thirst any more—*" Her chin started wobbling and she paused. Breathed deeply. Sniffed. Stared for a long moment at Joseph's face.

Maryam's shaking was now uncontrollable, her knees so weak she feared she would fall. She felt Lazarus's arm snake around her waist for support.

"Be strong," he whispered. "Show Joseph you can still be strong."

She blinked, unsure how to take his touch. But his words stuck in her mind and she roused herself, determined now to make Joseph proud. She looked to Ruth. "Go on," she said.

Ruth clutched the Holy Book so tight her knuckles showed white through her skin. She cleared her throat and finished the reading in a rush: "*. . . neither shall the sun light on them, nor any heat. For the Lamb which is in the midst of the throne shall feed them, and shall lead them unto living fountains of waters: and God shall wipe away all tears from their eyes.*" She closed the Book. "Rest easy with the Lord, Brother Joseph." Tears crawled down her cheeks as she turned to Maryam. "Is there anything else you'd like me to say?"

Maryam shook herself from Lazarus's clutch. Crossed to Joseph. Placed a tender kiss onto his forehead, shuddering as she felt his chill beneath the sunlit layer of skin. "Goodbye my friend . . . my love."

She watched with sick dizziness as Lazarus leaned over Joseph and kissed him as well. They had to do this now—get it over with before she lost her nerve. Together they hauled up Joseph's weighted body and pitched it clumsily into the sea. The water splashed up over them, smacking its lips as it received Joseph and swallowed him down. In only seconds he was gone.

Maryam sank down to her knees, her strength now spent. She raised her streaked face up to the heavens, releasing all her pain and anger in one almighty wail. Then, when no more air would feed her cry, she curled herself into a tiny ball of misery and blocked out the world.

*   *   *

As the day dragged on the wind picked up again, this time from the north. It buffeted the helpless boat at its will; the tiller was virtually useless without the steadying influence of the sails. The sea chopped up—nothing like the mountainous seas they'd already endured, but rough enough to make the ride uncomfortable and ripe for seasickness.

Maryam, Lazarus and Ruth lay on deck and did not speak. *It's all so pointless now*, Maryam thought. Her stomach groaned and grumbled but she had no desire to eat—she was sure she'd vomit food back up again as soon as it was swallowed down. Besides, there was very little left to tempt her. She was just so incredibly tired: tired of fighting, tired of running from danger, and tired, most of all, of the struggle to keep on living. She did not have the strength to feel angry any more, had slipped into a deadened state of limbo—flat and disconnected from the world at large.

Ruth seemed similarly afflicted, not even bothering to seek comfort from the Holy Book. Lazarus sat hunched against the shelter wall and stared blankly across the agitated swell. Defeat and hopelessness swarmed in the air around them. They were lost, and knew it; they were adrift at the feckless whim of wind and sea.

Late afternoon crept in barely noticed, and Lazarus finally rose from his refuge to relieve himself. "Holy Hell!" He flung himself onto the deck near Ruth and stared intently down into the bottom of the right-hand hull. At once he grabbed the jar he'd used to bail water earlier and yelled out to rouse the girls. "We're leaking bad!"

Ruth responded at once, snatching up a scoop and joining him in the hollow hull, where she began to bail as fast as she could go. "How can there be so much when we've already blocked the hole?"

Lazarus pointed to the planks that formed the hull. "The storm must've worked apart their seams." He glanced over at Maryam. "Come on, you have to help us here. It's serious."

She closed her eyes, feeling the wind snatch at her hair. *Serious? What could be more serious than Joseph's death?*

"Maryam!" It was Ruth this time. "Get over here. We're going to sink."

Then let us, Maryam thought. She had no fear with Joseph waiting down below.

"Maryam!" Ruth shouted at her now. "You have to help!"

The fear in Ruth's voice tugged her conscience: even if she wished death for herself, she couldn't let Ruth drown. She opened her eyes again, grunting as she rose, and it struck her how the deck leaned on an angle to the right. She moved more quickly now, rummaging through the debris until she found the fire-blackened pot they'd used for cooking.

The amount of water in the hull—the same hull that had hit the reef upon their entry to Marawa Island—shocked away the last of her haze. It was clear that the impact then, followed by the storm, had loosened all its joints. The water was nearly knee deep and steadily leaking in between the cracks as she started to bail with the pot, cursing under her breath as the motion of the boat kept jolting her off balance. With one arm useless, it was impossible to hold steady as she worked—she ended up kneeling in the bottom of the hull amid the sloshing water, bracing herself against its sides with her bare feet. She ached all over, certain that every part of her now bore some kind of bruise or scar. She'd been pitched straight back into another kind of Hell, the numbing peace of limbo denied her yet again. Had the Lord not already made His point? Why did He insist on piling punishment after punishment to make His case?

No matter how fast they bailed, the water level didn't seem to drop. As the sun lowered in the sky, Ruth called a halt.

"This is ridiculous. I need to eat and drink." She rose stiffly to her feet. "Maryam, you get yours while we keep on bailing, then when you're done we'll swap around."

Maryam clambered up the sloping deck, shocked to see the lean was worse: they'd been bailing for hours now and made no gains. She was so hungry her fingers trembled as she tried to peel a bruised banana one-handed; the moment she succeeded she stuffed it straight into her mouth. The fruit was over-ripe and sickly sweet, but insufficient to quell her gnawing hunger even though it stopped the shakes. She carefully measured out a third of a cup of water, closing her eyes to savour every soothing drop.

When she could no longer put off her return to work, she stretched and glanced out to the west to gauge the position of the sinking sun. They had perhaps another hour of light at most. The thought of bailing through the night, not knowing what lay in store for them—

Wait! There was a smudge to the north-west, something small and dark.

"You two, come up here quick!" She rubbed her eyes, desperately hoping they were not playing tricks.

Ruth and Lazarus leapt up to join her, tracking the direction of her pointing hand. There was definitely something there, but what?

"What on earth is it?" Lazarus squinted into the distance, biting at a piece of loose skin on his thumb.

Maryam stared so hard her eyes began to water and she cleared them with one impatient swipe of her hand. "Is it an island?" Something niggled at her brain. It was nothing like their first glimpse of Marawa; it did not look right. Too small, perhaps? Too indistinct?

Ruth's voice shook with uncertain awe. "Could it be another boat?"

Both Maryam and Lazarus turned to her, open-mouthed, then quickly swung back around again to see. Maryam's heart was racing now. What if, by some miracle, Ruth was right?

"Fire!" Maryam shouted now. "Let's build a fire! That's the only way anyone out there is going to see us."

Lazarus snorted. "Are you mad? This boat is made of wood."

"There has to be a way! If there *is* someone out there, we have to make them see." She cast about frantically for something that might form a base that would not burn. There was kindling enough from the wreckage of the boat, and piles of salvaged stores. She reached over to the heap of shattered earthenware, and dragged out the base of a huge broken urn that had once stored water. "Here!" She picked up a pile of clothes. "If we wet these and lay them under that base, they'll help to contain the heat."

Lazarus was shaking his head at her foolishness, when a flash of understanding dawned across his face. "It's crazy . . . but it just might work." He snatched the clothing from her hand and rushed over to the leaking hull, plunging the fabric under the rising tide of water with a decisive splash.

They set to work, one eye always to the north-western horizon. The shape was definitely still there, slowly taking on a more solid form. But the sun was sinking lower now, and time was short. They placed the makeshift fireplace near the leaking hull, close to water if it flared out of control. Besides, as soon as they had lit the fire, they'd have to resume bailing again. The water level had already risen higher and the boat heeled even further over to the right.

Thankfully, the sun had dried the thatch and wood, and Ruth had unearthed their flint and striker when she'd helped to clear the decks. As she and Maryam worked together to light the fire, Lazarus attacked the shelter's shattered framing, kicking and pulling at it until he'd hauled the whole thing down. He splintered the bamboo into strips to stop it spitting as it burnt; next he broke down the one remaining shelter wall: the pandanus thatch was excellent at producing smoke.

By the time the fire was sending forth a steady trail of thick white smoke, the last of the light was fading from the sky. They had eaten and drunk from their pitiful supplies, ready for the hard night of bailing ahead. But there was a feeling of desperate anticipation among them now—they'd watched the dark shape coming closer, even though the wind was blowing their own boat the other way. It *had* to be moving towards them. *It had to be.*

Maryam was left to tend the fire while Lazarus and Ruth reluctantly climbed back into the hull to bail. She locked her eyes on the last place she'd seen the mysterious shape before the light had gone, fighting her exhaustion to stay alert. But it was hard to concentrate. Her arm began to throb and her mind returned to Joseph—the sky pressing dark and heavy on her mood. It reminded her how small and insignificant they really were, how fragile the tipping point between death and life.

She tried to conjure up a picture of his smiling face but saw, instead, the ugly marks that pocked his skin and shuddered anew at the memory of his stiff, unyielding lips. *Joseph is dead.* The fire popped and crackled, sending a shower of sparks into the night, and she startled, turning her attention back to the distant dark horizon.

Suddenly she saw a flash of light, a beam that flared and swung in a slow arc across the ripples of the darkened sea. Then, as quickly as it had appeared, the light was gone. She blinked, and blinked again, her pulse now thrumming in her ears. Had she imagined it, that light? Conjured it up out of desperation from the far reaches of her mind?

But then it came again. Another flare! Another searchlight cutting through the inky night.

She roared for Ruth and Lazarus, her eyes locked on the beam of light. Someone else was out there; someone who could offer help was sending out a clear signal that they had been seen. It was a miracle.

CHAPTER ELEVEN

Huddled beside the signal fire on their listing boat, pinned by the searchlight's blinding glare, they could hear the ship before they saw it, the thunderous rumble much louder than the waste-powered engines used to heat the water and cookers in the Holy City back at home.

Maryam's stomach tied itself in anxious knots as a hulking black ship half the size of *Star of the Sea* slowly materialised from the darkness. Lights glowed from its control room, overshadowed by the searchlight as it made its way through the swell towards them. Maryam slipped her hand into Ruth's, and was momentarily comforted by her warm, familiar touch.

A disembodied voice barked out above the throbbing din. "Raise your hands above your heads."

They did as they were told, though Ruth held fast to her Holy Book and Maryam was only able to lift her one uninjured arm. Her initial relief at hearing English spoken was dissipated by the threatening tone of the command, and she felt exposed and vulnerable as the ship edged close enough for them to see the shadowy swarm of crew on its deck.

"Prepare to be boarded. Do not move." The man spoke curtly, his vowels flat and ugly to her ears.

"What are they doing?" Ruth whispered, her eyes wide and wild in the harsh stream of light.

"They mean to come aboard," Lazarus said. He looked pale and tense as he turned to Maryam. "I don't like the feel of this."

A cold shiver tiptoed down her spine as she watched them

lower a smaller craft down the big ship's side. It dropped into the swell, and she counted as six large men descended a swinging rope ladder to board it. Another motor whined and burst into life and then the little boat bounced across the narrow divide of sea. Oh, to have propulsion like that, Maryam thought, and not be reliant on wind and sail.

As soon as the craft drew near, a man stood up and threw a rope. Lazarus rushed to catch it, tying it off to the small remaining mast before stepping forward to greet the men as they boarded the stricken boat.

"Stand back!" a man's voice snapped. "Raise your hands."

Lazarus reeled backwards, flinging his arms into the air again. His face hardened now, jaw clenching and eyes narrowing as the first of the rescuers stepped aboard. As each of them approached, Lazarus seemed to straighten and grow taller, bearing himself like the arrogant Apostle Maryam had first met.

One by one the intimidating group lined up on the listing deck. They stood to attention, legs splayed to balance in the sloppy swell. They were dressed in a uniform of murky green, their heads encased in unearthly mask-like helmets, and each of them clutched tightly to a long, strange-looking metal stick.

"What are they holding?" Maryam whispered to Lazarus.

"My guess is some kind of gun."

She'd never heard this word before, but had no time to question him further as one of the men stepped forward and addressed Lazarus directly.

"You have entered our sovereign waters illegally. We order you to turn back now."

Turn back? Could they not see the boat was sinking?

Lazarus cleared his throat and puffed out his chest. "Our boat is damaged and we ask for refuge on your shores."

The man studied him from head to toe before turning his attention to the girls. Though his eyes were hidden by the strange mask, Maryam sensed his hostility. Her arm throbbed in time with her racing heart as he stepped closer and spoke to her. "You are injured?"

She nodded. "Yes. A broken arm."

"Anything else?"

She wondered if she should tell him about Joseph. *Joseph*. It hurt to even think his name. "No."

He turned back to Lazarus. "Where have you sailed from?"

"We left Marawa Island around two days ago, I think, when we were hit by a storm." Still holding his arms above his head, Lazarus's hands tightened to fists as he replied.

There was a ripple of movement from the men. One stepped forward and whispered in the interrogator's ear. They had an indecipherable exchange, before the leader addressed Lazarus again.

"All of you?"

"Yes."

"Were you the only boat to leave those shores?"

"Yes."

Again there was a brief whispered discussion between the two men, before another broke from the ranks and proceeded to turn the salvaged piles of debris over with his booted foot. The leader, though, approached Ruth and wrenched her copy of the Holy Book from her grasp.

"Where did you get this?"

Ruth shrugged, seemingly too terrified to reply. She shook uncontrollably as she struggled to keep her arms aloft.

The leader stared at Ruth for several long seconds before he shoved the Book back at her and spoke again. "We order you to turn back to the place of your departure. Should you fail to do so, you will be arrested and detained."

"That's impossible," Lazarus said. "We've lost the means to sail."

"Not our problem, boy. We'll tow you out of our waters and then you're on your own."

"You'd leave us out here to die?" Maryam could not contain her rage.

The man did not even deign to look at her, let alone answer. Instead, he signalled to one of his men, who retrieved a thick rope from the boarding craft and proceeded to tie it around the timbers that supported the figurehead at the bow. Once in place, the men retreated to their boat and made ready to return to the main ship to instigate the tow.

Ruth turned terrified eyes to Maryam. "They're not going to help us?"

"It appears not." She was so angry and shocked, she struggled to speak. These men could see they were defenceless, injured and about to sink, and yet they would not help.

They watched in disbelieving silence as the men retreated to the ship and scaled its sides. Once aboard they secured the tow rope to an aft bollard, and waited briefly while the engines roared back into life.

The ship turned to the east, its wash nearly swamping the smaller crippled craft that wallowed in its wake. As the rope stretched and grew taut between the two vessels, Maryam, Lazarus and Ruth were jerked off their feet as their craft began to move.

"I can't believe this," Maryam cried, awkwardly righting herself. "How can they just desert us?"

"Be warned," Lazarus said. "Guns can kill from a great distance. Don't do anything to rile them or they'll likely shoot us all."

"Shoot?" Maryam asked. "What do you mean?"

"I've seen one before, and read of them in books. They fire at great speed and can kill a man with just one strike."

"You've seen one? Where?"

"My father has one hidden in his private rooms. It looks quite different from those but I'm sure they must be just as deadly. Father's belonged to his forefather, the first of the Holy Fathers—Captain Saul."

"He's used it?"

Lazarus shrugged. "I don't know. But I've seen him take it out and clean it, just in case."

Ruth remained on her knees, moaning so miserably as she clutched her Book that Maryam automatically moved to comfort her, though her own head whirled with frightening thoughts. Even if they *could* stop the boat from sinking, they had too little food and water to survive for long. And the towing was already taking its toll on what little remained of their boat, forcing more water in through the widening cracks.

"Back to the bailing!" She dragged Ruth after her as she jumped down into the damaged hull. Their so-called rescuers were not only deserting them. Now they seemed intent on sinking them as well.

Maryam fumed as the three of them worked frantically to drain the hull, though the boat seemed to be leaking as fast as they were bailing out. She *had* to think of something. If there was only some way to convince those heartless men that it was better to take them in than to let them die at sea. There had to be some way to light a spark of human kindness in their hearts.

Light . . . Spark . . . Yes! Of course! *Surely they wouldn't desert us if the boat was destroyed right before their eyes?*

She stopped bailing and drew Lazarus's attention with a nudge of her arm. She slid her eyes to the smouldering fire and subtly jerked her head.

"What if the fire burnt out of control . . . ?"

She left the rest for him to imagine. What she was proposing was desperate and crazy, and just as likely to commit them to drowning as standing by helplessly as their boat was sunk. But, crazy or not, it just might work . . . might shame the foreign crew into rescuing them after all.

For a few heart-stopping seconds Lazarus just stared at her, his eyes flared in surprise, and she feared he had not understood. But then he nodded, his face grim as it set in a decisive scowl. "Are you prepared for the possible consequences if it doesn't work?"

She glanced at Ruth, her dearest friend, and nearly couldn't bring herself to follow through. But then her outrage won the battle for control. They had to try.

"Do we really have another choice?"

He downed his bailer and scrabbled back onto the deck, edging up to the fire as he held Maryam's watchful gaze. As unobtrusively as he could, first he moved the driest of the shredded thatch closer to the fire. Then he knocked the earthenware base of the fire off-balance with his toe and allowed the red-hot embers to spill out across the deck. Mission accomplished, he leapt back down to join Maryam and Ruth in the ruined hull.

Within seconds the flames caught on the piles of dry thatch and moved on to the kindling stored alongside. As the fire began to scorch the timbers of the deck, thick white smoke billowed up. *Forgive us*, Maryam cast out to Joseph's spirit, as she watched his father's precious handiwork succumb to the flames. She felt as if she had betrayed his whole family, destroying the one thing that had brought them hope.

"Fire! Help!" She shrieked as loudly as possible now, trying to project her desperation out above the rumbling of the big ship's motors.

Ruth took one look at the way the flames were licking at the timbers of the deck and screamed. As wild as a trapped animal, she fought off Maryam's reassuring hand to scoop up a pot of water to douse the flames.

"Leave it," Maryam ordered. "I'm sure that they won't let us burn." She glanced over at the towering ship, just able to make out a rush of silhouettes as the crew crowded the aft deck to watch.

Ruth struggled to push past her. "You're going to kill us all," she shrieked. But she was blocked now by Lazarus, who wrestled the pot from her hand and flung it over the side into the sea. She beat at him with her fists, wailing with such frustration and fear that Maryam could feel it pressing on her heart.

She lunged for Ruth, not sure how long Lazarus's restraint would hold, and dragged her out of his reach, feeling the heat of the fire as it ate into the boat's structural timbers and really started to take hold.

"Come on," she urged, the smoke stinging her eyes and making it ever more difficult to see. "If you want to yell at anyone, yell at *them*." She pointed through the smoke to the black ship, which had slowed its motors and now idled out of reach.

All three clambered to the very prow of their boat, where the carved warrior glared out at the foreign ship as though to curse it. "Help! Help!" They had no need to feign panic. The fire scorched at their backs and lit up the sea around them. Nor had they bargained on the acrid smoke that filled the sky, catching in their throats to set them coughing and spluttering.

"Why aren't they doing anything?" Maryam cried. She was terrified, trapped between the fire and the fathomless sea.

"We're going to die," Ruth wailed, before she was overcome by such a bad fit of coughing that she doubled over, wheezing, as she tried to catch her breath.

"We'll have to abandon ship," Lazarus shouted above the din. His eyes were streaming and bloodshot as he grabbed each girl roughly by one arm. "Whatever you do," he gasped, struggling to breathe through the stifling clouds of smoke, "just make sure we all go in together and hold on tight."

He did not give them time to argue, throwing himself off the side and pitching them over with him as he dropped. They splashed down in a struggling heap, wrenched from his grip as they plunged beneath the swell.

The water sucked Maryam under and, though she tried to surface, without the use of both her arms she could not seem to rise. Her chest was burning from the strain of holding her breath, her pulse beating fast and panicked in her ears. She was tumbled around beneath the swell, the unholy glow of the flames lighting the surface of the water like Hell's sunset as she forced her eyes open, trying to locate Lazarus or Ruth. But she could see nothing, her hair splaying out around her, tangling like unruly seaweed as it wound around her face. She could not hold her breath much longer now, her lungs so tight and bursting that she tried releasing the pressure inside one air bubble at a time—feeling the seductive urge to just give up the fight and seek out Joseph in the sea's dark depths.

But then Ruth's frightened face flashed through her mind, and she mustered up the strength for one last desperate bid to free her broken arm from its restrictive binding, to no avail. But the force of pain so ambushed her she automatically opened up her mouth to scream, and water started pouring down her throat.

Before panic could even set in, though, she felt herself being hauled up by her hair, and broke through the surface of the water in a coughing, retching, gasping mess. The swell slapped at her face, threatening to overwhelm her once again, and it was only Lazarus's quick actions that saved her, as he curled his arm around her neck to hold her head aloft.

He paddled with his free arm and legs, supporting Maryam on the surface as she struggled to regain her breath. Water streamed from her eyes and nose, blurring her vision. Then she saw Ruth bobbing next to them, and silently gave thanks that she was safe. Behind them, Joseph's father's boat lolled on the choppy swell like a burning pyre, the warrior's glistening shell eyes accusing her of his impending fate. But there was no going back on their rash decision: the fire was now way too fierce to fight.

Above the rasping of her breath Maryam heard the whining engine of the boarding craft before it emerged through the smoke. It surged towards them, and a man at its prow threw them a life-ring attached to a rope. All three of them lunged for it, holding on gratefully as the boat drew near. One by one they were fished up from the sea and hauled aboard, manhandled across the side of the small craft and flung onto the unforgiving floor. The air was filled with curses and shouts as the boat drifted in towards the burning wreckage, and they were knocked sideways as the pilot spun the boat away and returned, full throttle, to his ship.

There they were ordered to ascend the rope ladder that hung down the ship's rough steel sides. Lazarus took up the challenge first, clambering up unaided, followed by Ruth. But when it came time for Maryam to climb, she baulked, unsure how to tackle the ropes with just one working arm. Immediately a crewman moved in behind her, boosting her up to the first rung of the ladder before climbing up in tandem, using his rigid body to support her up the grimy ropes. His closeness petrified her and she was shaking uncontrollably by the time she finally reached the top.

The three castaways drew into a tight cluster, uneasy and unsure what would happen next. Once the pilot of the rescue craft had climbed aboard and the boat had been winched back up to its home, the crew formed a cordon around them, standing at attention as a white-skinned man emerged from the lit wheelhouse that overlooked the deck. He approached them now, his uniform so like the Apostles' that Maryam's heart lurched wildly in her chest: he wore virtually the same white jacket and pants, trimmed with gold braid and identical gold buttons. *This does not bode well.*

He fixed them with a steely stare, then appeared to dismiss the girls and focus in on Lazarus. "What do you think you're playing at?"

Lazarus raised his chin and met the captain's stare. "The motion knocked over our fire. We couldn't put it out."

The captain snorted. "Do you think I'm stupid, boy?" He didn't wait for Lazarus to respond, merely snapped his fingers at the cordon of guards and pointed to the three. "Take them below."

They were instantly surrounded by a jostling group of guards, who drove them like animals down into the very bowels of the ship. There they were pushed into a small, windowless room, so close to the engines the noise was deafening, and left alone. They were locked inside.

Ruth threw herself at Maryam, wrapping her in such a tight embrace that Maryam had to bite back a cry as her injured arm bemoaned the pressure. "I thought you'd drowned," Ruth sobbed.

"I would have, if Lazarus hadn't saved me." Over Ruth's shoulder, she met his eye. "I owe you thanks."

Lazarus shrugged and scanned their prison. "Don't thank me yet." He paced the room, taking in the tiered sleeping platforms that lined one of the metal walls. A lone grey blanket lay folded on each bare bed; the only other object visible in the room was an empty bucket by the door. The whole space reeked of stale sweat and urine.

For a few shocked moments after Lazarus's doleful response, no one spoke. They stood shivering as puddles formed at their feet from their dripping clothes, and listened for any hint of relief from outside the room. But the clamour of the engines over-rode every other noise, vibrating off the metal walls to drive right through Maryam's body with a force that set her teeth on edge, though whether she was shaking from terror or the cold it was hard to tell.

"Before we do anything else, we'd better get out of these wet clothes," Lazarus said at last, rolling his eyes at Maryam and Ruth's obvious alarm. "Oh, give me strength. I'll turn my back." He snatched a blanket off the closest bed and turned away, peeling off his sodden shirt as he did so.

Maryam knew he was right: they needed to dry off before the chill took hold. She shook out one of the blankets and held one corner in her teeth while she stretched the other end out in her good hand to screen Ruth while she stripped, then wrapped herself in another of the blankets. Before Ruth returned the favour, she carefully unbound the rope securing Maryam's arm. The release of pressure was a relief, but the moment was short-lived. As soon as Maryam moved her arm to undress, a stab of pain shot through her. *Would it never cease?*

She buckled onto the closest bed and ran her hand along the thick curtain of her hair to wring away the excess water. It pooled at her feet, its ebb and flow mesmerising as the ship rocked with the swell. She felt exhausted now and gave in to it, crumpling until she lay flat on her back and stared up at the wooden frame that supported the bed above. The surface of the wood was etched with roughly chiselled marks, telltale signs that others had once been detained in this dungeon too. She closed her eyes, desperate to block the whole world out, and the grief she'd pushed aside in these last few gruelling hours surfaced again. *Joseph is dead.* The knowledge lay like the anchor stone on her chest, restricting her breathing and pressing heavy on her heart.

A key turned in the lock and the door swung open. Two guards with guns stood watch outside, as the captain and one of his officers marched into the room. Maryam, struggling to sit up, gathered the blanket more tightly around herself and pressed back against the wall. Ruth huddled in beside her as

Lazarus, naked bar the blanket wrapped around his waist, glowered from the gloomy corner by the pile of his discarded clothes.

"Good," the captain said. "I see you've had the sense to
change." His attention was solely directed at Lazarus. The girls
may as well not have existed. "Now, no more games. Tell me
where you're from."

Lazarus weighed up the man before he answered, allowing
his distain to leak out through his eyes. "Originally from
Onewēre, but our boat got blown off course by a storm just a
few hours out from Marawa Island and was damaged beyond
repair."

"Onewēre, eh? That's a new one. And you were heading
for?" The man's face gave away nothing, good or bad.

"Anywhere we could find."

The captain frowned, tapping his boot impatiently on the floor.
What is Lazarus playing at? Why is he being so obscure? Maryam
cleared her throat and forced her words out past a nervous lump.
"We seek sanctuary. Somewhere safe where we can live."

"Indeed?" The captain did not even glance at her, his gaze
still locked on Lazarus. "These natives are your slaves, boy?"

Lazarus flinched and shook his head. "No . . ." He paused,
as if deciding how to answer this. "They are my—friends."

Maryam felt her face flush hot. *Since when did he promote
himself to friend?* She'd have laughed out loud had the captain's
words not jarred so uncomfortably in her head. *Natives? Slaves?*

The captain laughed crudely. "Two for one, eh boy? That's
quite a score." He turned to his companion and winked.

Lazarus shrugged. "Two is nothing, my father once—"

"Silence!" the captain barked, all signs of humour obliter-
ated by the impatient swipe of his hand. "As captain of this

vessel, I arrest you all for illegally entering our sovereign territorial waters. You will not be permitted to set foot on any Confederated Territory soil, and will be transferred to our detention centre for processing with all the other illegals, in compliance with our Sovereign Rights Act. Any non-compliance will be dealt with swiftly and assertively—so do not try." He waved his hand again, as if swatting away a fly. "That is all." He spun on his heel so quickly his threat still hung in the air after he had gone.

Confederated Territory? Where was that? Maryam was sure she'd never seen this written on the map.

Now his companion spoke. "You, girl," he said, indicating Maryam, "come with me. We will see to your arm."

Maryam just stared up at him, too scared to move.

The man snapped his fingers at her. "Come on. Do you want help or don't you? The choice is yours."

"Go, Maryam," Ruth whispered. "You need it fixed." She gently pushed Maryam towards the edge of the bed. "Go on. Go."

The vibration of the engines built inside Maryam's ears. She didn't want to go with him alone, undressed and vulnerable in a ship controlled by foreign white men. She shook her head, resisting Ruth's pressure on her back.

"I will accompany her," Lazarus declared in his most arrogant voice. "She is my woman, after all."

Maryam gasped. *How dare he?* She turned to skewer him with her gaze, but was sidetracked by Ruth's frightened voice.

"Don't leave me here alone." Her cheeks were so leached of colour they looked grey.

Maryam couldn't seem to piece her thoughts together in any logical way. She was too tired, too sore and too bereft to think this through. If she went alone, she left Ruth unprotected in the room with Lazarus, while opening herself up to possible abuse from the guards. If she left Ruth alone and took up Lazarus's outrageous offer, Ruth would be the vulnerable one. Then the answer came to her. It was so simple she flushed at her stupidity. *What is wrong with me?* She turned to the officer. "Could Ruth accompany me?"

The man shrugged. "Whatever. Just get moving. I have better things to do." He crossed to the doorway, drumming his fingers on the frame as the two girls stood and tucked the blankets more securely around themselves. "Oh, for heaven's sake, that's enough! Now come."

He herded them past the deafening engine room and up two narrow flights of stairs. Maryam's legs were trembling so badly she had to steady herself against Ruth. *What will they do?* The way she'd been treated by Mother Lilith, the only other healer she'd known except dear old Mother Evodia, played back in her mind. The humiliation. The pain. The total lack of care. But then these thoughts were shunted sideways as she recalled Lazarus's outrageous words. *She is my woman . . .*

She felt sick to her stomach, as it dawned on her that this was what he must have hoped for all along: he *knew* Joseph was going to die—oh Lord, had he not actively discouraged Joseph from taking her blood?—and, now that Joseph was out of the way, he'd staked his claim. His cold-hearted scheming disgusted her. How he'd fooled her with his act of grief . . . it was simply a ruse to soften her resistance to his game. *Once a shark, always a shark.* And now she and Ruth were cast to the bottom of the food chain again—aided, it seemed, by yet another group of uniformed, sadistic, white-skinned men.

CHAPTER TWELVE

Maryam lay curled up on her bunk, listening to the unending thump of the engines as the ship ploughed through the ocean. Apart from getting up to relieve herself in the bucket Ruth had screened off behind a blanket, she had not moved for what seemed like days. Neither had she eaten the stodgy tepid food; she had forced herself to drink the stale water only when her thirst was such she could no longer block it from her mind. Her arm had finally settled after the agony she'd endured when the ship's healer had hurriedly encased it from wrist to elbow in a sticky coating of white powder mixed with fibre. It had set hard now, and formed a buffer from further movement or knocks, but it did little to ease the ongoing discomfort.

She was so furious with Lazarus she could not even look in his direction without anger spiralling up like the waterspout that had nearly destroyed their boat. It almost threatened to outstrip her anger with the Lord, which sat inside her festering, as cold and domineering as Father Joshua's eyes. But the Lord had surpassed Himself, rubbed salt into her wound by making sure she'd seen a glimpse of Heaven with Joseph before He slammed the door shut in her face.

How she despised them all; hated the fact that *nothing* in her life was worth the effort even to breathe. The people she had loved were dead. And now she was trapped with the monster Lazarus, who had willed his cousin's death for his own greedy, selfish aims. Even Ruth was not immune to her unbridled fury: her ineffectual pleas for Maryam to rouse herself were as annoying as a buzzing fly.

To make things worse, Lazarus seemed to have brainwashed Ruth. She could hear them whispering in the bunk above, no doubt colluding in some cruel new game. She strained to hear what they were saying but the insufferable engine blocked their words. No mind. Let them scheme whatever they wanted: she no longer had the will to fight . . . no will, in fact, to live at all. She would starve herself until the end released her. She would welcome the descent into the eternal nothingness she now believed was really all that lay in store for those who died.

She drifted in and out of sleep, revelling in a bitter pleasure at the hollow rumbling in her gut. Then, during one of the long stretches staring morosely at the grimy wall, she heard a shift in the tempo of the big engines. The boat was slowing. From somewhere high above, the thud of feet and clank of chains reverberated down through the walls. Were the crew about to scoop up more deluded souls from the water, or had they reached their new island jail?

Ruth jumped down from the bunk. "Did you hear that, Maryam? I think it means we might be there." Her voice was pleading, urging Maryam to respond. She did not.

Now footsteps rang out close by, and Maryam heard the key turn in the lock of their prison door. Someone entered, clearing his throat before he spoke.

"We've arrived at the camp. Get ready to disembark." His voice was flat, as though he didn't care at all.

"Will we have a chance to plead our case?" Lazarus asked.

"*You* can try. Who knows? I've not seen any whites detained."

"And my companions?"

The man snorted. "I dunno about Onewēre, but surely you must know what happened to the last wave of illegals from Marawa Island?"

"What do you mean?" Ruth cut in.

"This was years ago, back in my grandpop's time . . ." Maryam could hear a shift in the man's tone, as if he was enjoying what he now revealed. "Hordes of them came—the whole fandango—deserting their poxy island for our tasty shores." *Whole fandango? What did he mean? That the entire population of the island had up and fled? But what of the bones?* She rolled over to study his pasty face. "Of course our blokes wouldn't let them in—we've had more than our share of useless bludgers in the past. No way were we gonna give up any of our own precious resources for a bunch of lazy heathen blacks . . ."

"They sent them back?" Lazarus asked. He stood facing the crewman with his arms folded across his chest. His cheeks were stained an unaccustomed red.

The crewman laughed. "Too right they did. Shipped them back and made damned sure they never bothered us again." He tapped the side of his nose and smirked. "Unfortunate collateral damage, mate. Couldn't be helped."

Maryam closed her eyes, picturing the sea of bones that littered the temple floor, the babies who had died wrapped in their mothers' arms. Were they wrong to have presumed the Tribulation had caused such slaughter? Were there other hands on which the blood of Marawa's people might be found?

"And it worked, you know, for bloody decades," the crewman continued. "But now you little bludgers are at us again." He punched his fist into his palm. "We'll whip you, though, just like *that*. The Confederated Territories are ours alone."

"Just where are these Territories?" Lazarus asked. "Anywhere near Australia?"

Again the man laughed. "Bugger me, I haven't heard *that* mentioned in a long time." He shook his head. "What's past is past. The Confederation Wars soon saw to that. Just you and your pretty little boongas here remember that we're all good Christians now, who've worked hard to shake off the effects of the radiation from the flares, and we're not letting any other useless bugger screw that up." The man looked pleased with himself, as if he alone held back the so-called heathen hordes.

Ruth's eyes widened as his words sank in. "You mean—"

"The Confederated Territories for Christian Territorials," he said smugly. "Cee Tees for Cee Tees. That's our motto." He snapped back into official mode. "Enough of this. Come with me now." He turned his gaze to Maryam, his lip curling as he surveyed her matted, filthy hair. "Get up, girl. In God's name, d'you have no pride?"

A kind of hysterical bubble surged up inside Maryam as she studied the man's ugly sharp-nosed face. He and his kind treated them like animals, yet expected them to come out looking fresh and clean? For a moment the old fire in her belly flared. *How dare he? How*—No. There was no point in fighting this. Let him think whatever he liked. Soon she would not be alive to care.

She rose, as if in a dream, to follow after Lazarus and Ruth, reaching out to steady herself as dizziness rocked her. The ascent through the ship seemed endless as she struggled to move her weak and wobbly legs, and she was so light-headed she could hardly see. It pleased her, in a disconnected way, just how much the lack of food affected her. Perhaps this would be over sooner than she thought.

The men working to ready the boat for arrival barely gave the passing group a glance. At last they emerged onto the deck, and Maryam was disoriented for a moment: the dawn was just breaking in the sky. Just how many days *had* it been since Joseph died?

After the putrid confines down below, the fresh air was welcome although the fumes from the engines—and something else, something faintly foul—masked the salty crispness of the breeze. Around their small huddled group the crew scrubbed decks and coiled ropes, preparing for their arrival at the unknown port that now lay directly up ahead.

The outer rim of the island crouched low in the water. Its raised central plateau was barren and windswept, and the thin sprinkling of trees on its lower coastal fringe looked scruffy and parched. Most of the buildings that bordered the decaying dock were patched and decrepit; only one gleamed white in the early morning light, and a startlingly bright pennant flew from its roof. It was blue, with a red and white criss-cross in the upper left-hand corner and, to Maryam's surprise, the stars of the Maiaki Cross. Its familiar aspect was strangely comforting amidst this jumble of unknowns.

As the ship drew up to its mooring, the acrid stench grew stronger on the air, like the stink of broken birds' eggs that had lain too long untended and turned rotten in their nests. It clung to the inside of Maryam's nose, feeding the nausea brought on by lack of food and sudden movement from their airless cell. The three of them were corralled together as a rickety set of stairs was pushed along the dock to be secured in place beside the ship. Strangest of all, an unfamiliar object was moving along the dock on six huge wheels. Many times bigger than the trolleys used to serve food back at the Holy City, it appeared to move all on its own. *What could it be?* Two men sat in the snout-like metal cabin, as if somehow guiding it, while at the rear a green cloth canopy and sides concealed whatever lay inside. It was the most peculiar thing she'd ever seen. The thing drew up next to the stairs, and the two uniformed men disembarked through doors cut into each side.

Lazarus was the first to descend the unstable grid of stairs. He stepped onto it suspiciously, testing its strength under his feet before he looked back over his shoulder and nodded reassuringly at Maryam and Ruth. His face had lost its certainty, and his skin was so pale the tired rings beneath his eyes stood out like the smears of charcoal used at ritual times to decorate the faces of the village chiefs.

Ruth scrabbled for Maryam's hand. "Please," she whispered uneasily, "don't let them split us up."

Maryam had no time to reassure her as she was prodded from behind towards the steps. With Ruth holding tight to one hand and the other stiff within its cast, she stepped onto the structure and began the slow journey down to the dock. Her knees were threatening to give out again, and she found herself leaning against the side railing for extra support. She dared not stop to stabilise herself further, only too aware of the guns slung over the shoulders of the crewmen who brought up the rear. Such an excessive show of power was laughable: just *what*, exactly, did they think she'd do? Make a break for it and run? Little did they know she'd never again give the Lord a chance to play such cruel games with her sense of hope.

As soon as they had reached the ground, all three were herded to the rear of the strange wheeled contraption and made to scramble in beneath the cloth. Inside, each side was lined by bench-seats formed from rough planks of wood. Two armed men climbed in, ordered the trio to sit, and took up positions opposite them.

"What is this thing?" Lazarus asked.

"What thing, mate?" the younger of the guards replied.

"This thing in which we now sit."

The guard laughed, nudging his companion. "Hoity toity, ain't he, Kev?" He pulled a face, as if he were sucking a lime, and spoke in a drawling parody of Lazarus. "This thing in which we sit is known as a truck. T. R. U. C. K."

The other guard sniggered. "Actually, Lord Muck, it's a bio-fuelled army personnel vehicle. Is there anything else Your Worship would like to know?"

Lazarus, his face suffused in red, ignored their game. "Where *exactly* are we being taken?" he demanded.

The young guard swallowed down his mirth. "Cee-One," he snapped. "You'll be processed and detained up there."

"I want to see your village chief." Lazarus spat out the words with gruff resolve, but Maryam could see his hands were shaking before he clamped them hard between his knees.

The guards' derision was drowned out as the truck lurched to life with a sudden roar. Maryam startled, trying to make sense of what was going on: it had to be some kind of engine, judging by the steady rumble and the vibration that rattled through their seats. Then, to her further astonishment, something graunched and juddered, and the whole thing began to move. Ruth still clutched desperately onto Maryam's hand; her other hand clasped firmly to the seat. She closed her eyes, mouthing prayers, no doubt wishing her Holy Book had not been swallowed by the sea as they'd leapt from the burning boat. *How hard Ruth will be feeling this*, Maryam thought. She reached inside her pocket for the small blue pebble Ruth had gifted her back on the atoll and pressed it hard into her palm as if the tiny talisman could somehow give her strength. It had, after all, survived her trials and flight from Onewēre, the storm, the fire, her plunge into the ocean . . . perhaps it contained more magic than she knew. Even just the thought of losing it now prompted nervous stirrings in her chest.

Poor Ruth. Whatever lay in store for them at this place, this Cee-One, she knew it would not be the answer to Ruth's rabid prayers. In truth, all they could hope for now was quick relief. She closed her eyes, willing the movement of the truck to bounce such bleak and frightening thoughts from her head.

It seemed a punishingly long time before the truck slowed back to an idle. Above the chug of its engine Maryam could make out men's voices, but was unable to identify the words. Then the truck jolted back to life, bumping over something that rocked them sideways; it made a sweeping turn and finally shuddered to a halt. In the ringing silence Maryam caught the dying whisper of Ruth's prayers.

"Right! Out you get." The older guard drew back the flap of the fabric and motioned for them to jump down from the truck.

One by one they set foot on the dusty ground and tried to take in their new surroundings. The truck had stopped just inside a towering barrier of netted steel topped by coils of fine-strung wire that budded lethal-looking barbs. Several more armed guards had arrived, and were hurrying to close the gates behind them. There was no mistaking it: they were locked in.

"This way." Their two guards pointed at a shabby building and pushed the trio roughly towards it.

"Leave the talking to me," Lazarus hissed to Maryam and Ruth. "I'm sure once they know the truth they'll set us free." He drew in a deep breath, as though pumping himself up, and took the lead.

Maryam bit back a sharp retort as she reminded herself that she no longer cared. *What did it matter who spoke for who?* The end result would be the same: Lazarus elevated back to his position of power, while she and Ruth were left to rot.

She couldn't help but glance around her, though. Beyond the building, another layer of netting rose just as high as the first, and beyond that again row upon row of squat, rusty metal structures packed the dusty, arid camp. Thin bedraggled chickens scratched around in the littered dirt and, through the gaps in the netting, a gaggle of dirty, wide-eyed children stood beside a group of men who seemed to be tracking their journey to the wooden building near the truck.

They were ushered into a stuffy room, where a fat balding man in uniform sat working behind an ornately carved desk. Without even glancing up, he barked out something she could not understand. "Nimes, pona deparcher, dytes a berth!"

Lazarus looked to Maryam and Ruth, and shrugged. It seemed he, too, had no idea what the man said. "I wish to speak to your chief. I am Lazarus, son of Holy Father Joshua, of the Lord's chosen Apostles of the Lamb."

How like him, Maryam thought. *Pulling rank to get his way.* But, to her surprise, the man did not appear the least impressed. He slowly placed a cap on some kind of writing implement and lowered it with such deliberation the hairs on the back of Maryam's neck stiffened and rose.

"And I'm bloody Ozymandias, sonny. King of Kings." The guards behind him sniggered, but were cut short by one glance of his cold blue eyes.

Lazarus straightened, obviously impressed by the man's status, bowing formally before offering his hand. "Then I am honoured to meet you, Bloody Ozymandias, King of Kings."

At this, the guards exploded into such snorts of laughter they struggled to rein themselves back under control. The King of Kings, however, was not amused. He rose from his seat, slapping his hands down onto the desktop as he eyeballed Lazarus, ignoring his outstretched hand.

"So you're a clever little bastard, eh?" He tapped his head. "Think you're much smarter than me? Yes? Well, you're the one in detention, bud, not me." He looked over at the older guard. "I can't be bothered with this today. Take Little Lord Lambie here and lock him up in solitary for a day or two, until he learns to show respect."

Lazarus shook his head, his face confused. "If I've somehow offended you—"

"Enough. I know your sort. You dip your wick into the ink, boy, you're bound to come out black." He nodded to the guard, who moved in now and wrenched Lazarus's arm up behind his back. "Take him away. I'm sick of smart-arsed little punks." He glanced up at something on the wall behind them. "Strewth, it's only seven-bloody-thirty in the morning and already some shithead winds me up."

Lazarus turned, trying to catch Maryam's eye as the guard made to march him out. "Tell him, Maryam. You explain." There was panic in his voice now, and Maryam felt a rush of guilty pleasure as he was wrestled from the room. *Let him discover how it feels to be the powerless one for once.*

Lazarus continued to argue his case as the guards hustled him away. Only when the commotion had faded completely did the man retake his seat.

"My name, girlies, is Sergeant Littlejohn, and I run this camp." He spoke more slowly now, as if they were dull in the head. "Now, before I lose my patience altogether, tell me this: your names, point of departure, dates of birth and nothing, do you understand me, *nothing* else." There was neither compassion nor interest in his face, just contempt.

Maryam took a tired breath and dropped her gaze to his short white fingers as they tapped the desk. "My name is Maryam. I come from Onewēre. I do not know the exact date of my birth but I believe I turn sixteen in spring."

At the mention of Onewēre, the sergeant's fingers stilled.

"And I am Ruth." Ruth wrung her hands, her voice quaking with fear. "I came from Onewēre too. I'm fourteen mid-autumn."

Sergeant Littlejohn leaned forward, studying them intently now. "Onewēre? I thought you came from Marawa Island?"

Maryam shook her head. "We sailed from Onewēre to Marawa Island first, then headed west from there."

"That's impossible," Sergeant Littlejohn said. "Everyone knows Onewēre was destroyed at the time of the flares . . . What are you playing at?"

Maryam had no idea what he was talking about. But when she looked up at him his eyes gave nothing away. He glowered at them, and waited for her to reply.

"I swear that what we say is true," she said.

Sergeant Littlejohn snatched up the writing implement and uncapped it again, then wrote something on the paper before him. "You'd better not be lying, girl." He jerked his head towards the door. "Take them away."

As the one remaining guard hurriedly escorted them from the room, Maryam tried to make sense of what the sergeant had said. Did no one in the outside world think of Onewēre at all? Was the sergeant saying no one even knew if it existed any more? No wonder they'd been left alone, trapped by the Apostles' rigid Rules.

"You'll be in with the other women and children," the guard explained, leading them over to the second wire fence. "In the next week or so someone will assess your status but, until then, remember you're here under arrest and any breaches of our rules will be dealt with, sharp and swift." He nodded to the guard at the gate of the enclosed area behind the fence, who unlocked the huge padlock to allow them through into the compound. "I take it you do know how to follow rules?"

Maryam met Ruth's eye. *Rules we know.* She nodded, feeling the tightness in her chest increase at the mere mention of the word.

The scraggly group of children had dispersed, but the cluster of men standing silently beside the fence remained. There must have been a dozen or so dressed in soiled white full-length robes, not unlike the gowns Maryam and the other Chosen wore each Judgement time, and many had their heads wrapped in coiled strips of cloth as well. But this was not what drew her eye or sent her empty stomach churning over in disgust. As she stumbled past, she was appalled to see that each man's mouth was roughly stitched to hold it shut: crusty ulcerating sores wept into their scruffy beards. *Was this the kind of punishment to which the guard referred?* She reached out for Ruth's hand.

It was possible to get some measure of how the camp was ordered as they were led down alleyways formed by blocks of the box-like metal structures. Passing the first doorway, Maryam glimpsed inside: five claustrophobic rooms sectioned into each box, each of them housing up to three or four sleeping mats that barely fitted such a confined space.

The smell of decayed eggs was much worse up here on the plateau, and it mixed with the stench of human waste and rubbish to make breathing almost impossible without the urge to gag. Maryam tucked her nose into the collar of her shirt, preferring the assault of her own stale sweat to the putrid air.

Chickens ran riot in and out of the so-called rooms, and mangy dogs lay listlessly in doorways, ribs sticking out against their matted, filthy fur. Sprawled out in the few patches of sunlight between the blocks, lay other animals that Maryam did not recognise: small furry creatures with long scrawny tails. These, too, seemed to lack the will to move.

Everything was covered in a layer of sticky white dust and not a scrap of greenery was visible between the rows. Inside some of the rooms, thin dark-skinned women lay about, barely stirring as the girls walked past. Now they crossed a barren courtyard between the rows of huts. Thick fabric had been slung between the roofs, forming a shade to block the sun. A group of thirty or so women and children sat cross-legged at its centre, listening attentively to a white woman as she showed them how to trace out letters in the dust. They were learning to write, Maryam realised, their thin faces etched with concentration as they formed whole words. It triggered memories of her own childhood on the atoll: her lessons with the Mothers when they learnt to copy out long passages from the Holy Book. Then, she and the other Blessed Sisters had complained about the long hours they were made to spend studying how to read and write; here, the women looked hungry with the desire to learn.

Finally the guard stopped outside one of the metal huts and gestured that they go inside. The space was barely large enough for the three stained sleeping mats that lay upon the floor. It had no windows, only the open doorway through which they'd come to offer any light or relief from the stifling heat.

"This is your new home!" the guard announced grandly, as if they should be grateful. "Settle in, and I'll let Aanjay know you're here. She's the unofficial leader of the women at Cee-One—she'll show you round." He left them standing awkwardly inside the doorway and hurried off.

Maryam flopped onto one of the sleeping mats, curling around the gnawing hunger in her gut. *Let it hurt.* Let it remind her of all the things she had lost.

She could feel Ruth's gaze upon her, prickling her back, but she did not bother looking around. There were others now— older and wiser and not so filled with grief—who could attend Ruth's needs. She closed her eyes, willing her life to reach its end.

"What now?" Ruth asked.

Maryam chose to ignore her, swatting the question away from her consciousness.

"I can't understand you. How can you just lie there while Lazarus is locked away for trying to speak up for us?"

Poor brainwashed Ruth, you have it so wrong. All Lazarus cares for is himself.

She heard Ruth move, her footsteps dull on the hard metal floor. Then she felt Ruth shaking her.

"Maryam! You have to help!"

"Do I?" Maryam snapped. She flipped over, breaking free of Ruth's grip. "He got what he deserves. You heard him dismiss us when I was summoned to the healer. We're nothing more than slaves to him."

Ruth's usually placid face was awash with fury. "He was trying to protect you! He didn't want to see you go off on your own!"

"That's ridiculous. When has he ever done anything that isn't purely for his own selfish ends? He's as deceitful and hard-hearted as his father. If he's suffering now, that's fine with me."

"He saved you from drowning! When you didn't rise he dived back down and dragged you up."

For a moment Maryam's mind flicked back to that desperate moment the sea water started flooding down her throat. To the relief as she was wrenched back to the surface by her hair.

"And I thanked him, if you remember, at the time. But one moment's humanity in a sea of crimes does not make him good," she spat. "He threatened to cut your throat when we escaped. Do *you* not remember *that*? Or what about on Onewēre, when he tried to force himself on me? *And* he poisoned Joseph's heart against seeking my help—he willed him dead."

"You're talking like you're crazy," Ruth shouted. "You saw how Joseph's death hurt him." She took a shuddering breath, trying to calm herself. "I've always looked up to you, Maryam—you've always been so wise and brave—but in this I think you're very wrong. He may have been a bad person back home, but Joseph's passing to Heaven has shaken him. I really do believe he's changed."

Maryam jumped to her feet. "Joseph has not *passed to Heaven*, he is dead."

"I'm trying to save your soul—"

Maryam clasped Ruth by her broad shoulders. "Why can't you just leave me be? *I'm* not the one who's done you wrong. I've tried my best to keep you safe—and I'm sorry I've failed, Ruthie, I really am—but now, please leave me. I've had enough. I want to die."

To her utter amazement, sweet docile Ruth slapped her so hard across the face she reeled back and bumped her head against the wall. "How can you say that? Do you think that's what Joseph would've wanted or expected from you? He loved you because you're special; because you, alone, had the will to fight. That's why we all love you."

Ruth's words were affecting Maryam in a way she could not explain. Her whole body was trembling, tears falling freely down her face. "And what of the Lord, Ruthie? Is *this* how He shows His love?"

Ruth bit down on her bottom lip. "I don't know. But I do know He tells us that to throw away our life is wrong. And He taught us to forgive, to give us all a second chance. Is it not just possible that Lazarus has seen the light?"

"You see good where none exists." Maryam slumped back against the wall and slithered down until she crouched on the floor, her head dropping into her hands. She had such hate for Lazarus and everything he stood for. To forgive him seemed impossible and foolish when he'd proved over and over again he was not worthy of her trust.

She had no power over the shaking that consumed her; it was as if the turmoil in her heart had set it free. She just couldn't bear the thought of going on without Joseph in her life. Somehow *he* had made her strong, given her the will to fight. And now that he was gone, that will to fight was gone as well. Every time she looked at Lazarus now, all she could see was the injustice: Lazarus had been chosen to live, while Joseph, who was good and pure, was gone. It was all the wrong way around.

Ruth wiped her eyes, sniffing loudly as she squatted to wrap her arm around Maryam's shoulders. "Please," she urged, her voice little more than a whisper, "don't give up now." She turned a wry, watery smile on Maryam. "Isn't that what you've been telling me, over and over, since we left Onewēre?" She nudged Maryam in the ribs, trying to force a returning smile. "See, even when you thought I wasn't listening, it seems I did!"

What is the point in fighting? Maryam tried a smile. "I've taught you too well. Now you're just as fierce as me!" She watched relief engulf Ruth's face, and sighed deeply to expel the last of the shakes. "But I still think you're totally wrong about Lazarus," she added stubbornly.

"Just speak with him. Please. For me. I think you'll be surprised."

"And I think you'll be disappointed."

"Maybe I will . . . but maybe I won't."

"Maybe when you see I'm right you'll leave me be."

"I'll not leave you be if you go on refusing to eat or drink."

Maryam shrugged. "You don't understand . . . when I think of food, it makes me sick."

"Then don't think about it first! Just put it in your mouth and think of something else."

"Like what? That Joseph is dead? That I dragged my best friend across the sea only to replace one kind of imprisonment with another?"

Ruth rolled her eyes. "Or maybe that despite the odds we're still alive?"

Maryam smiled at Ruth's about-face. "When did *you* become the strong, optimistic one? That job was mine!"

"That's right and don't forget it now!" Ruth grinned. "But you still have to find the strength to eat . . . and, by the way, you need to wash! You truly stink!"

This Maryam did not expect. She laughed, and felt a little of the pressure inside her ease. "You don't smell so good yourself!"

Ruth sent her a beatific smile and pushed herself up to her feet. "I can't believe you'd be so rude!" She held out her hand to Maryam. "Come on, then . . . let's go find a place to wash!"

Maryam looked at Ruth's outstretched hand, thinking how it symbolised the choice that confronted her: between doggedly fighting on or ending the torment, now, through death. She closed her eyes, picturing this awful camp and what, no doubt, lay in store. But rather than convince her there was no point in persevering, the image chastised her for her selfishness. Now was not the time to leave her one remaining friend unprotected and alone. Even in her pain she knew that *this* was wrong. So, in the end, despite the emptiness inside her heart, she took Ruth's hand.

CHAPTER THIRTEEN

Maryam and Ruth were hovering in the doorway of their meagre room, trying to decide where they might find somewhere to wash, when a small dark-skinned woman approached them with a welcoming smile. She wore a long beige tunic and trousers, and her head was covered in a frayed white scarf that gathered loosely around her neck. Her eyes were large and very dark, bordered by a network of tired lines.

"My name is Aanjay," she said in a soft unfamiliar accent. The fact that she spoke English—that *all* of them spoke English, yet each had their own peculiar way of forming the words—struck Maryam as she smiled in welcome. Why would this be? "You must be Maryam and Ruth." The woman pressed her hands together as if in prayer and bobbed her head in greeting. "I have come to show you around the camp."

Maryam returned the greeting as best she could. "I am Maryam and this is Ruth." Ruth, too, pressed her hands together and nodded her head.

"I am so sorry you find yourselves here," Aanjay said. "This is not a good place to be." A wave of sadness rippled across her face. "Did you lose many others on the way?"

How could she have known this? "Yes, our dear friend Joseph died." She hated how saying the words aloud made his death seem so much more irreversible and real.

"Ah, to lose even one is hard," Aanjay said. She turned then and beckoned them to follow her. "Come and I will show you around."

They set off along the narrow pathway between the huts until they came to a large roofed shelter where a group of women dressed much the same as Aanjay were rinsing everything from dishes to babies in a row of rust-specked metal sinks. On the opposite side of the shelter stood a small free-standing building. The stench of human waste that came from it drew a cloud of large black buzzing flies that honed in on the children who dabbled in the dregs of water at their mothers' feet.

"These are your closest toilets," Aanjay explained. Then she pointed to a line of partitioned cubicles beyond the row of sinks. "The water in the showers is salty and cold, but once a day they bring hot water in as well."

"Showers?" Maryam asked. "What are they?"

Aanjay smiled. "Come and I'll show you." She led them over to a cubicle and reached inside to turn a rusty tap. The two girls jumped backwards as water burst from the showerhead like summer rain. "The hot water arrives just after lunch. The first to use it find it much too hot, and the last too cold, but we make do. Only one tank is delivered to our area each day."

Maryam had to concentrate hard to understand the woman's words. Her accent spun the sounds around in complicated ways. "How many are here altogether?" she asked.

"It changes all the time," Aanjay replied. "People come and go, and many die."

"You mean there's a chance we could get out of here?" Excitement lifted Ruth's voice.

"We are given a choice: stay imprisoned here or return home. For most of us, to go back home is certain death."

"*No one* gets into The Confederated Territories?" Maryam asked.

Aanjay shook her head. "Unless we denounce our own faith and take up theirs, we have no chance. And, even then, it's very rare. They do not trust our kind at all."

"Your kind?" asked Ruth.

"Buddhist, Hindu or Islamic . . . people of all the different faiths wash up here."

"You don't worship the Lord and His Lamb?" Ruth backed behind Maryam, as if Aanjay could somehow do her harm.

"Faith is a choice, child. Here we try to respect every one."

Maryam blinked back her surprise. She had no idea there were so many alternative faiths. Beside her, Ruth was bristling, so she spluttered out another question to prevent Ruth from antagonising Aanjay right away. She pointed to the row of taps. "Is this water good enough to drink?"

"It does not taste very good," Aanjay said. "But after a while you will get used to it."

Maryam crossed to an unoccupied sink and cupped her hand under the running tap. The water looked clean enough, but as she swallowed she pulled a face and the nearby women laughed behind their hands. Aanjay was right. It tasted foul. She slunk back to Ruth's side.

"What about food?" she asked.

"We have rice for breakfast and lunch, and a thin hot soup for our evening meal. Sometimes, if we're lucky, the chickens lay fresh eggs—and a group of us have tried to cultivate gardens to grow vegetables. But the phosphate in the soil is harsh."

"Phosphate?"

"In the rocks. They used to mine it many generations ago. Now it blows around as dust." She bent down and combed the white layer of dust with her fingers, then waved her hand under the girls' noses. The scent of decaying eggs was much stronger now. "It is this dust that causes the smell."

Maryam met Ruth's eyes. So *that* was the source. "How many people did you say were held here altogether?" Maryam asked.

"Right now about eight hundred . . . maybe more."

"So many? From where?"

Aanjay shrugged. "All the islands in the sea. Life is very hard for all the generations who managed to survive the flares. Those of us caught up here desired a better life."

"You came from a small island too?"

"Indeed. But, unlike many whose islands can no longer sustain them, my people seek to escape the tyranny on our shores." She beckoned them onwards, moving with such grace her small feet barely seemed to touch the ground.

In the next courtyard a crush of women and children sat cross-legged eating bowls of lumpy rice. Maryam studied them shyly, struck by their many different shades: from the mellow creamy ambers of the fine-boned women like Aanjay to the same rich brown as she and Ruth—and some so dark their skin took on the indigo hue of midnight skies. Lazarus would be the outsider here, something he'd find hard to bear.

Maryam and Ruth squatted on the outskirts of the group as Aanjay volunteered to collect their lunch. It was a sobering sight: many of the detainees were so thin and frail it was hard to believe they received any food at all. Some rocked in a demented way, their eyes wide and haunted, while others stared into space with such desolation Maryam's pulse grew jittery at the sight. Many suffered weeping sores, a few the milky-eyed curse of the blind, and nearly all the grizzling children had tight protruding bellies and bowed, painfully thin legs. Perhaps she had died and come to Hell already, here amidst the other disbelievers of the Lord? Only Ruth's presence contradicted this possibility, just as only Ruth still kept her from succumbing to the void.

When Aanjay returned with three small bowls of the rice, the girls fell hungrily upon their share. Above them, gulls reeled in the updrafts, seeming to taunt Maryam's inability to refuse the food as they called out their raucous symphony to the wild and free.

The heat of the day was building now, and her own stale body odours rose above the general stench. If only she was back home on the atoll, where old Zakariya would heat clean water for the metal bath and throw in a handful of the pandanus leaves to perfume it. How they'd all taken such luxuries for granted, never for a moment thinking life might not continue so comfortably or peacefully.

"Where are all the men?" Maryam asked, as she scooped the last few grains of rice from her bowl and licked them from her fingers.

Aanjay pointed off to their right. "Unless they're here with family, the men are kept apart at night. You'll see them start to mingle soon, when the last of the breakfast has been cleared away." She gestured to the group. "We eat in shifts, as there is not enough room for all of us to join together in one place." She lowered her voice, as though she risked being overheard. "The guards use divisions such as these to keep us from uniting to fight for our rights."

"Has anyone ever managed to escape?" Maryam asked, thinking how her own people on Onewēre had also lost the will to fight.

"It is impossible," Aanjay said flatly. "The guards patrol the fences and the people of the island here are far too scared to help. They, too, rely on The Confederated Territories for their survival—without the camp, they'd have no aid at all."

"And the people of The Confederated Territories don't think this is wrong?"

Aanjay ran her finger around the rim of her empty bowl. "From time to time someone tries to tell our stories to their people, but even when they do it seems no one cares." She met Maryam's gaze. "Those few of us who can speak English do what we can, but every week more like you arrive and others die until, one by one, we lose the will to fight."

The rice in Maryam's stomach felt as though it had turned to stone. To be trapped in this place was to be caught inside a sticky web, suspended and helpless until the spider was due its next meal. And, sooner or later, she saw now, that meal would be her.

*   *   *

Maryam perched with Ruth in the doorway of the hut, teasing out the tangles from their long wiry hair. They had rinsed their heads in fresh water to rid them of the sticky coating left by the salt-water shower: it felt so good to be clean again. But the activity had stirred the pain in Maryam's arm, and she found it hard to block the throbbing from her mind.

The camp was busier now, men mixing with the women as the day progressed. "What I don't understand," Ruth said, "is why we're being held here if the Territorials are Believers too? And Lazarus? He's a Believer *and* he's white. Why are they still holding him?"

Maryam shrugged. "I don't know." She nearly added that she didn't care, but did not want to fight with Ruth. She stretched, looking for distraction. "Come on, let's take a walk."

Ruth pulled back her hair and smiled. "Maybe we can find out where Lazarus is being held."

"Maybe."

She struggled to her feet, still weighted by the deep sense of exhaustion that had struck her down with Joseph's death. She didn't care about Lazarus, and she hated that he lived while Joseph did not. Despite trying for Ruth's sake to rouse herself from her despair, she couldn't shake the grief of losing him. And, in a way, she didn't want to—for to stop feeling his loss was to forget him, and she vowed that this would never be.

They wandered aimlessly down the dusty walkways, getting a measure of the vastness of the camp. It seemed to go on forever, bigger by far than all Onewēre's villages combined. Eventually they came upon a patch of cultivated ground where women and children toiled beneath the punishing late-morning sun to work the dusty soil. The plants were withered and their fruits were small, though the children worked intently to water each thirsty plant. The more Maryam saw, the more her horror of the place increased. The smell, the heat, the lack of fresh clean water, the misery of knowing they were trapped within these barren bounds . . . this camp was not a waypoint in some journey, it was the end.

By the time they'd circled the barracks and come back to the place where they'd first entered the camp, the sun had reached its highest point. The same group of men stood stock-still beside the gate, their accusing eyes locked on the guards through the netting of the fence. Up close, the rough stitching of their mouths made Maryam's stomach churn all the more. *What kind of humans could do such a dreadful thing?*

Beyond the fence, Maryam recognised one of the guards who'd brought them here. He glared back at the men, his fingers fidgeting with the mechanism of his gun. To Maryam's surprise, Ruth sidled over to the wire and called to him directly.

"Why have you done this?" Her voice shook with nerves as she pointed to the tortured men.

"Don't blame us," the guard replied. "They've done this to themselves."

Ruth's face grew pale. "But why?"

"Ask them yourself!" He chuckled at his joke. "The stupid rag-heads think that by starving themselves they'll shame us into giving in." He snorted. "But they'll crack eventually—they always do."

The men's bravery touched something deep inside Maryam. If they could fight in the face of so little hope, then so must she. Fury overtook her as she, too, challenged the guard. "We demand that you release us. We've done nothing wrong!"

The guard laughed. "Oh yeah? You and whose army, sweetheart?" He raised his gun towards her. "Now get the hell out of here before I lock you up with that poncy little traitor you arrived with."

Everything she'd endured since she'd first Crossed seemed to boil up inside her. How dare this man think he could treat them like this! A surge of energy flowed through her, as if Joseph's spirit somehow buoyed her up and urged her to act.

She wrapped her fingers into the netting of the fence and shook it, yelling loudly: "Let us out! You have no right to hold us here."

Ruth put her hand on Maryam's shoulder. "Don't. You'll end up locked away as well."

"I don't care," Maryam said. "I'll not sit back quietly and let them steal away our lives."

The guard, on high alert, took a step towards her, and others ran over to his side. But she found she was no longer alone, for several of the men joined with her in beating at the fence. Ruth, however, backed away, a look of terror on her face as the guards dragged over a long flexible pipe and aimed it straight at Maryam. A furious jet of water shot from its end, hitting her square in her stomach and knocking her off her feet. One by one, the others were sent sprawling by the blast of stinging rain.

Maryam scrambled up, launching herself back at the fence as her anger and pain at Joseph's death recharged her words. "Let me out!" Again she was struck down by the water, and again she rose. But now the guards were swarming in through the gate. They swooped on her, and she screamed as they seized her broken arm and jerked it roughly behind her back. Then they took her other arm, then her legs, and swept her off the ground in a writhing ball of fury. She twisted, trying to locate Ruth, and glimpsed her panicked face through a frame of other arms and legs. But she couldn't hear what Ruth was shouting, her heart pummelling so hard its pulse filled up her ears.

The guards had trussed her like a sacrificial goat; now they snapped restrictive metal cuffs around her ankles and her wrists—right over the plaster cast. She struggled, powerless to do anything but submit as they hauled her, squirming and kicking and biting, to a stone building and dragged her to a tiny cell. There they left her, bound and panting and sodden. Locked her in.

For several minutes more the storm raged on within her. When it finally abated she cried, howling like a baby as the last of her bottled-up emotions were purged, until nothing more was left inside.

In the aftermath, she couldn't believe what she had done. Had she been possessed? But she didn't regret it, despite the terrible burning in her injured arm. On the contrary, she felt as if she'd rid herself of something festering and poisonous that could have done her harm. Besides, at least in here, alone, that nightmare world was held at bay.

Then she recalled Ruth's words as they'd stepped off the ship: *Please don't let them split us up.* Too late. Less than a day, and already Ruth's worst fears had been realised. What had got into her? All she could hope was that Aanjay would befriend Ruth now and keep her safe until Maryam was released. *If* she was released. *Oh Lord, what if they just leave me here to die?*

She twisted her neck around until she could see up to the ceiling of the cell. Cobwebs draped between the rough timber rafters, their fine-spun silk accentuated by thin layers of white phosphate dust. She could hear birds clattering across the roof and, closer still, in the cells beyond her own, the unnerving sound of a man sobbing and an incessant mumbling from someone else.

She snaked over to the metal grille that separated her from the corridor beyond and tried to peer into the next-door cell, but she could not. The mumbling continued, disconnected, from a cell much further down. It didn't sound like Lazarus— though she had no real idea of whether he was held here as well.

Now the outside door burst open again and one of the hunger strikers was escorted past her cell, two burly guards forcing his shackled arms unnaturally high behind his back. His eyes met hers and she nodded, acknowledging their bond as he was led away. Their footsteps echoed off the hard stone walls, and she heard the scrape of lock and key.

As they passed on their way out, one of the guards noticed Maryam's vigil by the bars and lashed out, his boot stamping only inches from her face. "Crazy black bitch," he spat at her. "They should've left you in the sea to die."

"I wish they had," she shot back, turning her face from him and holding her breath until she heard the outer door slam shut.

"Maryam! Is that you?"

"Lazarus?" She pressed her ear up to the bars to see if she could track his voice.

"I think I'm in the cell right next to you." There was a banging on the bars to her left and she swivelled around in time to spy his fingers reach out into the corridor and wave.

"Yes, I see your hand."

"What happened? Why are you here?"

She laughed, surprising herself by the cheerful nature of the sound. "I don't think they like to be reminded of their evil ways."

"You challenged them?"

"It seems I did." Despite her antagonism towards him, it was a relief to hear his voice. She felt small and vulnerable, and very scared.

"Did they hurt you too?" His question sounded strangely charged.

"Nothing I couldn't bear." She rolled her wrist within the cuff, trying to slide her right hand from the metal ring. No luck. "Are you bound as well?"

"Bound? No. Are you?"

One rule for brown, another for white. Her heart hardened towards him again. "Forget it."

"But I heard crying. Was that you?"

What pleasure it would give him to think this so. "It was an act to shame them." She was determined not to feed his prejudices, knowing he already thought her foolish and weak.

Lazarus did not reply, and she sensed that he didn't believe the lie. The floor was hard beneath her hips now, so she wriggled over to the side of the cell and pushed herself up until her back was propped against the wall. This eased her hips but put more pressure on her throbbing arm, still pinned behind her back. Again she shifted, leaning sideways against the wall, which eased her arm but did little to aid her overall comfort while her clothes still dripped and her hair hung lank and tickly around her face.

Even though she didn't want to talk to him, Lazarus's silence now unsettled her. *What was he thinking?* Was he sitting there judging her as harshly as she judged him? In the unnatural lull, she heard a dog barking and the nagging, plaintive cry of a child in pain. She closed her eyes, thrown back into a childhood memory of a time when she'd been ill and forced to stay in bed: how she'd so resented being stuck inside, forced to play eavesdropper to the happy voices of her playmates as they'd romped free, without her, in the sun. But Mother Elizabeth had come to comfort her, retelling stories from the Holy Book. She'd felt so special, tucked up next to her. How long ago that seemed. How distant and unreal.

CHAPTER FOURTEEN

A cough broke through her thoughts, and Lazarus cleared his throat. "I know you may not want to hear this but I have something I really need to say . . ."

Maryam could not reply. Her heart beat double time as she worked through every possibility. Perhaps he was going to admit the truth: that he had planned Joseph's elimination and his own rise to power from the start . . . or that now he planned to dump them here and travel on to The Confederated Territories alone? Whatever it was, she knew it was momentous by the nervous catch he hadn't quite managed to disguise.

She nibbled at a flake of dry skin on her bottom lip and steeled herself for what was coming next. "All right. What?"

Again he cleared his throat, as if he had to force the words to come. "I've had a lot of time to think," he said. "Way too much time." He paused. "I want you to know that I'm—that I'm . . . sorry. I've behaved . . . badly."

Was this another of her hallucinations, like the disconnected voices she'd heard on the boat? A huge churning stirred in her chest as she remembered the humiliation and terror that she—and poor dear Ruth—had suffered at his hands. The churning cemented into a cold fist of fury that dropped into her gut. *Did he think he could make everything right by a few trite words?* He had tormented her, terrorised and tried to force himself on her; treated everyone around him with disdain. Did she have it in her to forgive him? She wasn't sure. Not sure at all.

"Right," she murmured, knowing he was waiting for some

kind of response but truly not able to give him more. The hurt—the hate—she felt was still too raw, and she dared not soften her stance to him, lest he still do her more harm.

"Look, I know you probably find this hard to believe—"

She snorted, unable to hold back her bitterness.

"Okay, I guess you can't." He sounded less guarded now, and she knew by his tone that her response had rankled him. *What did he expect?* "When Joseph died—"

"You mean when you *killed* him," she spat.

Even through the stone wall of the cell she heard him gasp. "What in all Hell is *that* supposed to mean?"

Maryam leaned over, hissing out her accusation through the bars. "It means you planned to see him dead. I had the equipment there to save him—keep him alive until we found him help—but *you* poisoned his mind to this. You let him die."

"That's totally ridiculous! He was never going to take your blood. I told you that. I warned you that even if he did, he still would die."

"That's what *you* say. I guess we'll never know now if that was true."

"Why would I do that? He was my only cousin. I loved him too."

A bleak laugh escaped her lips. "Love? I doubt you even understand the word."

She could feel his rage fly from his cell towards her like a whirlwind. "What? And you, who teased him with your precious virgin state, showed him love? You played him like a nareau plant that first seduces and then eats the fly."

Her face burnt at the impact of his words. "No—you would

be the expert at *that* game. How many Sisters did you drug on the toddy and defile? Ten? Twenty? Perhaps more?"

"Bitch," she heard him mutter, though she was puzzled by his choice of word. Why call her a female dog? Perhaps he thought them lowly, as he did all other female things.

She found herself holding her breath, waiting for his next retort, but as the seconds stretched out she gave in to the urge to breathe. Her accusations had obviously hit the mark, and she was pleased.

Outside, she could hear a man shouting in a foreign tongue, his words unknown but the tone so full of anguish it burrowed deep into her brain. Try as she might, she couldn't erase the nightmare image of those roughly sewn lips. Was there no let-up in the torment of this place? Was everyone here as broken and as full of rage as she?

Just then a guard she hadn't seen before came past and stopped outside her cell. He was juggling a sleeping mat and bucket as well as a large bunch of keys.

"Here," he said, unlocking her door and depositing his load in the middle of her cell with a tired grunt. He approached her tentatively now, keys still in hand, and unlocked the cuffs to free her hands and feet. "In the future, missy," he said, "think more carefully before you stir up trouble, eh?"

She didn't answer him, frightened by her own newly dis-covered capacity for hot-headed rage. She daren't risk another outburst now, unsure just how far they'd go in punishing her again. But she was pleased to be free of the cuffs, which had left painful welts where they'd rubbed at her skin. Inside its cast her arm still throbbed, and she longed for one of Mother Evodia's herbal tonics to ease her misery.

As soon as the guard had left, she dragged the sleeping mat over to the corner furthest from the door. The mat was stained and lumpy, but she dropped down onto it thankfully.

Slowly her pulse began to calm, and the exhaustion she had fought since Joseph's death fell back over her in one sweeping wave. It was as if her bones had weathered into stone, and no amount of effort would move them from the mat. She gave herself over to it, willing herself to sleep now to block out the world. Yet, every time she slipped into a soothing dream, she'd startle and it seemed not even her subconscious would allow her to escape. As the afternoon dragged on, the heat intensified, slicking her hair to cloying fingers that wound around her neck each time she rolled and turned. But at last heat and exhaustion overrode her brain, and pitched her straight into an intense dream.

She was in the atoll's maneaba, kneeling beneath its cool thatched roof before the sculpted image of the Lamb. Somewhere in the distance she could hear the cheerful laughter of the little Sisters as they romped beneath the palms. Above, the Lamb watched down on her with mournful eyes. It was as if He saw right through her to the doubt that filled her heart.

As soon as the awareness of this doubt entered her mind she saw Him stir, the nails that fixed his hands and feet flying out unaided to land before her on the ground. Next, He stepped down from the Cross and stood before her, holding out His hand for her to take. She could not shift her gaze from His, their eyes locked in a timeless duel—neither was willing to be the first to look away.

"Come," He said, "and I will lead you safely Home." His voice filled the high reaches of the maneaba, as soft and soothing as the eternal whisperings of the sea.

She looked now to His outstretched hand, transfixed by the gaping wound that rent his palm. She wanted to accept His call, to bury herself in the familiar comfort of His warm embrace, but she could not. All sound had ceased, and all she was aware of was the reverberation of her own ragged breath. He made it seem so easy, as though all she had to do was lift her arm and reach out for His proffered hand. But still her limbs refused to move.

Over His shoulder another deity stood by: that man—the one from the temple on Marawa Island—his calm face breaking into a beatific smile as she caught his gaze. He bowed in greeting, his plump hands pressed neatly before him as he dipped his head. And above him now, squinting from the dark recesses of the maneaba roof, the masks of her ancestors came alive, their eyes flashing red and angry in the filtered light.

"Your heart is mine," the Lamb proclaimed, and He leaned forward, wrenching her to her feet so suddenly she had no time to argue or resist.

He pressed her to his sculpted wooden chest, locking His arms around her so tightly she had to fight to breathe. He laughed and, in a flash of cold recognition, she knew that laugh and tried to pull away—for it was not the Lamb who pressed her to his rigid body but Holy Father Joshua, his breath leaking the stench of phosphate as he crushed his shark's mouth over hers . . .

Maryam jerked awake with a cry.

"Are you all right?"

It was Lazarus calling from the next-door cell. He must have heard her cry out as she'd fled the dream.

"I'm fine," she croaked, her throat so dry it did not want to work. *What would he know of nightmares when he'd had so little in his life to fear?*

She heard him stir, and then a scraping sound as something scuffed across the floor. "Here," he called again. "I've pushed a cup of water out into the corridor. See if you can reach."

Already the little saliva she had left was pooling at the thought, so she crossed to the bars, relieved to see he'd placed the cup within her reach. She squeezed her arm through awkwardly, managing to hook the rim of the cup with her finger to drag it to her side. The water tasted oily, but it helped to soothe the swollen, prickly feeling in her throat.

"Thank you," she said, once she'd drained the cup. She pushed it back across the void.

"Look . . ." Lazarus said. "I know you won't believe this, but that time you caught me in the cellar was the first."

"You're right," she agreed, picturing the poor server as Lazarus forced the anga kerea toddy down her throat then stripped her bare. "I find it very hard."

"Just listen to me for a moment, will you?" He was almost pleading now. "Since Joseph died, my head's so full of all this . . . stuff . . . I just want you to understand."

"Why me? Why not confess your sins to the Lord, if that's what you want?"

"That's not what I want," he snapped. "Look, it's hard for me to admit this . . . but here's the thing: I want *you* to forgive me. From the moment I set eyes on you, I knew that you had something special—something that I . . . lacked."

This jolted her. In all her dealings with him she'd never heard him admit weakness or inferiority of any kind. "If that's the case, you have an odd way of showing it."

"Please, just try to understand . . . When I was young, Uncle Jonah and Aunt Deborah were the only ones who ever showed me love—and Joseph, of course. My own mother and father were totally self-absorbed. I spent my whole childhood trying to do something that would please them—make them notice me and show me love."

"But you had everything—"

"That's where you're wrong. I was raised to believe my father was a living god—a god who had no time for snivelling little boys."

"What of all the wonderful things in the Holy City? You can hardly complain about growing up in a place like that while those stuck on Onewēre struggled to survive."

"It's easy to see that now, but for years it coloured everything I thought and did. So when, three years ago, my father suddenly announced the time had come to train me up to take his place, I saw it as my chance to win his love."

"So?" Maryam challenged him. "Did that give you the right to treat the rest of us like slaves?"

"In an odd kind of way it did. I watched how my father treated you all and I followed his lead—and he'd praise me, tell me I was finally acting like a man." He laughed bitterly, then grunted, as if he was in pain. "It got to the point where I used to do things just to test him, thinking that surely *now* he'd chastise me and tell me "no". But it turned out that the worse I behaved, the more he drew me to his side."

"You did these things, even when you knew they were wrong?"

"It got out of control." His voice was wavering, and he cleared his throat. "I used to wonder why you servers never questioned him or called his bluff—always blindly believing everything he said or did. And then that passiveness started to annoy me—drive me mad."

"Mad?"

"Angry. Look, it sounds stupid now I say it, but I reached the stage where I truly started to believe you servers got what you were asking for—that your obedience and blind acceptance meant you deserved everything my father could dish out. And the angrier I got, the more I wanted to punish you all for being so gullible and ignorant." Again he paused, and she thought she heard him sniff. "It's like I said before—it just all got out of control."

There was an awful kind of logic in his words. Had he not accused her of this passivity the very day he'd trapped her near Joseph's house?

"But when I challenged you about it at the pool that day," she said, "you mocked me and told me to grow up." If only she could see his face, see whether he was smirking as he recalled her nakedness.

"I know," he said. "And do you remember what you said to me?"

"No. I was rightly fearing for my life."

"Oh hell . . . I'm sorry." He sniffed again. *Could he really be crying?* "Respect. That's what you said. That you would never respect me, no matter what I did. And, though I refused to admit it at the time, that really hurt. And the more I thought about it, the more it got to me." He sniffed once more, and when he spoke his voice was thick with suppressed tears. "*You* got to me."

Charming words, but she was not a fool. "I see . . . you were so moved you thought you'd put a knife to my best friend's throat and force yourself on us all so we'd be friends?"

"It was cruel and stupid, I know that now—and I'm really, really sorry, all right?" She heard a dull thud, as though he'd punched the wall. "How many times do you want me to say it? But I couldn't stop thinking about you, so then I started following you, and when I discovered what you were up to I realised it might be my only chance to get away and live my own life."

She felt so confused. Part of her was totally disgusted that he'd tracked her, while a tiny part was flattered, though it made her sick. "It didn't occur to you just to ask Joseph and tell him the truth?"

"It did. But do you think you'd have agreed to take me even if Joseph said I could go?"

In this, at least, Lazarus was right. "Never in a million years!" She stood now and paced the cell, needing the motion to clear her head. She was not so much shocked by his words as by the fact he said them at all. In truth, everything he said made sense in a twisted and deluded way. "And Joseph . . . do you *swear* to me you didn't mean him harm?"

"I can't believe you even have to ask." Now he sounded more like the Lazarus of old.

"Well I do," she insisted, staring at the wall as if he'd feel her eyes upon him now and have to tell the truth. "I need to know you grieve for him as well."

"Do you think I was feigning tears back on the boat? Of course I grieve his loss. But if you're asking me to grieve *for him*, then no."

His words pierced like a blade straight to her heart. "Why not?"

"Why grieve for him when he was the lucky one? From the moment he was born he knew he was loved."

"But it isn't fair. He didn't have to die."

"Fair or not, I still say he was lucky . . . He had you."

What on earth? She shook her head, uncertain if she even wanted to know what he was trying to say.

"You understand that I can never trust you?" she said at last. "Too much has happened to ignore."

"I know," he said. "And *that* grieves me."

This was too much to take in. Everything she'd believed had shifted beneath her feet like wind-blown sand, leaving her unbalanced and unsettled in its midst.

Their conversation was interrupted as the outer door slammed open and the guard wheeled in a trolley carrying fresh cups of water and small bowls of soup. Maryam watched, relieved to have this break to gather up her scattered thoughts, as the guard placed the food and drink within reach of each cell for the prisoners to either take or leave. Maryam retrieved her share and sipped the watery broth, all plans of self-denial swept away. The broth contained nothing identifiable in its stock, yet its warmth was soothing and she gulped it down. Outside she could hear a jumble of voices and guessed that the others were gathering for their evening meal. She could only hope that someone had befriended Ruth so she would not have to sleep inside that awful little room alone.

Now her bladder ached with fullness and she eyed the bucket the kind guard had left. The thought of using it in such a place embarrassed her, but she had no choice. She squatted over it, the sound of her splashing waters loud in her ears. Just as she had finished and moved the bucket as far away as possible, a woman entered the building and Maryam recognised the white woman she'd seen teaching in the courtyard when they'd first arrived. Her face was pocked with scars; her hair greying and very short. But her manner was reassuring, and she smiled as she stationed herself in the corridor so that she could see into the two adjoining cells. She acknowledged Maryam first, and then turned her attention to Lazarus. As she did so, her smile dropped.

"You are Lazarus?" she said. She spoke in the same flat accent as the guards.

"Yes."

The woman pointed at him. "Those are fresh?"

Again Lazarus merely said yes. Now she turned to Maryam, scrutinising her carefully from head to toe, her gaze coming to rest on the grubby plaster cast.

"And I take it you are Maryam? My name is Jo Sinclair. I wonder if we could talk?"

Maryam nodded, trying to read the woman's status from her clothes. She wore men's trousers made from thick faded blue fabric and a short-sleeved orange shirt. There was nothing to indicate just who or what she might be.

Jo Sinclair retrieved a chair from further along the corridor and placed it so she could be seen by both Maryam and Lazarus. "I belong to a human rights group that tries to help the detainees."

"Can you get us out of here?" Lazarus asked.

"I don't know. I'd like to hear your stories, though, so I can see."

Maryam was still trying to decide if it was safe to speak. Her only interactions with white people—apart from Joseph and his mother, Deborah—had been so painful she wasn't sure if it was worth the risk. Lazarus, however, had no such prejudice, and launched into an account of what had happened to them.

"We sailed from Marawa Island a few days ago—I've lost track of time a bit—and then—"

Jo held up her hand to halt him. "Hold on. I've just spoken with your friend Ruth. She said you came from Onewēre?"

"She told you that?" Lazarus broke in, sounding annoyed.

"It's the truth," Maryam snapped back. "What's wrong with that?"

"I'll tell you later when we can talk alone."

Jo raised an eyebrow at Maryam and shrugged before directing her attention back to Lazarus. "Okay. I don't think you realise how serious this situation is. Unless you can trust me, there's no way I can even try to help. As it is, my powers are limited, but, believe me, I'm the best—and possibly the only—chance you've got."

"Why should we trust you?" Lazarus asked.

Why was he being so pig-headed now, Maryam wondered, when only moments ago he'd seemed so keen to talk?

"Because you have no other choice."

Something about the frankness of the woman's approach convinced Maryam that she spoke the truth. "This is foolish, Lazarus. She's right, we need her help."

For a long moment Lazarus did not reply and Jo said nothing, obviously waiting for him to make up his mind without trying to interfere. At last he said, "I want to speak with Maryam first—alone—and, meanwhile, if you can convince them to let us all meet together in the same room then I'll agree. I need to see her face to face. These are my terms."

Is he mad? He was no longer the Holy Father's son but someone with no power to make such stupid demands. Jo's face remained passive, however, as she rose from the chair. "Rightio, I'll see what I can do." She turned to Maryam and winked. "Men!" she mouthed, and rolled her eyes. Maryam grinned, despite herself.

The moment Jo was gone, Maryam called to Lazarus, "What on earth are you up to?"

"Look, you can guess what they did to the people of Marawa Island—if they think we're the first of some great exodus, it's possible they'll try the same thing at home. Do you really want Onewēre invaded by this lot?"

"I can't believe you . . . here's a chance to tell someone what's really going on back there, yet you're perfectly willing to let your father's wrongdoing go unpunished so he can keep it up? Can't you see he's used our isolation as an excuse to trap us all under his rule? I'll have no part in keeping him in power."

"And I'll have no part in opening our doors to these thugs."

Why was *everything* so complicated where Lazarus was concerned? Just when she'd almost let her guard down with him, this new argument saw them back where they had started: totally at odds.

"The Confederated Territories or Apostles . . . they're all the same."

"Look, if you'd just see this logically—"

She cut him off. "If you tell me to *look* just one more time, I swear I'll scream."

"Now you're being childish," he snarled.

"Maybe I am," she bit right back. "But what do you know of being oppressed? You've been stuck in a cell for one day and you think you understand how it feels to have no power? To fear for your life?"

"You'd be surpri—"

His reply caught in his throat as the outer door was flung back open to admit Jo again.

She was followed into the building by the guard who had unshackled Maryam. He pulled his keys from his pocket and unlocked Maryam's door, ushering Jo into the cell and carrying the chair in after her so she had somewhere to sit. "Behave yourself, missie," he warned Maryam, shaking his finger at her to underline his words.

"Thank you," she said. "I promise I will." She smiled her thanks.

Next the guard approached Lazarus's cell and unlocked the door. "Listen to me, bucko. I'll put you in together, "cause I happen to think this fine lady here can do some good—and, god knows, someone needs to—but if you do *one* thing that brings me grief you'll get your arse whipped again, no two ways. You comprendo?"

Maryam was still struggling to decipher the meaning of the man's strange words when she heard Lazarus sullenly agree. She had to hand it to him: it seemed he'd got his way. *The Confederated Territories for Christian Territorials . . . whites for whites.* She heard his door creak open and waited for the guard to lead him to her cell, dreading the pompous look of triumph he'd have slathered on his face.

When Lazarus appeared, she was so shocked she cried aloud. Both his eyes were buried in a swollen mess of angry red and blue bruising, and a gaping cut on his left cheekbone still oozed with blood. He moved like an old man, favouring one side, one arm wrapped around his lower ribs to hold them firm.

"What in the Lord's name happened?" she whispered, automatically crossing to him to help ease him down onto the sleeping mat.

Behind her, the guard locked the door. "There's people here don't like so-called wiggers and boonga-jockeys, miss." He shrugged and looked at Jo. "No rewards for guessing whose handiwork this is, eh? Anyways, I'll be back in half an hour to let you out."

Jo shook her head slowly, her frown deepening. "Thanks, Charlie," she said. "I owe you one."

CHAPTER FIFTEEN

Maryam looked from Lazarus's messed-up face to Jo. "What did he mean?"

"It seems one of the guards objected to Lazarus's allegiances."

"His what?"

"Allegiances. His loyalties . . . his friends."

"But why?" She didn't understand. Why beat up on Lazarus when he was white?

"We've been taught, over the years, to loathe and fear anyone who doesn't look or act or think like us. So when some people see one of us mixing with the 'other side'—" she raised two fingers from each hand and wiggled them strangely as she spoke—"they see it as a betrayal of our race."

"You mean it's *our* fault Lazarus has ended up like this? Ruth's and mine?" *Oh great.*

"Forget it," Lazarus said. "I'm fine." Beneath his swollen bruises, his face set hard. "Let's just get on with this."

Maryam studied him from the corner of her eyes. He'd insisted that they speak together in this one room, so obviously he'd wanted her to see his injuries, yet now he told her to forget it. That made no sense. Still, now wasn't the time to pursue it. She might have only this one chance to tell someone what was going on back in Onewēre and she didn't want to waste it. "I'm ready to tell you why we left our home."

She could feel Lazarus glaring at her, but refused to let him put her off. She closed her eyes to block him out and began to tell her tale. At first the words came in nervous bursts but, as she proceeded, the horror of the Apostles' treatment of her—of all the Sisters—took over; her heart pounded hard and fast now as she relived the days and weeks since her Crossing. She found herself thinking ahead, trying to decide how much of Lazarus's involvement she should reveal. His presence in the story loomed large in her mind, but she was uncertain of what would be achieved by inviting a direct confrontation with him. By the time she'd told of Joseph's death, words were sticking dry and awkward in her throat, and she skipped ahead, ending in one breathless rush at the point where they'd been plucked from the sea. She glanced across at Lazarus, but he was staring steadfastly at the floor.

"My god," said Jo. "I had no idea." She shook her head, as though trying to fit in place everything she'd heard. "Onewēre's literally been off the radar for decades, like all the other outer islands. Everyone just presumed they were totally annihilated. When the first wave of refugees started arriving after the flares, our government made it policy simply to ignore any islands that hadn't been heard from—that any contact would just encourage further floods of refugees. And the government certainly didn't want that—especially with the start of the Confederation Wars. The people of those islands were literally abandoned then and left to rot."

"They didn't care that we might need their help?" *So much for their claiming to follow the Holy Book's teachings. Goodness and mercy . . . what a lie.*

Lazarus broke in now. "Come on! Even if they had shown up, do you really think my father's predecessors would've welcomed them? I'd be prepared to wager that if anyone had arrived in our lifetime, my father would've had them killed. The first Apostles set things up exactly as they wanted—and the fact you lot swallowed the line that you were the only ones Chosen to be saved just made you all the more compliant to their Rules."

"There you go again, blaming us. You haven't changed your thoughts at all."

"These are facts. It doesn't mean that I condone them."

Bitterness hardened Maryam's laugh. "Fancy words. To see something is wrong and do nothing is just as much a sin."

Lazarus bristled. "I'm merely pointing out that any kind of attempted contact would've met with grief." He shifted in his chair with a pained grunt. "This is stupid. They didn't even try to help—isn't that the point?"

Maryam turned away from him, sickened by his slick answers, and spoke instead to Jo. "But we're supposedly *all* the Lord's chosen children—His followers—the same as them."

"I'm certainly not excusing us," Jo answered. "But you have to understand what was going on at the time. Governments disintegrated, services collapsed. Only the toughest and the most powerful survived—just like your so-called Apostles—who were able to manipulate people's fear to seize control of the few resources the world had left. It really *was* a case of survival of the fittest—and often the fittest meant those prepared to stamp on the heads of others to survive."

"But don't you think the Territorials would act to put things right if they knew?"

Lazarus grabbed her arm and held it tight. "Don't do this, Maryam. Think about what I said before."

"I can't believe they wouldn't care."

"You're being foolishly naive." He released her arm, but not before he squeezed it so she could feel the imprint of his fingers well after his hand had dropped. "Look around this place and then tell me again that they'd care. Look at *me*." He thrust his battered face in front of her. "This is what I got just for mixing with you and Ruth. Imagine what they'd do to your people if they went there with their guards and guns."

"I'm afraid he's right," Jo said. "Go look around this place. You think the filth and squalor here is an accident? It's not. This camp has been used to detain refugees since well before your so-called Tribulation, and they've done nothing—absolutely *nothing*—to improve it since that time." She tipped her face towards the ceiling and drew a long slow breath, as though to rein her anger back under control. "It's designed to break wills and strip away dignity, while feeding the prejudices and fears of the people back at home. Calculated but clever, eh?"

"But if they'd just let us speak—"

"Your plea for help would fall on deaf ears. Most people in the Territories are struggling to survive—and they're not about to share what little power and property they *do* have." She massaged her temples for a moment before she continued. "Besides, unless the authorities think you're the first of a new wave of boat people from there, they'll not bother helping Onewēre even if you ask. They've got enough to contend with, given the number of people who still keep arriving."

"What *I* don't understand is why anyone is trying to come at all, when they must know the Territorials don't want them," Lazarus said.

"Because you don't know where they're coming *from*." Jo turned to Maryam again. "I wish I could tell you how much your story shocks me but, believe me, there are many people out there who suffer as much as you . . . in fact, the depth of human depravity does my head in sometimes."

Jo talked so fast and used such foreign words that Maryam struggled to understand her. "So there's nothing you can do to get us out of here?"

"I'll try. The fact that you share the same beliefs and that Lazarus is white may help." She sighed. "But, if you want my advice, I'd tell them you were the last of the people from Onewēre, otherwise god only knows what they might do if they thought the remaining population might look to The Confederated Territories for sanctuary or support. Remember the lessons of Marawa Island. I wouldn't want to see that kind of genocide take place again."

"Genocide?" What did this flat-voiced woman mean?

"Oh, they never admitted to it, of course. But a whole race of people doesn't suddenly drop dead for no reason. And our government had had a gutsful of boat people and made it plain they'd not stand for more."

"But The Confederated Territories must be huge—"

Jo laughed caustically. "Life's never quite so straight forward. After the solar flares there was precious little left for us, let alone all the other people decamping to our shores. It's said that some of our top brass decided to teach the poor people of Marawa a lesson—one the rest of the region wouldn't soon forget. Some say they were herded into the temple and gassed; others claim that they were shot . . ." Her voice drifted off and she shuddered.

Maryam pressed her hand over her eyes, trying to block out the picture of those tangled bones. *How could one human do that to another, in cold blood?*

Lazarus nodded his head and prodded Maryam. "See? Do you still want to send them to Onewēre now?"

He seemed so smug, so unaffected by what Jo was telling them. Maryam felt her fury rise again. She jumped to her feet, facing Jo accusingly. "Then what's the point of your even being here? You said that you could help."

Jo stood up. "I come as a witness, Maryam, to let you know there are still people out here in the world who care. And if I can help in any small way I will certainly try."

"Then I will do something myself. There has to be a way . . ."

Jo placed her hand on Maryam's arm. "I'm sorry," she said, "I'll speak to Sergeant Littlejohn myself, and see if he will let you put your case for settling on the mainland . . ."

She was interrupted as another group of hunger strikers were wrestled into the building. One of the guards pressed his face up to the bars of Maryam's cell.

"You kids can beat it now—we need the room." He nodded at Jo, unlocked the door and waved the three of them out. They did not need to be told twice.

The air was cooler outside the cell, but the stench of phosphate and human excrement still hung in the evening air. Somewhere an engine was thumping, setting up a dull reverberation, and lights were coming on in the walkways like scraps of weak winter sun between the clouds.

Jo and Lazarus looked at Maryam, as if waiting on what she would do next. She had no idea. All she knew was that they appeared to expect something from her, just as Ruth would, back in their airless little hut. But she had no plan and no reassurance to give. All she knew was she had to get away. Without any destination in mind, Maryam ran. She dared not look back as she dodged down an alleyway between two buildings. Lazarus called out after her, but she did not stop. All anyone had done since she'd been rescued was talk, talk, talk, bombarding her until she truly thought her head would burst. There were too many words she didn't understand—too many *things* she didn't understand—when all the time she felt as young and ignorant as a newly fledged chick.

The huts that butted up against the shadowy paths pressed in on her, and she tried to focus on her breathing, on the way the air rasped in and out of her lungs, rather than acknowledge the hum of human desperation that leaked out from the gaping doorways of the huts. Too much. Too much.

Eventually she turned a corner and found her way blocked by another fence. But the gateway remained open and she slipped through it, uncertain now of her direction or of whether this was the route Aanjay had shown them on their morning tour. She stuck to the fenceline, scanning ahead of each footfall to avoid the animal droppings and rubbish that lay in stinking piles. She ran on until the fence turned abruptly at a large building. Rounding a corner, she nearly crashed into a tall, bearded man.

"No girl, no girl," he shouted, holding out his hands to bar her way. The rest of his words were indecipherable, but his tone was not. She guessed she must be trespassing on the place reserved for men and turned on her heel, backtracking fast, and didn't stop until she'd traced the fence back to its start.

She dropped to her haunches then, panting out the stitch that knotted up her sides. When the pain had subsided, she set off in the opposite direction, turning down alleyways solely on the basis that they were deserted. At last, just as darkness swelled the shadows at the edges of the camp, she found herself out in the open ground.

A gaggle of young men were kicking a ball around on a patch of dirt. She slipped past and took herself off to the garden, crouching in amongst the malnourished plants to breathe in their dry leafy scents. Closed her eyes, trying to conjure up a picture of Joseph's face. If only he were here to talk with her, to help her understand what was going on. She felt tears rising as she pictured his vibrant blue eyes and the way his mouth curled and puckered as he leaned in for a kiss. The memory of his kisses tweaked low inside and she wrapped her arms around herself to try to hold the memory of him close. But the presence of the unyielding plaster cast that pressed against her breasts and the ragging laughter of the ball-players shattered her whimsy, sharply reminding her that Joseph was gone and there was no one to replace him.

What, then, would he do?

The answer to that question was not the one she wanted and she tried to bat it away again, but it persisted, knocking at her conscience until she had to give it space. Joseph would tell her to return to Ruth, who would be fretting once she heard that Maryam had been released. She could not add to Ruth's despair. So she rose and tried to retrace her steps, even harder now the natural light had gone and the man-made lights strung overhead cast little more than a watery glow. The mood of the camp was changing now, winding down. Babies cried weakly in their mothers' arms; women whispered and crooned as they rocked children to sleep; and the adults who clustered together by their small open fires murmured quietly—some even broke into laughter and sang plaintive songs that dissipated quickly in the thick night air.

She thought about the people back home on Onewēre

who lived according to the Apostles' Rules. They were not, as Lazarus had thought, foolish or ignorant or, as she herself had once said, weak. Most were merely doing as the people here were: making the best of what they had. They understood they were reliant on the Apostles' goodwill to keep them safe, but within those bounds they tried to build families and communities to ease the burdens in their hearts. It took a special kind of strength to go on caring for each other when life was limiting and tough. It was a kind of strength her father, for all his posturing, did not have.

The only difference between Onewēre and the camp was that the people here already understood that they weren't free. Would she have believed it if someone had told her of the horrors in the Holy City before she'd Crossed? Certainly not. It was only by hearing what had happened to Sarah, Rebecca, Ruth and Mark, and then experiencing it for herself, that her understanding of the world was reshaped. But how would her fellow islanders ever understand the controls and pressures on them to conform, when the Apostles used their power to silence every dissenting voice? They confused the thoughts of those repressed with tirades from the Holy Book, washed down with the anga kerea toddy to dull the servers' minds.

Reluctant but at least a little calmer now, Maryam tried to find the hut she shared with Ruth. Every pathway looked the same, every crossroad a random decision that she hoped was right. The accumulated effects of the day were now taking their toll, and she felt exhausted: her feet dragging and her brain growing ever more confused. Just as she began to think she'd never find her way back, she spotted Ruth standing anxiously beneath the flickering light outside their door.

"Finally! Where have you been?" Ruth scolded like a flustered mother hen before she scooped Maryam up into her arms and squeezed her so tightly Maryam had to push away to relieve the pressure on her arm.

"Sorry," Maryam said. "I needed some time alone to think."

"You saw what they did to Lazarus?"

"I did."

"Don't tell anyone," Ruth whispered, "but Jo and Aanjay helped me smuggle him into our room for the night, so we can tend to him."

"You what?"

"They were worried that his being white might get him into trouble with the other men. They say he won't be missed tonight—the guards have made a move on the men who refused to eat and Aanjay's sure there'll be some kind of trouble, otherwise they'd never have let him out of their sight."

All Maryam could do then was laugh. No matter how much she wanted to shun responsibility, the fates worked against her. Like it or not, it seemed she had an obligation towards Lazarus that no amount of personal antipathy could shake.

"What are you laughing at?" Ruth asked, looking suspicious and slightly hurt.

Maryam wrapped her arm around Ruth's shoulder. "Nothing, Ruthie. Nothing. I'm glad to see you're all right." She steered Ruth towards the door of their hut, and took a deep breath to ready herself for more of Lazarus's scorn.

He was lying on the sleeping mat furthest from the door and appeared to be asleep. He lay at an odd angle, protecting his left side, and in the small amount of light that bled in through the doorway the whole of his face shone black and blue.

"Has anyone checked his ribs?" Maryam whispered.

Ruth shook her head. "Aanjay says there's no point; that the healers here just hand out some weak pain potion, even if someone is about to die. She suggests we soak rags in cold water and lay them on his bruises to bring down the swelling and to make sure any cuts are clean." She raised a hand to her mouth, funnelling her whisper so only Maryam would hear. "I didn't want to do it until you came. The thought of touching him . . ."

"You have some rags?" Maryam's desire to laugh again was almost overpowering, but she knew that Ruth wouldn't understand. It just seemed so typical of her bad luck that now she'd have to bathe the one person she'd tried to escape. If the Lord was trying to rankle her again, he sure had picked the perfect way.

Ruth pointed to a bucket tucked inside the door. "I've got them ready over there. And there are some candles too." Now her face brightened. "You should see the miraculous things Aanjay gave me to light them with." She opened her hand to reveal a tiny box. Inside, miniature pink-tipped fire sticks lay in a neat row. She drew one out, struck it against the side of the box, and a flame flared immediately at the tip of the stick.

"Truly miraculous," Maryam agreed. She took the tiny burning stick from Ruth and examined it closely, dropping it with a little cry as it burned down and scorched her finger. She sucked the skin to dampen the worst of the pain, then shrugged. "All right, we may as well do this now so we can get some sleep."

Together Maryam and Ruth wrung the surplus water from the rags, lit two of the candles and knelt down beside the mat where Lazarus lay. Maryam's hand was trembling as she shook Lazarus's shoulder and called his name.

He startled, rearing up before he realised who had called. The shock fell away from his face and he lay back, staring up at Maryam through puffy eyes. "You returned."

She nodded. "I'm going to put some cool cloths on your bruises and wash out the cut on your cheekbone," she said, her tone as matter-of-fact as she could manage. "If I hurt you, just tell me and I'll stop."

"Don't worry about the pain—it's not so bad." He tried to sound casual but he winced as he straightened out on the mat.

Maryam was thankful for the way the candles' flickering light masked the shaking of her hands as she clumsily unbuttoned his shirt. It was too uncanny: not so long ago she'd stripped off Joseph's shirt with much the same intent. But she'd wanted so dearly to touch Joseph, to run her hands over his soft pale skin; now the very thought of touching Lazarus brought a lump of fear and disgust up into her throat. To make it worse, he never for a moment shifted his gaze away from her face as she bared his chest and leaned in a little to study his wounds.

There was a swollen, angry bruise shaped suspiciously like the tread of a boot on the left side of his chest where it dipped down towards his stomach. His chest was so thin she could see each rib delineated beneath the skin, except where the swelling had thickened it. Very gently, she placed the tips of her fingers to his side, and ran them along the structure of each bone. As she probed the swollen area, Lazarus bit his bottom lip to hold in a groan, but still his eyes never left her face. It unnerved her, this intense scrutiny, and she decided the only way she could continue was to pretend that it was Joseph, not Lazarus, who needed her help. She dropped her gaze, amazed at how similar the two cousins were in build: the same lean frame, the same soft golden wisps of hair . . .

No! To think of him as Joseph would not help. She must focus simply on the task at hand.

She could feel the unbroken lines of bone—a sure sign that, although badly bruised, the ribs remained intact.

"They're fine," she reassured him. "I can't feel anything like a break."

She placed the cool soaked rags over the worst of the bruising in the hope that they would help to bring the swelling down. A drip ran down his stomach, pooling in the indent of his belly-button, and instinctively she wiped it clear. His muscles tensed beneath her hand, and she cursed herself for her thoughtlessness. Heat blazed up her neck.

She wrung out another rag and placed it over one of his eyes to help to reduce the swelling, repeating the procedure with his other eye to free her at last of his disconcerting gaze. Then she turned her attention to the cut on his cheekbone. She looked to Ruth, who sat at her side with the lighted candles. "I wish I knew what to do now. If only we had some matutu leaves, the sap would draw the skin together and seal it tight," she said.

"So long as we clean it," Ruth whispered. "Aanjay says the biggest killer here's infection caused from festered wounds."

Maryam swallowed back nausea as she started to clean out the wound. The gash was long though not deep, but the skin around it had split and Lazarus flinched as she dabbed the open flesh. "Sorry," she muttered. Instinctively, she slowed the pace, working more carefully and gently to avoid causing him additional pain.

Once she'd cleaned the wound as best she could, she took the candle from Ruth and passed it up and down his body to check she'd missed nothing that needed care. His collarbones were caked in dried blood from his face wound, and she gave the candle back to Ruth to rinse the blood away. She could see his pulse running quickly at the base of his throat and, though she did not look at it directly, was conscious of the rise and fall of his flat pale belly as he breathed. Despite the relative warmth of the evening, his skin was ridged with goose bumps and his nipples stood out small and pert upon his chest.

As she began to wipe away the last of the blood from his upper body, she sensed that his skin did not look altogether right. There was the shadow in the creases of his collar bones, discolouration at the base of his neck. She retrieved the candle from Ruth again, and leaned in now to take a closer look.

As the soft yellow light spilled over him, she felt as though a hand had crept around her throat and pressed in tight. *No! It could not be.* This had to be some phantom trick, some tired flashback to Joseph's death.

With shaking hands, she ran her index finger along the purple-stained shadow. The discoloured skin was hot and raised, and she gasped, drawing away so fast she nearly knocked the other candle from Ruth's hand.

"What is it?" Ruth asked.

Maryam was unsure whether she could speak. She pointed to the purple marks and mouthed to Ruth through trembling lips:

"Te Matee Iai."

CHAPTER SIXTEEN

For a long moment Maryam and Ruth simply stared at the telltale marks on Lazarus's skin. The air in the hut seemed to condense suddenly, and all Maryam could hear was the thrumming of blood in her ears.

Lazarus stirred. "Well?" he said, "what have you found?"

Maryam glanced up at Ruth, shaking her head to warn her not to reveal what they had seen. "It's nothing." She faked a laugh. "A big insect that gave us both a fright!"

She returned to rinsing his skin, fumbling as her fingers told their own tale of shock. As quickly as she could now she wiped away the last of the blood and used a fresh cloth to pat him dry.

"I think you should keep the compresses on your eyes a bit longer," she said. "They'll help to bring the swelling down." She shifted on her knees to catch Ruth's attention, and jerked her head towards the door. "You rest now," she told Lazarus. "We'll go away and leave you in peace. Just call us if you need us—we'll be near the door."

"Thanks," he murmured, his voice thick with tiredness.

Maryam led Ruth as far from the doorway as possible, while still making sure she was within hearing distance should Lazarus call.

"It could just *look* like Te Matee Iai," Ruth said, though her tone suggested she knew better than to believe it.

Maryam shook her head. "I've seen too much of it now ever to mistake it. I can't believe he has it too."

"You don't think the Mothers were wrong when they taught us it couldn't be caught from someone else?" Ruth asked.

The thought made Maryam sick to her gut. And scared. She'd held Joseph close to her for hours on end. "I don't know, Ruthie. But right now we have to figure out what to do. Should we tell him what we've seen?"

"What do you think?" Ruth asked.

Maryam knew that even if they didn't tell Lazarus, it wouldn't be long before the symptoms of the plague grew obvious to him as well. But what purpose would it serve to tell him now? Why prolong the agony of knowing? However much she disliked him, she hated that he might think she'd told him out of spite. "I say for now we tell him nothing and wait to see what happens next. Besides, I suppose we could be wrong."

"Maybe," Ruth replied, sounding equally unconvinced. "We could try speaking privately with Aanjay. She might know what's best to do."

"Good idea!" Maryam had become so accustomed to dealing with problems on her own, the thought of seeking adult help— of even having it available—hadn't occurred to her.

She was about to suggest she seek out Aanjay straight away, leaving Ruth to look after Lazarus, when a sudden series of explosions split the night. There was a moment's dreadful hush, then came the sound of a woman screaming, followed by a storm of wailing that built into a high-pitched ululation of grief and rage.

"You stay with Lazarus," Maryam said. "I'll go and see what's happening."

"No!" Ruth grabbed Maryam's arm. "Don't get involved."

Maryam shook her off. "You forget we're trapped in this

camp. What goes on inside here affects us all." She was already making her way towards the central courtyard near the gates. "Whatever you do, keep Lazarus inside."

"But how?"

"I don't know," Maryam shot back. "If you need to, tie him down!"

She knew there was little Ruth could do to stop Lazarus from trying anything, but she had to find out what was going on. Dozens of angry voices had now joined the commotion, and she could hear the distant clattering of metal and wood, and the ferocious barking of dogs. All around her people milled in panic and confusion. As she pushed her way through the crowd she caught sight of Aanjay, who was rocking a sobbing toddler in her arms.

"Go back to your hut, Maryam," Aanjay called. "It is not safe."

"But what's happening? Has there been an accident? Have people been hurt?"

"They are moving on the hunger strikers."

"They're what? What does that mean?"

"It means Zia Kalily has been shot and killed. You should get back to your hut and keep as quiet as possible for now. It will likely take a few days for this to calm—and until that happens, the guards will be on high alert." The child was grizzling in her arms and Aanjay waved Maryam away. "Please, return to your hut now. I'll come and see you when I get the chance."

Someone killed? Maryam watched as Aanjay headed back into the crowd and for a moment she was tempted to follow. But then she remembered Ruth, and how she'd worry if she stayed away for long, especially with Lazarus needing their care.

Yet before she'd even made it halfway back to the hut, Lazarus himself emerged from the crowd like a nightmare ghoul.

"Come on," Maryam pre-empted him, seizing him by the elbow to swivel him around. She raised her chin to deflect any argument, acutely aware of how pale and strained he looked beneath his camouflage of black and blue. She knew that look. It wasn't good. "Aanjay says one of the hunger strikers has been killed."

Lazarus stumbled. "The guards used their guns?"

"I guess." She was distracted by the strong smell of smoke in the air, and an unsettling mass chanting that carried through the night like the agitated call of a strange flock of birds.

The crowd of women around them peeled away at the sight of Lazarus in their midst, and Maryam hurried him on, knowing if any of them objected to his presence he'd be sent back to the men's camp for the night. There was too much tension in the air already to risk further confrontation.

"Hurry up," she hissed, towing him back between the buildings to the relative sanctuary of the hut.

But it took a long time to settle. Ruth was anxious and dissatisfied with Maryam's scant account of what had happened, and kept up a barrage of questions, and it was impossible to ignore the continuing clamour from outside. For at least another hour the entire camp seemed to be in chaos, and it was hopeless even to contemplate sleep. Later still, as Maryam lay tossing on the lumpy mat beside the door, the memory of that unearthly chorus came back to her, the sound so ancient and innate she'd felt her ancestors stirring in her bones.

Even when the moon was well past its midway point sleep still eluded her. Outside there was no movement now, except for the fat brown-winged moths that batted up against the lights above the walkway, easy prey for the dusty little lizards that roamed the walkway's roof. Try as she might, she couldn't wipe the images of Lazarus's plague-pocked skin from her mind; she knew full well that her life would have been forfeited for his if they'd remained in the Holy City. There was no doubt her blood could gift him precious time, and she knew that he would think on this when he finally recognised the symptoms for himself. With Joseph it had been easy—she would have done anything, *anything*, to have saved his life. But Lazarus?

As if her thoughts had brushed with his, he whispered through the gloom, "Maryam? Are you still awake?"

"Yes."

"Are you thinking of Joseph?"

Again she had an uneasy sense that he had tapped into her brain. "I never stop."

"He did love you, you know? Every time he looked at you it was written in his eyes."

His words made her want to cry. How dare it be Lazarus who offered her comfort! Whenever he spoke to her in this way it made her nervous in a manner she couldn't quite explain—she just knew she was always waiting for the trap. But it occurred to her now that perhaps she could prey upon his pensive mood to pick his brain.

"Actually, I've been thinking about Te Matee Iai." She took a deep breath, trying to make the motivation for her words as obscure as a ruffled sea. "I wondered—do you think that being so close to . . . someone . . . when they died of it puts that person at risk as well?" She hated how selfish and uncaring this sounded, knowing he'd assume she was referring to Joseph, but it was the only way she could find out what he knew without giving her real motives away.

She heard him roll over in his bed with a painful grunt, no doubt prompted by his bruised ribs. "No, I'm quite sure that . . . someone . . . would be safe." There was disappointment in his voice, as though he'd exposed her as shallow and undeserving of Joseph's love.

She tried a new tack. "So how does someone get it then?"

"There's definitely some kind of family link, and my mother has this theory that it can sit inside someone from the time they're born, then suddenly emerge if something causes pain or stress."

Family link? Had not her own mother been taken by the plague? The hairs on the back of her neck prickled at the thought. "So Joseph got it because his father had it too?"

"In part. And Uncle Jonah got it from *his* father—my grandfather Moses." He coughed a little, as if his throat were dry. "You know, it was my great-grandfather who figured out about the transfusions and set up the first Judgements to source the blood."

"How did he even know what to try?" Maryam asked, curiosity getting the better of her.

"According to my father, he was the Holy City's physician and he scoured the ship's library until he worked it out—though I gather there were a few disastrous attempts before he got it right."

Maryam shuddered. He could only mean that many Sisters had been sacrificed in the process. "It seems one way or another your family has a lot to answer for."

"I know. I know." Lazarus paused for a moment. "You know my father has it?"

"What?" Maryam sat up. "But he's—"

Lazarus snorted. "Don't say it. You think because he's the Holy Father he's exempt? He's been living off the blood of Sisters for a good twelve years or so by now."

A ball of disgust rose up from Maryam's stomach. She had to swallow hard, pressing her hand over her mouth to hold it in. Was incapable of saying anything.

"Anyway, *my* theory, based on what Mother thinks, is that after Uncle Jonah argued with my father and left the City, he didn't know about Father having Te Matee Iai until about two years ago, when I said something to him on a visit there. He already knew Mother's theory about it being brought on by stress, and blamed their rift for Father's illness . . . Maybe he was so grieved about this, he triggered his own."

She tried to put aside the fact that Lazarus did not know the full story of why his uncle had left the Holy City and focused on the rest of his words. *Did Lazarus now somehow feel responsible for his uncle's death as well?* She was about to sound him out, when he began to speak again.

"Poor Uncle Jonah," he murmured. "To think he built that beautiful boat. I reckon that's why the plague hit Joseph too— because he was so distraught when he found out that Uncle Jonah was going to die."

And that's why it has now hit you? The stress of watching Joseph die was lethal enough for anyone, even without Te Matee Iai. How he must miss Joseph, the only one who ever really noticed him and cared about what he did. Joseph had that unique quality, the ability to make you feel special—a better person than you were.

She peered over at the shadowy outline of Lazarus's bruised

and battered body, and saw the awkward way he hunched against the wall. Outside, beyond the fence, stood guards who'd kill them if they tried to leave or even made a fuss. Was this not enough to trigger stress? The plague? The rash she'd seen on Lazarus's skin made tragic sense. *Surely he has thought this deadly inheritance through to its end?*

"My father said my mother died from it," she confessed. "Do you think it's in me too?"

She saw Lazarus sit straighter and felt his disappointment in her soften now. If he thought her questions sprang from this, then it was good: it would deflect from her real reasons for asking and set off a whole new chain of thought to distract his mind.

"Hold on," he said, rising to his feet and carefully stepping over Ruth until he hovered at the edge of Maryam's mat. He slithered down the wall and crouched there at her feet. For once she didn't feel threatened by his presence, sensing he came close to try to ease her fears. "I wouldn't let it worry you. For one thing, it's much more commonly passed down through men." He snorted softly. "And, anyway, what's the point? Worrying changes nothing—why spend your whole life waiting for the worst?"

"It doesn't scare you?"

Lazarus did not reply immediately. In the silence she heard agitated voices in the distance again, building like the sea when it was driven by wind onto the reef.

"Only the thought of going through what my poor uncle and cousin did," he said at last. "If or when that time comes, I think I'll just kill myself and get it over with as quickly as possible."

If or when . . . Almost as if he knew. How could she tell him now, knowing what he'd do? His blood would be forever on her hands.

All she could think to do was change the subject fast. And keep talking: it was strange how easy it was to chat when she couldn't see him clearly, didn't have to meet his eye. Here was the perfect opportunity to discover more of the Apostles' world and explore the inner workings of Lazarus's mind.

"Tell me," she said. "What do *you* think happens when we die?"

He laughed quietly, yet there was no hint of derision in his tone. "Do you mean do I believe in Heaven and Hell?"

"Maybe. That's what we've been taught."

"Do you?" She could hear the smile in his voice and caught the faint glow of his teeth through the gloom.

"That's not fair! I asked you first!"

"I think Hell is a great way for people like my father to frighten others into doing what he wants." He yawned. "And as for Heaven, I think it's much the same. It's like saying to someone: "Do what I tell you, and you'll be rewarded. Not in this life, though. In this life you have to keep on suffering because it reminds you who's in charge." Whichever way you look at it, my father wins."

Maryam was well past being shocked by anything that Lazarus said, but she would never have imagined she'd hear the Holy Father's son voice the same kind of doubts that swilled inside her own head. "So you don't believe the Holy Book?" she asked.

"Now *that's* a different question." He was quiet for a while. "You know," he finally said, "I haven't really decided yet. I think that once I would have said yes and never doubted it, but after spending the last three years so close to my father, I'm just not sure. All I know is that I despise the way it's used." He cleared his throat. "What about you?"

"It doesn't make sense to me," Maryam answered, feeling all her doubts and disillusionment swell up inside her again. "I mean, if the Lord is really up there watching us all, how can He be letting all these terrible things happen to his flock? Did Joseph sin? No! Or Ruth, who loves Him and would never sin? Does *she* deserve what's happened to her? Or think about the people in this camp: did that man tonight deserve to die for standing up for what was right?"

Ruth's sleepy voice broke in. "You forget that he's a heathen—that he didn't love the Lord."

Maryam startled. "Ruthie! You gave me such a fright! Did we wake you?"

"It's all right." Ruth yawned. "I was only dozing anyway." She rolled over to face them, her voice still thick with sleep. "He clearly tells us it's a sin to worship anyone but Him."

"But what about the children here? Do they deserve to be punished because their parents do not love the same Lord as us? And what of the Territorials? The guards? They love the Lamb and yet they're just as cruel as the Apostles back at home."

"Maryam's right," Lazarus said. "Do you really think—" But he was overcome by a fit of coughing so sudden and intense he doubled over as the spasms rocked through his body.

Ruth reached out for Maryam and jabbed at her, her meaning clear. The final stage of the sickness had already begun. Maryam jumped up from her mat. "I'll fetch you some water," she said as Lazarus gasped between the spasms.

She ran for the taps, aware of the tension in the air as enraged voices ebbed and flowed on the cool night breeze. She filled a cup and ran back to their hut to find Lazarus quiet again on his mat. When she passed the water he rose up on one elbow and to drink it down in one loud gulp.

"Thanks," he rasped. "I don't know what brought that on. All this dust, I guess." He winced as he lowered himself back down. "My ribs don't like that coughing one little bit."

"Try to sleep now," Maryam murmured, guilt at withholding the truth from him stealing her breath. "By the sound of things outside, tomorrow could be another long unsettled day."

She lay down herself now, listening to his breathing until it finally slowed into a more relaxed rhythm. As sleep drew her towards its depths, something Joseph had said to her about Lazarus came back and lingered in the shadowy place before her conscious mind let go. *Give him a chance.* It was as if Joseph was reaching out to her, sending her a message from his watery grave.

She rolled over, staring out the open doorway at the crack of sky visible beyond the walkway's roof. Stars twinkled down from their bed in the heavens, a thousand tiny eyes that seemed to urge her to take up Joseph's plea and act. "All right, all right," she whispered, so tired now she wished for nothing more than the abyss of sleep. Tomorrow she would act on Joseph's words, and seek out Aanjay's help.

* * *

The camp was well astir before Maryam and Ruth were ready to venture outside. The toilet block already reeked with the

morning's ablutions and they had to queue for even the briefest
of cold showers.

As they waited, Ruth chatted with a young girl next in line,
gesturing and laughing as each did their best to understand
the other's words. It seemed the girl and her family had been
detained over three years—half this little one's entire life. What
must that do to someone? Maryam wondered. To grow up here,
thrust together with others, so displaced that memories of your
former life ceased to exist, except in some strange half-dream
that slid away as soon as it was nearly grasped? Was this now
to be her fate as well? Locked up here and left to watch as, one
by one, through plague, infection or other illness—or through
some brutal action of the guards—they all would die?

By the time she and Ruth returned to the hut and made
ready for the day, the atmosphere in the camp had grown as
tense again as the previous night. From what Maryam could
gather through broken exchanges with the women in the next-
door hut, the guards had now decided to punish everyone for the
unrest, and were denying all so-called privileges until they were
brought back into line. No hot water, no hot food. No mixing
of the men with their families. In other words, no freedom and
no aid at all. As a consequence, Lazarus was now trapped inside
their hut, unable to show his face for fear of anger from the
guards or backlash from the women who might turn him in. The
bruises on his face had deepened to indigo, fringed by a rainbow
of dirty yellow, puce and red, and he seemed lethargic—not his
usual acerbic self. He was content to lie on his mat and rely on
news from Maryam or Ruth whenever they ventured out. But
if he worried that his health was failing for any reason other
than the beating, he did not acknowledge it, instead putting

his increasing breathing difficulties down to the dust and his bruised ribs. Meanwhile, Maryam and Ruth kept up a surreptitious watch on the marks of Te Matee Iai. Already his neck was nearly ringed by the ugly purple marks.

Finally, after an unsatisfying snack of cold, day-old rice, Maryam slipped away to find Aanjay and seek her help. It was not as easy as she'd hoped: the little woman so busy trying to calm the situation, Maryam had to wait in line. Distressed mothers fought to control agitated children, and the mood of discontent was all-pervasive.

At last, when the noontime sun was at its most searing, she got her chance to speak with Aanjay, who looked so harassed Maryam felt guilty for taking up her time. She carefully outlined her own understanding of the plague and told Aanjay about Joseph's death. She was amazed at how calmly she spoke of it. It was as if there was a glass wall between her grief and the outside world, making the telling somehow distant and removed.

"Already he's started coughing, and the marks are spreading and deepening—just like they did before Joseph died."

"These marks, do they look as though the blood is leaking and then hardening in dark clots beneath the skin?"

"Yes. And he is growing feverish and lethargic, and I think, though he won't admit it, he's in much pain." She looked into Aanjay's tired eyes. "Does this sound at all familiar? Is it something you know?"

Aanjay nodded her head slowly. "Yes. Here we call it Sumber Kemusnahan."

Maryam's heart missed a beat. "You do? And is there any way to stop people dying from it?"

"Indeed." Aanjay swatted a fly away from her face. "In fact, the cure turned out to be relatively straightforward: they discovered a tonic made from the mahkota bunga tree and the Territorials dispense it in tablets they have called Imatinibiate."

"You've seen it work? Save people's lives?"

"Yes, of course. There are many ills the Territorials can cure if they have the will."

It was unbelievable! A tonic made from leaves? Maryam felt herself teeter between joy and grief. To think that if they'd reached these shores just days before, Joseph might still be alive! The unfairness of it hit her like another of the storm's rogue waves, sucking the air from her, driving stinging tears into her eyes. But the possibility of respite for Lazarus was breathtaking news, too. Was it truly possible there was relief in sight? She skipped from foot to foot, astonished that, for once, the Lord had seen fit to undo some bad with good. What one cousin had not lived to use, the other would now receive. Joseph would be so happy if he knew.

"Can we get Lazarus some?" she asked, her pulse trying to leap right from her throat as she waited for Aanjay to reply.

But now Aanjay shook her head, her mouth drawing down in an unhappy frown. "I wish I could say yes, child. I know the trees grow wild on many of the islands, and that there is plenty of Imatinibiate stored at the hospital in town. But I've never seen it used to save a life in here."

"You mean that even though they have it, they'd not save Lazarus's life?"

"I wish I could give you hope . . . but it is better that you realise now that there is none." She rested her small brown hand on Maryam's cheek for a moment, and the sadness in her eyes leaked out and formed a band of pain around Maryam's heart.

Already others were pressing in and demanding Aanjay's time, pushing Maryam aside as she digested this bitter news. To know that somewhere close by there was a cure for Te Matee Iai yet she did not have the power to access it was almost worse than finding it did not exist at all. How would she and Ruth be able to stomach it, watching Lazarus succumb to the plague when the possibility to ease him was so close at hand?

The rage that had so often fuelled her actions in the past once again began to build. She could not accept this—*would* not accept this—while she still had breath in her to fight. There had to be some way, *someone*, who could help.

Then it came to her, the glimmer of hope that she so desperately sought: the person most likely to help her—the white woman Jo.

CHAPTER SEVENTEEN

t was not as easy as Maryam had hoped to find Jo amidst the turmoil of the camp. The gates between the men's and women's section remained locked and the guards had retreated behind the outer fence as well. They stood warily to attention, guns in hand, refusing to be drawn by the angry accusations of the detainees who lined the fence.

Beyond, their captors seemed in turmoil too: noisy trucks were coming and going up the dusty road and men in uniforms were milling in doorways as Sergeant Littlejohn prowled the grounds, barking orders as he went. Maryam had no doubt he could direct her to Jo, but she dared not draw his attention for fear of provoking him. Instead she scanned along the line of guards, trying to identify the one lone man—the one Jo had called Charlie—who'd seemed more sympathetic to her plight.

At last she saw him emerge from behind the main administration building and begin to direct the transfer of the delayed midday meal while the rest of the guards held the restless, agitated crowd at bay. He was about her father's age, she thought, his hair thinning to a peak above his sunburnt forehead and his washed-out eyes sunken and hooded in their sockets. Maryam pushed through the press of people until she finally arrived at his side.

He was arguing with an imposing detainee who spat on the ground and shouted angrily before stalking away. "Bloody impossible," Charlie muttered, before noticing Maryam waiting patiently at his elbow. "You, girlie, should get back to your hut. This's no place for a lass like you."

"Please," she said. "I must speak to the kind woman, Jo. It's a matter of life or death." She held his gaze, trying to transmit her urgent need.

"Isn't everything here?" His eyes were bloodshot and framed by sun-etched lines. "Anyway, I'm not sure if she's in today. This lock-down's screwed everything over and all our routines have gone down the chute."

It took Maryam a moment to understand what he was saying. "Please," she urged again. "My friend will die unless I speak with Jo—" For a moment the words caught in her throat, though she wasn't sure if it was Lazarus's sickness that choked her or the fact that she had instinctively called him "friend." But she could see that Charlie thought she was about to cry, and decided to play it up lest she lose her one chance of keeping his attention. She thought of Joseph, of how his life had slipped away in her arms, and the tears that were only ever a heartbeat away welled in her eyes. "She's our only hope and time is short."

He briefly patted her shoulder. "Okay. I'll see what I can do. But promise me for now you'll stay clear of this palaver here."

She nodded, though she was uncertain quite what he meant. "I promise. Thank you, Brother Charlie. You are a good man."

A smile flicked across his face, then he was once again caught up by the jostle of the complaining crowd. When at last she found her way back to the hut, her arrival prompted Ruth and Lazarus to cut short their conversation. She looked from one to the other, trying to read from their expressions what they'd been talking about, but it was as if a door had slammed on her.

"Where have you been?" Lazarus asked. He was propped against the wall, cradling his ribs, and the skin not already bruised by his attack was pale and slicked with sweat.

"Just checking what's going on. The gates are still locked between the two sides of the camp, and they've just delivered more cold rice."

"Did you bring some back?" Ruth asked. "I'm starving."

"Sorry. There was such a crush I thought I'd wait." She was hurt that Ruth would speak to Lazarus of something secret behind her back, and her tone was terse.

"I'll help," Ruth said, standing up suddenly and taking hold of Maryam's hand. "Let's go get some now." She did not wait for Maryam to answer, just towed her from the hut, turning to call back to Lazarus as they disappeared: "We won't be long."

As soon as they were clear of the hut, Ruth could contain herself no longer. "He told me he was sorry for what he'd done— that he never would have hurt me when he grabbed me with the knife! Can you believe that?"

Could she? All the usual arguments for not trusting him rose up in Maryam's mind, but somehow they had lost their bite. She thought about what he'd said when he had poured his heart out to her in the cells.

"You know, Ruthie, I think I do." She laughed, not quite sure how this transformation in her feelings for him had come about. But, somehow—between the urgency of his tone, his obvious and genuine love for Joseph, and the fact that he'd apologised to her and Ruth—the bitterness she'd felt towards him had dissolved. It was the act of apology that mattered most: she knew him well enough by now to realise that the word "sorry" came to him hard. The things he'd done in the past were cruel and wrong, but it seemed he now genuinely wanted to atone. The power he'd once held over her—the fear—was gone.

"But that's not all," Ruth burbled on, and she nudged Maryam in the ribs. "I think he likes you!"

"That's ridiculous!"

"He goes on and on about how brave you are. How different you are from any other girl."

"How can you even joke about it?" She didn't want to know this now; *this* she did not need—or believe. "What about Joseph? Am I supposed to forget him just like that?" She snapped her fingers, all her fury channelled into the sound.

"I know it's awful," Ruth said. "And I miss him too. But you've only known him since you Crossed." She shrugged. "It's not like you were married . . ."

Maryam could only stare at her friend open-mouthed. She would never, *ever*, forget Joseph. Just the thought of his memory fading from her mind made her feel panicky and short of breath. He had loved her, protected her from those who meant to do her harm. He'd thought her beautiful. And brave. Had offered up his life for hers. But before she had time to think how to reply she was rescued by the welcome sight of Jo, who was making her way towards them from the direction of the gates.

"You go get us some food and I'll speak to Jo," Maryam snapped at Ruth. She couldn't even look at her.

"Charlie said you wanted me?" Jo said as she approached. "Come on, I've got a minute, so why don't we sit over there in the shade and you can tell me all about it."

Immediately Maryam launched into her tale of Lazarus and Te Matee Iai.

"He doesn't know?" Jo asked.

"Not yet. But already I can see the symptoms worsening. We have little time."

"Well, I can continue to put a case for him to resettle on the mainland—"

"How long would that take?"

"Too long, I fear. I've had no luck for months, and with all the fighting to the north now, the government is even more reluctant to resettle anyone from outside our borders. They see terrorists in every shadow."

"Terrorists?"

"It's a handy label. What they fail to understand is that most of their so-called terrorists—" Jo held up her hands as if to stop herself. "Whoa! Tangent alert!" She laughed. "That's my little hobby horse, sorry. But it doesn't help you or your friend."

Hobby horse? How strange the words these people used. "There's no other way? Can't you just get the medicine he needs—the Imatib—no, Imatinibiate—from the hospital and bring it here?"

Jo didn't speak for several minutes, but sat picking the grime from her fingernails. Finally, she returned her gaze to Maryam. "If they'd let me into the hospital it would be easy enough to find the drug and slip some out, but conditions are so bad at the moment there's no way they'd let me see what's going on. They already view me as a troublemaker . . . Besides, even if I *could* get in, if Littlejohn found out I'd gone against his rules, I'd jeopardise the other work I'm doing here." She paused again, looking off into the distance as though trying to pluck another solution from the air.

It took several minutes for Maryam to process what Jo had said. *So many strangely accented words.* "What if I was to go?" she urged. She waved her grubby plaster cast. "Couldn't I convince them to send me there for my arm?"

Jo shook her head sadly. "No chance. I've seen women dying in childbirth who've been refused. Even those with the same illness as your friend are left untreated in this camp. The hospital is purely for guards and islanders alone." Two bright red slaps of fury painted her cheeks. "The only way a detainee gets access to the hospital is if they've lost the plot. It's too disruptive to the others—too likely to aggravate their discontent. Only then they'll take them to the hospital and dose them full of pills to shut them down, then bring them back."

"Lost the plot? What does this mean?"

"Mental breakdown. It's common here. People have already experienced much trauma in the countries they've fled, and then they find themselves locked up here with little hope of ever getting out. It messes with their brains. Deeply depresses them." She tapped her forehead. "Sends them insane."

Maryam tried to piece together what Jo had said. "You mean there's absolutely no way we can get what Lazarus needs?"

"No. I'm sorry, but the consequences would be too disruptive." She stood up and stretched. "Look, I'll do some asking around, see what I can come up with, but I'm going back to the mainland early tomorrow morning. My father's very ill."

"I'm sorry," Maryam said automatically, any hope she'd had of Jo being able to help them slipping away. "I hope he will recover soon."

"He's a tough old bird," Jo said, brushing off Maryam's sympathy. Then, suddenly, her whole aspect changed. "Oh my god, I can't believe I've been so dense! I've been so caught up in what happened last night and worrying about my father I'm not thinking straight! Of course I can help! I'm sure I can get access to the Imatinibiate you need from the mainland! I'll try to bring some back with me. Why didn't I think of that right away?"

"You can? When will you be back?"

"I'm not sure exactly, but it shouldn't be too long. I'll send a message via Charlie once I know."

"Thank you," Maryam cried, giving Jo a grateful hug. "I knew you'd help!"

"I must go," Jo said. "I'm acting as a mediator between the hunger strikers and the guards. Things are still very tense. I'll see you as soon as I get back. Take care now."

*　　*　　*

Lazarus and Ruth were already eating their rice when she returned to the hut, and she fell upon her portion hungrily, trying to ignore the cold gritty blandness of the food. How she longed for the fresh fruit and fish of home. She studied Lazarus furtively. He was merely toying with the rice, shifting it around the small chipped bowl, but barely eating any at all. His breathing was more strained now and the purple marks were tracking down across his chest. Before long he'd discover their existence for himself and the awful truth would be revealed. Would he thank them for keeping the knowledge from him when he did? She wasn't sure. But to tell him, when he'd spoken so openly of ending his life, was a risk Maryam wasn't ready to take.

She could feel Ruth's anxious gaze on her and nodded slightly to reassure her all was well. It was a strange juggling act, this trying to keep everyone appeased and safe, and she ached for Joseph by her side. What she'd give for just one more hour with him to talk this through. He'd know what to do, she was sure of it.

The stifling afternoon was drawing to its close and light rain had begun to fall when Maryam next ventured outside. They'd spent the long dreary hours talking of the old days, she and Ruth competing to name every Sister on the atoll to fill in the time. Ruth had won, crowing over her victory with the same exaggerated glee as when she'd trounced the Sisters in their running races back at home. Lazarus appeared content to listen, drifting in and out of restless sleep. Some of his lethargy Maryam put down to Te Matee Iai, but it seemed more than this—as if all the fight had gone out of him and the beating had left him shaken to his core.

Now she left the hut to seek the latest news from Aanjay. The drizzle had dispersed the family groups that usually met together in the courtyards, driving everyone under the cover of the walkways or back into their huts. But even with the stench that rose up from the toilets, the air outside was better than the stale confines of their tiny room.

She found Aanjay cross-legged on the floor of her hut, gently teasing out the knots in an old woman's long thin hair.

"Ah, Maryam. Is everything all right?" The fading light emphasised how tired and fragile she looked, her skin as dry and translucent as butterfly wings.

"I came for news." Maryam squatted in the doorway, embarrassed now, not wanting to intrude on the tiny space. "I'm sorry, I will leave you be."

"No need," said Aanjay. "My mother here can neither hear nor see. You won't disturb her."

On the far wall of the hut a makeshift shrine glowed in the

light of two fluttering candles, and Maryam recognised the image of the man they'd seen depicted on the buildings at Marawa Island.

"Who's that?" she asked, inclining her head towards the shrine. "I've seen him before."

"That is the Buddha," Aanjay said.

"He is your god?"

"No, not god. Merely the wise one who showed us how to start the journey towards enlightenment."

Enlightenment? What does she mean? "Then who is your god?"

Aanjay laughed. "No god. Instead, we try to find the godlike qualities in each of us. It is a personal journey, one that takes many, many different lifetimes to achieve." She looked at her mother and smiled. "Only when we release our attachment to desire and to the self can we reach Nirvana. My venerable mother is now very close."

Many lifetimes? "You mean that we come back again after we die?" This she could not comprehend. Was death not final—the destination either Heaven or Hell?

"When the withering leaf falls, a new leaf grows to replace it. It is similar to the old leaf, but not identical. This is the way of all life."

"But how do people know how to act if they have no god to make the rules?"

"We must discover the compassion and love inside ourselves for others, and forget our own desires, then we are truly on the right path." Aanjay gathered up her mother's hair and split it into three thin strands to plait. "But this is not what you came here for. Tell me what you want."

"Just news." She shrugged, her mind still juggling every-thing Aanjay had said. It didn't sound so very heathen . . .

"The hunger strikers have been convinced to eat. Our good friend Jo leaked word of the trouble back on the mainland and Sergeant Littlejohn will do anything to shut the protest down. It is heartening to know that some over there still care about our fate—although I've been here long enough to know that any gains are only temporary."

"So not all Territorials support what's happening at this camp?"

"Most believe what they're told—that we're a threat to their security. But there are some who still speak out."

Try as she might, Maryam could not conjure up a picture of The Confederated Territories in her mind. Was it all one big country or many joined together under the same rule? "What is it like there?"

Aanjay sighed. "Most people still have very hard lives, but there are a few who control the power and wealth and live extremely well. This is why so many are desperate to go there—they're all hoping to escape the tyranny at home and somehow join that select few."

"But it's not right! The Holy Book says the Lord will feed the righteous and thwart the craving of the wicked." The teachings of her childhood welled up in her like a jungle stream after the rains. Was not the Holy Book written in the Lamb's own words?

"Your Holy Book can say whatever it likes, but if there is greed and evil in a man's heart, he will always find the words to justify his acts."

The old woman yawned and murmured to Aanjay, and Maryam sensed she was taking up too much precious time. She thanked them both and ran back through the drizzly evening, their curious conversation still tumbling over in her head. If the goal was this Nirvana, not Heaven or Hell, and lives could be relived, did that mean one day Joseph might be reborn? Every cell in her body wanted it so, yet the concept fought with everything she knew. Only the Lamb had ever been reborn, to prove His rightful place beside the Lord. Surely it was sacrilege to think mere human beings could do the same—however much she wished it to be true?

As she approached the hut she saw Ruth waiting anxiously at the doorway. "What took you so long?" she snapped. "You're needed here."

"Sorry," Maryam puffed. "What's wrong?"

"Lazarus," Ruth hissed through barely moving lips. "He knows."

"How?"

"He sneaked over to the showers for a wash, and saw."

Maryam pushed past her through the doorway, but his sleeping mat was bare. "Where is he?" All her hope dissolved. *What now?* Would he make real his threat to end his life? Her knees buckled and she had to reach out for the wall to brace herself.

"I don't know." Ruth's voice rose to a frightened wail. "He came back and started yelling at me, telling me we're both liars and cheats. I tried to explain why we'd kept it secret and that Jo said she'd help, but he just took off. I started to chase after him, but he threatened to hit me . . . I didn't know what to do, Maryam. I'm so sorry. He looked so hot and sticky and I thought a shower would do him good."

"It's not your fault, Ruthie. He was always going to have to know sooner or later." She pulled Ruth towards her and hugged her tight. "You stay here, in case he returns. I'll go and see if I can find him."

"But what if he's still really mad?" There was real fear in her voice and Maryam realised that, for all Ruth's apparent acceptance of his apology, his violence haunted her still. Words could only heal so much.

"Then scream. The other women here will help." Already she was trying to imagine where Lazarus might have gone. The gates were still locked to the men's side, so at least her search would not have to take her there. She squeezed Ruth one last time for good measure, then released her. "I'll be back soon."

Her first stop was the shower blocks: perhaps he'd returned to the mirrors to check for the signs of Te Matee Iai again. But the place was packed with mothers bathing children before bed, and it was obvious he'd not still be close by.

She searched one walkway after another, weaving in and out of the labyrinth of huts, hoping to catch sight of his blond hair among the mass of people preparing for their night. She startled chickens from their roosts and turned the heads of many puzzled onlookers as she ran from block to block, calling out his name. Finally, as the night was closing in around her and the drizzle transformed the air to mist, she found herself out on the open ground beyond the huts. She skirted the gardens, checking down between the rows. Her lungs burned from the effort of running, and her broken arm throbbed hard within its plaster cast. It was hopeless. He could be anywhere. Could already be planning some means to end his life. As she spun her head from side to side for fear she'd miss him in her panic, she could hear Joseph's voice whispering that same urgent message in her ears: *Give him a chance.*

What more do you want of me? she threw back into the night. *I'm doing everything I can.* But he did not answer, just filled her with a sense of failure and disappointment that seemed to burden her further as she tripped over loose rocks and stumbled in the waning light. Her hair was soaked now, plastered to her head, and despite the heat that still rose up from the ground she shivered uncontrollably as she ran on.

She'd almost reached the very back boundary of the camp, where the looming fence bordered a craggy sea of knife-sharp rocks that fell away steeply to the bay below, when the rain came down in earnest. It stabbed the rocky ground, disturbing the layer of phosphate so it ran in white rivulets at her feet. It was hopeless, the rain so dense it was impossible to see ahead. She could only trust that Lazarus had by now returned to the hut of his own accord. If he was still out in the open, the chill would feed the hungry plague more greedily than ever . . . She found herself crying from frustration and helplessness—at the awful sense of having been through this same ordeal once before. She hadn't been able to save Joseph, and now it seemed she'd fail to save his cousin as well.

Above her, a clap of thunder sucked the air out of the sky, shaking the world by its throat. "Typical!" she screamed to the heavens, the rain pummelling her face and driving into her open mouth. She stamped the ground, making the stinking white sludge splash up around her, and raised her clenched fists at the Lord.

A great bolt of lightning ripped across the sky, blasting the landscape with a flash that brought everything around her into stark relief. There, at the very edge of her vision, something moved. The light was gone before she had a chance to identify it, but she ran towards the phantom movement in one last stubborn surge. The thunder roared at her again, mocking her feeble body as the force of it shook the ground. It was as though her words had called the Lord's wrath down to make His dominance over His wayward creation plain.

She was nearly at the fenceline now, could hear the rain pinging off the wire above her ragged breath. Then, as another fork of lightning flared overhead, she saw Lazarus, scrabbling up the wires of the razor-topped fence. She pitched herself over to him, too tired to call out, and flung herself up at his legs. He yelped, surprised as she took hold of his ankles now, the drag on her arm so painful it felt as if it would snap off at the point of the break. But, though he tried to kick her off, she steadfastly held on.

"Leave me alone," he fumed, his voice competing with the clatter of the rain. He twisted beneath her grasp and she nearly lost him, the shift in position almost breaking her hold. But she refused to let Joseph down; would not allow another life to slip away. She held on to Lazarus for all she was worth, crying out as she swung her weight into action while he struggled to hold his grip on the slippery wire.

In one final desperate surge she tugged as hard as possible, a cry fuelled by pain and fury breaking from her as she fought to bring him down. Then, as the sky lit up again above them, he dropped.

He fell heavily on top of her. Together, they were sent sprawling out across the sodden earth.

CHAPTER EIGHTEEN

The fall winded Lazarus. He rolled away from Maryam, clutching his ribs and gasping to regain his breath. She sat up gingerly and wiped away the mud that caked her face, raising it into the driving rain to rinse the grit from her eyes.

"Get away from me," he snarled between his laboured breaths. He scrambled to his feet, headed straight back to the fence and, once again, prepared to climb.

"Stop it!" Maryam shouted, forcing herself up off the ground. She grabbed at his muddy shirt and held on tight. "I won't let you do this."

"I don't care. Don't you understand?" He reached for her wrists, trying to break her hold on him, and she nearly cried out again as renewed pain shot through her arm.

"Don't you dare give up," she yelled. His shirt was ripping and she couldn't keep her hold on it beneath his brutal grasp.

She let him go, and for a moment they stood face to face, glaring at each other through the sheets of rain. Then he turned his back on her and began to climb again, pushing his bare toes into the footholds formed by the mesh of wires. Once more she threw herself at him, wrapping her good arm around his waist and reaching around with the other to lock her hands together in a stranglehold below his ribs. He writhed within her grasp, trying to dislodge her, and one of his elbows smashed into her nose.

A starburst exploded behind her eyes, and she fell back with a splash into the stinking sludge. Her nose felt as if it had been flattened, and tears welled in her eyes. The whole situation was absurd, futile. Still she heard Joseph's voice inside her head: *Give him a chance.* Why, oh why, did his spirit have to nag her so? He asked too much of her; forgot that she was nothing but a puny runt who had a knack for losing everyone she cared about and infuriating everybody else.

"Go on then," she hurled at Lazarus above the throbbing pain, vaguely aware that he had stopped in his tracks and turned to her as she fell. "Take your life! See if I care!" She staggered up, light-headed, and spat the words at him. "I knew you wouldn't have the courage to see this out."

Lazarus reeled at her taunt, but she pressed on. If he climbed again, she knew she no longer had the strength to pull him back.

"That's right, leave Ruth and me to suffer here all on our own. It's more than obvious you never really cared." Her anger was taking over now. "I never should have believed you when you said you'd changed. All you ever think of is yourself."

"That's not fair," he shrieked back at her. "I'm doing this for you."

How dare he lay this at my feet? "You think this is what I want? You think you understand my mind?"

"I'm going to die. You know it and I know it. Why make you suffer through this too?"

"How will you smashing yourself to pieces on those rocks below make me feel better, Lazarus? You selfish pig. Joseph would despise you for running away when things got rough."

She saw him flinch at her words. They were both shaking violently, chilled to the bone. Lazarus was so pale his face glowed, wraith-like, through the darkness. Maryam realised that if she didn't get him under shelter she may as well leave him to die right where he was. She reached over and took his hand, her own so numb she barely felt his fingers.

"Come on," she said.

Lazarus was strangely compliant as she hauled him back across the muddy ground. Once at the gardens she made for the hut that housed the tools. It was barely standing, but the timber roof would at least hold out the worst of the rain.

Inside it was drier than Maryam expected. Moonlight seeped in through the holes in the walls, illuminating an old blanket hanging by the door. She took it down and told Lazarus to peel off his muddy shirt. He didn't even try to fight her, just stood there with a blank expression as she wrapped the blanket around his shoulders and began to rub him down.

The friction revived him a little. "N-now you," he stammered, holding the damp blanket out to her. She took it from him, and he squatted down against the wall, dropping his head into his hands.

She draped the blanket around her, and carefully removed her sodden shirt. Wrung out the fabric then wrestled the shirt back on over her clammy skin. She felt colder than ever, but she didn't want to keep the blanket any longer when Lazarus had greater need of its warmth. She dropped it back over his shoulders and squatted down beside him. "I'm sorry for what I said."

Lazarus didn't respond, so she tried again.

"I didn't mean any of it. I just wanted you to stop."

"But what's the point?" he mumbled through his hands.

"Ruth told you. Jo can get you something that will make you well. I spoke with her today."

Slowly he raised his head. "Why didn't you tell me the marks were there?"

She swallowed hard. This was the question she had dreaded all day. "I didn't know what to do. I went and talked to Aanjay, and that's when she told me there's a cure." She shook him by the shoulder. "Do you hear me? There *is* a cure!"

He coughed, struggling to catch his breath. "You think if it's so simple my mother wouldn't know?"

It was a fair question and she took a moment to think it through. "Surely if she'd known she would have used it to cure your father?"

"No one survives Te Matee Iai. That's the truth."

"How can you say that? There's so much we didn't know about back home. Did you ever think you'd see a boat that moves without the need for sails? A truck? Aanjay says she's seen people cured of the plague."

He glanced over at her. "Totally cured?"

"So she says. I have no reason to doubt her. Why would she lie?"

The tiny spark of interest she'd ignited in him petered back out. "All people lie," he said flatly.

"I've never lied to you." As soon as she said this, she tried to reach back in her mind and reassure herself that it was true. Had she? She wasn't so sure. "But I *am* sorry I got angry back there—I was scared." She was so cold now she could hardly speak. Her teeth chattered each time she closed her mouth.

"Here," he said, and he held the blanket open so she could share its warmth.

She moved in closer to him, too cold to worry about how near he was, and gratefully wrapped the blanket around her shoulders. Heat was radiating off his body, no doubt caused by fever, but it helped to warm her all the same. "Thanks."

"Look," Lazarus said, "I'm sorry I scared you and yelled at Ruth, but my anger wasn't really meant for her. It's just—even though I half suspected it—seeing the proof in the mirror took me by surprise."

"You suspected it?"

He nodded. "To be honest I've felt run down for ages."

"How long?" To think he'd kept his fears about his own health locked inside while Joseph died.

He sniffed, and she could tell by the way he swallowed so compulsively that he was fighting back a cough.

"I don't remember now for sure, but it was around the time we first learnt Uncle Jonah had it too." He moved towards her slightly, until his shoulder pressed against her own and she could feel how he shivered still. "I had a big fight with Mother. Couldn't believe she'd refused to help. I told her it was wrong to let my uncle die, even if he had turned down her help before."

"What did she say?"

"She slapped my face. Told me it was time I grew up; that Father had worked hard to leave his son in a better position than the one he had inherited from his. She said something ridiculous, along the lines that I should be grateful Father had let Uncle Jonah live as long as that, given he'd defied him—"

"It's true." The words flew from her lips before she had time to stop them.

"What do you mean? What's true?"

"Your father. He threatened your uncle with death if he did not leave the Holy City and stay away." She could feel the shock rippling off him like heat. "It *is* true. Joseph told me at Marawa Island."

Lazarus slammed his fist against his forehead, as though

trying to lodge this new revelation in his brain. "Of course. Why did I listen to his lies? That all makes sordid sense." He shuddered, whether from disgust or cold she couldn't tell. "Lord, I hate him."

For several minutes he just sat in silence, fuming over what she'd said. Then he snorted, the sound filled with bitter self-contempt. "You know what I couldn't stomach in the end? My mother harping on about how I had the potential to be just like him and how I should be proud of what my father had achieved."

"I guess she *is* his wife . . ."

"She truly thinks he's a living god. She does, honestly. I swear on the Holy Book, she said it to my face. It wouldn't have been so bad if she'd just been saying it for show, but she believed it, Maryam. She bought the lot. When I realised this for sure, I knew I had to get away from them or else I'd end up crazy too . . . and then I found out you and Joseph had access to a boat." He rushed the last part of the sentence, anticipating another prolonged fit of coughing.

When the spasm had died down Maryam pressed on, determined that nothing more would stand between them from this time on. "So why did you continue to be so cruel yourself?"

He groaned deep inside his throat. "I *told* you. I was furious with everyone." He shrugged, and a damp blast of air slipped in under the blanket. "Besides, I knew the power my father could exert over people who criticised him or crossed his path . . ." His voice dwindled away to nothing and when he continued it was little more than a whisper. "If what you say is true, then Uncle Jonah wasn't alone in fearing for his life . . . to be honest, I was scared to death of what would happen if I didn't toe the line." He sniffed again. "Pathetic, I know, and, honestly, I see now that it's no excuse."

For the first time Maryam *could* at least partly excuse him. If Joseph and his family were so intimidated by Father Joshua's threat that Joseph could not reveal it until safely away from Onewēre, then Lazarus was right to fear the man as well. Father or not, he was not someone to challenge. She did not even want to think about what it must have meant to try to please him. He and his cold-hearted wife really were insane.

All of a sudden Lazarus began to cry. He buried his face in his hands as huge shuddering sobs consumed him. She did the only thing she could, wrapping her arm around him to help disperse his pain. But the crying made his coughing worse, and she could feel the bones of his back straining as his lungs worked overtime to dredge in air.

Outside, the storm had done its worst; the rain was easing as the thunder and lightning moved away. Maryam felt stiff from squatting so awkwardly but for a long time dared not move. He needed to let this out. Only when Lazarus's sobbing had slowed did she drop her arm from his shoulder.

"Come on," she said. "Let's go back to the hut and get you properly dry. Ruth will be frantic by now."

She leaned forward to give herself enough momentum to stand, and as she did so he turned and kissed her quickly on the cheek. "You're quite a girl," he said. "It's no wonder my cousin loved you so."

She blushed, feeling the rising tide of heat sweep over her neck and face, and tried to make light of it, though she could still feel the place his lips branded her cheek. "He probably wouldn't if he saw me now. I must look a real sight!"

"You and me both."

Relieved to hear him rallying, Maryam helped him to his feet. Together they trudged back through the water-logged camp, three times forced to stop as Lazarus was wracked by coughs. Finally they reached the hut to find a very agitated Ruth.

"Praise the Lord!" she cried, rushing forward to meet them. "I was worried you'd be struck by lightning."

"Close," Maryam muttered, automatically fingering her nose. It was not broken, she was sure of that, but it felt tender and swollen all the same. "Do you think you could find something to help get us dry?"

As Ruth scurried off Maryam sank gratefully onto the doorstep. She glanced over at Lazarus, who crouched in a growing puddle against the wall, able to see him properly now beneath the walkway lights. He looked a wreck: his eyes puffy and red from crying and his rash raised and purple on his neck. Yet, beneath the coating of mud and bruises, he was deathly pale. She thought instantly of Joseph. The fact he'd been drenched by rain after the climb down the mountain at Marawa, and later by the storm at sea, had undoubtedly hastened his end. It would surely be the same for Lazarus, unless Jo came back quickly with the cure.

Ruth returned with two thin moth-eaten blankets and two strips of cloth the women in the camp called sarongs. She had also conjured up another bowl of rice and, as soon as they were dried and changed, Maryam tucked into it ravenously while trying to coax Lazarus to eat as well. But he took only two or three mouthfuls before he sank onto a sleeping mat and wound the damp blanket tightly around himself for extra warmth. Within a matter of minutes he fell into a fitful doze.

Now Maryam was able to tell Ruth what had happened. "You mean he was scared of his own father?" Ruth said at last.

"Wouldn't you be?" The words were out before Maryam had thought through their impact, and she chided herself when she saw the way Ruth's face instantly paled. Of course she'd be scared. Hadn't she already fallen prey to Father Joshua? How could she be so stupid as to say such a thing?

As she watched Ruth's quivering chin, it suddenly struck her that she should stop assuming Ruth was blocking out her trauma through some misguided faithfulness to the Lord. Rather, she should admire Ruth's brave attempts to put what had happened from her mind—especially when Maryam herself struggled to push down her fears and keep self-pity at bay. *And* Ruth was two years younger. It made her feel ashamed. "I'm sorry, Ruthie, you've always had the courage of King David in the Holy Book. I wish that I was half as brave."

She saw Ruth's eyes swill with tears, even as her cheeks darkened with a flattered glow. "I try." She glanced over at Lazarus. "Do you really think we can save him?"

"Just pray that Jo can find the medicine he needs and comes back soon." She yawned. "I think I should try to get some sleep. It's been quite a day."

She pulled her mat over next to Ruth's and snuggled down beside her. Closed her eyes and tried to pretend they were still on the atoll in their own pandanus-thatched hut, and everything that had happened since then was a dreadful dream. She fingered the small blue stone Ruth had given her, now her only tactile link to home, drawing comfort from the warmth it seemed to store deep in its dark crystalline core. Somewhere in her mind she could still hear the soft, hypnotic whisper of the sea upon the reef, and matched it to her breathing, willing the sweet relief of sleep to take hold and temporarily set her free.

* * *

When a nearby rooster marked the arrival of the dawn, Maryam gave up trying to chase elusive sleep. The night had not been good: Lazarus had tossed and turned and coughed. Sweat pasted his fine hair against his skull, and his wheeze was rattly, his breathing way too shallow and fast.

Now he lay lethargically and made no effort to move or speak. When their neighbour came to the door to tell them that the hot water was to be restored and the cooked meals resumed, he barely reacted. It was like watching Joseph die all over again. *If only Jo would send word.* Maryam was furious with herself for not having asked how long it took to reach the mainland or when she could expect to hear; she'd been too caught up in the excitement to think ahead. Now these questions loomed large and serious, and there was no one to answer them. By lunchtime, as she and Ruth queued with the others for their food, Maryam was so jittery and anxious she could hardly breathe herself. It was as if Joseph and Lazarus had merged to one inside her mind. Not even the surprisingly tasty chicken soup could distract her, and her hands shook so badly as she helped spoon some into Lazarus's mouth Ruth had to take over the job.

Half an hour later and the effort of feeding him seemed all the more futile when Lazarus coughed so violently he brought the soup back up. The vomit sprayed across his chest, soaking the blanket and leaving him so exhausted he felt like a dead weight as they rolled him to clean up the mess.

Later, as Maryam leaned against the doorway while waiting for Ruth to return from the showers, she noticed the guard, Charlie, rounding the corner. She ran to him, deliberately diverting him away from their hut.

"You've heard from Jo?"

Charlie did not return her smile. "I'm sorry, love, the news is bad." He paused. "She said to tell you Littlejohn's used her father's illness as an excuse to shut her out. He won't allow her to come back." He placed a gentle hand on her shoulder. "It gets worse."

"Worse?"

"He's sussed that Jo leaked news of the protests and he's spewing. Says she and her kind are putting dangerous ideas into the minds of the detainees." He kept up the steady pressure on her shoulder. "No aid workers will be allowed back into the camp until he gives further notice. It could be weeks. That bastard's word is law."

Weeks? This could not be. If she did not get the cure for Lazarus, he would die. A howl broke from her as she shook off Charlie's restraining hand. She'd promised Lazarus a cure, held it up as bait so he wouldn't end his life. And now he'd think she'd lied. This was too much. *Too much.*

"It's only a few weeks," Charlie tried to comfort her. "You can bet your butt she'll be fighting his decision with every card she's got."

"You don't understand." There was nothing more to say to him. She had to get away from his uncomprehending gaze.

She started to run, pushing past a dawdling group of women as she made for open ground. Her feelings were too enormous to be contained within the confines of the huts—she needed space around her now so she could think. She thundered down the walkways until she reached the very spot where just the previous night she'd fought Lazarus to save his life. But that counted for nothing now. She had failed.

A great ball of grief churned around inside her and she sicked it up, retching painfully until there was nothing left to purge. She leaned against the wire mesh and tried to think. *Had* to think. *Come on, come on.* Lazarus was lying in their hut on the brink of death and now it fell to her alone to come up with a plan to save his life. She couldn't bear to let Joseph down— would be haunted by it forever if she failed.

It seemed cruelly unfair that the miraculous cure lay so close at hand. If only she could get into the hospital and find it for herself. There *had* to be a way. *Come on, what was it Jo had said?* That only those who lost their minds were taken there . . . ? That you had to be crazy? Then that was it! It wasn't as if she'd even have to feign madness, for surely she would lose her mind if Lazarus died.

Little by little her breathing slowed as she pieced together a scrappy plan. She'd have to convince them she needed to be drugged, otherwise all she'd achieve was being thrown back into the cells. Just, what, exactly, would she need to do? Something so radical that even those who knew her would doubt she was in her right mind.

She started back, step by step planning what must be done. It was her only hope—Lazarus's only hope. By the time she reached the doorway of the hut she'd come to a place of frightening clarity and calm inside herself. She knelt down beside the feverish Lazarus and gently shook him, sorry to wake him but never more sure of what she was about to say.

He rolled over and opened his eyes, and a welcoming smile lifted his lips. This nearly destroyed her, the way he looked at her with such trust; it took the very last of her strength not to cry as she brushed his sticky hair out of his eyes.

"Listen to me carefully," she said. "I have to go somewhere for a while, but I will return with what you need. You have to trust me—whatever you might hear. Promise me you won't give up."

"I—"

"Promise me—on Joseph's memory—you will *not* give up until I can return."

He dragged himself onto one elbow, trying to read her face. "What's going on?"

"*Promise me.*"

"I promise, in the memory of my cousin, I'll do my best. Now tell me what's going on." The effort to stay upright was too much for him. He dropped back on the sleeping mat with a sickening grunt.

"I'll bring you back the cure. That's all you need to know." She leaned over and briefly pecked him on the forehead, guilty and saddened by the way his eyes lit up at the touch of her lips. Now she rose. "Wait for me. I *will* be back." When she reached the door she turned to find he was still watching her, his face flushed with pink. "Tell Ruth I'm sorry, and to hold on to her faith." She ran from the hut now, before her resolve withered and failed.

"Maryam!" Lazarus cried out after her, but she dared not stop.

She skirted around the main courtyard, taking just a moment to stop and observe Ruth, surrounded by a laughing group of children and their mothers as she neatly traced out simple words in the stinking white dust at her feet. *Such a heart*, Maryam thought. She hoped Ruth would not believe what she would hear.

At the main gates a group of men prowled the boundary fence and, out beyond, bored guards patrolled the grounds. She had expected this, but now that she was here her plan seemed suddenly ridiculous. Would her nerve—her desperation— hold? She thought about how she'd been stripped bare before the congregation of *Star of the Sea* when first she'd Crossed. How innocent she'd been. How totally humiliated. But she had survived it, and would survive this too. She *had* to, if the promise she'd just forced from Lazarus had any worth.

She ran up to the locked gates and started to scream. "Never," she cried. "It was the source, the end, the morning and the night . . ." On and on, jumbling her words, making sure they made no sense while fervently hoping this was what a person did when they went mad. As she shrieked she clawed at her clothes and hair so that strands of it tangled in her fingers and came away in her hands. It was oddly exhilarating—releasing all her pent-up grief and shame.

Item by item she stripped off her clothes—her mind fixed on her goal, not daring to focus on her actions—until she writhed virtually naked before the whistling, jeering detainees. The guards were running nervously towards her now. And still she ranted, rolling her eyes and spitting as though possessed.

As the guards scrabbled for the keys to the gate, and the crowd of men beyond the fence grew ever bigger and more vocal, she threw herself onto the ground and thrashed there like a stranded fish. Two minutes more and the guards were upon her, hauling her back to her feet while trying to press her clothing back around her. They grappled her around the neck, forcing her hands behind her back, but still she kept up an attack that only the insane would fight. When, finally, they dragged her through the open gates, she felt a ball of triumph bursting in her heart. The first small step! And she laughed right in their faces as they bundled her, bound and semi-naked, into a truck.

CHAPTER NINETEEN

It took all Maryam's determination not to cower as they slapped metal restraints around her wrists and locked her arms behind her back. The pressure on her broken arm was excruciating, and however much she twisted and contorted, she couldn't ease the strain. It was hard to know which was worse—the pain from her arm or the humiliation of sitting naked, apart from underpants, in front of two antagonistic white guards. For a moment she was frozen by fear—but then she glimpsed the disgust in the men's eyes—the trigger she needed to renew her act. She'd not let them see past her madness to the skin beneath.

"Beware of false prophets, which come to you in sheep's clothing, but inwardly they are ravening wolves . . ." She so surprised herself with these words she chortled aloud, thinking of Father Joshua and his brainwashed Apostles. Then her mind flitted to another verse: *". . . and above all, love each other deeply, because love covers over a multitude of sins."* Joseph now sprang to her thoughts and she had to push his memory away. Thinking of him made her feel too vulnerable. She wracked her brain for more quotes, astounded by the aptness of the words her memory threw up. It was as if her mind had split in two: one side maintained this insane ruse while the other had never been so lucid or still. She kept the barrage of words flowing, hurling out the next quotation as if she were the Lord Himself.

"I will deal with them according to their conduct, and by their own standards I will judge them . . ." Again her rational mind chipped in: *If only that were really true.*

On and on she raved, allowing spit to gather at the corners of her mouth and fly out to fleck her skin. But there was no response from her captors now. The guards said nothing as the truck bumped down the winding road towards—she hoped—the hospital. She rocked her head backwards and forwards until her hair unravelled and fell across her face to form a camouflaging veil. To her surprise both guards looked pale, as if they were uncomfortable with what she was venting. *And so they should be.* Again she allowed her maniacal laughter to overflow—and revelled in the sense of power such lack of inhibition brought. She could say anything, *do* anything, and not be held responsible for it, other than earning the label "mad." It was a heady feeling, and she milked it for all it was worth.

At last the truck appeared to slow. It turned sharply now before stopping altogether. The guards waited for the driver to unlock the rear doors, then pushed her out ahead of them. Her hands were still cuffed behind her back, so she stumbled, trying to get her balance, and fell awkwardly to the ground. Shockwaves coursed through her broken arm.

As they hauled her roughly to her feet, she saw ahead of her a dilapidated huddle of buildings bleached silver by the sun. They marched her up a flight of steps, in through guarded doors, and past a group of uniformed women who eyed her nakedness with bored contempt. Exhausted by her efforts and smarting from her fall, she didn't speak now, just writhed beneath her captive's grip and rolled her head rhythmically from side to side to maintain her ruse.

The guards led her down the long dingy corridor that linked all the shabby buildings into one. Finally, they stopped before a set of reinforced locked doors and knocked loudly. Two men in grimy white coats peered out through the bars. They were not white-skinned as she'd expected, their faces sun-kissed like her own, yet their eyes appeared disinterested, almost dead.

"Another for the loony bin," one of her guards muttered. He thrust her forward, and retreated quickly as one of the white-coated men reached for her and dragged her across the threshold, locking the door behind him with a resounding bang.

She felt so foolish, so defeated: it hadn't occurred to her she'd be locked in. How could she find the cure if she wasn't free to search? None of this was going to plan—for immediately the two new guards grabbed an elbow each, hauled her down another corridor towards a row of doors, and flung her into a small room.

They pushed her onto the solitary bed, and came at her. She backed against the wall, trying to shield herself as a blinding white panic consumed her mind. As they threw her face down on the bed, she fought back nausea . . . but all they did was release the restraints around her wrists.

"What's your name?" one of them shouted, perhaps believing her to be deaf. She merely hung her head and growled, shaky with relief.

"Another Jane Doe, eh?"

"Or Jane Doggy," the other added, sniggering. "At least this one is easy on the eye." His hand whipped out and tweaked her breast. Instantly she parried his arm away with her plaster cast, the smack resounding in the room. "Crazy little bitch," he hissed, and cuffed her ear.

She recoiled, fleeing the bed and backing herself into a corner where she curled into a ball. With her arms wrapped tightly around her calves, she tucked her throbbing head down on her knees, her hair forming a wiry shield. *You can do this*, she told herself. *Focus on the reason you are here.*

The trouble was, she hadn't planned it through this far, and was uncertain now if she should sustain the act. Here, inside the hospital, if she was to pretend insanity—even for a short while—she'd have to up her game. Yet if she acted *too* crazy they'd drug her so she couldn't think. Why, oh why, hadn't she waited just a little longer to think it properly through?

The two men exchanged words in a language she didn't understand, laughing as they locked the door and left. She could hear footsteps in the corridor outside and tensed up every time they passed her door, but it seemed an age before the key again turned in the lock. She prepared herself, ready to revert to her demented role.

A fat middle-aged native woman entered the room and carefully shut the door behind her. She carried a metal bowl in which something clattered, and a pile of folded clothes.

"So, missy," she said, not without sympathy, "do you know who you are and why you're here?"

Maryam thought it best not to respond. Instead, she kept her face masked by her long swathe of hair, winding her fingers through it to form tangly knots.

"Okay, sweetheart. I'll take it that's a no." She squatted down next to Maryam, grunting at the discomfort. "Come on, now. Let's get you dressed."

Maryam allowed the woman to ease her up and lead her back over to the bed, reassured by her kind words and gentle hands. The woman picked up a folded garment from the pile and shook it out. It was made from thick grey fabric, with overly long sleeves and straps, and she draped it casually across her arm.

"That's it, love. We'll have you right in no time now." Her tone was soothing and her movements so calm that Maryam decided not to struggle as she gently worked one of the sleeves over the grimy cast.

Maryam couldn't figure out the purpose of the garment—the sleeves hung way down past her fingers and the straps dangled almost to the ground. By now the woman had fastened it at her back, and was taking each sleeve and crossing it over Maryam's chest. Before Maryam could comprehend what was happening, the woman spun her around, tightly tying up the sleeves behind.

No! She saw now what this garment was—some kind of restraining jacket that bound her arms. She started to resist, trying to free her arms, but the woman just pulled tighter and the jacket pinned her arms awkwardly against her body and wouldn't budge. Her plaster cast pressed hard up against her breasts, while the unnatural angle strained all the muscles in her shoulders and upper arms.

"Let me out of this!" she cried as the woman deftly tied the straps in place behind her back.

"It's for your own good," the woman snapped. Maryam thrashed and kicked out at her. "Calm down or I'll call in the men." She pressed Maryam down firmly onto the bed. "Sit there and don't move a muscle, or this is going to hurt you more."

She reached for the metal bowl, and Maryam's eyes widened in panic as she caught sight of the hypodermic needle the woman held in her other hand. Memories of Mother Lilith and her tortuous bloodletting flooded her mind, and her heart raced so fast she feared she'd sick it up.

"Don't steal my blood," she begged. She leapt up from the bed and threw herself back into the corner.

"No one's going to steal your blood, honey," the woman laughed. She held up the syringe and pressed its end, causing a tiny stream of clear liquid to spurt from the needle's tip.

In one long stride she stood at Maryam's side, her bulk blocking her only route to escape. Then she jabbed the needle into Maryam's thigh and pushed down the plunger. Maryam felt a burning pain as she watched the liquid disappear into her leg. It was more than she could stand.

"I'm sorry," she sobbed. "I was just pretending to be mad." She tried to catch the woman's gaze, to convince her she was telling the truth.

Again the woman laughed. "That's what they all say, love." She pulled the needle out and briskly rubbed the site, then patted Maryam on the cheek. "There, you see. That wasn't so bad now, was it? And soon you'll be in happy land. What's wrong with that?"

"You don't understand—"

"Of course I don't," the woman responded in a sing-song voice. "I don't understand. You don't understand. No one here understands a jolly thing!" She dropped the syringe back in the bowl with a decisive clang. Then she ran her hands down her white skirt and turned back to Maryam with a beaming smile. "Come, lie down now, honey. Trust me, in another ten minutes you won't be able to feel your feet."

She began to sing then. *"Father of Heaven, Whose love profound, A ransom for our souls hath found . . ."* She walked to the door, unlocked it and left, though for some seconds afterwards Maryam could hear her voice trailing off down the corridor.

Already Maryam felt woozy, much as she had after drinking the anga kerea toddy when she Crossed. Her brain grew foggy, her limbs ever heavier; with some difficulty she got up from the floor and staggered over to the bed. It was impossible to get comfortable with her arms crossed and bound in front of her, and the ties bunched and pressed behind. The site of her broken arm burned as if an ember had been slipped inside the cast, stealing what little capacity she had left to think. But she had to make a plan, figure out something—something about what to do next. An urgent . . . thing . . . this thing . . . what thing? . . . she had to, had to . . . had to do.

"To do, todo, to dododo . . ." she sang, smiling at the sound, lulling her, spinning around inside her head as her eyelids drifted down.

* * *

It was dark, and she couldn't move her arms. They were stuck to her somehow, and she didn't have the strength to peel them off. And they hurt. Hurt so badly she felt the pain as a pulsing heat. She couldn't hear the distant sea or ebb and flow of Ruth's calming breath beside her. *Where am I?* Her head felt heavy, and when she tried to turn it she felt dizzy and sick. *What is going on?* Somewhere, somebody was calling out in a desperate voice, but she couldn't catch the meaning, just the anguish in the cry. Her mouth was dry and she ran her tongue over her teeth to free them from her lips, shocked to feel her tongue so thick and ridged.

Nothing made sense. It was as if she'd been left for dead, buried alive. Thoughts of worms and the shiny blue beetles that devoured the decomposing birds amidst the leaf litter of the jungle came to her mind and were made real. *Lord in*

Heaven, what is going on? She tried to twist away from the creatures, feeling how they crawled across her naked skin, terrified they were going to eat her whole. She screamed, sure she could smell the fetid stench of death. Her legs were twitching uncontrollably, her heart pounding so hard she felt it bursting out between her ribs. The night creatures were gnawing at her broken arm now, burrowing beneath the cast and tearing all her flesh straight from her bones. Sweat poured off her in cold running streams, yet still those harbingers of decay nipped on and on at her and no one came to heed her calls.

At last they overwhelmed her and she gave in to her fate, moaning only slightly now as she felt the hungry little creatures crawl up towards her mouth and nose and start to feed . . .

*   *   *

It was light when next she woke. She stared up at the fly-specked ceiling, running her tongue over her lips. They felt dry and cracked and tasted of blood, as if she'd chewed them in the night, and her broken arm was throbbing mercilessly within its restrictive shell.

The terrors of the night came back to her, and she wriggled up against the wall until she could properly see her legs. They were covered with bloody scratch-marks, and her stomach lurched at the terrifying memory of the marauding beetles and the worms. But then she saw the blood that caked her ragged toenails, and it dawned on her she might well have done this damage to herself.

Everything came back to her now: the guards . . . the truck . . . the needle in her skin . . . her stupid plan. What had she been thinking? She was worse off than ever now and of no use to Lazarus whatsoever. Was he even still alive? She tried to push this new fear from her mind. Her predicament was bad enough already without the added possibility that all her terror and humiliation had been for nothing. Footsteps thudded in the hall outside, and she could hear voices and the opening and shutting of doors. She had to think quickly, figure out how to extricate herself from this mess. And most urgent of all, she had to find a way to stay in the hospital without remaining trussed up like a chicken ready for the pot. But now the key scraped in the lock and the same fat woman who had drugged her appeared again.

"Morning, cherub!" she said. "How did you sleep?"

Maryam studied her closely for a moment, sizing her up.

"Much better," she croaked. Her voice was hoarse from screaming. "Thank you for your help." She smiled, hoping the woman would see by her demeanour how truly sane she was. "Who are you?"

"Veramina," the woman replied. She checked the bucket by the door and picked it up. "I'll be back in a minute with a clean one and then we'll fix you up with breakfast. I bet you're hungry, eh?"

Maryam nodded, trying to look enthused. "Yes," she said, although the aching in her arm blocked all desire for food.

As she waited for Veramina to return, she tried again to think through some conceivable course of action. First she must convince them to release her from this foul restraint—but not appear too well or they would send her straight back to the camp. It was hard to focus when her head felt thick and heavy and the pressure on her broken arm was this intense. If only it would settle so she could plan. Would the cursed thing never heal? Self-pity threatened to overwhelm her but she pulled herself back from it. Until she heard for sure that Lazarus was dead, she would not give up.

Veramina finally came back, carrying a faded dress and a bowl of runny scrambled eggs. She placed the food down on the floor next to Maryam's bed and studied her with a practised eye. "If I take off that strait-jacket so you can eat and have a wash, you're not going to do anything silly now, are you, dear?"

"No," Maryam assured her, trying not to show the breadth of her relief. Step One. Now she had to convince Veramina not to tie her back into that dreadful thing once she had washed.

She stood and waited patiently for Veramina to untie the straps. As the pressure came off, her arm dropped to her side and she moaned in pain at the sudden movement.

"What's wrong?" Veramina asked.

"My broken arm," she said. "They put it in this cast, but it hurts so much it drives me mad."

"But child, that doesn't sound right. Usually with a plaster cast—"

With a flash of pure inspiration Maryam interrupted her. "In fact, that's what got me here. It's been unbearable, and yesterday I couldn't stand it any longer—I just snapped."

"Pain, you say?" A deep frown formed between Veramina's eyes. "Before they set it, did they x-ray it?"

"X-ray?" Maryam shook her head, genuinely confused. "All they did was cover it in this hard plaster. They didn't even set the break." This was true. She'd seen how Mother Evodia treated breaks, sometimes having to force the bones back into place. She'd dared not question the ship's doctor when he'd merely slopped the white plaster over top of the break and ordered her to hold it still until it set. Besides, what had she cared? Joseph was dead.

Veramina's frown transformed into a snarl. "They're animals. They really are." She shook her head and sighed before flashing a quick smile. "Now, child, we can't have you wandering around naked. Let's get you into some clothes." She held up the shabby floral shift. "It may not be the latest fashion, love, but it'll keep you decent enough for now. And pop these clean underpants on too."

She busied herself folding up the strait-jacket, allowing Maryam a little privacy as she dressed. When she was done, Maryam perched on the bed to eat. The eggs tasted watery and stale, nothing like the fresh ones she'd collected at home, but she forced them down, hoping the food might settle her stomach and help to clear her head.

Veramina bustled from the room, telling her she'd return as soon as she'd spoken with the doctors down the hall. All Maryam could do was hope this would somehow play into her hands—anything that kept her free of the restraint and of whatever they'd injected into her thigh last night must be useful to her plan.

When Veramina returned, she presented Maryam with four small objects she called pills and instructed her to swallow them.

"What are they for?" Maryam asked.

"The two white ones," Veramina said, "are paracetamol. They'll help ease the pain in your arm. The little blue ones will keep you calm—the same drug as I used last night. It obviously suits you, given how much better you are today." She crossed her arms across her ample bosom and waited for Maryam to swallow them down.

"Do I chew them?" she asked, stalling, trying to decide what on earth to do.

"Heavens no! Just swallow them whole."

Maryam tried the white ones first, having no gripe with wanting to relieve her pain. They were harder to swallow than she'd imagined; she gagged on the first and needed to drink nearly all the remaining water to wash the other one down. Now she was faced with the two little blue pills. She placed them both together on her tongue, surprised to find they tasted sweet. She raised the glass, surreptitiously spat the pills down the side of her plaster cast and swigged the rest of the water.

Oblivious, the woman patted her shoulder. "Good girl. Now we'll get you freshened up and then I'll get Henry to take you down to check that arm."

She'd got away with it! She could feel the sticky pills inside the cast. All she had to do now was make sure they didn't fall out when she lowered her arm. She nursed the cast against her chest—which had the added boon of helping ease the pain.

Veramina draped her arm around Maryam's shoulder and guided her down a hallway to a small tiled room, not unlike the bathroom she'd had back on *Star of the Sea*. As Maryam made to enter Veramina held her back.

"I'll give you a little privacy, honey, if you promise me you'll not do anything silly. All right?"

Maryam couldn't believe her luck. She met Veramina's eye and smiled as sanely as she could. "Of course."

"In you go then. I'll just be here outside the door."

As soon as the door closed behind her, Maryam rushed to the

hand basin, shook out the little pills and swilled them down the drain. Step Two accomplished, she rinsed her face in fresh water and ran her fingers through her hair to smooth its wiry mass. Above the basin, a small mirror reflected back an unfamiliar face. Lord in Heaven, she looked bad: her cheeks so sunken and her eyes dark-ringed and shot with blood.

Later, after Veramina had returned her to the room to wait, one of the white-suited men she'd seen the previous night arrived to escort her back out through the barred doors.

"See you later, honey," Veramina called. Despite the woman's kindness, Maryam sincerely hoped she would not. To do so would mean she had failed in her quest.

The man barely spoke as he led her through the building and handed her over to a white-skinned nurse, who ushered Maryam into what appeared to be a small treatment room. It contained a single bed, a basin and a long cluttered bench, its walls lined with heavily stocked shelves. It reminded Maryam of the room on *Star of the Sea* where she'd been bled, and the memory of it did nothing to calm her unease. At once, the nurse began to cut away the cast, struggling to wrench the seamless plaster apart. Maryam tried to distract herself from crying out by studying the boxes and bottles that lined the shelves. There were dozens of them, all containing different coloured pills. She recognised the word "paracetamol" and ran her eyes along the labels, trying to decipher the tiny printed words. Xanax, Staphcillin, Librium, Augmentin, Valium, Ativan. Such strange names. Fentanyl, Thorazine, Amoxicillin, Tofranil, Tegretol, Imatinibiate, Midazolam—wait! She scrolled backwards. There it was! Imatinibiate. She was sure that was the name Aanjay had used. *At last, a real piece of luck.*

A terrible stench rose from her arm, and she looked down reluctantly as the nurse peeled the shredded cast away. The woman wrinkled her nose and tossed the cast into a bin, as if it were a rotting limb. Maryam's arm was badly swollen, and an open wound wept pus where the jutting bone had rubbed against the inside of the cast. No wonder the injury had refused to heal.

"Shit, you're lucky we found this, kid," the nurse muttered. "Otherwise you'd probably have lost your arm." She leaned forward and studied the wound, her lips puckering as she drew close to the source of the rot. "We'll have to operate to sort this out."

"*Operate?* What do you mean?"

"We'll have to knock you out and scrape out the infection, then reset the bone and put you on a whopping great dose of antibiotics. You've no idea how lucky you are that you're already in the hospital—they never would've sent you here for this."

"I'll have to stay?"

"I know, it's good luck, eh?" The nurse patted her on the knee. "Not all of us are as heartless as those inhumane pricks who run the camp. A few days of good food and the correct medication, and you'll be feeling right as rain."

A few days? Maryam groaned. Even if she *could* steal the Imatinibiate, by the time she got it back to Lazarus he would surely be dead. Sweat broke out on her forehead and she felt tears pricking in her eyes. What a choice: if she stole the cure and made a break for it, she might save Lazarus's life but lose her arm. The Lord really was mocking her, playing cruel games. Was an arm worth someone's life?

The nurse was busying herself over by the basin. Now she came towards Maryam, another hypodermic needle at the ready.

"No!" Maryam cried. "Please don't give me that awful stuff again."

The nurse eyed her sympathetically. "I don't know what else you've been given, but this is only some Amoxicillin to treat the infection. It'll help you heal. Come now, you can look away if you like . . ." She injected the drug into Maryam's arm. "There, that wasn't so bad, was it?"

Maryam held her breath, waiting for the terrible mind-bending effects to hit her. What a fool she'd been: she should have run while she still had the chance. Lazarus could be dying at this very moment and now she'd let him down—and Joseph too. She was a failure and a liar, both. But as the minutes ticked away and the nurse began to gently clean around the wound, she realised the woman had spoken the truth. Her mind remained clear.

The nurse wrapped a loose bandage over the wound and tied a sling around Maryam's neck to support the arm. "Wait here and I'll check if we can fix you up a bed in the ward." She smiled for the first time. "Don't worry, kid, it'll be okay."

As soon as she left the room Maryam leapt down from the bed. She had no idea how she was going to see her mission through to its end, but she knew she had to take advantage of any opportunity that came her way. It was now or never. She grabbed a whole box of the Imatinibiate and slipped it into her sling, quickly realigning the other boxes on the shelf to hide the gap. All the time she strained to hear the nurse's return, her pulse hammering and her breathing light and way too fast. Now came the really hard part.

She peered around the doorframe. A woman sat at a desk directly opposite, but luckily her back was to the door. Maryam took the plunge: she stepped out into the corridor with her head held high, as though she had every right to stroll through the building alone. She passed behind the woman and, as calmly as possible, ambled out through another set of doors, relieved to find herself in the main corridor. There were people rushing in both directions and she joined the throng. Her legs were weak and wobbly and she felt as if she couldn't suck in enough air. All the time she was aware that at any minute the nurse would return to the room and find her gone. She could feel the seconds marking off inside her head, convinced her face must show her guilty secret like an open book.

By the time she spied the exit doors ahead she had to fight a powerful ingrained urge to run. But this was both foolish and impossible, as two uniformed guards flanked the doorway. She'd have to pass them to make her escape. To her left she spotted a small storeroom stacked high with chairs. Sidestepping into it, she gained a few more precious seconds to think. Did she have the nerve to stroll past the guards and on out the door as if she were quite entitled to do so? Would the colour of her skin tip the men off to her game? She had no idea. As she hovered, sick with indecision, a large family group, brown skinned just like her, wandered down the corridor beside her. It was another chance too good to miss. She slipped in behind them, trailing close enough to give any casual observer the impression she might well belong. The adults were laughing and chatting, teasing a teenage boy who limped along on crutches in their midst. They appeared not to notice she had joined their ranks.

Now they approached the exit and one of the guards stepped forward as if to bar their way. Maryam's heart faltered as he scanned the group and spoke to them in a language she did not recognise. She huddled down behind the others, for once pleased to be so small, and prayed that she would not be seen. Then she heard the big door swing open, and realised the guard was ushering them through. She bustled into the centre of the group, keeping her eyes averted as they were herded out.

Just as they were about to go down the steps, the guard cried out and the adults leading the group turned back to him. She could feel the acid taste of bile rising in her throat, and a panicked buzzing filled her head. She was standing next to a small girl; she grabbed her hand, and the child stared up at her with startled eyes. Maryam smiled, trying to reassure her, while the guard at the doors shouted something else. Her knees were now so weak she thought she'd fall, and she dropped down next to the child and stroked her on the head to soothe her, one knee on the ground to steady her legs. Above her, the father figure called back to the guard and laughed, playfully cuffing the blushing teenage boy around the ear.

At last it seemed she was free. But she waited until they were well clear of the doors before she made a move. At the driveway, she peeled away from the group and sprinted along the gravel road, holding tight to the sling to stop the drugs from falling out and to help stabilise her arm. Every footfall jolted the broken bone, and tears flowed freely down her cheeks. Ahead, the road split into two, one fork winding further down the hill, the other heading up. Which way, which way? She tried to recall the feeling of the truck journey, and made a snap decision that they'd journeyed down.

She threw herself towards the incline now, relieved to see the tip of the fences gradually coming into view, but they looked much further away than she'd imagined. Ahead, a truck drove down towards her, and she swerved off the road and hunkered behind some bushes until she heard it rattle past. Then up again she flew, her lungs burning and her arm screaming out its discomfort. It was intensely hot, and her mouth filled with stringy phlegm she had to spit to clear. And still the road stretched on and on.

Sweat was pouring into her eyes and her muscles were cramping by the time she finally rounded a corner and saw the camp's administration building against the skyline up ahead. But her relief was short-lived. How on earth would she get back inside the camp without bringing down the wrath of the guards? Her only hope was to hide until an opportunity arrived—a delivery by truck, perhaps, or a disruption while the gates were open so she could sneak back in. This strategy was ridiculously vague: she couldn't guarantee there'd even be an opportunity, never mind succeeding at such a reckless plan. Yet she had no other choice but take that risk.

As she neared the buildings she left the road and made for the rocky ground that led to the far side of the complex that flanked the outer gates. At every sound she checked over her shoulder; every movement in the edges of her vision caused her to flinch and freeze. The tension was exhausting and it seemed an age before she reached the rear of the weathered administration building. She pressed herself flat against its dusty timber boards, then edged around the building's side to confirm what was happening at the gates.

The usual complement of armed men, their guns cocked and glinting in the sun, stood guard, facing off with the protestors inside the fence. Maryam paused again, trying to compose herself. If she blew this now, all chance of saving Lazarus was gone. At least the guards' focus was turned inwards towards the camp and not out towards the road. It seemed they had not factored in anyone being reckless or crazy enough to sneak *in* rather than out.

She summoned up a picture of Joseph in her mind, using his faith in her as a touchstone to contain her fear. He had believed in her, told her she was brave. She couldn't let him down.

The waiting seemed interminable in the heat, and her body ached from the uphill grind. It felt like a good hour or so passed before she snapped back to attention at the rumble of an approaching truck. She flung herself onto the ground, biting hard on her bottom lip and cursing her own stupidity as she knocked her arm. For several seconds she couldn't see past the red burst of pain behind her eyes. But still she had to keep moving.

She snaked along the baking, rocky ground until she could just make out the truck through the straggly clumps of flax and grasses. It was idling, waiting to enter through the gates. She could see metal vats between the flaps in its canvas siding, and picked it as the water truck delivering hot water for the daily showers. Perhaps this was her lucky day, after all.

With her stomach twisting in a ball of nerves, she made her break, launching herself up off the ground and sprinting as fast as her legs could carry her over the open ground. All she could hear was the thumping of her feet; her eyes were fixed on that small gap in the canvas and everything else became a blur. *Help me, Joseph!* she begged him. Then, miraculously, she had somehow reached the rear of the truck without anyone seeing her. She scrabbled up, hauling herself over the tailgate to fall, shattered and exhausted, onto the tray inside.

CHAPTER TWENTY

The truck shuddered as it began to accelerate forwards, and Maryam quickly wriggled around until she was better hidden by the canvas flaps. She grasped hold of a strut to prevent being jostled too close to the water tanks, which radiated boiling heat from their tarnished sides. She couldn't believe she'd managed to elude the guards! Had she the energy to do so, she'd have danced on the spot.

The vehicle travelled at walking pace, and Maryam fought the urge to check their exact whereabouts until she was certain they were safely through both sets of gates. At last she peered out through a rip in the canvas and saw the ugly metal sidings of the huts. She'd made it! Whoever or whatever had aided her this day, she owed them thanks.

When she felt the truck slowing as it readied for the corner near the ablution blocks, she seized her chance. She edged back over to the opening in the canvas and launched herself out over the tailgate. Her landing was harder than expected, her ankles jarring and her arm complaining as she hit the dusty ground. But the thrill she felt, the elation as she waved to a group of girls who watched her with their mouths agog, pitched her forward, and she broke into a limping jog, on the home stretch now and feeling as if she was about to win the race.

She slowed to catch her breath as she reached the walkway that led directly to her hut. Only now was she suddenly over-come with a scalp-prickling sense of dread. What if Lazarus had succumbed more quickly than Joseph and the whole ghastly episode at the hospital had been in vain? She tried to push such doubts away, to hold on to the triumph of having made it back here at all, but the fear stayed with her, plodding at her side as she approached the hut.

And it seemed her dread was justified. Ruth sat slumped against the doorway of the hut, her head in her hands, elbows braced against raised knees, blocking any sign of Lazarus from Maryam's field of view. There was such an air of sadness that Maryam baulked.

"Ruthie," she whispered.

Ruth's face crumpled as she recognised Maryam's voice. She lurched to her feet, and threw herself at Maryam, sobbing as she obstructed entry to the hut and pulled Maryam away.

Ruth couldn't get one rational word out. Her hot tears dripped down Maryam's neck, and the truth hit Maryam like a thunderclap—she was too late. Her knees gave out from under her, and she buckled to the walkway.

It was as though the rest of the world hung in silent suspension around them; as if nothing outside this one painful drawn-out moment was real. *To get so close . . .* Now Maryam too started to cry, and she clung to Ruth, her whole body shaking as she tried to process this latest cruel stroke of fate.

At last she found the courage to speak. "When?" she asked.

Ruth sniffed loudly and wiped her nose against Maryam's shoulder. Her eyes were bloodshot and puffy, ringed with red. "How could you do that to me? I thought I'd never see you again."

"I'm sorry," Maryam murmured. "I never should have left you here to cope alone." She swallowed, having to force herself to ask again: "When did he . . . go?"

"Who? What are you talking about?"

"Lazarus," she whispered, a burning pressure building in her chest as she said his name. "When did he die?"

Ruth drew back, her hand flying to her mouth. "You mean you . . . ?" She shook her head vigorously. "No, no. He's weaker, but he's still alive." She towed Maryam towards the doorway now and Maryam saw his prone silhouette on the mattress inside.

"You're certain?" Maryam pressed. Lazarus lay so still, it was impossible to tell if he was alive or dead.

Ruth nodded.

"Oh, thank the Lord!" Maryam started to cry again, all her accumulated tension and worry purging with the hiccuping sobs.

At last she composed herself. "You'll never guess what I've found." She slipped her hand into the sling and withdrew the box of pills with a grand flourish. "I have the cure."

"You're joking me?" Ruth's face was lit by a wobbly smile. "How on earth did you manage that? *I* tried last night to get him help, but all they gave me were these things called paracetamol. They helped him for a little while, but by the middle of the night he was worse than ever."

"Paracetamol's for pain," Maryam said. "It's not a cure."

"And this remedy you've brought back really can cure him? That's unbelievable." She prodded Maryam's chest. "I could kill you, you know. You've no idea what you put me through—you had me scared half to death."

"I'm sorry! All right? And I promise I'll tell you everything. But first let's show Lazarus these pills."

"In a minute. First tell me if you're all right. Why are your legs so scratched? And where's the plaster on your arm gone? Did they hurt you?"

"There's plenty of time for that later, Ruthie. Let's attend to Lazarus first."

She opened the box and pulled out a small silver sheet of foil encasing several rows of pills. How was she supposed to get them out? She pushed and prodded, eventually managing to pop one through the silver foil.

"What do they do?" asked Ruth.

"You have to swallow them, like the paracetamol."

"All at once?"

"I'm not sure." She felt stupid now. There were no instructions inside the box that she could see, and guessing might be as dangerous as no medicine at all. Why hadn't she thought of this? She was an impulsive fool. "Maybe Aanjay will know," she said.

"Do you think she can be trusted?"

"Absolutely." She thought of the Buddha in Aanjay's room, and how she'd spoken of compassion and love. She'd understand.

"Then shall I go find her?" Ruth offered. "I need the air."

"Yes please. You go, and I'll tell Lazarus I'm here."

The smell of sweat and stale breath hit her as soon as she entered the hut. She understood now why Ruth was eager to take a break: the air was so steeped with the stench of plague she felt it settle in her pores.

She leaned over Lazarus and watched his pulse fluttering fast and pronounced beneath the inflamed rash that ringed his neck. There was still so much bruising on his face from the beating it was hard to tell if the rash had spread, but so little of his own white skin was visible she knew it could not be good. The plague was like a jungle creeper, slowly strangling and consuming him, just as it had poor Joseph. A day or so longer at most, she figured, and she really would have been too late.

She knelt down beside him now, noting the full cup of water and the empty soup bowl on the floor beside his mat. *Bless Ruth for looking after him so well.* She gently shook him by the shoulder, shocked by how thin he was: his bones were clearly defined beneath his discoloured skin. He reminded her so much of Joseph that she had to glance away before she looked again.

"Lazarus," she called, her voice barely more than a whisper. "I'm back." She watched his eyeballs slide beneath their fragile lids, but he didn't rouse. "Lazarus," she tried again, louder this time. "Wake up! I have the cure!"

His eyes fluttered open but it seemed an age before they focused on her own. He tried to smile but his lips were so cracked and dry he had to moisten them before they'd move. "You came."

She was taken aback by how much his smile pleased her, and covered her awkwardness by rattling the box before his face. "I told you I would find the cure." She couldn't help grinning, the enormity of what she'd risked only now really starting to sink in. "You need to get started on these right away."

He rolled over, painfully slowly, and reached for the cup. His hand was shaking as he picked it up, and she wrapped her own over the top of his to steady it so he could drink. "Ah, that's good." He sank back onto the mat, not for a moment taking his eyes off her face. "Tell me what happened." He paused to regain his breath. "How you are."

She laughed. "Ruth will not forgive me if I tell you first! I'll reveal everything once she returns and you've taken these."

His eyes flicked to her arm. "The cast?" It was obvious that speaking took a heavy toll. Between each short sentence he had to gasp for air.

"It's fine," she said. She was interrupted by the sound of heavy footsteps thundering down the walkway, and hadn't even time to get up from where she knelt when Charlie, the guard, burst in.

"What the hell is going on? They're looking for you over at the hospital!" His gaze picked up Lazarus beyond. "And what the crap's *he* doing here?"

Maryam slipped the box of pills under Lazarus's blanket and sprang to her feet. "He's dying," she said bluntly, hating to say it in front of Lazarus but needing Charlie to understand that hers was no ordinary transgression.

"How'd you get back in?" His eyes burned with fury.

"He needed my help," Maryam said, and she raised her chin defiantly. "How did you know that I'd be here?"

He snorted. "I didn't. I was coming to ask your friend Ruth what was going on. My wife, Veramina, works down at the hospital. She's says you did a runner when you heard they were going to operate on your arm."

"She's your wife?" Something in her brain went *click*. No wonder Charlie was so different from the rest of the guards. He loved someone with brown skin.

"Yeah." His face softened for a moment. "But why on earth risk an amputation and hightail it back to this shit hole? If you were going to run, you should've had the op, then run the hell away from here."

"An amputation?" Lazarus broke in.

"Nothing," she hissed back over her shoulder. She met Charlie's uncomprehending gaze. "Don't you see? I couldn't leave him here to die."

"When Vera told me about your breakdown yesterday, I

didn't believe it, but now you're starting to convince me . . . *No one* breaks back into here, you crazy kid—except the odd crusading reporter from time to time. You're bloody lucky I'm the only one, so far, who's figured out the girl who had the meltdown yesterday was *you*." He sighed, looking more tired than angry now. He jerked his head at Lazarus. "What the hell did you think you could do for him? Lay on your hands?" He ran his fingers through his thinning hair. "Listen, missy, I know you think you're helping, but if someone in *my* position can't convince the boss to get proper treatment for you lot, what makes you think *you* can somehow save his life?"

Maryam folded her arms across her chest, feeling like a chastised child. If only she could make him *understand* . . . She sized him up, from his weary face down to his scuffed black boots. If she took him into her confidence—somehow managed to move his heart—then maybe he could find out how to use the pills. But if he chose instead to uphold the law of the camp, he'd confiscate the pills, punish her for stealing and leave Lazarus to die. Was it worth this risk?

Now Ruth appeared in the doorway. "It's all right," Maryam reassured her. But she caught Ruth's gaze and slid her eyes to Charlie to warn her to be guarded. "Did you have any luck?"

Ruth shook her head. "No help."

Aanjay refused? Why would she do that? Had she been brainwashed by the white men too? Behind her, Lazarus succumbed to a fit of coughing, a terrible barking sound that resounded off the metal walls. Maryam shook aside her disappointment and knelt beside him. There was little she could do but offer him another sip of water once the final spasm had passed. When she'd helped Lazarus to settle comfortably again, she looked up at Charlie, whose brow was creased with concern. With Aanjay refusing to help, she'd have to make use of his good heart and take the risk of trusting him. "Can we speak outside?" she said.

Charlie nodded, glancing back at Lazarus as he left. "Take it easy, matey. I never saw you here, you understand?"

"Thanks," Lazarus rasped.

Outside the hut, Maryam shuffled awkwardly from foot to foot, trying to decide how best to confess. "Lazarus has Te Matee Iai," she started. "Aanjay says you know it as Sumber Kem—" She racked her brain, trying to recall the word.

"Sumber Kemusnahan," Charlie prompted. He nodded thoughtfully. "Yes, that makes sense."

She blurted out her story now: how Joseph had already died, how Lazarus had tried to end his life when he learnt the plague had struck him too. Charlie didn't interrupt, merely raised an eyebrow when she told him how she'd concocted her desperate plan. "I can't let him die, not now I know there's a cure." She told him of the hospital, of Veramina's kindness, and how she stole the pills.

"You're gutsy and inventive, I'll give you that . . . But do you understand the consequences if they find out you stole the drugs?"

She didn't want to think of this right now, it scared her so. "Wouldn't you have done the same?"

Charlie gazed off into the distance for a moment, as though he searched for the answer to her question there. "What if I was to assure you that I'll get him help, if you agree to go back to the hospital and let them fix your arm?"

She shook her head reluctantly. "No," she said. "I need to stay with him until I know for sure that he's cured. I gave my word to him—I can't let him down." Her pulse was crashing round inside her head like footsteps in an empty room.

Charlie slipped his hands into his pockets and whistled tunelessly under his breath as he considered her words. Then the whistling stopped. "Okay, here's what we'll do. I'll get Vera to tell me how to administer the pills and to explain away your absence from the hospital before it reaches my boss's ears. But, once your friend is well, you have to promise me you'll return for the operation and make no more fuss."

"All right," she agreed, too in need of Veramina's expertise to argue the point. "Thank you. But please don't put yourself at risk." She thought of Brother Mark back in the Holy City, and how he'd died trying to aid her.

Charlie waved her worry away. "Let me tell you something so you'll understand. When Vera and me first met, we had a child—a girl." His eyes grew distant for a moment and a soft smile lit his face. "We called her Sarwendah. It means wholly beautiful, and she was . . . She'd be about your age now if she'd lived."

"What happened?" Maryam prompted. She didn't want to rush him but she could hear Lazarus coughing again inside the hut.

"We lived on a small island some way from here—my parents went bush to escape the madness of the mainland and the endless wars—but the downside was we had no access to medical supplies. Sarwendah was two when she slipped one day on toxic coral down at the wharf. The wound on her leg got horribly infected and, no matter what we did, it wouldn't heal. We were advised to amputate, and in the end we had no choice but to agree. It made no difference. Without antibiotics she still died." He blinked his eyes as though damming back his tears.

"When we found Vera was expecting our second child, our son Lemah, we decided to shift somewhere with doctors and drugs on hand. Vera got a job at the hospital when the kids were older, but the only work I could find was here."

"I'm so sorry," Maryam said.

He shrugged. "I try to do what I can here in my own small way. But you, Maryam, must not throw your life away. It's hard in here, I know, but you *must* keep faith that things will change."

Maryam smiled, thinking that faith was the very thing she'd lost. But she knew *that* wasn't the kind of faith he meant, and she appreciated his kindness. "I'll try," she said. "But now I have to get back to Lazarus. That coughing is only going to get worse. How long will it take for you to find out about the pills?"

"I'll go and call Vera now and come back right away." He charged off down the walkway, leaving Maryam to wonder how he could speak to his wife without having to leave the camp. There was still so much she didn't know about this complex new world.

Ruth, meantime, was hovering in the shadows of the hut. "It's all right," Maryam reassured her. "He's going to find out how to use the pills."

"Thank the Lord," Ruth burst out. "Aanjay simply doesn't know."

As Maryam took up her place at Lazarus's side, Ruth told of her conversation with Aanjay. "She said the locals cure the plague by boiling up the leaves and flowers of a special tree—it's that essence the Territorials use to make their drugs—but she doesn't know anything about the right dose of pills and says it's far too dangerous for her to guess."

Maryam could tell that Lazarus was listening by the way his eyes clouded as this news hit him hard.

"It's all right," she reassured him, "Charlie's wife works at the hospital and will tell us how to use the pills." Now she told them about Veramina and how she stumbled on the cure, downplaying the part about her arm. *Now is not the time.*

There was nothing to do at her tale's end but wait for Charlie to return. Each minute felt like an hour as the girls tried to lower Lazarus's temperature by sponging down his feverish face and neck. At last they heard Charlie's heavy tread on the walkway outside.

"Mission accomplished," he announced as he entered the hut. "Give him six immediately and then two every four hours until all the symptoms pass. She says the one box should be enough, but that if you need more she'll see what she can do."

Maryam couldn't help herself: she leapt up and hugged him. "Thank you," she said. To think this white man had risked his job for her—for Lazarus. This was a rare and wondrous gift.

Charlie patted her awkwardly, then backed away. "Don't forget our deal. I'll come and check up on you before I end my shift."

As soon as he was gone Maryam counted out the first six pills and coaxed Lazarus to swallow them, taking a sip of water after each to wash it down. Still, he gagged on every pill, but when the last of them was taken relief flooded over her like summer rain. For the first time in so long she felt light, tentative flutters of hope.

All through the afternoon she kept watch on the position of the sun, trying to gauge the passing of each four hours so she could give Lazarus his next dose of pills. He dozed fitfully, his fever ravaging his strength, and she tried in vain to convince him to eat. In the end she gave up. She was giddy with tiredness herself. The pain-dulling effects of the paracetamol she'd taken that morning had worn off, too, and the burning in her infected arm was so unrelenting she had to grit her teeth to hold back tears. But when Ruth suggested she seek out more paracetamol, Maryam brushed the offer away. They daren't draw any attention to themselves while Lazarus still lay hidden in their hut.

Later, as evening fell, Lazarus grew agitated and bad-tempered, his fever rising so sharply he began to rave. To make it worse, he stubbornly refused to take the pills, spitting them out and rolling away to face the wall so that no one could coax him further. When Charlie called by to say that he was going home, he found Maryam pacing the hut in exasperation.

"You're sure I'm giving him the proper dose?" she asked, so tired and sore herself she could hardly speak.

Charlie gave her and Ruth an assessing look. "You've both done all you can. Now it's up to him. For goodness sake, get some rest."

"But he's worse!"

Charlie sighed. "You have to prepare yourself—even if he takes all the pills, they can't work miracles. Vera says that if the Sumber Kemusnahan is too far down the track, then not even the pills can bring him back."

"But they're supposed to be a cure."

"Bodies can only take so much strain. Now you have to leave it in the hands of God. I'll be back in the morning to see how you are. Get some rest in the meantime, for pity's sake."

Neither Maryam nor Ruth could speak as they watched Charlie leave. Maryam was the first to find words, though they were hardly coherent. "But Aanjay said . . . and Jo . . ."

Ruth took comfort in what she knew best. "If he's right," she said, "why don't we pray? The Lord will help."

"No!" Maryam couldn't take this now. She ran outside and leaned against the outer wall, watching as a cloud of moths beat themselves to death on the bare walkway lights. It occurred to her that this was how she felt: every time she moved towards the light, it turned out to be an illusion, a cruel trick of fate. Let Ruth pray to the Lord if it helped her, but Maryam would *never* again seek His help. The only person she could totally rely on was herself. And she would not let Lazarus die. Somehow she had to find the will, the strength inside, to take her life in hand and stop merely reacting to every new problem as it struck her down. If this *was* her only life, then she determined now to make it count. Or if, as Aanjay believed, it was only one step upon the road to something better—the thing Aanjay called enlightenment—then she must learn the lessons that might reward her with a better lifetime in the next. Whichever way, she was certain now her fate rested solely in her own hands.

She let out a long slow breath and felt a kind of peace descend on her. She could hear Ruth inside the hut, praying above Lazarus's reedy feverish ravings, and as she listened to their desperate duet she suddenly knew what to do.

She stormed back inside, apologised to Ruth for her rudeness, then popped two more pills from the foil. Too quickly for Lazarus to fight her off, she pushed them into the corner of his mouth and used her index finger to force them down his throat. He gagged but automatically swallowed before flailing her with a torrent of feverish abuse.

"You bitch. You total lying whore . . ." On and on he shouted, but whether he flung the words at her, or at someone in his past—perhaps his mother—Maryam didn't care. It was poisonous Te Matee Iai that spoke, not the boy.

She grabbed his arm, jerked him up until he was high enough off the mat to slip his arm over her good shoulder, and lugged him to his feet. She was so determined now, her own pain merely fuelled her strength as she forcibly began to march him out the door.

"What are you doing?" Ruth cried, buzzing around them like a worried bee. "You can't take him outside. The women will see . . ."

"I need to cool him down." She didn't wait to argue the point, just dragged him, struggling and cursing, over to the showers.

She pushed Lazarus into the first empty stall she came to, propping him up against the wall with her shoulder while she turned on the tap. Cold salty water rained down on them both as she manoeuvred him to a sitting position on the ground under the shower's cool but patchy flow.

Gradually his curses petered out and Lazarus slipped back into a listless doze. His forehead was growing cooler, and the ugly marks that marred his skin began to lose their angry bloom. Maryam let the water flow for a little longer, trying to judge the delicate balance between cooling him enough to bring his fever down and giving him a further deadly chill. At last she turned off the tap and, with Ruth's help, dragged him back to his feet.

As they dripped their way along the walkway, Maryam was no longer bothered about the curious stares of onlookers. She sensed she could rely on the unspoken unity between the detainees to keep Lazarus's presence secret for now. Back at the hut they stripped him of his sodden clothes, averting their eyes from his private places, and lay him back under a dry blanket on his mat.

The whole episode had eaten every last scrap of Maryam's strength. She stripped off her own soaked dress and wrapped another thin blanket around her like a sarong. Then she lay down to rest. She drifted off to the musical whisperings of Ruth's rekindled prayers, setting an alarm in her subconscious so she wouldn't sleep too long. Lazarus would need another dose of pills four hours from now.

She stirred from a muddled dream of Joseph to find Ruth sound asleep and the camp deathly quiet. For a moment she just lay there, trying to determine why this silence should matter so; then, with a sickening lurch, she realised she could no longer hear Lazarus's rasping breaths.

What if she had chilled him so much he was dead? She sprang up from her mat and stumbled over to his side. Her eyes had not yet adjusted to the dark and she couldn't tell if his chest still moved, so she dipped her head down, placing her cheek close to his mouth and nose to see if she could feel any shift of air.

"A naked angel," Lazarus croaked, as Maryam reeled upwards with shock. She'd forgotten her blanket! "Heaven is better than I hoped!"

"Pig!" But she laughed too, and gathered the rug around herself as she settled by his side. "How are you feeling now? You gave us quite a scare."

"Really? I don't remember much." Lazarus fumbled for the cup she offered and took a sip. "I *did* have a nightmare about some crazy girl trying to drown me, though." He chuckled, but instantly it brought on another fit of coughing.

Maryam retrieved his next dose of pills. "Take these, or that same crazy girl will stuff them down your throat again."

This time Lazarus swallowed the pills without a fuss. He groaned as he flopped back on the mat. "I feel like I've been beaten up again, only this time from the inside out."

To hear him speak like this, still groggy but lucid and cracking jokes, gladdened Maryam's heart. He was going to survive, she was sure of it now. Like the Lazarus of old, he'd come back from the dead. "Try to get some sleep," she urged him. "I'm sorry I woke you."

"I'm not." He reached out a hand and placed it on her knee. "I owe you a lot. Everything, really. How can I ever thank you?"

She pressed her hand over his for a moment then firmly lifted it back onto his chest. "Get better. That will be enough."

She tiptoed outside, hoisting her blanket up over her shoulders. She was too stirred up to sleep. The site of her infected wound burnt as if branded by a red-hot ember and she feared the outcome for her arm, but for the moment she would push back her anxiety and try to focus on the good. *Joseph, do you hear me? He's going to live.* She thought how joyful he would be, how happy that his cousin had been saved.

An unannounced tear tracked down her cheek. Then another. And another. *If only it were Joseph who now lay inside the hut reborn . . .* She retrieved the small blue stone, her talisman, from the place where she had stashed it on the crudely formed shelf beside the door, and pressed it to her forehead, right between her two closed eyes—sure she could feel its cobalt magic permeating the layers of skin right to her brain. It encircled the gnawing pain in her, diffusing it with coloured calm. Behind her eyelids the swirl of blue summoned up the mainstays of her past: the blue-eyed boy she had loved and lost . . . the pristine lagoon around that special island, Onewēre, where her mother's bones now lay . . .

To think that all along Te Matee Iai could be cured. A miracle far more convincing and enduring, surely, than any Father Joshua could conjure up. Imagine what it would mean to the people of Onewēre if they had access to it: no more families torn apart, no more painful deaths. And no more bleeding of the Sisters—in fact, no more excuse to hold the Sisters hostage at all.

Suddenly a hand dropped onto her shoulder, and she reeled around to find Lazarus propped in the doorway, a sarong wrapped clumsily around his waist.

"Go back to bed!" she hissed, seeing how he swayed. "You must rest."

"I need fresh air," he said. "It's like a burial cave in there." He stepped out onto the walkway beside her. "What were you thinking about so hard?"

Maryam laughed. "You really want to know?"

"It's got to be better than lying there choking on my own bad breath."

"Fair enough," she conceded, "but please don't catch a chill." She ducked back into the hut to retrieve his blanket and draped it around him.

"Thank you Mother Maryam," he said. "Now to your thoughts."

"All right, all right. If you must know, I was thinking about Te Matee Iai—and how the Apostles use their so-called resistance to it as proof they were chosen by the Lord." She glanced up at him. His face gave nothing away. "Imagine what would happen if the people learnt about the cure. Surely then they'd realise the Apostles had lied?"

"You think they'd believe it if my father told them it was merely Lucifer tempting them and playing tricks?"

"But don't you see? If the proof was right there, in front of their eyes, they'd *have* to believe. And then they could reclaim their lives—be rid of the Apostles once and for all. Set themselves free." She felt suddenly light and buoyant.

"And how do you propose to do that? Steal more pills?" He laughed softly. "Ask the Territorials to drop them off?"

She brushed aside his mocking, intent on plucking out some sense from the bombardment of thoughts inside her head. "No. Not the pills." *They mustn't rely on the Territorials or anybody else.* "There'd have to be a way to take the cure itself. The tree. Our climates are almost the same. I'm sure the tree would grow. Why not? With the help of all the good people we've met here—Aanjay and Jo, Charlie and Veramina, and Ruthie of course—there must be a way."

She glanced at Lazarus, blushing as she found him looking intently at her, and quickly looked away. What of him? Was it time to put his past behind him, truly to forgive him for his sins? Nothing that went through fire was left unchanged, and he *had* survived the feverish flames of Te Matee Iai . . . He'd have to prove himself, though, and in return she would have to equal his efforts—give him a fair chance. But could she do so after everything he'd put her through? She wasn't sure. Perhaps the most she could offer him right now was that she'd wait and see.

Suddenly it felt as if a fog had lifted from her mind. She raised her chin and placed her feet firmly on the ground. It was all so clear now. Such a relief to know what to do next. The death of Joseph and his wise boat-building father would not be in vain.

At last she could meet Lazarus's eye without any sense of inferiority or shame.

"It seems, Brother Lazarus, I have a plan. And I believe that, one way or another, I can make it work." She sent him a beatific smile and let the words fall calmly off her tongue. "I'm going back."

ACKNOWLEDGMENTS

Especial thanks to Mohammad Yasin Hamzaie for sharing his story. Much appreciation to Rose Lawson (my first and most enthusiastic reader) and to Thom Lawson, Brian Laird, Belinda Hager, Nicky Hager, Debbie Hager, and Julia Wells for their careful reading and suggestions. Also to Jane Parkin, Jenny Hellen, and the team at Random House NZ; Lou Anders and his team at Pyr; Joe Monti from the Barry Goldblatt Literary Agency for believing in me and making this possible; and last, but by no means least, my love and thanks to all my family and friends who, through their generosity and love, make living in this crazy world worthwhile.

ABOUT THE AUTHOR

MANDY HAGER is an award-winning writer and educator based in Wellington, New Zealand. She has a drive to tell stories that matter—direct, powerful stories with something to say. She won the 2010 New Zealand Post Children's Book Award for Young Adult Fiction for *The Crossing*. Visit her online at www.mandyhager.com, at www.facebook.com/BloodOfTheLambTrilogy, and on Twitter @MandyHager.